Post Mortem

Kate London

W F HOWES LTD

This large print edition published in 2015 by
W F Howes Ltd
Unit 4, Rearsby Business Park, Gaddesby Lane,
Rearsby, Leicester LE7 4YH

1 3 5 7 9 10 8 6 4 2

First published in the United Kingdom in 2015
by Corvus

A CIP catalogue record for this book is available
from the British Library

ISBN 978 1 51001 223 3

Typeset by Palimpsest Book Production Limited,
Falkirk, Stirlingshire

Printed and bound in Great Britain
by TJ International Ltd, Padstow, Cornwall

MIX
Paper from
responsible sources
FSC
www.fsc.org FSC® C013056

For Uri

Post Mortem

17 APRIL

CHAPTER 1

Detective Sergeant Sarah Collins and Detective Constable Steve Bradshaw had been close by when the call came out. It had taken them only a matter of minutes to get to the scene, but emergency vehicles already blocked the approach to the service road that led to Portland Tower. Collins stopped the car in the middle of the road, leaving its lights flashing.

'You control the scene,' she said. 'I'll go to the roof.'

Collins ran ahead. Bradshaw moved more slowly, walking round to the boot of the car to collect his grab bag. Collins, pulling her warrant card out of her jacket pocket, pushed her way through the group of onlookers who were crowding forward, struggling to snatch a glimpse. She pressed through them – the smell of their sweat, their sharp elbows, their panting curiosity.

'Police. Out of my way.'

As she reached the front, she was hit by the sudden revelation of the bodies, spread on the tarmac of the square in plain view.

Face down was a white uniformed male. Overweight. Late forties, early fifties. One arm was crushed beneath his chest. The other, flung out wide, was clearly fractured. Blood had burst out of the dead man's stomach and splattered across the ground.

The teenage girl lay face up, head back, arms spread, mouth open, like a pale doll thrown pitilessly on to the concrete. A few feet away from her, incongruous against the paving slabs, was a pink polka-dot backpack. The girl's face was dark-skinned – North African, Collins thought. She was wearing jeans and a T-shirt with a cat printed on the front. The cat's head was disproportionately large for its body, with even bigger eyes. It had an arching tail that snaked over the girl's shoulder. The dead man's blood had splashed across the T-shirt and the girl's face. There was something about the blood that was uncanny, the fact that it lay undisturbed, uncleaned.

Collins tried to dismiss the anguish that swept suddenly through her. Briefly it incapacitated her and she stood rooted to the spot. The paramedics were clearing up their equipment. It was only protocol that they had been called: someone had to pronounce life extinct. She looked upwards into the brightness of the cold blue sky. Even imagining the unstoppable fall gave her vertigo. The high-rise loomed above, casting her into shadow. These lives were beyond help, she told herself. She had a job to do; she would concentrate on that. Steve would secure the scene.

A uniformed sergeant was mustering shocked

officers to push people back. He had blue plastic gloves on and a roll of blue and white tape in his hand. Directly in front of her was a young Asian officer. He looked drawn and pale. Collins showed him her warrant card and spoke quietly, as if confiding a secret.

'Detective Sergeant Collins, Directorate of Special Investigations. My colleague Detective Constable Steve Bradshaw will be here in a moment. He's going to help you establish the scene.'

The officer waved her through and she set off quickly across the open concourse, around the building towards the entrance. In spite of herself her heart was pounding. She repeated her investigator's mantra. *One thing at a time. One decision at a time.* Every detail could be significant and every decision she made might prove much later, in a cold and unforgiving court, to have unimagined consequences. The universe was turning and she wanted to slow it down and hold on to every particle, to have time to examine it, to revolve it slowly in the light. Every human action contaminated. Still, she would go to the roof. To hesitate might mean she would lose other evidence. Like who was there right now.

The door to the stairs was propped open. She paused and considered the Coke can that someone had slid between the door and its frame. She called Steve on her mobile.

'Get someone on the door, quick. Nothing moves. No one goes up or down. There's a Coke can here needs seizing.'

She felt in her trouser pocket and took out a pair of blue plastic gloves, identical to those the uniformed sergeant had been wearing. As she put them on, she scanned the length of the building, taking in the CCTV camera that was pointing towards the door. She stepped into the lobby. It was dimly lit by the pallid light seeping through the glass bricks that formed part of the exterior wall. On the right was an abandoned caretaker's office, in front of her two dark lift doors and to the left, the door to the fire stairwell. She paused to consider which route they had taken to the roof. Had it been the lift or the stairs? She would order a search team to do a fingertip examination of the whole area, but in the meantime she'd risk the contamination and take the stinking lift. She pulled a pen from her pocket and used it to press the request button.

The lift walls were dappled stained metal. There was burnt aluminium foil on the floor. She prayed the lift wouldn't break down. It creaked steadily upwards, sending vibrations echoing along the shaft. The doors opened on to the final landing. Above her the service stairs climbed into darkness, broken by a square of light that was the opening on to the roof.

As she climbed, she heard distant low voices. Stepping out from the sheltered stairway, she was blasted by the wind. The sheer height made her want to retreat. Clouds were whipping across the blue sky. From where she stood, there was no view of the ground, just the white concrete platform of the roof, and the spinning sky.

A foot away from the edge, a male inspector in uniform faced a female uniformed police constable. The female was young, about twenty-two. Slim, athletic build. She didn't have a hat on, and Collins could see blonde hair pulled back into a plait. She was sitting down; on her lap, with his arm round her neck, was a small boy in a bear suit.

Collins held out her warrant card. 'Detective Sergeant Sarah Collins.'

The inspector stepped towards her. He was tall, a streak of grey in his hair. 'What are you doing up here? This is a crime scene.'

'I could ask the same of you, sir.'

Something like anger flushed briefly through his face.

'Kieran Shaw, I'm the duty inspector. It's clear enough what *I'm* doing here. One of my officers is dead. Another is up here on her own with a missing child. I'm here to make sure no one else falls off this fucking roof.' He turned away and spoke into his radio. 'Control receiving Inspector Shaw. An officer to close off the stairs with tape immediately. And any other entrances to the building to be closed off. No one else to go up or down. This is a critical incident.' He turned back to the female officer and the boy in the bear suit. 'We'll get you both down.'

Collins considered the female PC. She wanted to speak to her then and there. To spirit her away

7

from this duty inspector and find out what had happened before anyone else could brief her. But the PC was ashen and her lips were blue. She was beginning to shake as though she had been immersed in very cold water for far too long. Collins spoke into her own radio. 'Control receiving DS Collins, DSI. I'm going to be running this from now on. DC Steve Bradshaw is supervising the establishment of a crime scene. We need medical assistance for an adult female believed going into shock. Breathing and conscious. I'll meet London Ambulance at the bottom of the stairs.'

Collins left the PC sitting in an ambulance being assessed by paramedics. She noted the officer's name in her notebook: Police Constable Lizzie Griffiths.

The mother of the boy was waiting in the back of a marked car. Collins let go of his hand and watched the little bear running towards her. As soon as she saw him, she threw open the car door and ran to meet him. She flew him up into the air and then squeezed him tightly against her chest, pressing her face into his until he cried out: 'Mummy!' She pulled the bear hood down and buried her nose in him. The uniformed PC who had been driving the car gave them a moment before ushering them both into the vehicle and away from the waiting bank of press. Collins watched it turn slowly away from the scene.

From then on, she knew, it would be a race not

to lose evidence, like trying to gather up shells before the tide swept in and claimed them for oblivion. No, not just gathering the shells but also carefully cataloguing and recording the damn things. She looked up. The sky was grey. The weather was turning and the spring sunlight was already paling. They would have to work quickly. She went back to the car, grabbing a forensic suit and a decision log from the boot.

She met up with Steve on the edge of the crime scene. He lit two cigarettes and passed her one. They inhaled together as they stood watching the local officers struggling to erect the white tents that had arrived on blue lights.

'Never find it easy, do they?' Steve said.

Together they allocated the many tasks that lay ahead. There was so much to do – informing the families, deciding the forensic strategy, door-to-door, CCTV, witnesses, debriefing the response team. Steve called the bus company and the local-authority CCTV office. He would go with another DC and see if he could grab some footage before the operators went home. Collins checked her watch. People would be looking forward to leaving work. Soon they would struggle to get hold of the civilians they needed. As every moment passed opportunities were being lost to preserve evidence. Secondary-school children were traipsing home, walking along the perimeter of the scene with their scruffy bags and dusty shoes.

CHAPTER 2

In the back of the ambulance, a paramedic was talking to Lizzie and filling in a yellow sheet fastened to a clipboard by a large bulldog clip. He leant over and slipped the cuff of the sphygmomanometer around her upper arm. She felt it inflate and constrict the flow of blood. It was as if everything was happening to someone else. The paramedic said something to her. She wasn't sure what it was, but it was definitely a question and he smiled as he spoke.

She said, 'OK,' and smiled back.

She found herself very interested in the paramedic's clipboard – in the diamond hatching of the board and the dark bulldog clip. She wondered how hard it would be to press the butterfly of the clip open. Some of them were very stiff, after all. The door of the ambulance opened. Her sergeant was standing just outside, speaking into his radio. He nodded at her and she nodded back. 'Sarge.' She dragged her bottom teeth hard across her top lip. It felt like she'd had an anaesthetic.

A skinny man with a crumpled face stepped into the ambulance. He was wearing a dark blue suit.

He flashed a warrant card at the paramedic and sat down opposite her. She noticed nicotine staining on his third finger. The paramedic and the man were talking, but she couldn't make sense of what was being said. The man leaned forward and put his hand gently on her shoulder.

'Lizzie. It is Lizzie, isn't it?'

'Yes.'

'Here's my card, Lizzie. DC Steve Bradshaw. Look, pass me your warrant card. I'll pop it inside there and then you'll know you've got it. That mobile's on 24/7 and it's always OK to ring me. We'll catch up with you when the medics give us the thumbs-up.'

'Yes, thank you.'

He smiled. 'OK, I'll leave you to it.'

Then he was gone. The paramedic reached over and attached something to her index finger. Another butterfly clip. She noticed that it had a red light on it. Her pulse, the beat of her heart. She closed her eyes. She felt as though she was lying on the bottom of a swimming pool looking up. She allowed herself to relax and look at the surface of the water, how it formed into shifting blue polygons. And then unbidden, and for just a brief moment, she had a sudden flash of the roof. Of the girl, Farah, and of Ben in his bear suit, the blue sky behind them, the clouds scudding past.

Lizzie shuddered violently, as if she had nausea. The paramedic, she realized, was offering her a bowl to vomit into. She could see his wide, kind, tired face. The comforting green of his uniform, those trousers with the side pockets. She had pockets like that, she remembered, but black, not green. She waved him away. 'No, I'm fine, thanks.' With determination she brought her attention back to the clipboard. She thought about how old-fashioned they were. Who would have imagined that paramedics still used them?

Inspector Shaw stepped into the ambulance. 'All right, Lizzie?'

She nodded. 'Guv.'

She observed him. He was being efficient, she understood that. He was making arrangements for her. He was looking after her.

CHAPTER 3

The ambulances and fire engines had gone and Collins had moved her car up into the outer cordon. She sat in the front seat working through the printouts of the linked dispatches that were the police records of the incident. Head down, she scribbled in her counsel's notebook.

There was a tap on her car window. Detective Chief Inspector Baillie was leaning down looking at her. His thin, intelligent face was dusted with freckles, and above his pale blue eyes was a shock of flaxen hair. He smiled, pleased to have caught her off guard. She flicked open the door lock so that he could join her on the passenger side. As he crossed in front of the car, she saw how his dark pinstriped suit hung off his coat-hanger shoulders. He slid the seat back to its full extent and stretched his legs into the footwell.

'Bit of a problem, Sarah. Don't know whether you are aware? We've been looking at informing the families. Turns out that Younes Mehenni, the father of the dead teenager, is currently in police custody on remand to court tomorrow.'

Collins felt immediately wrong-footed: she should have known this. 'I'm sorry, sir . . .'

'It's OK, you've been a bit busy. I've appointed Alice as family liaison. She's at Farlow nick now, organizing bail on compassionate grounds. We're going to escort him to court in the morning and see if we can sort it out quickly. The advice is that legally there's no other way round it. It doesn't look like it's a particularly serious matter – criminal damage with a linked malicious communications. We're just getting to the bottom of it now. What do you have about the dead officer?'

'PC Hadley Matthews, sir. Fifty-two years old. Three years to go before retirement. Inspector Shaw, Matthews' line manager, is informing his family. Shaw was the duty inspector today.'

Baillie nodded. 'Yes, I've come across Kieran Shaw.'

'You've worked with him?'

'No, not at all. Don't worry, no conflict of interest there. But from what I've heard, he's a good man.' Baillie stretched his arms behind his head. 'All right, Sarah, I'll let you get on. We'll use Farlow nick as our base for the initial response. I'll see you back there for a more detailed briefing. How much time do you need? Shall we say twenty hundred hours?'

'Yes, boss.'

Baillie nodded reluctantly towards the outer cordon, where the bank of press were loitering.

'And in the meantime, I need to face that lot. Any suggestions as to what I might say to them?'

Collins turned in the direction he had indicated and saw a thicket of zoom lenses pointed towards the scene.

'As little as possible as far as I'm concerned. We are still investigating. All lines of inquiry still open, that sort of thing?'

There was a brief silence. Baillie palmed his car keys and flicked the door lock open.

'Well,' he said. 'Our first job together, you and me, and it's a big one. I hope you're a safe pair of hands.'

CHAPTER 4

The marked car drew up outside PC Lizzie Griffiths' flat. Arif was in the driving seat, Lizzie beside him. He switched the engine off.

'Are you sure you're going to be all right?'

'Yes, I'll be fine.'

Arif, like Lizzie, was young in service. In fact, because she had just a couple of months' more experience than him, Lizzie was even the slightly senior officer. She knew he had been first on scene, had probably even seen the fall. She wondered how he was coping. They sat together in silence.

'I don't know,' Arif said finally. 'It just doesn't feel right. Leaving you. I can sit with you for a bit if you want. We can have some tea.'

There was a pause.

'Or something stronger.'

'No, Arif. It's all right. I'll be fine. Thanks.'

She got out of the car. She was aware of Arif waiting, watching her while she walked down the driveway and then fumbled with her keys. She had a ridiculous sensation, as though she were pretending to unlock the door. When she had got it open, she turned and waved. Everything was hunky-dory. Still, he hesitated for a moment before nodding and driving off.

As soon as the door was shut, she crouched down on the floor and put her head in her hands.

Lizzie sat motionless on the edge of her bed. She didn't know how long she had been there and had no recollection of how she had navigated the distance from the hallway to her bedroom. Her mind felt like a wide-open blank. She picked up her phone and glanced at the screen. She had seven missed calls. She had been distantly aware of the phone ringing, but it had not crossed her mind to answer.

Tapping on the images application, she flicked through the pictures until she found a picture of herself with PC Hadley Matthews, his arm round her. She considered this for some time until the phone rang again, interrupting the screen.

Unknown number.

Immediately she rejected the call. She could think of no one to whom she could speak. She could think of nothing.

She tried to pull herself together.

In the back of the ambulance, a female detective constable had seized her uniform and put it into brown evidence bags. Lizzie was sitting now in a white top, white tracksuit bottoms and black pumps provided by the detective when she took her uniform. Lizzie knew these clothes. They were the type given to prisoners in custody when their own clothes were seized for forensic examination.

Her mind scanned around like a slow computer system conducting a search that never resolved. Or like a freeze frame that wouldn't play. The edge of the roof, the wind blowing across. In spite of the futility, she kept on struggling to find a way to make it not true, to make it come right, like a dream dreamt again. She could almost see the rainbow wheel in her head endlessly whirring and reaching no conclusion. No results. Disk irretrievably damaged.

Suddenly she felt that the clothes she had been given were repulsive to her. She got up and changed into some of her own jogging trousers and a T-shirt. She threw the clothes she had been given into her bin.

The small effort had exhausted her. She lay on the bed and stared at the ceiling. She couldn't see any way forward beyond this present moment.

CHAPTER 5

Collins stepped out of the scene tent that sheltered the body of PC Hadley Matthews. She peeled her forensic suit down to her waist, removed her plastic gloves and reached for her cigarettes. Both bodies were ready at last to be bagged up and moved.

At the outer cordon onlookers were still standing. What on earth, she wondered, could they be hoping for? There was nothing to see now except the tents, and the officers and SOCOs moving around in forensic suits. Nevertheless, it was the usual street party that accompanied catastrophe. Mixed-race and white boys in hoodies were fooling around and giving the uniformed officer on the tape a hard time. An elderly lady in a hijab and a cardigan was staring with fixed concentration towards the concourse. Collins would task one of the PCs to make sure this woman's details had been taken. A white man wearing the paint-splashed dungarees and boots of a decorator was filming it all on his phone. A TV cameraman was also still lingering, hoping probably for footage of the bodies being moved into the vans and driven out. She should warn the forensic team about him. They could back the van right up to the tents, obscure the body bags.

Collins lit her cigarette then moved over to her car. She pulled out her notebook and, leaning against the vehicle, glanced down at her list of actions. A box was inked and doodled around the words 'PC Lizzie Griffiths'. The young female constable from the roof had to be the next priority.

Collins radioed Control and then waited on the spare channel while the operator checked the dispatch.

'PC Griffiths hasn't gone to hospital, Sarge.'

'Not gone to hospital?'

'No, Sarge.'

'OK, what does it say on the dispatch? Where has she gone?'

Collins scratched her forehead irritably while she waited for the operator to get back to her. Finally the radio crackled. 'The officer has been dismissed from duty. The CAD shows a car taking her home.'

'Home? Who authorized that?'

'The duty officer, Sarge. Mr Shaw.'

Collins threw her cigarette on the ground and lit another one-handed. 'OK. Thank you, Control.' She dialled into her mobile. 'Steve, Lizzie Griffiths, the female PC—'

'It's all right, Sarah, I called for an update myself. Tried to talk to her in the ambulance but the paramedic said she wasn't ready. She's on her own, apparently. God knows what Shaw was thinking.

I'm on my way; turning into her street right now, actually.'

'Thank God. Take her over to Victoria House. We don't want her anywhere near her own nick. I'll meet up with you as soon as I've seen Baillie.'

CHAPTER 6

Lizzie had fallen into a stupor and the knock at the front door startled her. For a moment, she froze. Then she began to act swiftly, throwing her phone, some pants, a couple of T-shirts and a utility bill into a small backpack. The plate of the letter box lifted quietly and she paused. *A cop at the door, then.* There was no access to her garden from the front of the building. She would be OK if she moved quickly.

A male voice called into the hallway.
'Lizzie?'
She stopped moving, hoping he would not realize she was at home. After a pause, the voice continued.
'Lizzie, it's only me, Steve. You remember me? I came and said hello to you in the ambulance . . .'
The letter box shut. Lizzie bent down and quietly slipped some trainers on, but as she did so, her phone began to ring. *Beginner's mistake.* She heard the letter box open again.
'Lizzie, I know you're there. I can hear your phone ringing.'

Lizzie reached into her bag and grabbed her phone. She rejected the call and switched it off. Then she threw the bag over her shoulder and ran into the hallway. She had to go this way to get out of the French windows into the garden. She could see the fingers of a white male hand holding the letter box open. She heard his voice again.

'Don't be ridiculous, Lizzie. I can see you. This looks terrible, me talking to you through the door and you running away. It's bloody silly, for a start. We'll both look bad.'

She hesitated. He spoke again.

'Lizzie, look, I understand. You feel dreadful. You're still in shock. Stay and talk to me. You can trust me . . .'

She turned away from the front door and began to run down the hall. Behind her she could hear the unmistakable sound of the detective constable trying to force his way in. The door was shaking in its frame. He would be in the house within a minute. Quickly she opened the French window and slipped into the garden. The side entrance was protected by a tall fence. The gate at the back led into the park. She unlocked it and pulled the hood of her tracksuit top up. Sunset was beginning to draw in. The fading city sky was streaked with vapour trails and pink clouds. She broke into a run, crossing the darkening park and turning towards the high street.

★   ★   ★

Her bank was already closed. She withdrew the maximum amount from the cashpoint. She paused, instinctively looking up and around for CCTV cameras. Then she decided it didn't matter.

She turned off the high street and ran about a mile along the back streets, towards the offices under the railway arches.

CHAPTER 7

A fat PCSO pointed Collins in the right direction. Baillie had commandeered an office at Farlow police station, up some stairs and along a corridor. As she struggled through the station with her heavy old laptop and her pile of papers, Collins could feel the local officers' eyes clocking her lanyard. The door of the office was half-glazed, and before she knocked, she caught sight of the back of Inspector Shaw. He was sitting down, facing away from her towards the desk, where, presumably, Baillie was also sitting, just out of view. She hesitated, then tapped on the door and entered.

Baillie smiled at her. 'Sarah.'

'Boss.'

Inspector Shaw had stood up, and now he turned and offered Collins his hand. The top button of his shirt was open and his police tie was threaded through the retainer on his shirt. He looked exhausted, but he was a good-looking man, she realized. Tall, athletic. Hair streaked with grey.

'Sergeant. Collins, isn't it?'

She felt the DCI's eyes on her. 'Sarah,' she said, accepting Shaw's hand.

'Sarah.' He paused. 'Kieran.' He waved her towards the seat he had been sitting in. 'No, please, sit. I'm on my way now anyway. I was just updating the boss before I go off duty. Unless you need anything from me?'

She shook her head. 'No.'

He turned to the DCI. 'With your permission then, sir?'

'Yes, thanks for your help.'

Shaw turned to go, then hesitated. 'Look, Sarah, I'm sorry if we got off to a bad start. I was in shock myself.'

Collins nodded. 'Yes, of course you were.'

'I've never lost an officer before.'

'Really, I understand completely. It's terrible.'

There was a pause.

'Still, no excuse for not being professional. What is it they used to say to us at training school?' He gave a half-laugh. 'You only get one chance to make a first impression?' He smiled complacently at the worn-out cliché. It was a reference to a shared experience – training school, years of policing – an appeal perhaps to Collins' better nature, but she was not put at her ease by his confidence and the cliché, she realized, cut both ways. She too, of course, had made a first impression, one that she felt sure he hadn't liked.

'Yes,' she said, attempting a smile. 'That's right.'

'You getting all the help you need? My team being cooperative?'

'Yes, thank you.'

'I'll let you get on then, but if you need anything, call me.'

'Yes, I will. Thank you.'

Collins' eyes flickered involuntarily towards the DCI. He caught her glance and held it as the door closed behind Kieran Shaw.

'Not like him much?' Baillie said.

Collins shrugged. 'No opinion. Don't know the man yet, sir.'

It took them a moment to get the laptop plugged in and up and running. The password was the usual struggle, but eventually the media programme opened. They leaned over the computer, watching.

First: jump frames of colour CCTV. Farah and Ben on a bus. A dark-skinned teenage girl in a cat-print T-shirt and a small boy in a bear suit. Farah holding on to the standing rail. The boy sitting separately but close to her on one of the high seats at the front. Passengers getting on and off. Farah jumping Ben down from the seat in three bites of images. Then, a different media file: council CCTV, black and white. Farah and Ben walking hand-in-hand through the estate. Now, by the entrance to the estate. Then a remote view: the slight figure of a teenage girl and a small boy crossing the central square. A local-authority camera showed two marked police cars entering the estate separately. Their flashing lights flared, whiting out the grey tones of the film.

The media window went black. Collins closed the program.

Baillie said, 'That it?'

'Yes, sir. That's all we've managed to recover so far.'

'Still, not a bad effort. Is there anything you need to tell me about it?'

Collins picked up the sheaf of papers she had left on the seat of her chair. She handed them to Baillie.

'Just the timings, sir.'

Something wary, something usually hidden, flitted across Baillie's face, and Collins thought, *No one gets to DCI without some steel in the soul.* He sat at the desk, put on his reading glasses and glanced at the papers. After a minute he removed the glasses and held them in his right hand. He looked up at Collins.

'It's going to be quicker if you explain this to me.'

'The first printout, sir, top of your bundle. The 999 call shows that the boy's mother, Mrs Stewart, called police at 15:48 hours to report Ben missing. At 15:51, the incident goes out over the radio with a description of the boy and a request for officers to attend the home address to take the report. No one knows the location of Ben at that time. In all likelihood he's already at Portland Tower with the girl, Farah. We've got CCTV of them already on the bus before the mother dials 999. In any case, the unit reports Ben as a high-risk missing person. At 15:54, the duty inspector deploys units to conduct a search of the area surrounding the boy's home address.'

Baillie leafed through the papers. 'OK.'

'If you turn to the next dispatch, sir . . . At 15:53, a new report has opened. It's a member of the public calling 999. She's seen some figures standing on the roof of Portland Tower. The informant's not good on description, but she's sure there are two people, and thinks one may be a child. She's run into her home to make the call and can no longer see the roof. That's transmitted over the main channel at 15:56. The call's treated as an immediate suicide risk, and at 16:00, two units are dispatched on blue lights. No one links the two incidents at this point, at least not officially they don't.'

Collins felt Baillie's eyes flick to her. She found herself swallowing before continuing. It was important not to seem worked up.

'So, neither PC Hadley Matthews nor PC Lizzie Griffiths is on the log as putting up for either call. I've examined the duty slate – that's the fourth printout, sir. PC Matthews is assigned to a non-suspicious death and he's shown making his way to that call. PC Griffiths is shown in the police station, unavailable. Her sergeant has told us she was assigned to complete an outstanding file for court. There's no indication why she suddenly abandons her case file and drives on blue lights – for which, incidentally, she's not authorized – to Portland Tower.

'If you go back to that earlier dispatch . . . At 16:07, the first unit to attend Portland Tower notifies Control that it has arrived. At 16:09, this same unit radios. The officer can see three figures on the roof. Two together and one slightly further off. The figure standing a little further off is wearing a police uniform. The officer on the ground cautiously identifies this person as PC Matthews.

'Control calls PC Matthews on his radio. There's no reply. Then if you go to the radio log – at the back of your bundle, sir – at 16:10, PC Matthews switches his radio off.'

Baillie put the papers down on the table. 'Sarah, where's this going?'

'Sir, the timings should be just the usual recording of a team responding to an emergency. But the dispatches look wrong for that. The log of the movements of PC Matthews' car show that at 15:57, without notifying Control, he diverted from his assigned call. That's just one minute *after* the transmission of the call from the member of the public regarding the suicide risk. So, the instant it's broadcast, Hadley Matthews decides to divert. And he must have driven like the clappers. He arrived at Portland Tower at 16:00. That's just four minutes after he hears the report of the figures on the roof, and seven minutes before any other

30

officer arrives. In short, sir, the behaviour of PC Matthews and PC Griffiths seems irregular to me. They both get to Portland Tower too quickly.'

Baillie tidied the papers and added them to his case file. 'It doesn't seem much, to be honest. If it's suspicious, I'm going to need a lot more than a couple of PCs getting there quickly.'

'Of course. I understand that.'

It wasn't a good time for Collins' phone to ring. Steve's name flashed up on the screen. Baillie waved his hand for her to take the call.

'Right, OK. Thanks, Steve. I'll tell the DCI. I'm with him now. Ask Jez to obtain an out-of-hours warrant. I'll get back to you in a moment.'

She closed the call.

The DCI said, 'An out-of-hours warrant? What's that for then?'

There was no avoiding it.

'Sir, I'm sorry. I've got bad news.'

CHAPTER 8

Lizzie had been aware of this place and its big orange sign, but she had never been inside before. She knew it was where the drug dealers went to get their cars when they had a stash to sell. The man behind the counter leaned away from her as if to take a better look.

'Wolverhampton Wanderers,' he said.

'I'm sorry?'

'You're wearing Wolverhampton Wanderers colours.'

'Oh.'

He seemed pleased with his joke, if that was what it was, smiling to himself as though he had said something very funny. He took his time filling out the paperwork and checking her driving licence.

'Doesn't do you justice,' he said, handing back the photocard and casting his eyes over her approvingly. 'Going anywhere special?'

'Not really.'

'Fancy some company?'

She gave a laugh and said, 'You're working.'

'I'm off in a moment. You were lucky to catch

us open, actually. I'm waiting for a customer, then I'm out of here.'

He passed her the card reader. She tapped in a number and then shook her head. How could she have been so stupid? She tried again, but she could not for the life of her remember her credit card PIN.

'I can't believe it,' she said.

'Don't put it in again. You'll lock it.'

'Oh shoot.'

'You got any other card?'

'Not really. Should I risk trying it again?'

'Up to you.'

'Don't suppose you'd take cash?'

'Against the rules, love. I need a card as a deposit.'

'Damn. I'm going to a funeral tomorrow and I've got to be there first thing in the morning. I really need a car. Mine's suddenly gone to shit. I think it's the clutch.'

'Sorry about that, love.'

'If it helps . . .' She pulled out her warrant card.

'Oh. I see.' He took in the fact of it with something like disappointment. 'I would never have guessed.' He considered her with an appraising eye, as though her appearance and the warrant card contained confusingly contradictory information. 'One of those volunteers, are you? You're too pretty to be arresting people.'

She smiled. 'Look, I know it's a bit irregular, but I can pay cash and leave you my credit card number for the deposit.'

He tapped his cheek with his index finger. 'OK. How long do you want it for?'

'Just a couple of days.'

'It's more than two hundred quid. You've got that much cash?'

She started to open her purse. 'Thanks, really. You've got my details and you know you'll be able to find me. I am a cop, after all. I've just got myself into such a state.'

Even at this time of night, the traffic crawled. The suburbs rolled slowly past: shuttered dress shops, twenty-four-hour corner shops with metal grilles, the empty tarmac expanses of superstore car parks. Lizzie's hands were shaking on the steering wheel.

After about forty-five minutes, she pulled over and went into an all-night café. There was a strong smell of cooking fat. An overweight woman with a purple chiffon scarf on her head was sitting in the corner. She had a small white dog on her lap. It had pink weepy eyes and its skin showed through its fur. The man standing at the counter swiftly stubbed out his cigarette and stashed the ashtray. He waved his hands about in a vain attempt to dispel the smoke.

'Sorry, darling.'

Lizzie shook her head. 'No, not a problem. Buttered toast and coffee, please.'

'White bread's all we've got.'

'That'll be fine.'

At the table was a well-read *Evening Standard*,

probably abandoned by some other customer. She unfolded it and saw that the story had made the front page of the late edition. *Police officer and teenage girl in death fall.* The man came over with her order and she put the paper down. He wiped the table with a dirty rag.

'You look as though you need a bit more than coffee and toast.'

'No, that's great. Looks delicious.'

She stared at the photo on the front of the *Standard.* It was the usual impersonal crime-scene cliché: blue and white plastic tape, the concrete concourse, figures in white forensic suits, and in the background, the tower itself.

The call that had begun it so many weeks ago had come over the airwaves graded *Soon.* The traffic had been moving sluggishly that day too, and the police car had nudged forward slowly. It had not been an emergency, not something requiring an immediate response, just an outstanding dispatch from the day before that the night duty had managed to avoid. It had been routine activity. Anyone could have taken it.

The early-morning streets had been busy with the legitimately purposeful: the employed making their way to work, shopkeepers rolling up blinds and setting out vegetable stalls on lead-drenched pavements. The tall buildings, like needles on a sun dial, had cast sharp cold shadows on the waking streets. The name of the ubiquitous

London Road suggested that the city was not here but further on: a place to which one journeyed from a rural village. But the streets with their pastoral echoes had long since merged into the metropolis. Heath Lane, Chase Road, The Green: all were concrete and tarmac, lined with halal takeaway shops, cash converters, pound stores, Tesco Metros.

Lizzie had turned her head and read, *Unblock your phone here.* This was the place where robbers came to offer up their pickings, BlackBerries and iPhones that had made their owners suddenly vulnerable and fearful. The premises were still shuttered: the shops' suppliers would be sleeping. Staring at the cold streets, Lizzie imagined them in their Victorian squats, in 1930s estates, in 1970s tower blocks, sprawled across unmade beds, on sofas, prostrate on floors, sleeping off the effects of late-night fighting and crack use. But the police were always on duty and they woke early. Alarms prodded them from their beds before the light had broken and they dressed in the other room so as not to wake their partners. The marked cars cruised aimlessly, five at a time flocking to any *Immediate* call that promised action. Police officers drifted around in the morning sunlight like tired crows, waiting to see if they were needed and dreaming of breakfast.

She could so easily have ignored the call – as indeed all the other cars had – but she liked to work and for the team to know she was working, and so she had put up for the uninspiring dispatch that everyone else was avoiding.

'OK for that?' she had said to Hadley, and he had put his blue lights on just to make the traffic give way and to turn the car in the direction of the call.

'Yes. OK. Why not?'

Number 5 Kenley Villas was part of a Victorian terrace on one of the gentrified streets of the borough – media types living next door to drug dealers. A street that was asking for trouble. Lizzie noticed that it had a heavy Victorian-style door – hardwood, with leaded lights in the top panes.

Hadley turned off the engine.

'We'll do this,' he said, 'and then go back to the nick for breakfast. See if you can get it done in fifteen minutes. I'll set the alarm on my watch. If you succeed, I'll buy breakfast. Otherwise it's on you.'

Lizzie slipped quickly out of the car. Hadley followed slowly behind. In a gesture of anticipatory politeness, he hitched up his trousers – a useless action, the belt fighting its habitual losing battle with his belly. His gut had a physical presence as solid as a watermelon, and Hadley's bulk created the impression of settled indolence, however urgent the call.

Carrie Stewart answered the door. She was pleasantly scruffy in an affluent, educated style: leggings, blonde hair tied back with a scarf, green cardigan. Without make-up her face was pretty, faintly dappled with freckles, and tired. There was a dog, a spaniel, jumping up behind her. A boy with the same colour hair as his mother pulled the dog back by its collar and said, 'Charlie, Charlie.' The boy was wearing a bear suit. He stared at the police officers, his cheeks red from heat. The dog wagged its tail enthusiastically.

'He won't take it off,' the woman said, her hand on her son's shoulder. She led the way along stripped wooden floorboards, past some large framed black-and-white photos in the hall: children on swings, the perspective making their feet big, Carrie Stewart herself in a white linen suit and a just-too-large hat, the glamorous incarnation that was implicit in her house and her clothing. 'He even wants to sleep in it. I don't know what to do.'

She stepped down into the kitchen.

'Can I get you tea?' she asked. Her voice was low and the accent was what Lizzie's fellow officers would call well-spoken.

'No thank you,' said Hadley.

'A glass of water would be nice . . .'

Carrie's back was turned as she reached for a glass. The shelves, Lizzie noticed, had no Delia Smith or Jamie Oliver on them, but a cut above – torn covers of River Café, olive-oil-stained Marcella Cucina. Crowded amongst them were novels, Booker Prize winners, a commentary on the Middle East, a history of the Ottoman Empire.

Through the wooden-framed windows the garden was shady. York stone dusted with moss. A wrought-iron bench; beside it on the ground a discarded novel. A trough of bluebells not yet flowering. A red plastic child's tricycle. Hadley caught Lizzie's eye and tapped his watch face.

As the glass filled with water and bubbles, Lizzie said, 'Why don't you tell me what this is all about?'

It was a minor offence, which Mrs Stewart recounted in too much detail. Hadley looked as patient as stone as the woman took out a large lined diary. But Lizzie wasn't fooled by his manner: Hadley's was the patience of a man who had spent a long career enduring the folly of others. Lizzie saw names and times scribbled in black italic handwriting. Carrie was explaining: she had taken notes of the dates and the increasing frequency and violence of the damage to her property. She knew who was doing it: it was her neighbour. She did not know why he had taken against her. She had always been friendly. She had cut back a buddleia that was growing in his garden. It had been blocking her light. But she couldn't think it was this that had made him angry. Well, the garden was hardly well tended and the buddleia had obviously self-seeded. It was one of those pale purple ones you saw on railway tracks. And it had only been the branches on her property. She had been careful about that. She hadn't put the cut branches back on his land. She believed that was the law but it seemed so rude. She leafed through the diary. Hadley caught Lizzie's eyes and his own rolled heavenwards. Lizzie knew she should hurry the woman up but she didn't know how.

Hadley said, 'Nothing else?'

'Not really. I did have a word with his housing officer. I'd asked him to move some of his stuff off the pavement. He had dumped it out there and it wasn't nice going past it. He didn't do anything about it. It's not a lot to ask, to keep the front of the property clean. I don't like to interfere, but I didn't have any choice but to make a formal complaint. It all amounts to nothing much really, no reason to provoke this behaviour.'

'How long have they been there?'

'Oh, not long. A month maybe? I can give you the details of the housing officer if you need them.'

Lizzie said, 'No, that won't be necessary, thanks.'

Hadley shifted in his seat. There was a pause.

'You are sure it's him?' said Lizzie.

'Absolutely positive.'

It was the worst possible outcome. A seething neighbour dispute; an educated victim who would not drop it easily; a minor offence without evidence to support an arrest and charge.

Lizzie said, 'Do you have any proof?'

And here was the surprise, for Carrie did. For the first time she brightened up and Lizzie saw in her the determined nature that lay hidden beneath her urbane vagueness. 'Yes, I've got photos. Would you like to see them?'

The Mac was perched on a desk in the small front bedroom. Outside the window a cherry tree was in full bloom. The screen saver was passing through images of family holidays. A boy doing a handstand. Children playing with a plastic bucket and a net by a broad green river. This house, thought Lizzie, was an oasis, a force field of advantage. She knew the crime statistics for the area. It seemed fairly mad for this family to live here. And yet here they were, the adventurous middle classes, colonizing, transforming, improving the local schools, pushing property values up. And they got so much more for their money.

'Please – sit,' said Carrie.

Lizzie took the chair before the desk. Hadley crammed himself into the doorway, making the wooden frame seem like a cartoon drawing and himself a milder version of Desperate Dan. Carrie leaned over Lizzie, moving the mouse and flicking through the images. There he was, this unknown neighbour. The photos were sequential and conclusive.

The man was dark, thin. He wore the uniform of the street – jeans, a hooded zipped jacket, trainers. He had a child with him, a girl with dark skin and long dark curly hair. She was caught at angles, turning away. One image had her at three quarters to the camera, her face tipped downwards. She would be pretty were it not for something caught fleetingly, something watchful, nervous in the face. She looked about fourteen years old.

41

Father and daughter paused in the photos as a woman with a buggy passed by. The father glanced about him. He took out a can of paint. He sprayed it down the fence. A close-up of the word: *Bastards*.

It was the perfect montage of the offence. Suddenly the matter had gone from a dull report to an easy detection.

'And who's the girl with him?' Lizzie asked.

Using the cursor, Carrie flicked back through the images. There was the teenager, small, a dark figure standing back from the action. Watching.

'Oh, that's his daughter,' she said. 'I think her name is Farah. What a pity he's sucking her into this.'

'Do you mind?' Lizzie said, taking the mouse.

'Please, go ahead.'

She zoomed in on the figure, but the image of the girl blurred and fragmented into its constituent pixels.

Hadley's watch beeped. Lizzie winced.

'What's that?' said Carrie, looking up. 'Do you need to go?'

Hadley caught Lizzie's eye and smiled. She owed him breakfast.

'I don't know,' said Lizzie. 'It's not my watch. Hadley?'

Hadley smiled again. 'Sorry,' he said blithely. 'I must have set it off by accident.'

Carrie glanced between the two of them, as if she sensed she was missing something.

Lizzie stood up. 'I've got all the details.'

Carrie stepped back into the hallway. 'What I don't understand,' she said, and this seemed suddenly to be the heart of the matter, the thing that was really troubling her. 'What I don't understand is *why*. Why is he doing this? That's what really troubles me. Perhaps if we spoke with him . . .'

'Yes, I will be speaking with him.'

'I understand that. But I wondered whether instead . . . that is, whether you offered some kind of mediation?'

Hadley intervened. 'We're the police,' he said. 'We deal with criminal matters. We don't do mediation.'

The boy, still in his bear suit, was standing on the landing behind Hadley, watching warily. Instinctively, perhaps sensing the tone change, he grabbed on to his mother's leg. Lizzie thought how impressive they must seem to the boy, the two uniformed officers, with handcuffs and CS gas and radios chattering quietly away in this small room in the shade of the cherry blossom.

'It's all right, Ben,' his mother said with an encouraging smile. 'These officers are here to help us.'

Unlike in other houses Lizzie had visited, where the children watched warily from behind the legs of their parents, or stared at her, faces blank with an inherited hatred, the child in this house was trustfully curious. He must have been told that the officers were his friends. This was a vital part of his education, something essential to survival. Frontier people needed their children to trust the police. They needed them to learn not to try to deal with things themselves but to turn to the black uniform when matters got out of hand on the bus or when another child took their mobile phone at a street corner. It was the peculiar and relentless power of the privileged not to sink to the level of fisticuffs. Lizzie heard the bugle's reveille and saw herself and Hadley as the unlikely cavalry riding over the brow of the hill. Poor broken-backed horse that would have to carry Hadley! It was an image that also made her flinch: her sympathy had always been with the Indians rather than with the frontiersmen corralling their wagons in preparation for settling a prairie that did not belong to them.

A woman who had knocked on her parents' door a lifetime ago came to mind. Lizzie remembered her standing in the frame of the doorway with a tightly pursed smile.

'Can I speak to your mummy or daddy?'

They had lived in a new-build semi with a view over former farmland that had been converted into a municipal park and playing fields. Buying the house had been a move up in the world. As her father had contemplated the woman, an expression of satisfied fury had settled on his features.

'The gypsies have been there far longer than these houses,' he said.

The woman wriggled uncomfortably, as though

her underwear was too tight but she did not feel free to adjust it. 'But why can't they be *clean*?' she protested, in an outraged rejection of having been put so firmly and so unexpectedly in the wrong.

'I'm sorry,' said her father, already shutting the door. 'You've come to the wrong house with your petition.'

Lizzie gazed at the boy in his bear suit standing in the hallway. What did any of that have to do with him? He suddenly said, 'Mummy,' and raised his arms. As Carrie scooped up her hot little bear, like the sun being revealed by a gusting cloud Lizzie suddenly saw it differently and was ashamed. How frightened this woman was by the random and unexplained hatred of her neighbour. It turned out it wasn't complicated. The man lived next door. Carrie Stewart was at home with a young child: an easy target. And she was no settler – she was more likely to have been born in London than the man who was persecuting her. She wanted only to protect her family – this soft boy in his bear suit – from a mysterious hatred. It was her home and she had every right to live in it without fear.

'You've called the police,' Lizzie said. 'You don't really want mediation. What you want is for this to stop. You don't want to be sitting down talking to this person: you don't want any more to do with him. You want him to leave you and your family alone. That's why you've called the police and that's what we're here for. We'll make some

45

inquiries and be looking to arrest him. I'll keep you informed.'

Carrie smiled with relief. It was a smile that promised trust and confidence. 'Yes, you're right. Of course you are. Thank you so much.'

'Mediation,' Hadley had muttered contemptuously, as he slid behind the wheel and turned over the engine. 'She could have tried talking to her neighbour before she went to the bloody housing officer. Doesn't she know anything?'

'Yes, but I think she said she did try talking to him . . .'

'Do you know what, Lizzie, at the end of the day, who bloody cares? Let's keep it simple – criminal damage, arrest and charge.' He paused, and then laughed out loud. 'Mediation! You'll see. By the end, Carrie Stewart will not only want him hanged. She'll be quite happy to be the one to kick the stool away.'

CHAPTER 9

The twilight was a stained urban orange. Collins clipped the blue light on to the roof of her vehicle and pulled out of the yard. Headlights flared at her as she made steady progress across London.

The disappearance of PC Griffiths was perhaps the opportunity Baillie had been hoping for. It gave him the edge.

'For Chrissakes, Sarah, couldn't you have held on to her? What were you thinking?'

And although Collins knew she could have argued in her own defence – after all, it was Shaw, not her, who had sent Lizzie home – a quiet place inside her accepted that Baillie had a point. Every cop she knew would agree that she had taken her eye off the ball. She hadn't held on to Lizzie Griffiths, which – looking back – seemed now to have been the single most important thing to do. That was Baillie's brief: find the bloody PC before anything else went wrong. He had allowed himself to lose his rag a bit. Perhaps it had been a show, perhaps not.

'And while you're at it, find out what that fat

47

PC, poor bastard, was doing up on the roof. Don't get me wrong, Sarah. Do a good job. But I'd still appreciate you getting a bit of a fucking move on. We're going to have to organize a funeral soon enough and everyone will be anxious to know whether Old Bill will be wearing white gloves. For my part, I'd like to be able to stand in front of that revolving sign and say something nice and bulletproof. In case it's slipped your attention, the journos are also very keen to know what's going on. Just doing their job, I'm sure. But I don't think your press strategy of not telling them anything is going to wash for very long, to be honest. The only press release I can offer them right now is that following today's tragic events at Portland Tower, we've now mislaid the only witness, who is also, by the way, a serving police officer. It doesn't look good, Sarah. It doesn't look good.'

The street outside Lizzie Griffiths' flat was jammed with unmarked cars. The door was on the latch and Collins made her way in unannounced.

Inside, all the lights were on. It was a small flat, but neatly done. The warrant and the premises search book were on the sofa. Everyone was working in silence, the officers, all in forensic suits, searching systematically. Drawers and cupboards were being turned out. Lizzie's laptop had been placed on a pull-out desk and a technician was in front of it. One of the DCs was going

48

through her correspondence. Another held up an apricot silk cami and matching knickers.

'Nice,' he said.

Somebody coughed. The detective constable's face froze: he hadn't realized Collins was in the flat.

She spoke as if to a child. 'No, Jez, they wouldn't suit you. Now put them back.'

There was a short laugh from one of the other officers.

Steve said, 'I'm going outside for a smoke.'

Collins followed him out. She lit two cigarettes and passed him one.

'Filthy habit,' Steve commented as he inhaled with satisfaction.

'It is,' Collins agreed as she too inhaled.

In the tungsten light of the street lamp, Steve's face had something of a used paper bag about it. He reeked of tobacco. The middle finger of his right hand was stained yellow. The man was a ruin, emotionally and physically: a divorce behind him and duly signed up for child maintenance payments. He had given up on any form of optimism about the human race a long time ago. And in a funny way, Collins recognized that she loved him. Not the kind of love that ended up in bed or holding hands walking along a beach. No, it was pure detective love. A variation on the kind of recognition that Volkswagen beetle drivers experienced when they flashed their headlights at each other.

'There was no reply at the door,' he said. 'I checked the letter box. When I saw her making off, I put the door in. Figured I could justify it one way or another. Genuine fear for her safety, something like that. Better than losing her, anyway. When I finally got in, she'd gone. The doors to the garden were open. I did a drive around but I couldn't spot her.' He tipped his head towards the high wooden fence that blocked the side entrance to the garden. 'A few years ago I could have climbed that but now the damn thing's too tall for me. I'm getting old. I just wasn't quick enough.'

'It's OK.'

'No, it isn't. I'm sorry, Sarah.'

Baillie's words were still ringing in Collins' ears. 'Don't worry,' she said. 'It's my fault.'

There was silence for a moment.

'Her car's over there,' Steve said, pointing to a neat little Golf, five years old but in good condition.

'So she's left her vehicle. That's something, I suppose. Perhaps she's not planning to leave London. You've tried calling her, of course?'

'A couple of times before I went round. The phone's switched off now. Goes straight to voicemail.'

Collins sighed. 'Fuck.'

'Fuck indeed. How was Baillie?'

'As well as can be expected.'

Steve took another drag. 'That figures.' The cigarette crinkled red. It was burned almost to the filter. 'It could be nothing, Sarah. She could be shopping.'

'Shopping?'

He laughed. 'OK, that's unlikely—'

'But it could be a temporary disappearance, yes. Maybe she's just gone for a long walk to clear her head. But if it's not temporary, do we know what sort of risk she is? Why has she gone? Any chance she's going to kill herself? How much do we know about her?'

'Not much yet. She's young in service: only just out of probation.'

'Any issues around her?'

'Not at work. Top of the class. Nothing on her record except a borough commendation for her actions as first on scene for a sexual assault by touching. That was when she'd only been operational for six months. There's another one pending too, apparently. Domestic murder.'

Collins exhaled. 'OK. What about her family?'

'County officers have gone over to Mum. Mum's not heard from her. She's tried to ring her but no reply. Says Lizzie is bad at keeping in touch at the best of times. Sounds like they're not close.'

'Dad?'

'Dead.'

Collins found herself unaccountably furious. Only a few hours and somehow one of the lead subjects of the investigation had gone missing. 'Do we have her bank details? Can we run her credit card?'

'Financial are working on that. We'll have a full intelligence pack first thing in the morning.'

'Is it too late to start checking CCTV? Has anyone tried?'

'Yes, Carl drove over there. They've already closed. This borough's not twenty-four hours.'

'OK, we need to work out who stays and who goes. You should get off yourself. No point in running on empty. Boss wants us in bright-eyed and bushy-tailed at eight for a briefing.'

'I'll be all right. I was going to sleep at Victoria House, but if you're running the search, I'll go home.'

Steve offered another cigarette. Collins shook her head.

'They're no substitute for food, you know,' she said.

Steve lit up. 'I could actually *see* her through the letter box. I can't fucking believe it.'

'Get over it. Listen, I'll stay and supervise the search. But could you have a quick word with Jez before you go. Tell him not to behave like a cock.'

CHAPTER 10

Driving had become a consolation in itself. Lizzie followed signs towards the motorway. She was headed to no particular destination but still she wanted to drive fast, as though she could escape her own mind. She briefly considered making for Dover and crossing the Channel, where there would be no limit to her journey, no sea to hem her in. But passport control, with its possibilities of identification, deterred her. She wondered how it worked. Would they put a flag on her name? For now it seemed most important to get some distance between herself and the people who, she knew, were already seeking a quick resolution. The matter pressed inside her uncomfortably. It shifted its shape, appearing now one way and now another but mainly condensed in images – a face, a shadow in a hallway. And that terrible, stupid, catastrophic quote that rang in her ears.

Isn't that just like a wop – brings a knife to a gun fight.

She took the slip road and pushed her foot flat. The car roared forward. Fields and woods flashed by. She wanted to close her eyes. After about an hour she took an exit on to an A road. Roundabouts. A vehicle showroom. Horses, dark shapes moving through a field's darkness. She had found her way into a seaside town and wove through its traffic system. She parked parallel to the shoreline. The sea lapped blackly against the shingle. A woman was pushing a shopping trolley full of plastic bags along the concrete path. Lizzie let her pass and then walked down over the crunching pebbles towards the restless sea. A single running shoe sluiced back and forth in the tide's frothy edge.

She closed her eyes and saw, as if on a loop, a repeating backdrop of square windows, blue sky and concrete, spinning and passing, passing, passing. She could not escape the horror of it: falling unstoppably, irretrievably, until the hard concrete reached up.

That last glimpse of them at the edge.

She opened her eyes and let the wind blow cold into them. She saw the glinting dark sea. She swallowed and wished that it was the usual dream; the one that ended with a bump and an awakening.

There was loss, of course, but anger there too. She admitted that to herself. An overwhelming, pointless anger searching for something to fasten itself to. A bitter anger in the end, mainly with herself, as though she could easily have avoided the thing that had undone her. It felt like some monster species of the inattention that let a glass slip between the fingers and watched it shatter on a stone floor. The memory of the roof came to her again unbidden and she shied away, unable to bear it. Not inattention; that wasn't entirely accurate, no.

Well, people's lives went astray. Actions had unintended consequences.

A fatal road collision she'd attended came to mind. The car hadn't even been moving. The driver had been a bleary mother, distracted by extended sleep deprivation. She had just strapped her one-year-old into the car seat behind her and had thought to give him some milk for the journey. She'd opened the driver's door. Just – like – that. The cyclist had been a young woman. A student on a sit-up-and-beg with books in the wicker basket strapped under the handlebars. She had been dressed in a blue polka-dot dress: flared skirt, a broad brown leather belt around her narrow waist. *Dressed* had been the right verb, as though she were already prepared for the coffin. Apart from the head wound, she was unmarked by the collision. She had freckles across her snub nose and down her pale arms.

Lizzie could still see those symbols of the cyclist's bright future spread across the road. Kant's *Critique of Pure Reason* had been one of them. She remembered too the face of the driver, a young mother standing in the road with a look as blank as November. Fatal distraction: that was how she had tagged it in her internal list of unforgettable things already encountered in her brief service as a uniformed constable. Would she cover her own conduct with such pithiness? The thought of it hurt her. She shied away from the fact of what had happened, struggling to contain it within herself. It was absurd. She had joined the legions of people who could not put the clock back.

The cold water had seeped into Lizzie's running shoes. The tide had come in without her noticing its advance. There was a strong smell of brine and seaweed. The wind was bitter and the chill of the sea had penetrated into her bones. Her hands were frozen. She looked away from the water towards the seafront. Lights were on in the windows, and car headlights fanned across the beach. She imagined the town's cafés, its B&Bs crammed with bored asylum-seekers staring out of dirty windows at the dark ocean.

She took her phone out of her jacket and held it in her palm. It was a temptation. She wasn't exactly sure how phones were used to trace people – that was CID stuff, not the province of uniform. Could the police locate her, she wondered, just because the phone was switched on, or did she need to make a call? And how precise would any such location be? Would it illuminate her on some electronic map, a pinprick of light here on this lonely beach? She knew it couldn't possibly be like in the movies, where the cops turned up within minutes of a mobile phone being switched on anywhere in the world. She could only guess at the reality of trying to get local police to respond quickly to a phone trace in St Leonards.

The phone lay cold and dark in her hand. She longed to switch it on. It was as though its lit screen would offer her some primal warmth, some link to others. The retained voicemails, the texts, even the lists of contacts would place her somewhere in a world that had a matrix of connections. Standing here by the sea, she imagined herself slipping off the map, like Voyager travelling out into deep, deep space.

18 APRIL

CHAPTER 11

Collins turned the car into the concrete descent to the underground car park of Victoria House, swiping her warrant card at the gate and entering her PIN. The building was separate from the other police buildings, tucked away, anonymous. It was not a port of call for the public, not an address for anyone really except the people who worked there. She couldn't think of anyone, not one single interest group, who liked the cops who investigated cops.

Her alarm had gone off at 6 a.m. Outside her window it had still been dark and it had been desperately hard to be prodded from sleep by the alarm's insistent beeping. She had grabbed a short, hot shower. When she got out, the milk for her coffee had boiled over the stovetop. There were some advantages to living alone: she had made an ineffective stab at wiping it up and then given up. On the way in she had picked up what had turned out to be probably the most expensive coffee and muffin in the Western world – she'd stopped on a red route and been photographed by a mobile CCTV car.

A strong smell of buttered toast greeted her as she made her way down the corridor to her office. The door was propped open with a spoon in the hinge. The window to the office was open too, and Steve was standing on the low roof smoking. A crow hopped around warily within about a foot of him. More than a year ago Collins had named the bird Sid and begun to tame it – or perhaps, she acknowledged, it was the bird who had tamed her. Steve sometimes threw things at it: the roof was littered with fag packets and old biros, all of which had once been missiles. At other times she had seen him toss the bird the crust of a sandwich. He seemed to treat Sid like a low-level informant, despising and befriending him in equal measure.

Collins threw her car keys on the desk and the crow came hopping towards the window, its head on one side. She shouted over to Steve.

'My spoon in the door, is it?'

'No comment.'

'What time did you get home?'

'Not too bad. About midnight. I've been in for an hour. I've bashed out a briefing document on where we are with Ms Griffiths.'

'Thanks. Have I got time for a cigarette before I go up?'

'Sorry. He's already been down asking where you are. We'll mainline some decent coffee and fags when you get back. You look knackered.'

Collins smiled. 'Thanks for that. Tell it like it is, Steve, that's always the best policy. I'll be taking you up on the coffee and fags provided I'm not a hospital admission once he's finished with me.'

Baillie had moved into an expansive office on the sixth floor. His suit jacket was on a wooden hanger on a coat stand. He wore a beautifully pressed white shirt with an off-white and navy striped silk tie. He also wore, Collins noticed, very good brogues.

The DCI had only recently taken up post but the office, with its grand view of the Thames, already bore his imprint. Waiting while he read Steve's briefing document, Collins glanced at the shelf behind his desk, where a framed photograph of a small blond boy, aged about eight, had been given pride of place. The boy looked at the viewer with a solemn expression and held, in small, tense hands, a very big fish. We are normal people, the photograph seemed to announce: we share your concerns. How could we be anything other than normal, for *here is my son with a big fish*. On the desk itself was a button with the instruction to press in case of panic. DCI Baillie, Collins already suspected, was not the type to panic: the button must be intended for others.

Baillie put the briefing document down and looked up. 'So, Sarah, no phone use, no financial, no vehicle.'

'That's right, sir. She withdrew three hundred pounds from a cashpoint on Kilsby High Street at 19:32 hours. Nothing since.'

'What about the phone?'

'We've done urgent checks. Nothing. It must be switched off. She may even have got rid of it.'

'She's on a contract?'

'Yes, sir.'

'What about family? Friends?'

'Mum hasn't heard from her. We haven't had time to develop her lifestyle yet. We're working on it.'

'And she left her car behind?'

'Yes, sir.'

'You've started checking the CCTV?'

'Jez is down there with Alice. They only opened at eight.'

'OK. So she's not using her vehicle or her phone. She's not with any family that we know of.' He paused and looked at Collins. 'That's correct?'

'Afraid so, yes, sir.'

Baillie went and stood by his window, gazing out towards the Thames. Collins could see, beyond him, the opaque grey river, sinuous and cold.

'Sir, I wondered about publicity . . . Perhaps we should release that Lizzie is missing. She's a pretty girl, fairly recognizable.'

She waited while Baillie studied the river. Finally he spoke. 'No, I don't think so. Not yet, anyway. We don't know enough.'

'OK, sir.'

Baillie turned and considered Collins with interest, the ghost of a smile at the corner of his lips. 'You happy with that?'

'Of course, sir.'

He smiled. 'You don't *look* happy.'

'OK, well. Look, I take full responsibility for—'

'But that's not the issue, Sarah. We've moved on from that.'

'Thank you, sir.'

There was a silence. Baillie waited for Collins to continue. She spoke carefully.

'It's just that I don't know what's going on with Lizzie or how much time we have. I wouldn't want her coming to harm or to lose any evidence. And I'd rather not wait until she makes a mistake, because she's a cop and we might be waiting a while for that. She probably knows quite a lot about disappearing.'

'Sarah, Sarah, Sarah, hang on, hang on a minute. We don't need Lizzie Griffiths to *make a mistake*. We are better than that. We are going to deploy our resources and we are going to find her. I have a lot of confidence in you. You won't be coming to me in a couple of days and saying that she is still missing.'

'Well thank you for your confidence, sir.'

He smiled again, but there was, nevertheless, something undeniably irritated in his eyes. 'You've got Farah Mehenni's post-mortem this morning?'

'Yes, sir. In fact I'm sorry, Steve and I need to head over there now.'

'You'd better go. When you get back, I want an update on how you're getting on with locating Lizzie.'

CHAPTER 12

Lizzie shifted in the narrow single bed and drew her cold feet into the warmth of her body. Troubled by sudden remembrances, she had slept fitfully. All night she had recoiled from the bed's freezing edges as she struggled to fit beneath the too-small blanket. Street light had filtered purple through the curtains, and she could sense the imprint of others who had slept on the mattress before her. She had woken with a claustrophobic sensation: one day her own heart would stop beating; the blood would no longer move.

She swung her legs out of the bed and her bare feet recoiled from the sticky carpet. The water in the bathroom emitted from the plastic shower head in an irritating squirt that alternated between scalding and freezing. The smell of the drain was ineffectively masked by disinfectant.

Shivering, she put on clean pants and a fresh T-shirt.

The dining room was empty of other guests. Individual boxes of Rice Krispies and Alpen were lined up on the shiny paper tablecloth like cardboard soldiers on forlorn sentry duty. A glass bowl held segments of limp grapefruit in yellow fluid. A female teenager with spotty skin and chipped nail polish approached and asked if she would like a fried breakfast or porridge.

Lizzie declined both and asked for fresh coffee. 'Hot, please,' she emphasized. 'And strong.'

Home. Most people would go home.

The girl put a cafetière on the table in front of her and smiled. 'I made it as strong as I could.'

Lizzie could not look at her straight: she brought to mind her first sight of Farah, the figure in a dark hallway. She looked down. 'Yes, thanks, thanks for that. Thanks a lot.'

Through the smeary window she registered blindly the traffic queuing along the coast road.

Number 7 Kenley Villas; the house next to Carrie Stewart's. Hadley had insisted they park the police car round the corner, but Lizzie couldn't see the point. They were both in uniform, after all, and so the Mehennis would know they were police. They would either open the door or they wouldn't.

She had knelt down and opened the letter box. She could still feel, as she had felt it then, the stone of the doorstep against her bony knees – hard and cold through her uniform trousers. Through the narrow and awkward aperture she could see the darkened empty hallway. Hadley, standing beside her, put a hand on her shoulder and pulled her back a little.

'Never heard of the dog that didn't bark?'

She stood up and brushed down her knees. They exchanged glances. Lizzie imagined a bloody big dog banging its head against the door and giggled at the thought and at Hadley's wilful misappropriation of the Sherlock Holmes quote. Hadley feigned ignorance with a suppressed smile.

'Well?' he said. 'What?'

Lizzie pulled a straight face and knocked again. 'Police. Anyone home?'

The door opened a crack. Dark beady eyes, as alert as a mouse, peered at them. Lizzie craned round the half-closed door to see. The woman must have been about sixty years old. She had thin dark lips and olive skin. She wore a green cable cardigan and a pink and green patterned headscarf. Hadley stepped round Lizzie, pushing her gently aside. He put his shoe, a large black Doc Marten, on the threshold.

'Your son in?' he said. 'Younes?'

The woman shook her head and started speaking a language Lizzie did not know but recognized as Arabic or one of its brother languages.

'May we come in?'

'Yes, yes,' the woman replied, but it was not clear that she had understood the question.

Hadley stepped swiftly sideways into the hallway. He was so large that the woman was virtually pressed against the wall by his bulk. Lizzie followed him into the dark, narrow corridor. Hadley had already pushed open the door on the side of the hall. He disappeared into the room, leaving her with the woman. She was small and wiry, wearing a dark skirt and pink slippers. She kept speaking, moving her hand in a patting motion as if smoothing something down. It was a reassuring movement that suggested she was used to trying to appease. Appease whom? Men? White people? Police officers?

Younes Mehenni's mother was bewildered but also strangely tenacious. Lizzie followed her as she turned and walked down the hallway into the kitchen. The woman was still talking but was also now dialling a number into her phone. Lizzie was uneasy. She looked around her. The house had a strangeness about it – it was the same basic layout as Carrie Stewart's, which was only next door, and yet Lizzie's sense of it was so different. This woman, it seemed, lived only on the surface of the place and had in no way penetrated its core. It was mutual: the house had had no effect on her either. She seemed to move around these rooms, transposed as if by green screen from her North African city.

The kitchen, like the hall, was dark. There was the smell of foreign food. Although there was washing on the floor and dirty plates on the side, the room did not feel truly inhabited. It felt as though the family could leave in a matter of minutes and never again be found. The floor was cheap linoleum, an orange flowery pattern left over from the sixties. The work surfaces were Formica,

edged with pine panelling. Someone else's optimism, lingering long after its authors had
disappeared. There were no pictures on the walls,
no books, no clues as to the inner life of the place.

Mrs Mehenni passed Lizzie the phone.

'Yes, who are you?' The voice was female, heavily
accented, and angry.

'I'm a police officer.'

'I *know* that. What's your name?'

'PC Griffiths.'

'And your number?'

'611DW.'

'I've made a note of that, PC Griffiths. Now
tell me what are you doing there.'

'Who are you?'

'You are in my mother's house. I want you to
leave.'

'Your mother is Mrs Mehenni?'

Silence.

'We need to speak to your brother, Younes.'

'What about?'

'I'm not sure I can discuss that—'

Mrs Mehenni was talking loudly and gesturing
for the phone. Lizzie handed it to her. There was
a ring at the doorbell and she turned to see who
was there. But Mrs Mehenni was passing the
phone back and Lizzie was detained by the angry
voice on the other end of the line.

'My mother says Younes is not there. You can
look in the garden if you like.'

Mrs Mehenni had opened the back door and

was gesturing for Lizzie to go outside. Along the hallway Lizzie heard the click of the front door opening. She looked over her shoulder. Hadley was standing in the doorway. Just past his bulk she could see the slight figure of a girl dressed in school uniform. She could not concentrate on this new arrival – Mrs Mehenni was speaking and through the earpiece of the phone Lizzie also heard the other distant voice, imperious and seething with disdain.

'Have you been outside?'

Lizzie stepped into the yard. It was neglected, damp and cold under an overcast sky. Concrete paving slabs that she could see had once been yellow and pink were stained grey-green by lichen and rainfall. In the corner a neglected sandpit was filled with rain. Just over the fence she could see Ben Stewart's toppled red tricycle. The splat of a raindrop landed on the discarded novel that lay next to Carrie's bench. Another raindrop fell on Lizzie's hand.

'No one there?' Lizzie heard again the scornful disembodied voice down the phone. 'Now you've looked everywhere, please go. You are upsetting my mother.'

'Could you tell your mother we need to speak with her son? Does she know where he is?'

There was the sudden heavy patter of the rain shower bursting. Lizzie stepped back into the kitchen. The voice on the other end of the phone continued.

'Give me back to my mother.'

Mrs Mehenni spoke to her daughter in a torrent before handing the phone back to Lizzie with some urgency. The dam burst of words between mother and daughter was reported as a brief statement: 'My mother does not know where my brother is.'

'Can one of you tell him we need to speak to him? Can he come to the station?'

'Neither of us has spoken to him for more than a week. We don't know where he is. If you don't leave immediately, you can expect a formal complaint.'

Hadley was standing in the entrance to the kitchen. He was watching with the air of a sceptical observer and Lizzie felt a flash of irritation. She did not feel in control and she didn't feel as though she had any understanding with Hadley. What was the plan? Why were they still there when Mehenni was clearly not present?

Behind Hadley was the half-seen figure of the girl.

Lizzie tried to retrieve the memory of that first encounter. It was an image through a darkened, fragmented lens – a shifting shadow in the hallway and yet, somehow, a haunting integer. A thing complete in itself. Perhaps Lizzie was the fragmented one in the de-silvered glass. The voice was still rattling away angrily down the phone.

'What are you doing in my mother's house? I've told you to leave. Why are you still there?'

Hadley had been fully in the kitchen by now,

and the figure behind him had stepped forward into the light. Lizzie had realized then that this was the girl from Carrie Stewart's photos, suddenly there, standing in the doorway to the kitchen in her school uniform – baggy sweatshirt, green tartan skirt and soft green headscarf. She was slight of frame, with dark eyes in which a watchful intelligence flickered. Her name had come back to Lizzie: Farah.

Hadley's bulk, the vulnerability of the mother, the unnerving hostility of the teenager: the place had felt crowded. But Hadley as usual seemed at ease, unaware of peril perhaps, or accustomed to facing it down. An air of benign perplexity hung about him. It was the cloak that disguised him, or the shield that protected him.

The voice on the end of the phone had now been so loud that Lizzie had held the phone away from her ear. It was audible in the room: 'Do you have a warrant?'

Hadley spoke loudly and cheerfully. 'We don't need a warrant. Your mother has invited us in.' He gestured to Lizzie to give him the phone. He took it from her briskly and spoke over the rattling voice. 'Yes, I've got all that. Could you tell Younes when you see him that he'd better come down to the station? We'll have to keep coming here until we've spoken with him.'

The volume of the shouting at the other end of the phone increased. There was the sound of a click in the hallway.

Hadley said, 'I've got to go now. Cheerio.' He pressed the disconnect button and handed the phone back to the mother, then turned towards the hallway, but Farah was ahead of him, already running towards the door. She shouted something in that other language. Lizzie followed, realizing suddenly what was happening.

In the kitchen the phone was ringing incessantly but no one was answering it. Mrs Mehenni was pulling on Lizzie's arm, trying to hold her back. Lizzie shrugged her off. She followed Farah and Hadley down the hallway and out of the now open door. The street was dripping from the recent rainfall but the sky was suddenly a brilliant blue. Looking to her right, she saw a man running away: Younes Mehenni. Hadley was chasing – a fat man struggling to run. Lizzie transmitted. 'Suspect making off east down Kenley Villas, IC2 male, blue jeans, dark top, approximate age forty.' She began to run. Ahead of her Hadley turned off down the side street where they had left the car. Lizzie was fast. She was gaining on Farah and her father. She glanced ahead and then to her right; saw Hadley getting into the car. But Farah had retraced her footsteps and was also turning into the side street.

Lizzie slowed and looked down the road. The car's engine had started and she could see the front wheels turning, but Farah was in the road, beside the vehicle, obstructing its exit. Lizzie ran down the street. Farah was clambering on to the bonnet now and Hadley was opening the car door.

'Get off the bloody car.'

Lizzie shouted. 'It's all right, Hadley, I've got her.'

But Hadley was already there, outside the car. Farah was trying to grip on to the edges underneath the windscreen, her fingers clutching, white with effort, but Hadley had reached over and had a firm hold of her. He pulled her from the bonnet and lifted her, kicking like a child having a tantrum, towards the pavement. He set her down and stretched out his hand, stopping her getting any closer. The girl was shouting furiously at him in that unfamiliar language. Lizzie stepped between them, raising her left hand. 'Farah, stay back.' Her right hand was feeling for her cuffs. 'It's all right, Hadley,' she repeated. 'I've got her.'

But something was happening to Farah: she had started to suck in breath and was holding her ribs, arms wrapped tightly around her chest as if she were in pain. Behind her Lizzie heard the siren wail as the car swung round and roared off to search for Mehenni. Farah fell forward on to her knees. She seemed to be struggling for breath, taking deep inhales.

'Are you all right?' Lizzie moved forward, all thoughts of handcuffs long gone. 'Are you injured? What's happening?'

Farah did not respond. Suddenly there was a long, deep cry that seemed to come from deep within her. She shuddered and spluttered. Her face was contorted in a grimace, as if in pain. Then she was sobbing and wailing, rocking back

75

and forth, digging her nails into her arms. Down the street someone came out of a door and watched. Lizzie moved forward and crouched beside the girl. She seemed unreachable, somewhere other than the London street.

'Farah, what's happening? What's happening? Are you all right?' Lizzie put her arm around her. 'Do you need a doctor?'

Farah shook her off, throwing her arm wide. She had stopped wailing and she clenched her fists tightly. 'No. No doctor.' She stood up and turned away from Lizzie, starting back towards Kenley Villas. Lizzie put a hand on her shoulder.

'Hang on, Farah. Are you OK? Are you hurt? Do you need an ambulance?'

Farah turned on her. 'Don't touch me.' Her eyes were dark, hostile beads, her face a closed little circle as if it had been drawn tight by a string. She wiped the back of her hand across her mouth. 'No, I don't need an ambulance. Leave me alone.'

There was the sound of another siren. A marked car drew up beside them. Arif was in the passenger seat and he wound down the window. 'You all right, Lizzie?'

'Yes, I think so.'

'You sure?'

'Yes.'

'We'll crack on, then. There's a couple more cars out doing an area search.'

The car sped off. Farah had stopped to listen.

'Why have you got cars looking for my father? He is not a criminal.'

'Farah, let me take you back to the house. We can talk about this.'

'I don't want you anywhere near my house. You shouldn't have come in at all. Go away.'

'But Farah, you don't understand. We need to speak with your father. It's not such a big—'

'It's YOU who don't understand. Go away. Go away. Go away.' She started walking off briskly.

'Farah, hang on . . .'

There was the wail of an approaching siren and Hadley's car drew up beside them. He stopped in the middle of the road and got out, switching off the siren but leaving the blue lights flashing. Farah became still. She was pale, and mascara had smudged down her face in sad black streaks. Hadley stepped towards her.

'What on earth did you think you were doing, young lady?'

Farah tipped her head back. She couldn't have looked further from her earlier distress. He was an ignorant adult: she was indifferent, bored even.

'I repeat, what do you think you were doing? You could have been hurt.'

Lizzie tried to intervene. 'Hadley—'

He flashed her a look. 'Have you arrested her?'

Arrested her? It hadn't crossed her mind.

'No.'

Farah was standing up to the bulk of Hadley, as fierce as a weasel. He towered over her.

'You are very lucky my colleague has decided not to arrest you. That trick you played: it's called obstructing police. Don't ever try it again.' He turned back towards the car, the keys already in his hand. 'Come on, Lizzie, we're going to carry on looking for him.'

Farah was already walking quickly away from them back along the street towards her house. She had her arms wrapped tightly around her chest again. Hadley slowed the car and wound down his window, coasting alongside her.

'There's four cars out looking for your dad, and if we don't catch him now, that just means we are going to keep on looking until we do. You'd better tell him to hand himself in. This isn't going away.'

He hit the siren and the car accelerated. They turned on to the main road and past a row of shops, then off down a residential street a couple of miles from Kenley Villas. Hadley killed the siren and pulled over into a parking bay. He pushed his seat back, stretching out his big feet into the foot-well. After a brief silence he took out a tube of Rolos and emptied a handful into his mouth. He began to chew noisily. Lizzie braced herself – she was clearly due a bit of a lesson.

'You OK?' Hadley said between chews.

'Yep.'

'Mad cow.'

Lizzie nodded. She felt powerless, ineffective. 'I thought we were looking for Mehenni?'

'That was just a bit of theatre for the girl.

You not heard of rattling their cages yet? Mehenni's long gone.' He offered the tube of Rolos. 'Want one?'

'No thanks.'

'We'll have to write it up when we get back to the nick – that bit of soap opera on the car bonnet. Use of force, all that.'

'What was it? Common law or section 117 of PACE?'

'Search me. She was stopping us making an arrest, felt right to me.'

Lizzie didn't know if he was serious. She said, 'I think it was PACE 117.'

Hadley shrugged. 'You'll need to put a notification for her on the system as well. Every child matters, after all. Don't forget to mention that she's a nutcase. And say you considered arresting her but used your discretion – not in the public interest, all that.'

'It never crossed my mind to arrest her.'

'Well it bloody well should have.'

He was right, of course he was. Farah had been obstructing police, absolutely to the letter. It should have at least crossed her mind. It would have been perfectly lawful to arrest her. The girl's distress had overwhelmed her. It still overwhelmed her.

Hadley took out another couple of Rolos. They looked small in his big paw and were already beginning to melt. 'Sure you don't want one?'

Lizzie nodded. 'Mmm.'

'Suit yourself.' He emptied them into his mouth. 'What a pain it would have been to nick her.' He smacked his tongue loudly against the roof of his mouth. 'Frightened you a bit, did she?'

'She did, yes. A bit.'

'She's not top billing, keep that in mind. We'll refer her for some TLC, but let's not forget we are police, not bloody social workers, thank the Lord. We need to nick Mehenni, that's the main thing. A lot of that shouting stuff is just a smoke-screen. It's all right doing the bleeding-heart routine at the side of the road, but that girl stopped us catching him, which was what she wanted. Farah Mehenni needs to know we mean business. We can't have them taking the piss, Lizzie.'

CHAPTER 13

Fluorescent light. Stainless steel. White tiles. They dealt with the school bag first. At the scene it had been lying face down, but Collins now saw that it had a stylized drawing of a cat's face on the back flap. In addition to a maths textbook and a spotty pencil case, the bag also held a crumpled blue paisley headscarf, a pot of pink sparkly lip gloss, an embroidered purse containing 78p in change, a crushed pack of T-Zone nose pore strips and, in the front pocket, a small blue plastic horse with a silver nylon mane. Steve bagged up the items individually and made a note in the exhibit book.

The girl's face was spattered with dried blood, which ran down her neck. They swabbed her skin. It was chilled from the mortuary fridge, and stiff. The T-shirt, with its cat's face, was soaked in blood at the back and was still damp. The fabric peeled away from the cold skin as if it were a kind of thinly rolled sour pastry. Slowly they stripped the girl to nakedness, packaging the exhibits and making notes as they went. Farah's skinny jeans were cut away, the medical scissors drawn carefully to not damage her. Steve searched the pockets. A Zip card. In the other pocket, a torn piece of spiral-leaf notepaper. The paper was stained with blood, but the markings of black biro handwriting could just be made out: a telephone number. He made a note in the exhibit book and bagged the scrap of paper.

Finally Farah lay naked on the table. Collins felt an urge to shield the girl from her gaze, which reduced the body to mere evidence. Farah's skin had the blue-grey pallor of death. Blood had pooled along her back. Still she remained an effigy of womanhood just beginning. On the left of her flat stomach, just above the crest of her pelvis, was a small dark mole.

Steve lifted her left hand and rotated the wrist. On the inside of the forearm were five tiny parallel silver scars. Next to them, three fresh cuts.

Collins and Steve smoked in silence outside the morgue.

Collins' doctor had recently shown her a clear plastic cube containing a viscous brown liquid that slid about like poisonous treacle. 'That's how much tar you are putting in your lungs every month,' the doctor had said. There had been photographs on the wall of the doctor's children. Collins had no children to consider, and none of the deaths she had seen had much to recommend them. Cancer was probably as good as anything, she had concluded.

Finally Steve remembered something funny one of the uniformed officers had done and they both laughed. Collins wiped a tear from her eye. Anyone watching them would have thought them indifferent to the systematic undoing of the teenage body they had just witnessed.

CHAPTER 14

Lizzie zipped her jacket and walked along the seafront. Fog had fallen across the town and the view out to sea was a sheet of grey. It was not possible to make out where the water ended and the sky began. The pebbles were blue and grey and brown. The tide had swept the stones across the tarmac path that lay beneath the sea wall. Down the beach, Lizzie noticed, like a sleeping puppy, a fish balanced on one of the rocks. She walked towards it. The rock on which it lay was smoothed and sculpted by the tide, hollowed out into little pools empty of life. The fish was silvery grey, with brown spots along its spine. It seemed untroubled, as if merely resting on the stone. Out of its right side a red substance bloomed into the water like coral. Lizzie made herself look over and saw where the eye had been pecked out, an unflinching hole. She imagined the fish flung out of its element on to the sudden rock. Had death been instant? She pushed away the thoughts that came unbidden like rising nausea: the bodies falling, the white scene tents she had glimpsed as they took her to the ambulance, like euphemisms concealing the shattered bodies of Hadley and Farah. And she thought of the ambulance, of Shaw moving around, looking after her, arranging for her to go home. She reached for him, as if to know him.

After the arrest inquiries at Mehenni's house, she remembered, Shaw had sent a message asking to speak with her before she went off duty. On the stairs up to his office she had heard someone requesting him, and she had paused on the stone treads and cocked her head towards the radio on her stab vest to listen. She remembered the busy transmissions of a live firearms incident, the updates from the officers on scene, Control asking the inspector to agree the rendezvous point. Not wanting to disturb, she had not knocked at the door of the office but had instead slipped quietly inside. He had been standing, leaning over his computer screen.

'Yes,' he said to his radio, 'I'm reading it right now.'

She took the opportunity to observe him. His capable hands with clean moon nails, the firm jawline, a streak of grey in his hair. His collar was open, revealing the warm skin of his neck.

'In the forecourt of the BP, then.'

Aware perhaps that he was keeping her waiting, he looked up and she felt suddenly self-conscious, as if caught in the act of looking at him. She gestured that perhaps she should go and come back another time, but he smiled and shook his head. He gestured towards the chair. She sat and waited. His stab vest was sprawled out on the table and his radio chattered with the continuing call. On the ring finger of his left hand was a gold band: she knew he had a young daughter.

He stood up and logged off his computer. He smiled at her again.

'Sir, you're busy. I'll come back later.'

'No need, I'll be quick.'

He stepped out from behind the desk. She stood up and handed him his stab vest. He started to pull it on. 'You made unsuccessful arrest inquiries earlier today?'

'Yes, sir. Younes Mehenni. Criminal damage. He made off.'

He slotted his radio into the plastic grip on his stab vest. 'Bit of a drama, was it?'

'Sir—'

He waved his hand. 'No, don't worry, Lizzie. It's fine. Hadley said you wrote it up. Anyway, a couple of things. I had Mehenni's solicitor at the front desk earlier on. There's been a complaint.'

'Oh. OK. What was it about?'

'Walk with me.'

Shaw was zipping his stab vest as he walked quickly out of the office and down the stairs. She kept pace with him.

'Were you there when Hadley was talking to the girl?' he asked.

'What, the daughter? Farah? I was there for most of it. There was a bit when I was in the garden on my own.'

86

'OK. Have you covered what was said in your notes?'

'Well, I didn't hear it all.'

A pause

'Anything else, sir?'

They were already at the door to the yard.

'No, that's it. A shame. I'd hoped to bosh it. The family's alleging you entered the property unlawfully and that Hadley said something racist to the girl. Apparently she was very upset and they say that's why she acted the way she did. Doesn't make much sense to me. Have a think about it, see if you can, um, remember exactly what happened. I've got a lot of confidence in you. I'm sure you can shed some useful light on it all.'

She had almost lost the thread of what was being said. Her thoughts were whizzing, struggling to remember. What exactly *had* happened? There had been a period, she remembered, when she and Hadley had been separated – she had been in the garden and talking on the phone, Hadley had been in the corridor with Farah. Or was that later? In any case, what had happened subsequently – when they had chased the father – had seemed much more important. That had been the focus of her statement. Was there perhaps, she wondered, an expectation here? She wanted to ask the inspector exactly what he meant – if she couldn't remember it, had heard nothing, was that going to be a problem? But he had to go to the firearms incident. They couldn't talk. She'd look at her statement, check what she had written.

Shaw had paused with his hand on the open door of the car. He met her eyes and smiled, and Lizzie felt for a moment ridiculously happy. In spite of the wedding ring, she couldn't help wondering. She'd heard his family lived somewhere near the south coast: he kept a flat for himself in London for when he was on duty.

'Don't worry,' he said. 'Storm in a teacup. You want to come to this call?'

There was a moment's regret: it would, at the very least, have been a pleasure to sit next to him in the response car.

'No, sir, I can't. I've got a shoplifter to deal with.'

'Oh, good. Well done, you have been busy. Never mind. Another time.'

She had stood, she remembered, and watched as his car pulled out of the yard with its blue lights on.

CHAPTER 15

Collins' phone started ringing. She glanced down to where it sat in the plastic moulding by the handbrake and saw the name across the screen. *DCI Baillie*. She pulled over.

'Boss.'

'Any news for me?'

'We've released the body of the girl to the family.'

'Good. Well done.'

A pause.

'Did you get anything from the autopsy?'

'Looks like she self-harmed. Nothing dramatic. Just a few scars on her left arm and some recent cuts.'

'Makes sense. Anything else?

'A phone number. Could be nothing. We don't know whose it is yet.'

'OK. What about PC Griffiths? Any news on her?'

'Nothing new since we last spoke, sir.'

There was a pause. Baillie said, 'Well, I'll leave you to get on. Call if you've got anything new for me.'

'Yes, sir.'

★   ★   ★

Collins flashed her warrant card at the gate. She drove past a group of new recruits marching quickly towards the main building, their breath frosting in the morning air.

Training school: she still recoiled at the memory of it. In the dawning sunlight she had stared out across the playing fields and imagined herself elsewhere. A young ex-military man, Ian, had been put in charge of them. He was a recruit like the others, but because of his two years in the army, he knew how to march. Every morning he had shouted at her. 'Retard!' he called after her. 'Fuck-ing Christ!' The ordeal had not been the abuse, as some would think, but rather the uniquely stupid experience of being insulted while being made to stand to attention. She had passed out top of her class in tests and somewhere near the bottom in terms of popularity. She didn't like marching, she was bored by drunkenness and she wouldn't pretend to be like them. As soon as she could, she had stopped wearing the uniform. Nothing would ever convince her to put it on again. She would live and die in investigation even if it meant she never achieved any rank beyond sergeant.

She found her way along the corridor and knocked on the trainers' door. Even the waiting, she remembered bitterly, had been part of the experience. Trainee officers were not to put their hands in their pockets, not to lean on the wall. Today she opened the door without waiting for a response to her knock and stepped into the room. Three men in uniform were crowded together round a desk, staring at a computer screen. She wondered what could be so interesting. One of them clicked on the mouse. The others looked up, ready to deliver a bollocking.

She took another step forward and said, 'DS Collins.'

One of the men – short and somewhat fat, with the blotched skin of someone who ate too much red meat – came over to her. He did not offer his hand.

'Sergeant Hill,' he said. 'Alan.'

The tips of his shoes shone with a terrifying patina. His shirt was starched brilliant white. She guessed he must be ex-army, one of those Para types who had spent his whole police service in uniform and for whom it was a badge of honour to despise CID. He regarded her evenly – he had probably already identified her as a possible troublemaker. 'Sarah, isn't it?'

'That's right. Can we talk in private?'

The other two moved away from the desk and exited, stuffing their hands into their pockets. She noticed one of them catching the eye of the sergeant as he left. The door shut behind them.

'Thanks for the email,' Hill said. 'I was her training sergeant. She's not in any trouble, is she?' Collins made no reply, happy for him to lead the conversation. 'I saw it on the news,' he continued, somehow suggesting by this statement that he already knew as much about the incident as she did. 'Terrible. A few of the guys here knew Hadley. They say he was a decent cop.'

He was only marking out his territory – no different from a dog pissing on a post. Nevertheless, fifteen years in the job and Collins still struggled to hide her feelings from such men.

'Have you any idea yet exactly what happened?' he asked.

'We're still investigating.'

He looked at her and nodded as though he had anticipated this response. There was a pause. Then he said, 'I don't know how I can help you really.'

'I'm grateful for your time, Alan. I appreciate you're busy. I won't be long. I wondered, did Lizzie have any special friends? A boyfriend, perhaps?'

'Interesting question. Can't you ask her yourself?'

She cursed herself for not sending Steve. He would be sitting with one cheek perched on the desk by now, dishonestly hinting that he too had served a couple of years in the army and agreeing that the job wasn't what it used to be.

'Alan, I'd really appreciate you helping me out with this.'

'I'll get the class list.'

She watched as he pulled up the list on his terminal. He printed it out and started to underline some of the names. 'This was her class. She was friends with her, yes . . .'

He handed the sheet over. Collins was aware

that he was studying her as she scanned it. 'Thanks for that.' She put the paper in her bag and crossed her arms over her chest. She looked at the sergeant. Well, no harm in trying.

'Can you tell me anything more about her? I won't be taping this or recording it in any way. It's not hard evidence. I just want to get a sense of her. I'm sure you'll understand that. She was the only other adult on the roof when they fell and I haven't spoken to her yet.'

'You haven't spoken to her yet?'

'That's right.'

He paused.

'Missing, is she?'

Collins didn't answer. Hill smiled, pleased with himself.

'That must be a right hot potato.'

Collins nodded.

The piece of inside information did the trick. Sergeant Hill became much more forthcoming. He warmed to his theme. Idealistic: that was how he described Lizzie Griffiths. He gave an example. The group had spent the afternoon learning how to fill in a report. The afternoon had dragged on in the hot classroom. The sun had poured through the windows. The metal blinds were pulled but many did not shut properly: their slats were bent out of shape. The recruits moved their desks out of the blazing sunlight and took off their cravats and ties. They struggled over the horrid little forms: the small boxes that must all be filled. The lines that must be drawn with a ruler. The liturgy of paper-work. The sheer mindlessness of it, the detail. One of the recruits had made a joke. It was a bit off, no doubt about that, but at the same time . . . He broke off.

Collins prompted. 'Yes?'

'Well . . .'

She waited for him to elaborate, but he didn't. 'So?'

'So anyway, Lizzie raised her hand and repeated the comment, and made a complaint. Right thing to do, of course. She said she didn't want her objection to go any further. She just felt that what he'd said wasn't right and she didn't want it to pass without saying something.' Hill shook his head. 'Naïve.'

'Naïve?'

'You know: things said in public always go further, particularly if someone objects to them. That's the way it is in the job. She didn't under-stand that.'

Aware of Collins' eyes upon him, he covered his ground. The student who made the comment got a letter on his record and – he spoke with careful emphasis – that was a good thing, of course. The boy had to learn.

Collins said, 'But this student with the . . . the off comment. He wasn't the only one who needed to learn?'

Hill's face was exactly like the shine on his shoes: impenetrable. 'Things have changed a lot since I joined.'

'So . . .' Collins paused before finding the phrase. 'So Lizzie was as green as grass.'

'Idealistic.' She noted his repetition of the word. He must have been pleased with it. She wondered if he had found its ambivalence useful on many occasions since being posted to training school.

Hill had stopped speaking. It was as if he was observing whether she was getting the measure of his evidence.

Collins said, 'Thanks very much. You've been very helpful.'

He opened the door to see her out. 'Don't get me wrong, Sarah. I thought Lizzie Griffiths had the makings of a good officer. She just needed to go out there and get stuck in. Go into the real world and stop worrying about stuff that didn't really matter. Well, good luck with it all. I'll be interested to hear how you get on. I'll look out for it on the news.'

On the way back, Collins decided to make a detour.

Kilsby High Street held no surprises. The rolled-up sleeping bag in the doorway of a charity shop, the lines of chain shopfronts – Boots, Starbucks, Tesco – the queues of coated people waiting for buses.

Collins followed the route that Steve had told her CCTV showed Lizzie taking, walking north towards the Underground. Lizzie hadn't been shown on the camera that covered the entrance

95

to the tube station and she hadn't reached the camera at the far end of the street. The camera covering the middle section wasn't working, but she had disappeared from somewhere on this road. Collins went into a minicab office.

The man behind the counter wore a dirty silk waistcoat over a frayed shirt. He had a long beard and frizzy hair pulled back in a ponytail. His teeth were yellow.

'I can't remember anyone like that, but then there's people in and out all day,' he said. 'You're welcome to inspect the bookings.'

He had an old-fashioned ledger written out in ink. His handwriting was italic. Probably plays Dungeons and Dragons, Collins thought as she ran her finger down the entries and scribbled in her notebook the names and journeys of the single females who had used the service since the incident.

'Lisa Gardener?' she asked. 'Do you remember her?'

'Oh, she's a regular. Not your lady, for sure. Must be sixty if she's a day. Uses a cab because her legs are bad.'

'And Helen Thompson?'

'Can't remember. Oh no, hang on a minute. I think she had two kids with her. This lady got children?'

Collins went into Greggs and bought a cheese and pickle sandwich. Eating as she drove, with one hand on the wheel, she turned down a side street past the cab office that went towards the viaduct. After about a mile and a half, the street was lined with VWs and BMWs. Obscuring the Victorian brickwork was a large orange plastic sign: *Quick Car*.

The man behind the counter – a lean Asian man in a sharply cut suit – leaned away from Collins as if to get a better look. Collins got out her warrant card. 'Detective Sergeant Sarah Collins. Met Police.'

He took in the fact of it with evident pleasure. 'You lot are like buses,' he said.

'Oh yes?'

'Yes. Wearing an orange jacket. Paid cash. Said she couldn't remember her credit card PIN.'

Collins rang Steve.

'She leased a vehicle last night. I've checked the camera at the car hire office here and it's definitely her. Can you run the registration through ANPR?'

CHAPTER 16

Steps led up from the beach. A hotchpotch of buildings – fluted columns, Doric pilasters, castellated and gabled – rose away from the sea and sheltered a Victorian park. Lizzie sat on a bench. A duck and a drake were floating, asleep on a cold pond. The birds' necks were curved round, their heads nestling improbably into their backs, tucked between the blades of their wings. Like a model of domesticity the sleeping birds rose and fell with their breaths.

Lizzie took a roll from her pocket that she had buttered and wrapped in a paper napkin at break-fast. She just needed time, she told herself, time to think it through, to work it out.

She would sleep in the hire car tonight – pick it up later from the hotel car park and drive it up the coast. She still had plenty of petrol. She could run the engine to keep warm. She would be sure to find some off-road parking where no one would bother her. She shuddered. Pressure; there was always pressure. Pressure to decide, pressure to resolve, pressure to act.

★　　★　　★

Inspector Shaw had stood by the terminal flicking through the morning briefing – slides of burglars, boys on pushbikes snatching phones, a vehicle linked to drug dealing, a known gang member believed to be carrying a weapon. The newer officers, including Lizzie, had made notes in their pocket books. Hadley had sat back in his chair and watched the screen, interested but not sufficiently so to put pen to paper. At the end of the PowerPoint, Shaw asked Hadley and Lizzie to stay behind.

As the others filed off to breakfast, Hadley said quietly to Lizzie, 'Looks like we're on the naughty step. What have you done?'

She looked at him and he winked.

Shaw sat on the table. 'Carrie Stewart,' he said. 'Ring a bell, anyone?' Lizzie drew breath to answer but a slight pat on her knee and a smile from Hadley told her not to bother. Shaw was continuing. 'So, Mrs Stewart has been in to see the Chief Superintendent in person. Apparently Younes Mehenni rang her up last night and told her to back off or else.'

Hadley interrupted with a not-bad imitation of curiosity. 'Or else what, guv?'

In spite of himself Shaw smiled. 'Oh, you know, the usual nonsense. It's gone on as a malicious communications. At least we've managed not to record it as a threat to kill.'

Hadley said, 'OK, well that's something.'

'Mrs Stewart doesn't see it like that. She asked

the boss what on earth we are doing and why Mr Mehenni hasn't been arrested. She was quite upset, apparently, and now the Chief Superintendent is also quite upset.' Shaw pressed his fingers together. 'Now, starter for ten, anyone. The qualities of shit are?'

Hadley lifted his hand slowly. 'Oh, guv, pick me. I know that one.'

'Yes, Hadley then.'

'Shit rolls downhill, guv.'

'That's right. So, bearing that law of physics in mind, can you please make sure that Mr Mehenni is nicked as soon as possible.'

Hadley had pulled up and parked the car directly outside number 7 Kenley Villas.

'We're not hiding up the street today?' Lizzie asked.

'No, today we are not hiding because today our purpose is different. Today we are rattling cages. I am going to sit inside this nice warm identifiable police car and you are going to knock on the door and try your hand at rattling. If you are successful and Mehenni hands himself in during the next couple of days, I will be buying you a drink at Sergeant Thompson's leaving do. And vice versa, of course, so mine's a pint of London Pride. Should chummy, however, surprise us by being at home, I will be here waiting for him. I shall wedge myself into the gate. He will not be able to leave and you will be able to slip the cuffs on.'

Farah opened the door before Lizzie had even knocked. She was wearing the same shapeless green uniform of the local academy school and her bag was already slung over her shoulder. It was pink, polka-dotted and heavy – bulky and sharp with the corners of her school books. She had white headphones in and she left them in place.

'Come in.'

'No, that's OK. I don't want to make you late for school.'

'No, come in.'

She moved sideways to let Lizzie enter and began walking down the hallway. Lizzie turned briefly and gave Hadley the thumbs-up. She left the door on the latch and followed.

Farah had thrown her school bag on to the kitchen table. The bag, Lizzie noticed, was not all polka dots after all. The back pocket was white, with a big line drawing of the face of the Japanese cat Hello Kitty with a bow by her left ear. Farah had pulled off her headscarf and taken the buds out of her ears. Her hair was long and dark, tied back in a ponytail. From the trailing headphones Lizzie could hear tinny beats and a female voice singing something strident in a distant place. Mrs Mehenni hovered in the doorway but Farah spoke to her in that other language and she disappeared quickly down the hallway.

Farah said angrily, 'She's rung the housing officer again.'

'I'm sorry?'

The girl seemed to be entirely involved in her own concerns; seemed even to assume that Lizzie understood and shared them. 'That woman next door. She's rung the housing officer again. We've got a letter. They want to come round and see us. She won't be happy until she's got rid of us.'

Lizzie wasn't quite sure how to respond. She had the sensation of being pulled into something more entangled than a mere allegation of criminal damage, something that was beyond her powers to unravel. But it was simple, surely?

'Farah, your father needs to come in and see me. It's the only way to sort this out.'

'But we've only been here a few months. That woman won't ever leave us alone.'

Lizzie felt she had been given a sudden glimpse inside a desperate room. She said, 'Yes, I understand that . . .' But she wasn't sure she really did understand. 'Look, I can see you're upset . . .' Again she sensed that she was being pulled off course. She heard Hadley's rebuke. *We are police, not bloody social workers.* She tried to get back on track. 'This isn't going to go away, Farah, not until your father's spoken to police. Your dad won't be able to come home, not until it's sorted. But it's . . . how can I put it . . . it is serious but it's not the end of the world. If he comes in, that's the best thing. Then we can sort it out. I can talk to your housing officer. Explain the situation. Perhaps your father's suitable for a caution.'

There she was. It had felt like dry land.

'A caution, what's that?'

'A caution, that's like a warning.' Lizzie felt in her stab vest pockets but she knew without searching that she had forgotten to bring a memo pad with her. 'Look, give me a piece of paper and I'll scribble my number down for you. If your dad's prepared to come in, you can call me and I'll be sure to be there to deal.'

CHAPTER 17

Collins knocked at the glass door. Caroline Wilson was standing on a table, reaching up to stick a drawing pin into a Mollweide projection of the earth. Her jeans were too tight and her raised arms exposed her plump tanned bottom. She turned and smiled, embarrassed to be caught in this awkward position. She had curly dark hair and a round kind face; a face clearly moulded by years of giving encouraging smiles.

Collins showed her warrant card. 'Sarah Collins, Met Police. Thanks for making the time.'

Miss Wilson's smile contracted into something less welcoming. She reached out a hand to be helped down from the table. 'Yes, the office said you were coming.' She brushed herself down and went over to her computer, where something was printing off. With her back turned she said, 'I can't spare much time, I'm afraid. I'm going out.'

Collins glanced around the classroom. A poster proclaimed bravely: *Maths makes a difference to your future career.* Miss Wilson put a collection of papers on the table in front of Collins.

'A copy of her last report. Farah was particularly

talented at maths. I'm head of maths. I would have been expecting her to get an A star at GCSE. Of course that sounds ridiculous now.' She paused and briefly put her hand to her right eyebrow. Her tone was more constrained when she spoke again. 'That is, in the light of what's happened. Totally ridiculous.' She unexpectedly smiled self-effacingly. 'Do you think I'm a monster?'

Collins shook her head. 'A monster? Why on earth would I think that?' She looked at the teacher's kind face again. 'Certainly not.'

She sat down at one of the tables and began reading the report. *Farah is operating well above average. She has a desire to improve and succeed . . . Farah sits at the back of the class and is shy about contributing but her written work is of a high standard and she shows a good grasp of ideas and argument . . .* She put the paper down on the table and looked up. Miss Wilson had been studying her.

Collins said, 'She was doing well.'

'Very well, yes.'

'You were proud of her.'

'Yes.'

Collins hesitated. 'You're angry.' There was a pause. 'And sad. Yes, of course you are. I would be too.'

Miss Wilson exhaled. She muttered, 'Well . . .' She sat down opposite Collins. There was a brief silence. 'What I don't understand is the bit about her taking the child. That's what I read in the press. Can that be true? Are you absolutely sure she took him?'

Collins avoided the question. 'Why would you say that?'

'Farah was lonely, troubled even, but I never saw her cruel. Quite the opposite. There's a girl in her year with learning difficulties and Farah was one of the few children who was ever kind to her. I just can't believe that she took a child. What would make her do that?'

Collins allowed herself a moment to think. Then she said, 'Well, I suppose it's my job to find that out – to find out exactly what happened and why. And I don't have the answers yet.'

Miss Wilson looked her in the eyes. 'OK.'

'You're deciding whether to help?'

Miss Wilson smiled. 'No, I think I have decided. What did you want to know?'

'Tell me about Farah.'

'What about her?'

'You said she was troubled?'

'Yes, but I don't want you to think that explains—'

Collins reached her hand forward to interrupt. 'It's all right. I don't.'

Miss Wilson smiled. 'I'm sorry.'

Collins smiled too. 'That's OK.'

'So, OK. Farah was a troubled girl. That's definitely true, yes. She was shy, sat at the back of the class, hardly ever spoke. I'd noticed she'd been cutting. Her wrist . . .'

'Yes, I saw that too.'

Miss Wilson looked up, curious. 'How did you see it?'

'At the post-mortem.'

Miss Wilson's face closed in sudden horror and Collins remembered too late how unfamiliar and distasteful her profession must sometimes seem.

'I'm sorry. I should have thought . . .'

Miss Wilson smiled in a friendly way. 'No, no. That's OK. Of course, yes. Of course you did. How horrible that must be for you.'

'It's OK. It's just my job.'

There was silence. Then Miss Wilson said, 'I'd referred Farah to the school's counsellor but they hadn't met yet. Farah's mother is dead, of course. Died back home, I think, before she arrived in the UK.'

'And her father?'

'He always came to parent evenings but he was one of those parents . . . how can I say? I never really knew exactly *why* he was there. There was no dialogue. He didn't seem to understand any of it, just sat there. Hard to feel you ever made contact with him.'

'Did she have any friends?'

'None in particular. She was a lonely girl, I think.'

Collins' phone started ringing. She reached it out of her pocket and glanced at the screen.

'I'm really sorry. I'll have to take this.'

She went out into the corridor. A man was mopping down the far end and she took a few steps away from him. A young woman in flared

107

jeans and a checked shirt was coming towards her. Afro haircut, pale brown skin, pretty, with a wide face. Late twenties probably. She walked past Collins and into Miss Wilson's classroom.

Collins took the call. 'Steve . . .'

'The car pinged twice last night in St Leonards – once on the approach, the other time right on the seafront. Nothing since. They're quite well served for ANPR cameras. It's probably still there.'

'OK. Let's get over there. I'll pick you up in half an hour.'

Collins went back into the classroom. Miss Wilson was standing beneath one of the high Victorian windows. Her friend was perched on a desk, leafing through an exercise book.

Collins said, 'I'm sorry for interrupting.'

Miss Wilson said, 'No, no, come in. This is my girlfriend, Patti.'

Patti turned and smiled, and Collins felt a sudden pang sweep through her. The two women seemed so happy together, so optimistic, believing in the future and making the world a better place, all that stuff. And then she told herself that this imagining of them was just fantasy, of course. What did she know of them?

She said, 'I'm really sorry, I've got to go. Something urgent's cropped up. I can come back . . .'

'No, no, that's all right, if you've got everything you need.' Miss Wilson smiled. 'Good luck, Sarah.'

CHAPTER 18

With the expanse of sea as her only map, Lizzie walked. Her mind and the terrain were a blankness to her from which only the occasional object emerged: a lifebuoy on a stand, a level crossing that made her change her stride. The sun was suddenly low on the horizon and for a brief moment she did not know what to do as she stood alone on a darkening country road. With some effort she began to retrace her steps towards the car. That was her plan, she reminded herself; that was where she would sleep. She turned her mind towards her memories as if towards a difficult task, one avoided all day. Cars sped past, flashing at the lonely figure, their lights on full beam and their horns blaring.

Her mobile had rung with an unknown number. The voice had been faintly accented – one of those hybrid voices that could only belong in London.
'Hello. PC Griffiths?'
'Yes.'
'It's Farah Mehenni.'
'Oh, Farah, yes . . .'

'I spoke with my dad. He's going to come in to the police station in an hour or so. Will you be there?'

'Yes, of course, I'll get freed up.'

'PC Griffiths?'

'Yes.'

'Remember, you promised me. You remember? If my father came down you would look after him. You said that thing . . . a caution . . .'

'Well, I'll be there to deal, but I didn't—'

'You said it was serious but not the end of the world.'

'That's right.'

'If he came down you would sort it out.'

'Well, if he comes down it will get sorted, but I didn't promise—'

'We'll be there in an hour.'

'Farah, hang on . . .'

The line went dead.

Glancing through the glass of the station office counter, it had been immediately obvious which one was Mehenni: he was the dark-skinned man raising his voice and jabbing his finger.

'I came to this country because I like this country. English police, they are famous. Everyone tells me: English police are *fair*. They do not even carry guns. Now this man, Officer Matthews. He abuses my daughter. How dare he? I will not repeat what he said to her. And I? I am certainly not Bin Laden. He knows nothing about me . . .'

Farah was standing behind her father and she put her hand on his arm as if to hold him back. She looked embarrassed, self-conscious. The other people in the station office were staring openly and exchanging glances. An old lady pulled her bag close to her. The station officer raised his eyebrows at Hadley and Lizzie. *A right one.*

Lizzie approached cautiously. 'Mr Younes Mehenni?'

He turned on her. 'PC Griffiths?'

'Yes. Thank you for coming in—'

The man was immediately so angry that it was hard to get a word in edgeways. 'How dare you come to my house and speak to my mother—'

Lizzie interrupted. 'Mr Mehenni, there's been an allegation . . .'

But he was not listening. As he looked beyond her to Hadley, Mehenni's face had that elsewhere cast of someone deaf to all reason. He lunged forward, saying something guttural and unintelligible in his own language. Hadley, moving surprisingly gracefully for a man of such bulk, stepped to the side. Mehenni lost his balance.

Someone must have put up for assistance, because other officers were piling into the station office. Her team were there – Inspector Shaw and Arif and Sergeant Thompson. There was no room to move and these other officers, through sheer physical strength, were taking charge. The urgency of restraint had taken over all other considerations. Lizzie had her cuffs in her right hand. She glanced to her left. Hadley was standing well back, watching, and Lizzie thought, momentarily, *that's not like him.* And then she saw, out of the corner of her eye, Farah looking at Hadley with unmistakable hatred.

The old lady, still clutching her handbag, was hedged up against the wall. Mehenni was on the floor, face down. His arms were being forced behind his back. He was squeezing out words but they were mainly not in English. The only thing she heard clearly was *racists.* Kneeling, she slid the first cuff on to his right wrist. Sergeant Thompson pushed his left wrist towards her and she snapped the cuff over it. Shaw glanced at her, prompting her to say the words. 'Mr Mehenni, I'm arresting you on suspicion of criminal damage and malicious communications.'

She looked up at Farah, who had pressed herself back against the wall. Her face was knotted into a tight, angry frown behind which, Lizzie suddenly realized, tears were probably being held back.

Mehenni sat in the interview room barking out a furious discourse on the failings of the British police in general and PC Hadley Matthews specifically. The interpreter translated in a loud but neutral tone, automatically and indifferently processing words from one language to the other, like a driver switching lanes on the motorway.

'I like this country . . .'

Mehenni wore a loose grey suit, an open-necked shirt and black leather shoes. He had, Lizzie realized, dressed up smartly for the arrest. She imagined that in the street he would merge anonymously into the usual file of London immigrants. In his own home he might well be one of those extravagantly courteous and formal North Africans who offered coffee and sweet pastry. But watching him closely like this, she thought that he also had the thinness of a man who was systematically eating himself into a sack of angry bones.

The solicitor, a young, plump white man wearing trainers, jeans and a shiny Chelsea FC top, caught Lizzie's eye. Lizzie ran her nail down the groove where the plastic box of the tapes opened. The cellophane wrapper wouldn't easily break.

Mehenni had started to speak English. 'I *like* this country. I respect this country. This country has given me a home.'

Lizzie addressed the solicitor quietly. 'Are you certain that Mr Mehenni needs an interpreter?'

The solicitor said, 'I think it's for the best.'

He reached across the table and offered her his ballpoint. She jabbed at the cellophane. It puckered and tore like the fine skin of an onion. Mehenni, now back in his mother tongue, was continuing to talk loudly. Lizzie turned to the interpreter, raising her voice over the continuing diatribe.

'Would you explain to Mr Mehenni that I'm putting the tapes in now? Only then will the interview start.'

The interpreter was a fat, dark-skinned man with

a beard and a plastic name badge hanging from a lanyard round his neck. He had chubby hands with dark hairs on the back of his fingers and thick yellowish nails. He smiled at Lizzie as self-satisfied as the Cheshire cat – 'Of course, Officer' – and then switched language, speaking forcefully to Mehenni.

Mehenni stopped talking. He nodded and folded his arms across his chest as if waiting impatiently for an incompetent servant to complete some necessary task.

The tape emitted its harsh long tone. Lizzie read from the prompt. *This interview is being tape-recorded . . .*

There was never any question of a no-comment interview. Mehenni was incandescent. He kept interrupting as she went through the formalities, waving his hand impatiently like a member of the aristocracy who wished to be spared the details. No sooner had she finished the caution than he began to talk again in a ceaseless flow, like angry water tumbling over rapids. His tone was that of a man speaking to minions who had badly disappointed him and were about to be fired.

'My neighbour has been out to get us ever since we moved in. She doesn't like us living next door. We waited one year – one year! – in a bed and breakfast. Now she goes to the housing association. I have to sign a contract – a contract for what? For what? We live peacefully next door. All we want is peace. Why does this woman—'

Lizzie interrupted. 'Mr Mehenni—'

Mehenni continued, ignoring her, and Lizzie considered him as if a wall of glass were between them. She had given full disclosure to the solicitor, shown him the photographs, told him she would ask for a caution if Mehenni would make a full and frank admission. The solicitor caught her eye and shrugged. Mehenni was continuing, an uninterrupted stream of invective. He was on to Hadley now.

'And my name is not Mohammed either, or Bin Laden . . .'

Without her willing it, an imagining of the accusations came to Lizzie as real as if she had seen the events herself: she out of earshot in the garden with Mehenni's mother while Hadley was with the girl in the hallway, giving in to a bit of what he would probably consider harmless frankness. She could almost bloody see him, dammit. Farah in her school uniform, smaller than Hadley, awkward and crowded by his bulk in the narrow space. Hadley hitching up that gut of his and saying, 'All right, Miss Jihadi, can you tell your dad . . . What's his name now? I forget. Mohammed, is it? Bin Bloody Laden?' She hadn't of course heard him say it but that didn't mean he hadn't. Equally, she reminded herself, these were words that someone could easily make up and put in the mouth of a police officer. Which account you were inclined to believe depended largely on your own point of view. The complaint was a commonplace accusation. Just as plausible surely to believe Hadley's account: Farah's allegation was malicious, made simply to divert attention from the truth, which was, after all, no more than a routine enquiry into a sure-fire charge for a petty offence.

She needed to distance herself from the complaint. It wasn't her problem. It was outside her remit. It was her job to investigate Mrs Stewart's allegation of criminal damage. She raised her voice again.

'Mr Mehenni, if you won't let me speak, I'll have to stop the interview.'

There was a moment's silence. Mehenni folded his arms across his chest and gave her a look of fury, as if waiting for her explanation.

'Mr Mehenni, *I'm* interviewing *you*. I understand you've made a complaint. You have a solicitor. That matter will be dealt with, I can assure you, but separately, not by me.'

Mehenni denied all offences. Lizzie couldn't caution him and she couldn't charge him either – she needed to get the data for the threatening phone call to Carrie Stewart. She had no choice but to bail him. She had a word with his solicitor in the corridor.

'Please, try to explain to him. The best thing is for him just to stay away from Carrie Stewart. Tell him to think of his family.'

Bailing Mehenni had made her late. As she entered the bar, Sergeant Thompson, wearing a bright red wig, and Superman underpants over his trousers, was holding forth. Other drinkers were casting nervous glances at him.

'Lizzie!' Thompson shouted to her as though she were the most ardently wished-for member of the company, as if her arrival at last made the celebration complete. She smiled at the welcome.

'Drink, anyone?'

It was a large order: she paid with a card. The bar was crowded and dark. At the table they were reciting Monty Python sketches. She drank steadfastly, getting determinedly into the spirit of things. Thompson was making a speech. He was off to pastures new, where the women were better-looking and – more significantly – no one knew him yet. He held up the framed Polaroid photos they had given him of the team and waved the bottle of whisky.

'Seriously, thank you for this. It's been great. A very difficult decision to leave. If you believe that, you'll believe anything.'

Lizzie found the photo frame in her hands. Among the images was one of herself and two of the other girls draped across the bonnet of a police car.

'So that's how you spend your time,' commented Arif over her shoulder.

'Nobody knows exactly what *you* do all day,' she countered. 'Hiding in cupboards, is it?'

'I'm not hiding in any cupboards.'

'No, that's true enough.'

They clinked glasses. At a far table Hadley was drinking stolidly. He gestured to a tall glass standing on the table and waved for her to come over.

'You won the bet after all. Surprised me, well done. Bloody Mary your poison, isn't it?'

It was possible that, for all Sergeant Thompson's brief enthusiasm, Hadley was indeed her natural companion at this event. She took a seat next to him.

'Sorry I couldn't help you out with Mehenni,' he said. 'Guv'nor thought I ought to leave it alone. In view of the complaint, that is.'

'Yes, no worries.'

'What did he say?'

'Denied it.'

'Charge him?'

'No, on bail.'

'That's not a good idea, is it?'

'I need to get the phone data. Since Carrie Stewart put her oar in, the Superintendent's been taking an interest – told me I couldn't let the malicious comms drop because Mehenni wouldn't accept responsibility for the crim dam.'

Another Bloody Mary had appeared in front of her. Furtively someone passed Sergeant Thompson's card under the table for her to sign. She saw written, *Never liked you* and added her own inevitable insult: *Good riddance to bad rubbish.*

She glanced across at the other officers. Thompson had been given a plastic cock and it was being passed around, in and out of trouser flies. The team was like a pack of dogs, each fitting in as best they could, neither sweet-natured nor nasty, just a member of the group. She longed to merge herself in this identity and pull the sledge with the others. They were a breed apart, mysteriously but somehow unavoidably tainted by their labour. If you were one of them, it was best to be truly one of them.

Hadley was talking. 'I wanted to ask you about the complaint.'

It was a weary subject and she didn't want to get drawn in, but she was tired and it was easier to stay here than to make the effort to join in with the others. All that cock business would be really trying. Her fatigue was compounded by the increasing effect of alcohol. Perhaps she should give up and go home to her bed, but, she told herself, it would look bad to leave so early. Besides, as she barely admitted, even though it was silly, she couldn't help herself waiting, hoping. She glanced around the room. She could not see Shaw.

Hadley muttered into his beer, 'I've got a board coming up.'

'Yes?'

'It's for training school. If I get it, it'll take me off the streets.'

'You gonna be a shiny arse?'

'All right, Cagney, give me a break. I'm too old for early turn and freezing crime scenes. Only three more years to go and then I'm off.'

She glanced at her watch. If Shaw didn't turn up, she would give up and leave in five minutes. Then she saw him, standing at the bar. He was away from the main crowd, talking to one of the skippers. He glanced over to her and made a drinking gesture. She tapped her glass and gave a thumbs-up. There, in spite of herself, was that involuntary hope again, that excitement that was almost physical and had nothing to do with anything she had dared to even think through.

Hadley was still speaking. 'If you could just say you were in the room the whole time . . . Say it's not true what she's claiming.'

Arif gestured to her to come and join him in some dancing. He had somehow got hold of a feather boa. She waved back at him. *Later.* The evening's prospects were improving.

'But Hadley, I *wasn't* there . . .'

'It's not bloody true what she's saying – I'll tell you exactly what happened and you just repeat it in a statement. Then it'll be resolved locally. Otherwise it'll take bloody ages. The bloody inspector could have knocked it on the head, but he's got an eye on promotion.'

'That doesn't sound like the guv'nor.'

'I didn't mean *our* guv'nor. I meant Inspector Grosz. It wasn't passed to Shaw, was it? He wasn't allowed to deal.'

She remembered vaguely the mention of a solicitor at the front desk. Perhaps he'd insisted on a different, independent inspector.

'Hadley, it'll all get sorted . . .'

'But too late for the board.'

She couldn't see what the fuss was about. He could survive three more years of crime scenes, surely? This was the bit where cops were supposed to keep their head down and bide their time in anticipation of the handshake.

A Bloody Mary was placed on the table in front of her. The guv'nor joined them, taking a seat opposite her. She took a sip of her drink, trying not to betray her pleasure in his arrival. She had to work out how to enjoy rather than suffer these five minutes of his company.

'All right?' he said to Hadley.

'Yes, guv. Just heading home, as a matter of fact,' Hadley said, getting up. 'See you tomorrow, Lizzie.'

'Yeah, see you, Hadley.'

So they were to be alone for a moment. Lizzie resolved to get a grip on her feelings. Luckily, at the bar, voices were raised. 'What's the commotion?' she said.

'Arif's been ordering drinks on someone else's tab.'

She raised her eyebrows. 'Whose?'

'Sergeant Thompson's.'

She laughed. 'Definitely not wise.'

'No.'

'Still, you've got to admire the boy's courage.'

'True enough.'

They fell into silence. Lizzie stopped herself from making forced conversation. Her nervousness risked spilling out into unconstrained babble. Her fluster, she knew, did not stem from the inspector's rank. She had an ingrained contempt for grades of all varieties. She had an uneasy feeling, nevertheless, that she might be being seduced by a different variety of job bullshit. There were rumours that, before making inspector, Shaw had done interesting things, confidential stuff. Another man might have bragged, but not him. He might have stories but he was not telling them.

The silence had extended for too long and she began to feel a need for words. She took another sip at her drink and considered making her excuses, but this time he broke the silence.

'Enjoying yourself?'

Usually this kind of question was a form of team requirement, a kind of grand hurrah. *Are you enjoying yourself? Are we all enjoying ourselves?* However, this time it had the air of genuine enquiry about it. The guv'nor, she noticed, was drinking orange juice. He was stone-cold sober. To her surprise, he returned her gaze with steadiness. She laughed nervously at the imagining of kissing him that came unbidden to her, and said, with some truth, 'Yes.'

'I didn't think it was ever as simple for you as that.'

'Well, I'll admit I don't usually enjoy police piss-ups, but I'm enjoying this one.' She had nearly said *now*. She wanted to stay but decided to go before she made a total embarrassment of herself.

She grabbed her bag. 'Got to get up in the morning. I'd better be off.'

He reached out and touched the back of her hand.

'Don't go yet.'

The touch was – she had to admit, cliché as it was – like electricity. She blushed and then couldn't stop herself grinning. She had considered herself totally immune to the charms of any man with the power of arrest. How utterly *bored* she had been. She suddenly speculated what he would be like with his clothes off. She laughed again, and he laughed too.

'Or if you do have to go, let me drive you home. You're not far from me, are you?'

She tried to banish her imaginings. She summoned the image of his child. He had brought her into the station one Saturday: a blonde-haired girl with pink Crocs on her feet.

'I'll be fine on the tube. Really.'

He smiled. 'But it is a bit silly, isn't it – you getting the tube when I'm leaving too and only live a few streets away?'

She gathered her bag and her jacket. They were leaving unexpectedly quickly. It had turned out to be so easy. Was it the effect of the alcohol? She hoped she wasn't going to make a fool of herself. As she walked past the others, Arif caught her eye and winked. She wagged her finger at him with mock severity.

Shaw drove a Land Rover Discovery. She had to step up to sit in its plush leather seat. The darkness of the road was a change in key, and Lizzie felt the mood had shifted. She sat back in her seat and watched the orange tungsten of the street lights flaring rhythmically over the bonnet of the car.

But Shaw had not apparently caught the mood. Perhaps she had misread the lift home. He said, 'I took a look at your statement – the one about the incident at Mehenni's house. You hardly talk at all about the stuff before Mehenni turned up, before all the drama. Perhaps you just need to do a short further statement – clarify that you were with Hadley all the time when you were inside the house and that he didn't say anything offensive. Just a few lines, shouldn't take you long.'

Lizzie's attention shifted sharply, like a driver sobering up quickly when pulled over by a marked car.

'But I wasn't with him all the time. I was in the back garden for most of the time he was with Farah.'

Shaw nodded and sighed. 'Oh, OK.'

'I'm sorry?'

'Hadley wrote in his statement that you were with him the whole time.'

For a brief moment Lizzie could not think at all. Then, all at once, she was furious. Suddenly everything made sense. Hadley had lied in his statement and now he needed her to lie too! That was why

124

he had been going on and on. Immediately another, insidious suspicion dawned on her. Was that why he had been so quick to leave when the guv'nor sat down? Had they been discussing his little difficulty? Was that why Shaw had offered her a lift home, so they could talk about this? She felt cheated, stupid, humiliated.

'Why on earth would Hadley say I was there?' she said angrily. 'If he wanted me to lie, he should at least have asked me first.'

Shaw glanced in his mirror and indicated right to overtake an old Metro that was ambling along at 20 mph, apparently in no particular hurry to get anywhere. His tone was affable: he was, he seemed to imply, concentrating on his driving.

'Lizzie, slow down a moment. Don't jump to conclusions. You've been in the job long enough to know that people remember things differently. Perhaps he thought you were with him all the time. Perhaps he forgot you went into the garden.'

Lizzie sat back crossly in her seat. Hadley had thought she was there? Slowly she conceded to herself that yes, that was possible. She knew well enough how two people could have entirely different recollections of the same event. It was, after all, the everyday sport of defence lawyers. And the later incidents had seemed so much more important. Mehenni making off. Farah jumping on to the car bonnet. That had been the stuff she had been concerned to cover in her statement, the stuff that had worried her.

The late-night streets were spilling over with people. A girl on the pavement was falling about, drunk, or pretending to be so. It was hard to tell. The guv'nor had to brake to allow a couple leaning into each other's arms to cross in front of the car. He waited for them to pass.

'It isn't a big deal, Lizzie, really it isn't. Don't worry, it'll all get sorted one way or another.'

She tried to sound as though she agreed with him. Silly of her to think it might be a big deal. 'Yes. You're right.' The car pulled away again and accelerated. Then she said quietly the thing that was now on her mind. 'I suppose everyone's got an opinion about this.'

'You won't last long in the job if you worry what people say about you. Just ride it out. Stick to your guns.'

'Stick to my guns?'

The street light pulsed over Shaw's impassive face in waves of white and darkness. 'Well, you know what I mean.'

But she didn't know what he meant. That was the whole problem.

Shaw decelerated for the approach to the traffic lights, then, as the lights turned to green, swung out on to the speed and blankness of the A road. The car slowed for a speed camera and then accelerated to 80. Lizzie sank back into the leather seat and surrendered to the speed, to the night. A firearms car drew past, blue lights flashing, no siren. Another part of London; another drama.

They pulled off the main road and weaved through roundabouts and intersections before the car slowed to a halt. He said, 'Exactly where do you live?'

'It's a few streets up here. I'll direct you.' She gathered her things from the footwell. 'Or I can walk the last bit.'

'Don't be silly. I'm just here on the left. If you want a drink first.'

CHAPTER 19

Collins and Steve worked their way systematically from opposite ends of the seafront, trying every hotel. The Sea Crest, which had a dirty awning and condensation misting its windows, had its own little car park, from which Steve exited pulling his North Face jacket tight around him and lighting a cigarette. He called Collins on his phone.

'Bingo.'

They parked a little way down the front, facing the car towards Hastings with a good view of the hotel doors and the exit from the car park. Collins called for more troops to drive down and relieve them. Jez and Alice said they could work the overtime. They were on their way – drive time away. Collins needed some sleep. Ideally someone else would be responsible for detaining Lizzie if she turned up to retrieve the car.

They waited.

Night had fallen and the sea was an expanse of glassy blackness. In the distance Collins could just make out the spectre of the ruined pier. She slid her seat back and closed her eyes. When she woke, she was stiff and cold.

Steve said, 'Thank God you've woken up. I'm absolutely Hank Marvin.'

'What the hell's keeping them?'

'I got a text while you were sleeping. There's been an accident on the A21. They're stuck in traffic.'

'OK, get some chips for both of us. Plenty of salt—'

'And no vinegar. I'll be quick.'

'No problem.'

Collins got out of the car and stood by the iron balustrade that protected the fall to the beach. She lit a cigarette and imagined her empty house going through its solitary motions, the central heating clicking on.

She turned and leaned back against the balustrade, glancing to her left. A young woman was walking towards her, a slight figure in a hoody, jeans and trainers. Collins fished her phone out of her pocket and selected Steve from her favourites, but it rang unanswered. The young woman was getting closer. Collins ended the call and slipped her phone back into her pocket. She turned back towards the sea and leaned her weight against the railing. She would wait for Lizzie to pass. With any luck Steve might even be back by then. But the young woman's steps were slowing, and then she too paused and leant against the balustrade.

The countryside had given way to lights. The seafront was a half-night stained by neon and sodium. Lizzie turned her back to the town and gazed out towards the darkness of the sea. She listened to the sighing and pulsing, the stones shifting endlessly.

He had become Kieran to her that night; that was the detail she remembered now. Before, he had been the inspector, the guv'nor, sir, Mr Shaw. Now, with the physical act, came his name: Kieran. She could taste it still in her mouth, the voiceless velar stop, the vowel like a sigh, the sound travelling forward and turning like the roll of a wave to end with the soft touch of her tongue tapping the n. She remembered him leaning forward to kiss her. His lips, his tongue. The taste of him, the pressure of their desire, as if they wanted to swallow each other whole. Her hand around his neck, the short hair at the back of his head. His hand – how tender – flat against the small of her back. And yet, in spite of this moment of tenderness, the desperation, the hurry, like runners racing towards a finish line.

They had not moved from the sound system, as if they were teenagers; the coffee table cramped them. Somehow to go to his bed was out of the question. Their clothes were torn away, discarded, only half removed, and then, with a final impatience, they were naked. There was a moment's stillness. She had traced her finger along the line of darker tan where the short-sleeved police shirt ended. She was leaning backwards. There was a scar glimpsed on his arm, a tattoo on his chest and another on his bicep. Then, with the shock of intimacy, he was inside her. He leaned away from her. He smiled and said her name. *Lizzie*. As he reached towards her, she saw more clearly the tattoo on his arm: a rose blooming and winding. A sudden compassion arose in her: the mess of it, the pain, the urgency, the unexpected beauty, the awkwardness, the bloody stupid coffee table.

She rested both hands on the balustrade, felt the cold metal against them. The incontrovertible rightness of it: that was what she remembered. Even now her desire held its own justification, its own meaning.

The sea sighed and turned. Lizzie glanced to her left. A woman a few feet away was also leaning against the balustrade, smoking, looking out to sea. Lizzie watched her and wondered what thoughts were going through her head, what memories playing. What had brought her here on her own to contemplate the sea? She was older than Lizzie, wearing good flat leather shoes, and what looked like grey suit trousers, all incongruously topped by a zip-up waterproof jacket. Lizzie realized all at once that she was, of course, a cop. Then the woman turned slightly and Lizzie saw her on the roof, holding out her warrant card.

Startled out of her reverie, Lizzie turned immediately and started walking in the direction she had come from. The detective sergeant began to walk after her, calling her name. Lizzie quickened her pace and began to run.

★   ★   ★

After the first few steps, Collins turned and ran to the car. In defiance of the protesting horns, she swung the vehicle sharply round on the coast road. The seafront was busy, cars speeding. She could see Lizzie running ahead, her arms swinging easily. In a second she would be alongside her. She would head her off, run round, get hold of her. But Lizzie had looked over her shoulder towards the approaching car, and now she ran out sharply in front of it, forcing Collins to brake sharply. Collins was already getting out of the driver's seat, her right foot on the road. The traffic would stop Lizzie. She would be able to grab her. But then, to her horror, she saw Lizzie swerve away into the path of an oncoming car. The car blared its horn and screeched to a halt, avoiding her only by an inch. Lizzie almost lost her footing. She put her left hand on the bonnet to steady herself and then raced on, head down, running with a good stride. The driver was getting out of the car, a fat, angry man. Collins could see Lizzie turning up a side street. The fat man was shouting after her and shaking his fist. 'What the bloody hell?'

Collins ran, leaving the car in the road. Her phone was ringing. She could just see the back of Lizzie disappearing to the right on to the main street.

She pulled her phone from her pocket and answered as she turned and began to run back to the car.

'Steve, she's made off. I think she's gone up the

main street, towards the station. She's too fast for me. I'm getting back in the car to look for her.'

Fifteen minutes after Collins and Steve had given up searching, Jez and Alice had arrived in St Leonards. Now they all sat together in a bar on the first floor of a big old white hotel on the seafront, drinking orange juice and eating salted peanuts.

Collins was furious. Lizzie Griffiths was making a bloody fool of her. She had a strong image in her mind – an image that she felt would always be with her – of Lizzie's young, slim frame outpacing her effortlessly, as if she were the front-runner in a cross-country event.

Neither Collins nor Steve spoke.

Jez said, 'Look, it's not a bad thing. She's got no car now and she's running out of money. It's a small town and she hasn't got a vehicle. We can check the CCTV inside the hotel. Find out what she's wearing. Can't we get the local plod to help us?'

Steve shook his head. 'Baillie says no.'

'Call him. Get him to change his mind.'

Collins spoke for the first time. 'He's not answering his damn phone, is he? I'll have to talk to him in the morning.'

CHAPTER 20

Lizzie couldn't stop shivering. She knew how easy it could be to miss suspects when they were only a few feet away, so for a long time she had simply crouched down behind a shed in the dark corner of someone's garden. She didn't know how thorough they would be in looking for her, or how many of them there were. Finally she decided to risk moving. Perhaps they would send more officers, search systematically, even cordon off the area where she had been seen. She needed to get away, at least from the centre of town.

She walked quickly up and away from the sea through streets of ample Victorian villas, finding herself finally in a deserted business park. Workshops and warehouses, lonely offices with pictures of Alsatians in the windows. There was a row of garages, and she could see that on one of them the padlock only appeared to be closed. She pulled it open. Inside was a locked white transit van, and behind the van, some large cans of paint. Leaves had gathered along the wall.

She rested against the van and waited for things

to become clearer to her. It frightened her that they had identified the hire car. She felt the facts constricting around her, forcing her to some sort of ending that she dreaded. The cold was penetrating her body. She crouched down, took the T-shirts out of her backpack and put them on in layers, then zipped up her waterproof again. Her hands had a kind of luminosity in the darkness, white with cold.

The hire car, with its powerful heater had been a kind of refuge to her and it had given her a fantasy of escape, of driving for miles and miles, for ever and ever. She remembered bitterly the squishy leather seats of Kieran's Land Rover. The luxury and exuberance of the car. The blast of music from the iPhone in the dock.

She had been going home to her parents that first morning, and sex had made her late. Kieran had rolled her over on to her back like a lion playing with a willing cub and said, 'Plenty of time. I'll drive you to the station.' It had been as if they had wanted to enter through the wall of skin into each other's bodies. His smell, his taste – they had been a confirmation of what she had suspected. Her desire had been verified.

Afterwards the city had swept past in all its glorious grey, the huge buffeting sky framing the Westway flyover with its billboards and high-rises.

She said, 'A proper drug dealer's car.'

'That's right. Can't let them have all the good things.'

Kieran glanced to his left and put his free hand briefly on her knee. Then he indicated right to overtake and changed up a gear.

'Lizzie, about Hadley. You feeling better about that?'

'Mmm.'

She hadn't wanted to think about Hadley at all. She had wanted the drive to last for ever. She wanted to walk with Kieran along a pebbly beach. She wanted to eat breakfast with him in a small old-fashioned hotel. She wanted to know everything, every little detail about him. She wanted to ask what on earth they both thought they were playing at, and she wanted to fuck him again, soon.

He said, 'OK, listen.' She turned to him but he was concentrating on the road. 'We're not having this conversation, do you understand?'

She shrugged. 'OK.'

'And this is just my opinion. It has nothing to do with me being your guv'nor. It's just my opinion as your, your . . .' She squinted at him and thought, *lover*. He smiled briefly at her and said, '. . . friend.'

'Yeah. OK. Go on.'

'Lizzie, this is what I would do about Hadley. Of course I'll back you whatever you decide.'

There he was, twenty years' experience and no shit sticking to him. She said, 'OK, Kieran, guv'nor, whatever. Go ahead. I want to hear what you really think.'

And that had been the truth. She hadn't necessarily

intended to do what he told her, but she had wanted him to stop speaking in code.

'If it was me . . . I would talk to Hadley and find out what really happened when he was with Farah and you were in the kitchen. It needs to be just you and him and you need to talk bottom line. Then you'll know what to do.'

'So you haven't submitted the file yet.'

He shook his head. 'No, I was waiting for you to decide what you wanted to do.'

To decide? She hadn't quite realized that some sort of decision was expected from her.

'Be sure of yourself. Don't get yourself in the shit, Lizzie. Or me, for that matter. Have a think and let me know what you want to do. If you want to talk to Hadley, I'll make sure you're posted in a car on a night shift. Until then, you're not working together.'

He swung the car off the slip road and round the feed lane into Paddington station. Her hand was already on the door handle. She was in danger of missing her train. He had to get in for late turn and was now in a hurry. But he reached out and she felt his hand on her shoulder.

'Haven't you forgotten something?'

For a minute she felt as she did when she made some rookie error, like failing to enter an interview in the custody record. But Kieran was smiling at her. He leaned across the car to kiss her, his hand caressing the back of her neck.

'Mum's the word, eh?' he said.

★   ★   ★

137

The Asian taxi driver who picked Lizzie up at the station needed to unburden himself about his brother's success in investing in the local property market. Lizzie, making muted sounds of approval, tuned him out. How badly everyone needed to be listened to! She had read somewhere that people spent ninety per cent of their time thinking about themselves. Her phone pinged and she ferreted it out from her bag. It was a text from Kieran: *OK?*

She texted back: *OK. U?*

There was no reply and she put her phone back in her bag. Watching the suburban streets threading out with their PVC windows and waxy camellias in tidy front gardens, she battled an impulse to ask the driver to turn back to the station. She remembered spying through the open door of the kitchen. The window streaming with rivulets of condensed steam. Her mother hissing bitterly at her father: 'You refuse to do well.'

Too soon the cab was drawing up outside her parents' house. She paid the driver and let herself in quietly with her own key. Before stepping into the sitting room, she stood in the hallway for a moment like a diver slowly surfacing, carefully acclimatizing herself to a different atmospheric pressure.

Her father sat upright in the special chair her mother had bought for him. Tapestried upholstery struggled to hide the chair's nature, but a cable stretching from the back of it to the wall gave the game away. A cushion supported her father's back.

All around were the trappings of her mother's efforts to keep him alive. The sliding doors to the dining room were closed on the bed the hospital had provided. Lizzie could hear her mother fretting in the kitchen. She tried to hide her horror at her father's emaciated state. She said, 'Dad,' and attempted a smile that she felt emerged instead as a grimace.

'No,' he said, shaking his head at her brief confusion. 'No, no, don't worry, Lizzie.' He reached out a hand to her. It was skeletal, already mummified. 'What have you been up to?'

Her mother entered with optimistic tea and cake. 'Lizzie.' She hesitated briefly as though considering an embrace and then thinking better of it. She began to fuss around her husband, rearranging the cushion behind his back. He was a failing idol, rigid in his chair but still exacting tribute with his skull face.

'Will you be able to stay the night?'

'I told you, Mum. I'm on duty tomorrow. Early turn.'

The doorbell rang.

'That'll be the vicar,' said her mother.

Lizzie could not stifle it. 'Did you have to arrange for him to come the one afternoon I was here?'

Her mother matched her. She spoke in an angry hush. 'Your father asked to see him. Be polite.'

The vicar had a thin, drawn face and long-fingered hands. With his dog collar, dark jacket and comfortable crêpe-soled shoes, there was nothing to like about the man: he was no smiling Anglican in a rainbow surplice. Rather there was – it seemed to Lizzie in her temper – an unmerited complacency about him. Like an old copper who had got the job off pat. With the air of a man familiar with the preamble to death in centrally heated homes, he folded himself into one of the armchairs and commented favourably on the aspect across the road to the playing fields opposite.

'Yes, we bought it for the view,' her mother said, and Lizzie thought of bulrushes and bog land, long gone.

'The sun sets over the fields,' her father said.

Lizzie said, 'If you'll excuse me, Vicar.'

As she went to join her mother in the kitchen, her phone pinged again and she saw, with a sudden flash of joy, that it was another text from Kieran: *All good. OK?*

Good. Back for early turn tomorrow.

Her father had summoned her here, closed her within this semi-detached airlock of double-glazing and cavity wall insulation, but soon she would flee this place! Inside her a pocket of reverie was protecting her, a corner in which something was germinating, like a seed uncurling in a dark cellar. Perhaps this would become something more enduring than a one-night stand and the memory of a winding rose tattoo.

Pills were lined up on the side in a plastic container with multiple partitions. Yellows, light blues, cheerful reds. It occurred to Lizzie that someone had invented the specialized container: that somewhere there was a factory that made plastic boxes suitable only for holding different dosages of pills in promising colours. Her mother was tidying an already tidy kitchen, wiping down clean tops, dragging around a seething resentment. Her parents' life together seemed to be run along the lines of a barely concealed competition for moral superiority. Lizzie raged inwardly that neither of them was prepared to shoulder the blame for Eve biting the apple. Her mother's resentment was as threatening as a spark to tinder. Lizzie had a pile of it, a whole woodshed, inside her ready to flame. That's what I am, she thought, I'm an internal combustion engine. You could harness me to the National Grid and cut down on CO_2 emissions. Hardly a word had been spoken, but somehow she and her mother were already arguing. Lizzie stifled the flames: there would be no fight. Her father was dying.

'I'm going for a walk until the vicar leaves,' she said to her mother.

She walked out over the playing fields. They were hard and dry, firm underfoot, and she remembered a different time, when there had been marshland, and kestrels had hovered above. Once she had found a grass snake, emerald and jewelled against the new road's fresh black tarmac. It had seemed to her a visitor from a land as foreign as Narnia. And like such a visitor, it could not survive

141

long in the alien planet's atmosphere. One of the other children prodded it with a stick and it responded with a weary undulation that travelled like tired electricity through its coils.

Her sister had said, 'Lizzie, run and fetch Dad.'

He had arrived with a perfect understanding of the urgency and lifted the snake into his hands. The children gasped at his bravery. His hands seemed so strong and capable; the snake must now surely be saved. He turned it over and found the injury. 'The poor thing has probably been hit by a car,' he said. 'There's nothing we can do.' He had walked towards the longer grass, the children trailing behind him in the lengthening afternoon light. He bent down and placed the snake in a hollow in the earth. 'Its best chance,' he explained, 'is to leave it here quiet in the long grass. I want you children to leave it alone.'

He stood sentinel and the children wandered away in search of other activities. They knocked on neighbours' doors and asked for old newspapers for recycling, daring the adults not to believe them. They took the papers up the hill behind the house and set fire to them. In a ditch in the wood the glorious conflagration leapt and soared. The local constable arrived and they crouched in the bushes watching him stamping it out. It was Tracey's dad; he lived in one of the old police houses across the way.

Later, as the sun was setting, Lizzie had gazed out of the window towards the marshland where the snake still lay. Her parents were arguing in the kitchen, behind the half-closed door. Plumes of steam rose from the hob and condensed on the window in streams and pools.

'Why do you do it?' her mother hissed.

'Really, *Paki*?'

'OK, they shouldn't use words like that, but still . . . What one child says to another is not worth adults arguing about. There's a way to say things and the way you do it you won't make any difference. You won't change anyone's opinion. The only difference you will make is to your own family.'

Lizzie ran out of the side door.

Her mother called out to her, 'Don't be long. I'm serving.'

She ran across the road and through the boggy field to where they had left the snake. She was at the edge here – the house, with its orange electric light, was a remote outpost, a lighthouse winking on the meniscus of a darkening sea of rippling sedge. She found the snake a few feet away, dead. It seemed an almost wilful act, as though, in defiance of those who had come and invaded this previously remote place, it had chosen to die.

Over the following two years, as the fresh houses settled into the land, the earth had thrown up its treasures like one last offering. Clay pipes, fossils, dead birds; all were cast out. The land was shedding itself of colour and variety. Once Lizzie had wandered by herself the two or three miles down the lane and found the gypsy camp, tucked into a bend in the hedgerow. There were only a couple of caravans. She stood at the perimeter and watched. Catkins were hanging down like lambs' tails. Washing blew in the cold breeze. A child poked about with a stick in a muddy puddle.

The house now seemed peculiarly equal to her in all its different epochs, as though it existed outside time. Perched on the edge of land that had once been tussocky farmland but was now a bland suburban park, it had distilled into something smaller but more intense in her imagination.

Dusk was already drawing in, and against the darkening sky the clouds were washed with crimson light. She turned to study the house, imagining it holding the past, like a shaken snow globe with the snow still falling. But it was the present, and her parents were old and failing. An ambulance was pulling up outside. In the dusk, its lights were preternaturally blue, like strange celebrations.

She could not run fast enough. Still she tried, because that was always going to be preferable to surrendering to the other possibility: that she had spent long hours on the train but her mother had still contrived to cheat her of the moment her father needed her. She was a good sprinter and she concentrated on her technique. Head in line with the spine, chin down. Smooth action of the arms. Hands relaxed, fingers curled. She felt her power, the roll and drive of her feet. Her arms punching. Her lungs sucking in oxygen. The land climbed towards the house. The body might want to give up, but that was when you dug for a bit more strength. The last part of any race was all about being mentally stronger than your opponent. You thought running would kill you, but it didn't. And afterwards you were always stronger than you had been before.

She climbed the bank, still sprinting, to see the ambulance pulling away, its winking lights disappearing along the darkening road.

Her lungs hurt. She leaned over and spat.

Her father was dead before he reached the hospital.

19 APRIL

CHAPTER 21

The man was heavyset, maybe thirty or forty years old, wearing a parka with a furry hood, paint-stained trousers and trainers. Lizzie didn't know how she had fallen asleep in spite of the cold, but now she was confused and it was hard to wake. The man was standing over her, looking at her. He shook her shoulder and spoke with a foreign accent, Polish probably.

'You all right?'

'Mmm.'

'What you doing here?'

She was trying to get up, but it wasn't easy. 'Nothing,' she said. 'I'm going now.'

He reached down and helped her up. 'You cold. It's OK. I give you lift. You want lift? I go for breakfast. You want I buy you breakfast?'

In his van he took off his parka and switched the heating on full.

He said, 'You sleep in garage, you need keep warm.'

'Yeah, yeah. You're right.'

'Serious,' he insisted. 'Is serious.'

★　　★　　★

149

She ordered the full English – beans, sausages, fried eggs, bacon, bubble and squeak, the works – and tried to warm her hands with a big mug of milky coffee. At first the sounds of the place were distant, but gradually she felt the volume returning to normal. She was able to notice the pictures of footballers on the walls, the large-breasted woman serving behind the counter. The café, it turned out, was piping hot and smelled of fried meat.

He said his name was Janusz but he didn't say much else. He got himself a tabloid and leafed through it as if she wasn't really there. After about twenty minutes he gathered himself together and stood up to leave.

'You want sleep in garage?'

'Maybe.'

He nodded. 'OK. But you need keep warm.'

'Yes, I get it. Listen, thanks.'

She could not bring herself to relinquish the warmth and comfort of the café. She got her phone out of her bag and considered it for a while. It was, she recognized, another sort of warmth, and equally tempting. Could she perhaps just touch her index finger to his name? *Kieran.* She imagined him picking her up in the Land Rover. She imagined sinking into the leather seat and driving, driving away. She could picture the countryside, a cottage on a hill perhaps. Dry-stone walls. But she knew this was a fantasy. Her phone would summon police, or Kieran would inform – would have no choice perhaps other than to inform – Detective Sergeant Collins.

He had been her protector before, or at least she had thought so.

After her father's death, when she had found it hard to do anything for herself, she had stayed at his flat. He had bought her takeaways and cooked for her as though she were ill. He had gone to work; she lay in his bed wearing his old T-shirts and watching black-and-white films on his laptop.

Alone, while he was at work, she had wandered his flat. On the wall in the sitting room was a framed black-and-white photo of a six-year-old girl in a tutu. A skinny girl with fair hair tied up in a bun. Her right foot, clad in a ballet pump, pawed the ground in the manner of a horse before a set of Cavaletti jumps.

His bathroom was pungent with the smells of masculine soap and deodorant. The shelf held two toothbrushes in a cup, one a child's. Lizzie's face was pale in the steamy mirror as she brushed her teeth with her index finger.

When her mother had left, there had been no shouting, no door-slamming. Lizzie had come down for breakfast, and instead of being at work as usual, her dad had been there in her mother's place, making golden toast.

'This is always my favourite breakfast,' he had said. 'I can never have too much of it.'

She was putting her plate on the table, her back

to him, when he spoke. 'Mum's gone away for a bit. Try not to worry. Everything will work out.'

That afternoon her father had taken her on her favourite outing – the traditional sweet shop with the doorbell that pinged against its taut spring. She had stood at the counter and gazed at the panoply of sweets. Banana and custards, sherbert lemons, rosy apples. Her father bought her a mixed bag of stripy bullseyes, barley sugars and fruit rounders. Lizzie had walked out across the playing fields and sat on the stream's muddy bank. The sweets were like balls of tangy coloured glass, holding a mystery of sugary dissolution within them, but the bag had tipped over beside her and the sweets rolled down the hill, coating themselves in soil. She left them where they fell, like spilled treasure.

That was all she really remembered of that time. It was like a silence inside her. And then her mother had come back. Lizzie had watched from an upstairs window as her father helped unload her suitcases from the boot of the car. There was a little attaché case, pink leather with rounded edges and a zip.

Kieran, she remembered, had brought her gifts of old-edition Penguins from a local junk shop, and when the clothes she had brought with her ran out, he arrived with pants and shirts as though she were a child who had fallen in a stream.

He came home from work and cast off his T-shirt, kicking it to the bottom of the bed. When he slept, she put her hand against the muscle on the side of his neck where her teeth had left a mark.

He had taken his wedding ring off and driven her to her father's funeral. She didn't know what it meant that he was there with her except that, for this moment at least, he was by her side. He sat beside her in the chapel, holding her hand firmly.

Before the funeral, her mother had given her a box of photos. She had taken the lid off and flipped through the images. Her father teaching her to ride a bike. Pagham Beach on a summer day, the sky a brilliant blue and the sun shining off the bonnet of the family Volkswagen. On the front of the order of service had been a picture of her father, youthful, dashing in his army uniform, his dates in italics underneath. She had googled him on her phone but he was not to be found. He had left no mark at all. More obscure than an ammonite, he had fallen to the seabed leaving no trace.

His figure in the coffin had been a simulacrum. Her father was no more there than he was anywhere. Her mother had shown her halting colour-bleached Super 8 film: children in duffel coats at a zoo; her father looking at the camera and then pointing towards the penguins; her mother and father emerging laughing from a house in the rain and running to a car.

As they followed the coffin out into the sunlight, Kieran put his arm around her shoulders. The grave was a deep black mouth. Her sister's children ran to it as to a party and threw red rose petals on to the descending coffin.

After the burial, they cut across the countryside in Kieran's Land Rover. There had been a late hoar frost. The fields were white and the branches of the trees were crystalline. The lanes dipped into deep banks and threaded between high hedges from which birds exploded like gunfire. The coverage on Lizzie's iPhone kept vanishing. The Land Rover showed as a pulsating blue blip travelling through a limitless grey grid, as though what she saw through the windows was a mirage. They could be in a boat on an ocean. They could be travelling over the moon.

Kieran had got a handle on it. He didn't need the sat nav. Somehow he could follow the hopeless pencil-drawn map on the back of the order of service. He always seemed to know where he was.

He said, 'Have you got a charge agreed for Mehenni?'

Why, she had wondered, was he troubling her with this now?

'Yes,' she said. 'I'll charge him when he comes in on bail.'

The M40 had sped along, grey tarmac and white lines. She had not seen the landscape flashing by as the sun began to fall in the sky, but rather the memory of learning to ride her bicycle, her father running behind holding the seat.

CHAPTER 22

Steve was sliding open the office window to step out on to the low roof for a fag, but he paused when he saw Collins pushing open the door.

'What did Baillie say?'

'Yes, he's agreed to go public that she's missing. He's going to do a press release in about an hour. We're using screen grabs from the hotel CCTV.'

'Cigarette?'

She glanced at her watch: 7:30. If Arif was on time, he would be with them in half an hour.

'No, it's fine. I want to crack on.'

'We've got the subscriber's check back on the phone number in Farah's pocket.'

'And?'

'It's a historic number. Belonged to Lizzie Griffiths. She changed it on the thirteenth of April.'

A pause.

'And were there any phone calls between Farah and Lizzie?'

'Joe's checking that now.'

'OK.'

Collins watched Steve step outside. He leaned

155

with his back against the wall and began to smoke. The crow loitered at a discreet distance, hopping about on the edge of the roof.

She opened the working copy of the tape and slipped it into the player. It was the recording of the radio traffic during the incident; the nearest she could get to the experience of the officers at the time. She closed her eyes and listened, imagining it into life. The traffic over the main channel crackled. Officers cut in with routine requests and were told to move to the other channel. The call came out for the person on the roof. *Units to attend.* 761 showed himself on scene. He could see two figures on the roof, he reported. No, three figures.

The radio was busy. It was hard to make it all out. Commands from the duty inspector. Updates from the scene. Paramedics being assigned. She noted the absence: the continuing radio silence of 611 and 170, Griffiths and Matthews. Their silence was a void, a negative space where the important things were happening unrecorded.

She stopped the tape and slid open the window. 'Steve. Put that bloody cigarette out, would you, and come and listen with me?'

'OK. Stand by, Met Police.' He took a final deep inhale, trod on his cigarette and stepped in through the window. She rewound the tape and listened with the transcript in her hand.

Confirm two people on the roof, no, three people.

Go ahead, 761. Informant said two people. Confirm three people.

Steve wrote on a piece of scrap paper: *761?*
Collins took his biro from him and wrote: *Arif.*

A third figure has joined. Repeat: a third figure has joined. I can't identify them from this distance. They are right at the edge.

The transcript showed Inspector Shaw transmitting.

Control, show me making my way. ETA about a minute. I'll go up the stairs.

Control receiving 761.

Go ahead, 761.

One of the people on the roof appears to be a police officer.

Confirm, please. One of the people on the roof is a police officer?

Yes. Yes.

Can you identify the officer? Repeat, can you identify the officer?

I think it's 170.

Steve wrote: *170 – Hadley?* and Collins scribbled: *Yes.*

170 receiving Control. A pause. *Repeat, 170 receiving Control.*

Under the tape Steve said quietly, 'He'd already switched his radio off?'

Collins nodded. She closed her eyes again, straining to hear. She could not help but imagine it. The three figures on the roof, the boy in his bear suit at the edge. The duty inspector issuing commands into the radio. No to air support. London Ambulance Service to stand by. Everything correct, the timeline

157

of a critical incident unrolling. She could picture the resources being deployed. The officers in other boroughs turning their cars and switching on their blue lights. The centre of the storm sucking in backup like a typhoon snatching up street furniture as the borough reached out to the rest of London for aid. The incident in full play and all the power available to the state being deployed to contain and neutralize it. And then, in the midst of this radio traffic, 761 cutting in, as clear and final as bad news always was: a sudden dissipation.

They've fallen.

All units receiving Control. Radio silence please. 761 go again, go again.

They've fallen.

761 confirm, please. Confirm who has fallen.

Steve's mobile rang. Collins stopped the tape and waited as he spoke into the phone. He ended the call.

'Arif's waiting downstairs. I'll go and bring him up.'

The boy – for in spite of his office of sworn constable, that was how Arif Johar seemed to them both – was trim and lightly muscular. His skin was an even light brown, his cheeks marked by a hint of stubble. He wore jeans, a tight T-shirt and sporty shoes that closed over the top with Velcro straps. His hair was gelled. He smelled of fresh aftershave. He smiled shyly and his hands stayed in his pockets.

Steve stretched out his own hand with warm masculine enthusiasm. 'Thanks for coming in so early.'

Arif's right hand reached out. His shoulders relaxed. He smiled. 'No worries.'

Collins remembered him at the scene: a young officer sitting pale and shaking on a wall. Amidst all the shock, he had escaped the net of care that had wrapped around the response team. She had directed the paramedics towards him.

She unsealed blank tapes to record the interview and slotted them into the machine.

Arif was still standing. 'I don't think I've much information to offer really. I was on the ground. I saw it all at a distance.'

Steve said, 'That's all right. Sit yourself down.' He patted the table opposite the chair. 'We just need to get your account down on tape. You know all about that, yes? We have to record you because you're a sig wit – a significant witness.'

Arif cut in, naïvely keen to show he was not as green as grass. 'Yes, I know all that.' And then, rowing back hurriedly, 'Well, I've never done one myself, obviously. The guv'nor explained—'

Collins interrupted. 'Yes?'

Arif shot a sudden watchful glance between the two of them.

Steve intervened, casual. 'Well, that was good of him. He say anything else about this?'

'No. Nothing. Just talked me through the procedure, that's all.'

Collins avoided Steve's eye. Steve smiled. They had stumbled on something that gave an appearance of difficulty but needn't really bother anyone.

'Arif, you don't have to worry. I know you're new to the job. You've never been through anything like this before. We just need to get an account of what you saw, that's all. You're not under investigation. There's no trick questions. We just have to record your evidence. It needs to be done properly. You understand that? You've seen the press.'

'Yes, yes. Of course. I understand. It's not a problem.'

Steve sat back and let Collins ask the questions. She was clinical and swift in obtaining the account, as they had agreed she would be. Arif had been on foot patrol and had put up to take the report from the woman who'd called in the incident, who had first seen the figures on the roof. Her flat was on the ground floor of the building opposite. Spick and span. Lace curtains. Porcelain Siamese cats lined up on the mantelpiece next to some pictures of grandchildren. The woman was white, in her fifties, London working class; one of the estate's watchful inhabitants. Arif had been as quick as he could getting her details. Then he'd gone out to see what was happening. That was when he'd started transmitting on the main channel.

He could see three figures on the edge of the building. He thought he had seen the boy in his bear suit on the ledge. But he wasn't clear whether he could really make out that detail. Perhaps he'd

160

misremembered. He'd definitely seen a short figure anyway, and a taller one besides it, the third figure further off. Perhaps he was filling in his memory with what he knew had happened. They'd have to check his transmissions. People had started to gather, wanted to know what was going on. Rubberneckers. He had tried to push them back. He was on his own and had struggled to control the growing numbers. Some members of the crowd had been hostile. People were enjoying it: he was just getting in the way. One young man – he remembered him clearly – had snarled at him to fuck off.

In the middle of all this Arif had looked up and transmitted about the police officer on the roof. He'd been pretty sure from the start it was Hadley. But he'd been distracted by the public, had been trying to move people a safe distance from the building. They weren't listening to him and he wasn't sure of his powers or what to do. He'd called for backup, made an emergency transmission. That was when he'd turned round and seen Hadley. At the moment of falling. The sight was . . .

Arif paused. He tapped on the desk with his middle finger. He could not find the word. He had surprised himself by arriving at this moment. Finally the word came out of him like a guilty secret that still had the power to shock him.

'Funny.'

He pressed his lips together. They were a thin white line. Collins waited.

Arif went on. 'How can I explain it? Like a comic. Hadley was trying frantically to back-pedal as he fell, trying to get back to solid ground.'

Collins recognized that sensation of disbelief from numerous crime scenes and years of seeing the improbable. Arif was continuing, in the grip of memory now.

'Sarge, it was . . . how can I say?' He paused and then lighted on the word with something like satisfaction. 'Cartoonish – a fat man trying desperately not to fall. But then it wasn't at all, because it was . . .'

He trailed off, lost for words once more.

Collins said, 'Yes, of course. It was real.'

Arif drew his hand over his mouth and closed his eyes. When he opened them again he didn't seem to be seeing the office any more but something else, more compulsive.

'Hadley, he braced himself before he hit the concrete. He put his hands in front of his face. It was somehow the worst thing. As if there was any protection. From that fall. There was no way back.'

Collins waited, and then, when Arif seemed to have lost himself, prompted, 'And the girl?'

'The girl, yes. I think she fell slightly before Hadley but I can't picture it exactly. People fall at the same speed, do they? Irrespective of their weight, that is. I can't hold it in my mind. I can't be sure. I think she leaned out into the drop almost as though she could fly. I remember her thin in the sky like a branch. And then, close up. A girl.'

'Which one hit the ground first?'

'I don't know.' He paused and rubbed his eyes. 'The girl, I think. Yes. The girl.'

Collins said the time and stopped the tape.

Steve said, 'You all right?'

Arif gave a barely noticeable nod, just a tip of his nose.

'You want a cup of tea?'

Arif shook his head, another slight movement.

'Smoke?'

'No.'

Steve reached his cigarettes from his shirt pocket.

'I go out the window for a fag. The DS turns a blind eye. Feel like joining me on the roof terrace? We're a long way from the edge. Only danger is of falling in on a senior management meeting.'

They climbed through the window on to the moss-covered flat roof. Sid hopped about at the edge. Steve gestured towards the crow. 'Don't worry about that bastard. He *can* fly.'

Arif gave a half-smile.

Steve said, 'Well done. You shouldn't be in the job if you can't laugh at the worst things.'

Arif took a packet of gum from his pocket and offered it.

'No thanks.'

Steve turned towards Arif, using his back to shield the lighter from the wind. Arif popped the gum into his mouth. They both leaned against the wall and looked out towards the horizon.

Steve said, 'How much service you got?'

'I've been on borough three months.'

'Christ. Just three months.'

'I've been loving it, actually. I love the team. They've really welcomed me. I thought it might be an issue, me, well . . .'

'You being gay?'

Arif blinked. 'That obvious, is it?'

Steve flashed him a grin. 'Yep, it is.'

Arif laughed. 'OK, I guess it must be.' There was a pause. 'Anyway, it hasn't been a problem, not at all. Even Hadley. He was really old-school but he always welcomed me. I had to put up with the jokes, of course, but they don't bother me. It's just a way of people showing you they trust you not to be a cunt.'

Steve inhaled.

Arif said, 'Sounds corny, but I really loved them. All three of them.'

'Doesn't sound corny.'

'No?'

'Not at all.'

'Anyway, who cares, right?'

'Right.' Steve took a final drag on his cigarette and threw it on the roof. He stamped it out with his foot. 'What do you mean, all three of them?'

'Hadley, Lizzie, the guv'nor. I don't want Lizzie or the guv'nor to be in the shit.'

'Why would they be in the shit?'

'I dunno. Lizzie and the guv'nor, they've

been . . . well, you know.' Arif smiled, a bit embarrassed perhaps.

'I didn't know. He's married, isn't he?'

'Yep. I probably shouldn't say any more.'

'No, probably not.'

CHAPTER 23

Lizzie knew she had to keep moving. She put the silent phone back in her bag, then opened her wallet and counted her money. She left the café and walked up the street. Two PCSOs, their backs turned to her, were putting up a poster in the entrance to a Lidl. As she passed, Lizzie looked over her shoulder and saw that it was her own face sellotaped to the glass door. She recognized the Sea Crest Hotel, blurred in the background of the image – the photo must have been captured by the CCTV camera in the lobby.

On her left was a side street, and at the far end she could see a hairdresser's sign: *Hair Today*. As she approached, she saw that the shop was a converted chemist's. The windows still showed the stained-glass emblems of the pharmacist: large apothecary jars in green and blue and red. There was a television set mounted on the wall but the sound was off. A radio was playing. A woman was sitting behind the counter reading a John Grisham novel. Her hair was bleached blonde and her fake tan shone under the LED spotlights.

She put the book down on the counter and looked without expression at Lizzie.

'You're lucky. We can fit you in. What do you want?'

'A cut and colour, please.'

'Full head or highlights?'

Lizzie wanted a bob. She'd decided to go dark, she said. The woman sat her down and wheeled over the colouring tray.

'It'll suit you brown,' the woman said, looking at her in the mirror. 'Dramatic.'

'How long will it take?'

'About a couple of hours.'

The woman's eyes met Lizzie's, her gaze travelling over her with professional indifference. She began to paint her hair with a thick cream and wrap it in squares of foil.

From where she was sitting Lizzie watched absent-mindedly the television that was reflected in the mirror opposite. The screen showed a helicopter shot: night falling over London. Only gradually did Lizzie realise that the camera was focusing in on Portland Tower, circling the block and then travelling high and away, the drop to the concourse even more vertiginous than in memory.

Lizzie's hair was almost entirely covered in foils. She glanced in the direction of the hairdresser who seemed absorbed in the business of dabbing on the colour. Lizzie judged that from the angle she was standing she would not be able to see the television screen, but she couldn't be sure.

Her gaze went back to the television. The image had cut to a thin man with straw-coloured hair and a freckled face. Underneath him ticker tape writing spooled out but Lizzie could not read it – the script was reversed and illegible. Then Lizzie saw – the same image as the PCSOs had been putting up in the Lidl – her own unmoving face.

She glanced back to the hairdresser, who caught her eye in the mirror and frowned. 'Everything OK?'

'Yes. Thanks.'

Lizzie did not dare look back to the television. She stared forward while the hairdresser folded in the last few foils.

'It'll be about 45 minutes. OK?' she said.

'Yes, fine.' She flicked her eyes sideways for a second. The images had changed. Two glossy presenters were sitting on a couch holding mugs and talking. 'Do you mind if I see if I can find a film on the TV?'

The hairdresser was tidying up her trolley. She shrugged. 'Be my guest but please don't put the sound on. I like listening to the radio.'

CHAPTER 24

Outside the door of the male constables' locker room, someone had left a bunch of flowers in a glass jar. Collins put the takeaway coffees on the floor and bent down: bluebells, buttercups and cow parsley. There was no note.

She picked up the coffee, stood up and knocked at the door.

'Female,' she called out. 'I'm coming in.'

The room was subterranean and deserted. Light filtered through foxhole windows above head height. A narrow corridor ran down the right-hand side of the room, giving way on the left to rows of gunmetal-grey lockers. She walked to the end and turned along the furthest row. Sitting on the ground by a cordon of blue and white crime tape was Jez. He was reading a Jack Reacher. He put it down with a little embarrassed wag of his head and began to get up.

'Sarah.'

'I've got you a coffee. Two sugars, right?'

'Yeah. Do you want me to help?'

'Don't worry. Drink your coffee.'

A different DS would have let him go to the canteen while she cracked on with the search. Never mind. She didn't want any allegations. She did things by the book and so he'd have to stay to corroborate anything she found. She'd brought him a coffee. He'd have to be happy with that.

She was meeting Steve in an hour and a half and she needed to work quickly. Hadley had had two lockers. She slipped the key into the lock of the first. The door opened outwards. Taped to the inside was a photograph of a plump middle-aged woman sitting on a beach with four sunburned boys ranged around her. The eldest was about thirteen. The youngest was definitely primary-school age – seven perhaps. The eldest boy had his arm round a surfboard. The youngest was standing between the woman's legs, leaning his head against her chest. The woman's left arm was looped around his waist, her hand spread open on his chest. In her right hand was an ice cream with a flake. She had brown curly hair and was laughing towards the camera.

Collins photographed the locker with a digital camera and then began to empty it systematically. She started from the top shelf and worked towards the bottom, making a note of the contents as she went. A box of epaulettes. Plastic over-trousers. Still in its cellophane bag, the white cover that allowed a stab vest to be worn covertly. A jar of Brylcreem. Deodorant. Shower gel. A tin of biros. Too many shirts. At the bottom, a smelly towel.

A half-empty tube of mints. She returned every-thing to its place and closed the door.

The second locker was very much like the first. Crammed and disordered. On the door of this one was sellotaped a faded picture of a football team, cut from a newspaper. The players wore red jerseys and old-fashioned, endearingly brief white shorts. She recognized George Best in the middle row. Another face was familiar. Was that Bobby Charlton? She wasn't sure; football wasn't her thing. Anyway, it was clearly one of those football moments. They were all sitting in rows behind a cup and shield. Again she photographed the locker and listed its contents. More biros. A spare hand-cuff key. Two police jumpers. Cavernous trousers. Shirts on wire hangers. She checked each pocket and then hung them all back up. Old tissues, a packet of gum. A formal tunic on a wooden hanger. On the floor, an old-style truncheon and, in a box, a silver whistle on a chain.

She closed the locker and signed off the crime scene in the book. She signed paper seals and stuck them over the two doors.

Jez said, 'All done then?'

'Yes.'

'Do you want me to take the keys back?'

'No thanks. I'll do it.'

The civilian in Resources was past fifty and over-weight. Her breath was audible and she moved slowly. She wore tortoiseshell-framed glasses, a green Tyrol-style cardigan, a high-necked blouse, a brown pleated skirt.

Collins showed her warrant card. 'I wanted to return the key to PC Hadley's lockers. I'm Sarah, by the way – I'm the DS investigating PC Hadley's death.'

'Yes, dear, that's all right. I know who you are.'

She glanced at the warrant's detail nevertheless, and her small eyes briefly flickered towards Collins' face. She did not immediately accept the master key. Instead she took a key out of her handbag and used it to open her desk drawer. In it was another key that opened a metal cupboard on the wall. She unlocked the cupboard and then stretched out her hand to take the locker key from Collins. She hung it on a peg inside the cupboard labelled with a small laminated note: *M3*. Then she locked the cupboard and replaced the key in her drawer.

Collins said, 'I can see you do a good job of keeping everything in order.'

'You have to.' It was said with something like conceit.

Collins gave an exhale of agreement. 'Around coppers, I expect.'

'Well some of them can't be counted on. They'll always lose something.'

'And then blame you.'

'That's right.'

'So you must keep a record of the keys. Who has them, that sort of thing? That way you can prove it's not you who had them last.'

The civilian's head cocked to the side, suddenly careful.

Collins said, 'Well?'

'I do, yes.'

'Do you mind if I have a look at it?'

The civilian hesitated only briefly. 'Of course.' She went back to her desk, opened the drawer and handed Collins a hardback indexed book.

'I'll leave you to it,' she said, moving towards the door.

'Do you mind just hanging on a minute . . .'

The civilian looked at her warily and then moved away towards the franking machine. She showed her back, wrapped in green cardigan: she was busy with the registered post.

Collins opened the book to the day of the fall. She ran her finger down the entries. The key to the drying room. The key for the custody store. The master key for the men's lockers. There it was, the signature she had half expected.

The car was stationary, with the engine running and the heating fan on full. Collins' mobile was ringing. She was sitting with her head tilted back against the headrest and her eyes closed. With a sigh she opened her eyes and fished the phone out of her bag. DCI Baillie's name had appeared across the screen. She didn't want to speak to him, not now. She put the phone back in her bag, letting it ring to voicemail. She took a Marlboro out of its packet, lit it and pressed the button to lower her window. The smoke expanded into her lungs and the nicotine hit.

She was enduring the usual cold sensation that preceded post-mortems. Once it got started, she told herself, she would be fine. She would be busy. It was the anticipation that filled her with dread. She hated the reduction of a human being to its constituent parts, to bags of muscle and a jar of brain. Every time, it evoked an uncanny sensation. Warmth, desire, struggle, everything of interest to a detective reduced to the cold facts of biology. The heart that pumped, the body that acted, the grey sponge that desired and intended.

She called Jez and asked him to arrange for Inspector Shaw to come in. 'Late afternoon, please. After the PM.'

Then she leaned back against the headrest, closing her eyes and conjuring the memory of the young female PC, pale and shaking on the roof, the boy in the bear suit on her lap. She recognized that she had got her priorities wrong: she should have spirited Lizzie Griffiths away then. It was in those moments that people talked. Perhaps Inspector Kieran Shaw had been ahead of her in realizing that.

There was the noise of a car pulling into the yard. Collins opened her eyes. Steve was parking up parallel to her. His passenger window slid down and he leaned over.

'Have I got time for a fag?'

'Sorry, no.'

'OK, let me finish yours.'

She joined him on the tarmac and handed him her cigarette. He took a long drag and held the smoke in his lungs while he spoke. 'They've got the posters up and the boss has done a press release. We've got some officers down there looking and the locals are on board.'

'Great.'

'Has the boss rung you?'

'He's just tried. Why?'

'Because he rang me looking for you. Wants an update.'

'OK. I'll speak to him later. We'd better crack on. The pathologist's not going to be happy. We've kept her waiting. We'd better apologize.'

Steve took a last drag and threw the cigarette on to the ground, treading the stub into the paving.

'If you'll just help me roll him to the side . . . Richard, you put two hands on the abdomen. Careful, we don't want him to split.'

The body was heavy and hard to manipulate. Dr Graham went to the head, Steve to the top of the thighs. Collins put both hands behind the pelvis to assist. Richard, the mortuary assistant, had the worst job, holding the stomach in place, but he seemed as indifferent to it as he was to all aspects of autopsy.

Dr Graham was a neat, thin woman in her fifties. Her hair, drawn back in a twist at the back of her head, was streaked with steel grey. Her motivation in picking her particular specialism would always be a mystery to Collins, but she was grateful simply that Graham was not only methodical and professional but also sparing with the jokes.

Collins watched carefully, hoping for the unexpected, the thing that would leap out and give her something to go on. They rolled Hadley on to his back. His front was a mess. The face was fractured, covered in dried blood. The jumper was split open, soaked in blood and intestine. Through the split a sheet of bulging yellow plastic showed.

Richard cut the jumper off with medical scissors and Steve bagged it up. Underneath, the shirt was also stained and split, wet with the blood that had spread and seeped like an ink stain across the back and under the armpits. Hadley's warrant card was in the top pocket. Dr Graham passed it to Steve. He flicked through its contents, making notes in his exhibit book and bagging each item. A ten-pound note. PC Matthews' emergency life-support qualification. He passed the warrant card to Collins and she flicked it open. The photo was a flashback to the late eighties. It was faded through years of swiping, but she could still glimpse Hadley as a young man: whippet thin, shoulder-length hair, a moustache. He must have caught the tail end of Thatcher, when officers still patrolled in tunics. She pondered the fact that he had never had cause to change his original warrant card photograph. Twenty-seven years a uniform copper. That stood for something, even in her book: aching feet, cold crime scenes, early turns, late turns, night duties, fights and robberies, fatal traffic collisions, death messages – the whole catalogue of misery that was the lot of uniform.

She'd studied Hadley's record. He'd had a commissioner's commendation for an incident a few years earlier when a man had been threatening suicide with a razor blade. Another one pending for a domestic murder. He also had a couple of disciplinary incidents on his file. Two years ago, an allegation of improper use of force. Further back, another allegation of racism. He'd received warning letters for the two incidents but they'd both lapsed. And the man himself? One divorce, a successful second marriage. Three children, or four if you counted the one he'd raised that wasn't his. Three years from retirement and a full pension, and then he falls from a roof.

The trouser pockets were filled with loose change. Steve counted it out into an evidence bag: £8.30. He removed the notebook from the back pocket and passed it to Collins. It was wet with blood. She peeled back the pages, careful not to rip them. It was a neglected document; no date was even written in for the day he died. The assistant cut the remains of the shirt off. At the scene a yellow clinical-waste bag had been taped to the body to hold the stomach in place. Beneath this the intestine bulged, precarious, threatening to spill out in rolls. PC Matthews' underpants were predictable:

comic or tragic, she couldn't decide which – large Y-fronts that fell to the side.

Then it was done and PC Hadley Matthews was naked on the slab. The bruised, smashed face. The hairs on his arms oddly real in the waxy flesh. The bloated stomach still contained by the taped yellow plastic, the chest white and hairy. The penis grey and lifeless. Large white hands – the fingers stiff and claw-like in death. Here was the cadaver's usual enigma. The man himself, both here and not here. Collins had a strange urge to reach out and touch his arm. A fleeting desire to comfort.

The pathologist turned to her. 'Officer, are you ready for me to begin the examination proper?'

Collins took a breath. They had to proceed, even though the cause of death was evident enough.

'Yes, Doctor. Please go ahead.'

CHAPTER 25

'Family?' Hadley had muttered scornfully as he bit into his toast. 'Who on earth does he think disposes of the clothes after a stabbing? It's Mum running the washing machine or it's Dad with the bin bags.'

Lizzie was sitting with the foils in her hair. There was the pungent smell of chemicals and the radio was chirruping relentlessly. The hairdresser was back in her novel and the television was now safely showing a period drama. Women in Regency dresses walked through the countryside. Men rode horses. There was a dance: the women gossiped and wore gloves.

Lizzie's mind drifted: the first shift after her father's funeral. It had been a night duty. The team had been gathered in the canteen.

Radios were on the table, mugs of tea and crumpets. Calls were coming in. The news was unwinding only partially noticed on the canteen's plasma screen that had been taken off some handlers and recycled as an advert for the Proceeds of Crime Act. A politician was recommending the strengthening of the family as the key to reducing knife crime, and Hadley was holding forth.

A request to conduct a welfare check on a young woman believed to be suffering mental health problems had come over the radio. Lizzie looked at Hadley and he interrupted his speech and shrugged. 'Yes, OK. Put us up for it.'

Kieran came in, late for supper as usual. He had had to stay behind in the parade room and deal with something. His shirt was open at the neck, the police tie pulled through the cotton retainer stitched above his left breast pocket. He drew up a chair and Arif pushed a cup of tea towards him.

'Crumpet, sir?'

Everyone seemed suddenly very interested in the table. Arif sniggered.

Hadley cleared his throat at the interruption and returned to his theme. 'We did a warrant on a crack house: five kids, pikey mum handcuffed in the bedroom and Jamaican dad handcuffed in the living room. Auntie turns up to take the kids to school. Mum says to the little one, "You can't go to school in that shirt. It's not ironed."'

There was an appreciative laugh around the table. Kieran caught Lizzie's eye and smiled briefly. She concentrated on her toast. A domestic call came out over the radio and was ignored.

Hadley resumed his disquisition. 'Of course they *love* their children. Christ, you'd have to be an idiot not to see that. You can see it's completely genuine. Love isn't the issue. Or family, for that matter. Bloody politicians. *Family.* These people need *taking away* from their families, for God's sake. The kids are sweet enough right now, they look like the fucking Jackson Five, but if they stay with their mum and dad, don't tell me they won't be out dealing and robbing and carrying in a matter of years. Don't tell me anyone's got a believable plan to deal with that.'

The domestic came out again. No one was taking it. Hadley pushed his chair back. 'All right for that, Lizzie?'

'I put us up for the welfare check.'

'Get us de-assigned, then. That one's an emergency.' He stood up and addressed the table. 'And none of these lazy fuckers are taking it.'

Arif said, 'You'll be sorry.'

Hadley shook his head. 'You're probably just showing off, Arif, so I'll let you off this time, but please don't be learning bad habits from the others.'

Arif blushed and began to clear the table. Lizzie, by now also standing, pressed the transmit button on her radio and accepted the call. Other dispatches were coming out thick and fast. Chairs screeched across the floor as people got up and pulled on their Met vests. Hadley was already out the door and walking along the corridor towards the yard.

Lizzie settled into the passenger seat. The covers were frayed, the back collapsed. She opened the glove compartment, but it was stuffed with paperwork. She threw the breathalyser on to the back seat. Hadley slid the driver's seat back and turned the engine over. Lizzie tapped her code into the onboard computer, then opened her pocket book and began a new entry. She scribbled down the reference of the domestic and called up Control to send the dispatch to the computer. Hadley hit the siren and began to pull out of the yard.

'You OK to work?' he said.

'Yep. I'm better off working.'

'I'd be the same.'

The yard's gate slid open. A car flashed its headlights to let them out. Hadley turned hard right and drove up fast between the lines of traffic. The oncoming headlights were bright in the city's fluorescent night. Lizzie scanned through the dispatch on the computer. Intelligence showed the property occupied by squatters. A female, Cosmina Baicu, had come to notice for a non-crime domestic at the address. No other details known.

'No known risks,' she reported to Hadley. 'It's a squat, apparently.'

'Uh-huh.'

Hadley was driving fast, playing chicken with the oncoming traffic, bullying it into giving way. Lizzie pushed back into her seat and tried not to be afraid of the headlights that flared and turned away from them.

'This fucking job saved me, you know,' he said.

'What?'

'The job saved me.'

'Saved you, what do you mean? Saved you from what?'

'Well, no big deal, just from . . . you know, general fucking up. The job and my wife.'

'Your wife?'

'She saved me too. I was married before but it didn't work out. She took the house, left me with nothing. Women. What do you expect? But my new wife, I've got to admit she was exactly what I needed. Put me on the straight and narrow. We've raised four children together, one of mine, one of hers and two that are both of ours.'

Lizzie was running her biro over the computer screen, tracking their progress.

'Left here.'

As they turned, she saw a young black man in jeans standing on the steps of one of the houses. He spotted their vehicle and ran down the steps and along the pavement towards the car. Hadley slowed and the man knocked on the passenger window. Lizzie opened it. Gesturing to the house behind him, the man said, 'She's in there.'

'It was you who called us?'

'Yes. Joe Macintyre. She's in there. You'll have to get in. She's in a very bad way.'

Hadley switched off the engine. Lizzie, resisting the civilian's pressure to act without thinking, got out of the car trying not to betray undue haste and said, 'What did you see?'

'Nothing . . . just a man came out of the house and walked off. He was wiping his hands on his trousers. Sounds ridiculous but I thought it was blood. But it wasn't that. It was the screaming . . .' The witness shook himself, as if coming back to the present. 'It sounded as though someone was being murdered.' He paused before going on. 'No one's come out since. It's completely silent. She must still be in there. What took you so long—'

Lizzie cut him off, dismissing the thought of the call that had gone out several times over the radio. Nobody had wanted to get tied up with a DV incident.

'I'm sorry, Joe,' she said, resisting the instinctive lie – no cars available, too many calls. 'It is Joe, isn't it?'

He nodded.

'Joe, do you know if there's anyone else in there?'

'I don't know. There's a lot of them normally. Eastern Europeans, I think. There's always trouble.'

It was said without acrimony. He stood beside her like a dog straining on an invisible leash. Hadley shuffled off, mumbling something about checking out the door. Lizzie requested another unit over the radio, silent approach. DW27 put up. She switched to support to check an ambulance was running and to request the enforcer for the door. Back on the main channel, the radio, suddenly busy, chattered with other calls. A fight in the park. At the Arcadia shopping centre, a shoplifter detained.

Joe stood silently, insistent that something should be done *now*. He was young, good-looking. Short corkscrew hair, blue jeans, a checked shirt. Looking through the basement window of his flat, Lizzie could see the light from the screen of his computer. He had been distracted from something.

She said, 'You a student?'

'Yes.'

She glanced at him, aware amid the rush of imperatives that this man was that uncommon thing – someone who was prepared to get involved. He couldn't stop himself. He had been outside waiting for them. Something had prevented him from returning to his computer screen. She couldn't help but feel sorry for him, knowing that such people were always regarded with ambivalence by police and, indeed, everyone else. What was he? A nosy parker, an adventure hound, or that other much rarer and scarcely believed-in thing? One came across them: random individuals with their moral codes, people who couldn't stop themselves. The one in a hundred who gave a statement, who stood up in court. They could be young, old, black, white, fat, thin: the only thing that united them was their sense of obligation to complete strangers. Their nearest and dearest claimed to be proud of them, but there was always a nagging feeling that they would still rather they didn't do these things, put themselves in this place that made everyone uncomfortable and uneasy. Elsewhere, she and this young man would have nothing in common, but standing next to him on the street, she felt a link as deep and as troubling as DNA. She had an urge to reach out to him, even to thank him, but realized that this was out of place – anything so human would only cause him more apprehension. She was the police. He needed her to appear unmoved, in control.

'The other unit will be here in a minute.'

'You need to get to her quickly.'

Lizzie glanced towards the building. Hadley was sliding a piece of plastic from a weapons tube down between the lock and the door.

'Bloody thing,' he mouthed at her.

Lizzie turned back to the witness. 'Don't worry. We'll break the door down. I'm just waiting on the enforcer – you know, the thing we use to put the door in – and a couple more officers.'

Joe's eyes narrowed, as if he had had a brief glimpse into her world with its risk-assessed dangers. She smiled at him, feeling like a fraud but hoping to convey something capable and re-assuring. It was, she thought, peculiarly like waiting for a very important bus. As a way of passing time she said, 'It was you gave us her name?'

'Yes. I spoke to her once on the steps. She didn't look too good then either. Had a black eye. Look, I hear what you're saying, but you should hurry—'

'Will you give us a statement?'

'Of course.'

'Don't worry. We'll be going in just as soon as another unit arrives.'

She scribbled down his details. *Joe Macintyre.*
Date of birth 22/05/89. They continued to wait. She
pressed the transmit button on her radio. 'DW27
receiving?'

There was silence. She repeated the call.

She realized that her mouth was dry. This Joe
Macintyre had got her adrenalin going and she too
was impatient to get inside the house. Load of
bollocks, she told herself. There'll be no one inside,
or she'll be fine – watching TV and drinking lager
out of a can.

'Control receiving?'

'Unit calling, go ahead.'

'Yeah, sorry, we're trying to raise DW27.'

'Didn't you hear? The channels have been split.
Shooting at Ludlam Court.'

'DW27?'

The command was peremptory. 'Change channel.'
She felt embarrassed. She switched channel, her
fingers jumping over the buttons. 'DW27 receiving?
DW27?'

Joe said, 'Officer—'

'Excuse me for a moment.'

Lizzie turned and walked away up the stone
steps. Hadley had his hands on his hips. 'Yes?'

'Twenty-seven aren't answering. They've probably
been diverted. There's some big firearms incident.'

'Bloody hell.'

Lizzie glanced towards the witness. 'He says the
victim's still inside. He thinks she might be in a
bad way.'

187

Hadley gave a little cough – of course, she was stating the bleeding obvious and getting herself excited to no purpose.

Lizzie considered the property – a Victorian town house with two bay windows either side of the front door. The door was some squatter's expedient – palely washed in peeling grey paint, with a white steel lock. She slipped on her plastic gloves and lifted the letter box to see only a silent entrance hall abandoned in darkness. 'Police!' she shouted. 'Police. Open the door!'

'It's a shit door but a good lock,' Hadley commented. 'Stand back, Lizzie.'

He kicked the door, aiming his foot below the lock. There were a couple of loud bangs. The door shuddered but did not give. He stopped and, hands on knees, bent over, catching his breath and swearing quietly.

'It's no use. The door's too strong for me. I'm too bloody fat.' He gestured in the direction of the witness. 'What's his name?'

'Joe.'

They both looked at Joe, who gazed back up at them, less confident now as he observed the Old Bill, stripped to the bone, going about its business.

'Joe, come on up here, fella,' Hadley said.

Lizzie said quietly, 'You can't ask him . . .'

'Of course I can.'

Joe Macintyre hesitated. Perhaps, with a sixth sense, he was sensing his role shifting imperceptibly.

Then he started slowly up the stairs, almost giving the impression of going backwards. He tipped his head back as if in query.

Hadley said, 'Joe, you look like a strong fella. Work out, do you?'

He grimaced, unconvinced. 'Sometimes . . .'

'Joe, the guys with the enforcer have been diverted. Do me a favour and give the door a good kick.'

'I'm not sure . . .'

'It's perfectly legal. You're assisting a constable in the lawful execution et cetera. Section 17 of the Police and Criminal Evidence Act. That's all you have to do – give it a bloody good kick. You're a younger man than me, and in better shape. Shame to waste all that time at the gym, don't you think? You're not just doing it for the ladies, are you? The door'll give easily enough. And Lizzie here will be greatly impressed, won't you?'

Lizzie couldn't help smiling. 'I suppose so, yes, I will.'

Joe was not taken in by the humour. He wiped his hands down his thighs as though drying them from sweat.

'I dunno . . .'

But Hadley was in earnest. 'Listen, Joe, you seem like a good man. You said it sounded like she was being murdered. Someone's been shot somewhere else and there'll be no backup for a while now. Old Bill's a bit thin on the ground and we've got to do the best we can. It's perfectly fine. Just give the door a good kick and we'll do the rest. As I've said, you're assisting a constable in the lawful execution of his duty.'

Joe was studying his own feet. Hadley put his hand on his shoulder.

'Come on, lad. There's no one else. You said yourself she might be dying.'

Joe sucked his cheeks for a second. 'How long will they be?'

'Anybody's guess.'

His eyes moved from Hadley to Lizzie. 'What do you think?'

Her mouth was dry – they were going in on their own, then? – but she tried to sound cool, as though this kind of thing happened all the time. 'Like Hadley says, we'll do the rest.'

Hadley cut her off. 'There's a good lad. Just give it a kick here, mate. Just below the knob. Should shatter quite easily.'

'OK . . .'

Joe turned and faced the door. Hadley drew Lizzie to the edge of the steps and said quietly, 'Call Control again. Say we're going in and we need backup urgently. That'll force them to send another unit.'

As Hadley had said, Joe Macintyre was a strong lad. The door gave with two kicks. Hadley flicked the hall light but there was no electricity. The house was utterly silent but uncannily weighted with the lives of its absent occupants. The street lamps threw orange light on packing cases and cardboard boxes. It was a makeshift place, an encampment. The banisters had been broken. Hadley and Lizzie unshipped their torches and peeled off, following the narrow beams of light, each checking a room as they went. Hadley had the sitting room. Lizzie went ahead up the stairs' bare boards. Her breath sounded so noisy to her in the uncanny silence that she felt as though she were wearing a spacesuit. As she reached the landing she saw, through an open doorway, a woman motionless on a sofa. Her head was thrown back, her face catching the tungsten street light from the window.

For a brief moment Lizzie just stood. The woman's skin was green and blue and orange in the artificial light, the tones of oil paint in a modern American masterpiece. There was no movement. Christ, she's dead: that was the thought.

She remembered herself and shouted out, 'I've found her.' She called Control and requested an ambulance on the hurry-up. Then she moved towards the woman. 'I'm a police officer. Can you hear me?'

The left side of the woman's head was enormously swollen. It was a nonsense – the right side normal, the left side huge, like, like what? Like a movie make-up job, a medicine ball, a pillow, both hard and soft, the skin stretched over a tight swelling that came to a ridiculous point far higher and further out to the side than a head should ever be. It was a strangely captivating sight and

Lizzie stared as if waiting to come to terms with the fact that it was real. How could the human body become like this? Why would it do such a thing? Was it part of the body's defence, and if so, what benefit could there be in such monstrosity?

In the pallid light from the street, it was hard to judge the ashen shade of the woman's skin. Lizzie did not know whether she was alive or dead. The need to know was urgent, but respect or awe or plain inexperience slowed her. Touching this woman was like touching a shrine, a sacred object, a cracked plaster saint. The skin of the woman's chest was exposed by a round-neck T-shirt, and Lizzie gently put the flat of her hand against this exposed, uninjured skin. The body was warm. It was an intimate sensation – touching this stranger made unearthly by the room, the silence, the injury. Was this warmth vitality or just the fleeting imprint of a departing life?

Lizzie remembered with horror how she had sat in the canteen and not taken the call. Like the sea flooding in, she felt a sudden rush of pity for the woman. And then an immense regret that people did such things in darkened houses. She wanted to say, 'I'm sorry someone has done this to you,' but instead she said, 'I'm a police officer. I'm here to help you. The ambulance is on its way.'

She was aware suddenly of the witness, Joe, standing at her side. He had followed her up the stairs. He said quietly, 'Is she alive?' Lizzie wanted to reach out and take his hand. Instead she felt the side of the woman's neck, and there, beating, was the pulse of existence.

'Yes, she's alive.'

They both laughed, as if it was somehow funny.

Hadley, Lizzie realized, was still searching the property in case anyone was lurking in its unlit corners. Thank God for the experience of Hadley, who knew to make sure they were safe before worrying about victims. Thank God for Hadley, who, for all his palaver, had put up for the call. Lizzie pinched the woman's ear lobes. When this didn't work, she ran her knuckles across her collarbones to try and revive her. She remembered the woman's name from the dispatch. 'Cosmina. Cosmina. You've got to wake up.' She tried again, more savagely. The woman stirred and groaned. 'Cosmina, it's the police. An ambulance is on the way.'

The woman stirred again. She rolled her head slightly towards Lizzie and her right eye opened. She croaked something.

Lizzie leaned into her. 'I'm sorry, Cosmina, I didn't hear that.'

She croaked again, but this time it was more insistent and decipherable. 'Has he gone?'

The impulse to reassure was overwhelming. 'Yes, he's gone. He's gone. We're police. You're safe now.'

'Police?' She turned away and groaned. 'Shit.'

Lizzie was silent.

Cosmina turned back slowly and fixed Lizzie with her open eye. 'He's gone?'

'Yes, he's gone.'

She groaned again. 'Shit.' And then, 'I love him.'

Suddenly the ambulance crew were in the room. A man and a woman. A big bag. Green uniforms. A different competency that somehow made Lizzie inadequate with its straightforward ways. She stepped back to let them work.

'Her name's Cosmina?' the male paramedic said.

Cosmina was reviving and interrupted. 'Yes, I'm Cosmina. Leave me alone.'

Lizzie stepped further away, towards the window. It was a second wave of thought now and she relaxed briefly. The paramedics would do their thing. She was no longer alone and there was no danger. She called the section sergeant. Momentarily she cast around, remembering the imperative to investigate. The room was disordered. Empty beer cans. An ashtray filled with the dog ends of a hundred roll-ups. No curtains at the windows, but the place was warm. She noticed a large metal radiator. They must be abstracting the electricity.

Perhaps it was shock, or a general feeling of uselessness, that was making her drift off like this into irrelevancies. Her attention was drawn back to Cosmina by an increased sense of agitation. It took her a moment to make sense of it: things were not going as they were meant to. Voices were raised. The scoop lay untouched on the floor. Cosmina was protesting. She did not want to go to hospital. The female paramedic was having a go at persuading her. She was leaning over, holding a mirror to Cosmina's face so that she could see for herself the extent of her injury. But Lizzie heard the protests.

'No, no. I don't want to go. I'm staying here.'

The male paramedic stepped in.

'You have at least two injuries that are potentially life-threatening. You could have a fractured skull and you've almost definitely got a fractured rib, which could puncture a lung.'

'I don't care. I don't want to go.'

Joe broke in loudly. 'Didn't you hear? You might die.'

'I don't care. I don't want to go. I want to stay here. And I want you all to leave. You are trespassers, please get out of my house.'

Lizzie moved over and squatted down in front of Cosmina. 'Why don't you want to go?'

'Can you call him for me?'

Him – the man who had done this to her. Here was the copper's priority suddenly resurfacing: to catch the man who had done this. Lizzie, excited by the prospect of evidence, said, 'You've got his number?'

'07781 746341.'

Lizzie repeated it. 'What's his name?'

'Stefan.'

She wrote it in her pocket book.

'Stefan did this to you?'

'Yes.'

She wrote the exchange down verbatim and signed it off with pocket book rules.

Cosmina said, 'Can you ring him for me?'

The male paramedic interrupted, perhaps irritated by the police considerations. He had the high ground: the first priority was always life. He squatted beside Lizzie, pushing her gently to the side.

'Cosmina, we need to get you to hospital.'

Cosmina shook her head again, emphatically unpersuaded. 'No, I don't want to go. I'm staying here.'

Lizzie was surprised by how angry she had suddenly become with this pathetic woman who had been beaten within a shred of her life by her despicable boyfriend. She cast through her mind for a way to force her into the ambulance before she died.

'Imagine it was me lying there with my head like that. What would you tell me to do?'

'I would tell you to go to hospital.'

Hurrah. A roll of drums. Euphoria and enthusiasm all round: we can do our job.

Hadley wandered into the room and leant against the wall. People made ready to help lift Cosmina. The female paramedic said, 'Let's get you in the ambulance.' But the celebrations were premature. Cosmina, still resolute and calm, said, 'No. I would tell *you* to go, but still, *I* don't want to go.'

Hadley ambled over to Lizzie, taking her discreetly aside. He nodded in the direction of Joe, who was standing with the paramedics. She heard Joe say, 'Listen, if you don't go, you're going to die.'

Hadley said quietly, 'Get rid of him.'

Lizzie had the sensation of waking up from layers of sleep. Of course, Hadley was right: Joe had no place in this room. She went over and touched his arm.

'I'm sorry, you'll have to go.'

Joe looked blankly at her, and she said, as kindly as she could, 'This is a crime scene.'

It was the truth, of course, but the wording suddenly distanced Joe and in this way was unexpectedly effective. He realized all at once that he had been carried away by events. He became amazingly compliant, like a road-collision victim. Lizzie walked him down the stairs and down the street to his front door. He fiddled in his pocket for his keys.

'You'll be all right?' she asked.

'Yes.'

'Make yourself a cup of tea. Perhaps you should call a friend to come over. We'll be in touch.'

'You'll be in touch?'

'Yes, I'll let you know what happens. And we'll need a statement.'

Suddenly the street was full of vehicles with blue lights flashing in the night. The ambulance. A paramedic support car. Three marked police vehicles. Things had gone from a call that nobody wanted to a critical incident. While she was showing Joe back to his flat, the scene had filled with other officers from Lizzie's relief. As she went back up the stairs, she could hear raised voices.

Arif was speaking. 'If you carry on refusing to go in the ambulance, you're going to be arrested.'

Arrested. What was he talking about? Lizzie stepped into the room. Cosmina was speaking, calm and sweet, as lucid as a barrister.

'You can't arrest me. I haven't done anything wrong.'

Arif, Lizzie realized, was panicking. Furious at Cosmina's stupid passivity, he was stepping beyond the law. He moved away from her and whispered angrily to Lizzie, 'Fucking *victim*: she won't even save her own life.'

Lizzie stepped towards Cosmina, inside the circle of paramedics and police. 'No,' she said, thinking of safety and pity and keeping Cosmina on side and not getting anyone into trouble, even if they did have the best of intentions. 'No, Cosmina, we're not going to arrest you. You are the victim of an offence. We are going to take care of you.' She shot Arif a quick look and a smile and he retreated to the perimeter of events. But all Lizzie's goodwill was getting her nowhere.

'I'm not going and you can't make me. This is my home and I'm staying.'

Hadley was gazing out of the window across the street. Without turning from the view, he finally spoke in a tired voice.

'I don't much like it here and I'm due a cup of tea.'

Everyone, including Cosmina turned to Hadley. His heartlessness was curiously refreshing. Now

198

that he had their attention, he continued in his usual unconcerned tone. 'Think about it, Cosmina. I can't leave you. That means I'm stuck here until you agree to go to hospital. Arif here can't arrest you, but I have a power under the Mental Health Act and I'm about to use it. I'm going to section you because I believe you pose a danger to yourself. I'd like you to go to hospital voluntarily, but if you don't, I will force you.'

Cosmina looked around her at the others. She seemed dazed. Perhaps even pleased. This suggestion of force, of obligation, relieved her in a single sentence of all her protests. She could have it both ways: refuse to go to hospital and still be made to go by others.

Hadley glanced across at Lizzie and a brief smile passed his lips. This was not a lawful use of the power, he seemed to suggest, but who in the room would stand up for the law now?

'Can I have a cigarette before I go?'

Arif had his pack ready in his hand: it was impossible not to like the boy.

Lizzie said to the paramedics, 'Would that be all right?'

The man said, 'Yes, OK, but let's wait till we get her outside by the ambulance.'

Cosmina had refused to allow the paramedics to put her on the trolley bed. Assisted by the female paramedic, she chose a bag of stuff from her bedroom to take with her to hospital.

Lizzie stood on the landing and watched her being helped down the stairs. Hadley joined her.

'Happy with that, are you?'

'I'm sorry?'

'Hardly a lawful use of the Mental Health Act, was it? We're in a dwelling, for a start.'

He waited for her response.

'Of course I'm happy with it,' she said finally, irritated.

'Thought you would be,' he said mildly, and ambled off down the stairs.

The incident was resolving. The section sergeant arrived and called up a scenes-of-crime officer. Blue and white tape was stretched across the entrance to the property; poor Arif would be stuck there probably until morning. Cosmina was now sitting outside on the wall, smoking. Hadley sat beside her talking nonsense.

The female paramedic used the moment to take Lizzie quietly aside and lead her back to the room where she had packed Cosmina's bag. On the floor was an Oscar statuette. It was with this statuette, Cosmina had told the paramedic, that Stefan had struck her. Bending down, Lizzie could see blood on Oscar's hands and on his gold metal shoulder. She scribbled down the paramedic's details for a brief statement.

The section sergeant spoke to Lizzie in the corridor. 'Go with her in the ambulance. If she won't give a statement, get some Q and As in your pocket book. Do the best you can. Hadley will join you to bag up the clothing and take some pictures. He's going to pick up some evidence bags and a camera.'

At the hospital Lizzie had a renewed sense of purpose – a sense of doing something useful, effective. She hid her eagerness and aimed for a show of neutrality, disinterest. With only a vague sensation of betrayal, she scribbled down questions and answers in her notebook. She was, she thought, perhaps tricking Cosmina into giving the information, but she pressed on nevertheless, obtaining an account that she hoped would be good enough to send Stefan to prison. It wasn't clear to her why Cosmina was telling her story so painstakingly when she had refused a statement. Perhaps she just needed to talk it through. Or perhaps some repudiated part of her wanted Stefan to pay for nearly killing her.

Cosmina told her that she and Stefan had been drinking and had then had sex. Lizzie scribbled quickly, using her own made-up shorthand, struggling to get it all down verbatim.

A: Almost immediately Stefan starts up with his accusations. I shout back at him.
Q: Why did you shout?
A: Because it's so ridiculous that he's jealous. I love him. We are standing and he hits me several times with the Oscar. It was a joke, a gift from Stefan. When

he gave it to me he said that I am his star and I deserve an Oscar. Stefan does that sometimes: buys me nice things. You can never predict what he will bring home. He is so kind, so loving and gentle . . . Only gets like this when he has been drinking . . . Tried to defend myself but, you know, he is big. He accuse me. I am wrong sort of star: I am a hit with his best friend. So he gives me the Oscar over and over again.

Q: How many times?

A: I can't remember.

Q: Guess?

A: Five, perhaps?

Q: Then what?

A: I fall to the floor and Stefan kicks me in ribs.

Q: What is he wearing on his feet?

A: Boots.

Q: What kind of boots?

A: He works on building sites.

Q: Steel-toecapped boots?

A: I don't know, the kind they wear on building sites.

Q: Then what?

A: Then he stops kicking me and picks up his mobile. 'I'm going now,' he says and walks out. I follow him into the hallway but he won't stay. I can't remember going back upstairs, just waking on the sofa.

Lizzie ruled it off and signed it at the bottom as a true record. She offered it to Cosmina to sign but she refused. She was fussing instead, wanting to know what was happening. Were the police still at the house? Lizzie put her pocket book in her stab vest pocket.

'Cosmina, this is serious. You can't kid yourself that we are not going to be involved.'

'But where will I live? Where will I go? They won't let me back in the house now I've brought police there.'

'You didn't bring us there. Stefan did.'

Cosmina shook her head impatiently: logic was irrelevant. 'Where will I go?'

'You have no friends? No family?'

'No.'

Hadley arrived with paws full of evidence bags and a digital camera hanging daintily from his huge wrist.

'I hate these things,' he complained as he struggled to work out how to switch it on. His hands were too big for the tiny wheel and buttons. He looked like a benign gorilla in a nature documentary. Lizzie found herself smiling and had to remind herself that, for all his bluff, Hadley was the only officer on the ground who had put up for the call in the first place.

'You any good with them?' he asked Lizzie.

'No.'

Cosmina, pouring contempt on their incompetence, took hold of the camera. She turned out to be handy with technology and took pleasure in showing them all the switches. Finally she insisted on a picture of the two of them. In the tiny screen Hadley and Lizzie were a *Variety* throwback: Laurel and Hardy pretending to be cops in blue woolly jumpers. All three laughed at the image. Cosmina, studying the photograph, shook her head in disbelief and said, 'Christ help me.'

Hadley said, 'Best police force in the world, I think you'll find.'

Cosmina said, 'Not saying much, is it?'

'Your turn, clever clogs,' said Lizzie and turned the camera lens on Cosmina.

She had got used to the swollen bruise that was Cosmina's face, but seeing the fact of the injuries reduced to their forensic digital record renewed her shock. As she flipped through the images, Hadley, watching over her shoulder, said quietly, 'Get the bruises on her arm too. The defence wounds.' Only a fool would think that Hadley was not purposeful. Cosmina obliged, turning her right arm against the yellow coverlet.

Nurses and doctors passed in and out of the cubicle, taking temperatures and blood samples. A hospital porter turned up – a skinny Asian boy with shaved stripes along his skull. He eyed the police officers warily and muttered something about X-rays. He flipped the brakes on the trolley with his foot and expertly wheeled Cosmina out of the cubicle.

Hadley waited for her to be out of sight. Then

he said, 'Stefan's been arrested. He turned up at the crime scene and Arif nicked him. So Arif got something out of the night after all.'

'He'll be pleased. What's the arrest?'

'Attempted murder.'

They both smiled. Good boy: he'd aimed for the stars but they both knew he wouldn't get it. Best they could hope for was probably a Section 20 GBH.

'Fucker,' said Hadley.

'Bastard,' Lizzie concurred.

'Fucking bastard.'

They were silent.

Then Hadley said, 'Better bag up the clothing. Another job I hate.' They worked together putting Cosmina's jeans, her bloody T-shirt, bra and pants into brown paper bags. Hadley said, 'You exhibit them and I'll book them in. OK? The T-shirt will have to go in the drying room. Fuck, what weariness.'

Lizzie leaned over the side table and started writing out the labels. Hadley said, 'It's not too late for decent food. What do you fancy?'

'I don't know. Not a kebab.'

'Not a kebab, OK. BP?'

She imagined the fluorescent lights, the pale-faced Indian man behind the till, the aisles of chilled food. The pasta and pesto. The cherry tomatoes. All unnaturally bright behind clear plastic shells.

'No, not BP.'

'Curry?'

'Christ, not curry.'

'Difficult, aren't you?'

She rose to the challenge. 'Do you know what I really fancy?'

'Bloody hell, Lizzie, salmon and caviar? Bottle of Bolly? How the hell should I know?'

She made him wait.

'Fish and chips.'

'Fish and chips!' He rubbed his hands together in agreement, as if at a point well made, one that he would have to concede, then stood up with enthusiasm, unclipping the car key from his belt. 'Now you're talking. I *love* fish and chips. But I'll have to get a shifty on if I'm going to make it before they close.'

His large, sloppy uniformed bulk moved away between the hospital beds, the drawn plastic curtains. The electronic doors swished open into the night. Through the overhead windows above the central doctors' station Lizzie saw the reflection of the blue lights flashing. Perhaps under the circumstances fish and chips were a genuine emergency.

Casualty continued with its curiously relaxed but purposeful rhythm. The footfalls of nurses, the swish of curtains marked the progress of a job that would never be done. The DI called for an update. Lizzie made her way to the desk but was reluctant to disturb the fat Indonesian-looking woman sitting there. *Sarwendah Wahid*, stated the name badge. *Charge Nurse*. She answered Lizzie with placid bovine eyes and clicked on the computer.

'No, I don't have an update.'

Lizzie returned to the cubicle and flicked through her iPhone. These were the waiting moments. Soon Hadley would be back. A friendly fat male nurse took pity on her. 'Help yourself to coffee or tea from the nurses' station.'

'Thanks.'

She leaned back against the chair. It was warm in the hospital.

'Sleeping on duty?'

Hadley was standing over her with the fish and chips. She felt bleary and confused. He passed her a hot package and pulled up a chair for himself.

'Hang on,' she said, pulling a crushed and creased five-pound note from her warrant card and holding it out.

He already had his portion on his lap and was beginning to unfold the paper with the slow care of someone who never spilled a chip. He shook his head at the proffered note. 'Don't worry,' he said. 'Later.'

Steam and the smell of fried vegetable oil rose into the air.

'Lizzie, I'm sorry about your dad.'

Lizzie felt a sudden obstruction in her throat. 'Thanks. It was expected. He'd been ill for ages.'

'Still hurts, though, doesn't it?'

She cleared her throat. Hadley took his time selecting a particularly fat chip.

'I love fish and chips,' he said. 'I remember

picking it up for the whole family and sitting in the front of my dad's Ford Anglia. The hot paper used to burn my legs.'

Lizzie, unwrapping her own portion, summoned her own fish-and-chips memories. Queuing in the shop while her dad waited with the engine running. The yellow wall tiles interspersed with occasional pictures of fishing boats. An ample shake of salt over a hot bag of chips.

They ate, entirely absorbed. Lizzie reached the end of her appetite. She balled up her paper with some chips still in it. Hadley had finished too and wiped his huge paws on his trousers.

'Guv'nor said you wanted to speak to me about giving a statement.'

Lizzie broke the seal of her water bottle and swilled a mouthful. She tried to appear relaxed. 'Well. I thought we should talk about it, anyway.'

'Is it that you're worried about getting into trouble?'

'No, Hadley, not that. I just want to know what happened.'

He exhaled heavily. 'What happened?'

In spite of her efforts, she felt sick inside. 'Yes. Just that.'

'With a view to what exactly?'

She thought of those interviews where the suspects tried to ask the questions. She had to admit he had a point: with a view to what exactly?

'It's a straightforward question. You've pulled me into this . . .'

Even as the words emerged, she was wishing them unsaid. Exasperation flashed across Hadley's face.

'Pulled you into it?'

He was right: if the complaint was unfounded then it was Hadley who had been pulled into something. His annoyance was perhaps genuine, but Lizzie also suspected that he was satisfied to have kicked off the conversation with her already on the wrong foot.

'OK, maybe not. I don't know. Just tell me what happened, can't you?'

His exasperation was making it difficult to think. Kieran had said to talk to him and then she'd know what to do. Hadley stretched out into the back of his chair. He sounded bored.

'I don't mean to be rude, Lizzie, but I've got to be honest, I don't even know what this conversation's *for*. Either you believe what I told the guv'nor or you don't. Either you back me or you don't. I've got twenty-seven years in. No disrespect, but I'm not about to start justifying myself to you. What do you want to know? What will make you feel better?'

'What do you mean, what do I want? You've made it difficult for me, saying I was there.'

'You *were* there.'

'I wasn't. I was in the kitchen. I didn't hear a thing.'

'I'm sorry, then. I thought you'd heard everything.'

She pulled a face. He kissed his teeth, gangsta style. They both laughed.

There was a pause.

Hadley said, 'I didn't think it would be such a big deal.'

'It isn't a big deal if you don't mind me telling the truth.'

'*I'll* tell you the truth, Lizzie. Pay attention now. Are you listening carefully? The truth is that this girl has made up stuff I'm supposed to have said, and while the job fiddles around worrying itself sick about absolutely *nothing*, worrying that I might be a racist, oh dear God, I'm missing out on my board and a few years staying in the warm before I retire.'

She thought, is that really all the consequence you fear? Would there not be more serious repercussions for a racist comment made to a fourteen-year-old schoolgirl in her home? He had paused as if waiting for her to comment, but she was wary of voicing her suspicions and made no response. He went on.

'You forgot to caution that black boy the other day. What was his name? That's it: Jordan. Do you think I'd find it difficult to say you did? Do you think it would even *matter*?'

'That's not fair . . .'

'Yes, OK, you remembered. But that's not the point. What if it had become an issue?'

Lizzie shrugged. 'I don't know.'

Hadley nodded as though he had won the

point. He swigged from his water bottle and then resumed.

'Look, everyone's out to get us. The lawyers, the press, not to mention every other bloody arsehole that wants promotion. I think it's something about their mum and dad disappointing them, or maybe they just can't accept that the world is made of stone and blood and not fairy dust. It used to be about not beating people up in the back of vans. Not fitting people up. Now it's fart downwind and you'll be asked about it on the stand. I don't know any cop, good or bad, that hasn't been in trouble at some point. How can we stand if we don't back each other? You'll understand this when you've got more service. Obviously I won't back you if you take a bribe or send someone down who's not guilty. But the usual day-to-day stuff, the usual shit? The usual shit? Of course I'll back you. If I know you and I trust you, if you're basically sound, then I'll back you because that's how we play the game.'

She moved to interrupt but he waved his huge hands impatiently, talking over her.

'No, no, no, no, not *play the game*, that's wrong. That's just playing into your hands, those words. Not play the game; it's how we *survive*. Fucking *survive*, Lizzie. Pay our mortgages and make sure we go home every night rather than into a bloody cell.'

He paused again, waiting to see if she had a response now. She shrugged. He continued more quietly.

'What about me threatening to section Cosmina earlier on? That's not lawful. You going to write that up? Even if you don't, what if someone else does? You going to back me or you going to make me face a disciplinary for saving that girl's life?'

His impatience, his certainty were devastating. Her qualms felt trivial, her pristine conscience absurd. She remembered her mother hissing at her father, 'It's just a *word*.' Her father had not had many people at his funeral. She found herself in a difficult place.

'Hadley, I'm sorry. If I'd heard what had happened, of course I'd back you.'

He gave a snort of contempt. 'That's a fucking relief, I must say. If you'd heard me, you'd back me.'

They sat in an angry, wretched silence. The plastic curtain swished open. The Asian boy wheeled the bed back in. Cosmina was sleeping heavily. Her face was swollen and blue. The right arm, lying over the cover, was bandaged.

Hadley got up. He reached out, picked up Lizzie's fish-and-chip paper from the floor and shambled off in the direction of the A&E general waste bag.

CHAPTER 26

Lizzie was in Farlow nick, logging on to a computer. The early turn relief had passed through the parade room to go on duty but she had still to write her statement about Cosmina before she went home. Kieran put his head round the door and smiled.

'Well done for tonight. You and Hadley have done a good job.'

'Thanks.'

She kept her eyes firmly to the screen. He stood behind her and glanced towards the door before putting his hand on her shoulder. 'How was it with Hadley?'

She clicked on the program to open the statement pro forma. 'Fine, yes. OK.'

His hand was still on her shoulder. 'No news for me about that, then?'

'No, guv'nor.'

'OK.'

The program had loaded and she began to type. *On the night of Thursday 9 April I was on duty . . .*

'That's fine, then. No issues. Mark up your overtime.'

He bent down and kissed her neck, and of course at once she wanted to relent, to turn round and bury herself in him.

He said, 'Will I see you later?'

'Yes.'

She pushed him away and resumed typing.

She was alone with the day opening through the high parade-room windows. Briefly the night shuttered through her mind. So much could happen in one shift. The sight of Cosmina through the doorway with the lamplight falling on her tilted face. The silent, hostile drive back to the police station with Hadley.

Arif appeared, finally free from dealing with his prisoner in custody. He drew up a chair beside her and opened his arrest book to write his statement.

'Good arrest, Arif. Liked the offence.'

'You heard?' he said.

She shook her head.

'CID have already bumped it down to an ABH.'

'ABH?' It was unbelievable. Bloody CID. The last she'd heard, Cosmina had been taken back to theatre. 'What was he like, Stefan?'

'Evil bastard.'

'He just turned up at the address?'

'Yes. Said she's always drinking his stuff.'

'Did you hurt him?'

'Best I could. He tried to head-butt me. That gave me an excuse to get him on the ground, at least. I think Sergeant Thompson would have quite liked to drive over him.'

She gave a snort of agreement. 'Handcuffed?'

'Face down on the ground. Back to back. No other way to get them on. What a shame.'

It was a shock to Lizzie to realize that for the first time she was wishing they had the option of old-style policing, the stuff that leaked out in the anecdotes of old sweats. She would have quite liked for Stefan to have had a good kicking in the back of a van. Best they could do nowadays was to cuff him face down, with his hands behind his back. And then the Police and Criminal Evidence Act and all his rights back at the nick. The bastard would have an interpreter and a lawyer and the doctor to check he was OK. *And all these things are right, of course.* She shook her head and pressed her hands against her eyes. She saw her former self as if she were standing across an unbridgeable gulf as deep as the Grand Canyon. And she preferred this former self to the one who still had a crime report to complete before she crawled into bed in full daylight.

Arif finished his statement and went off duty. As the morning light widened, Lizzie rang the duty social worker to try to arrange emergency housing for Cosmina.

The voice on the other end of the line sounded tired and irritated. 'She'll have to go into the housing office when it opens at nine thirty and queue.'

'She can't queue, she's got a head injury.'

'Are you certain she is a resident of the borough?'

'Yes, I'm certain.' Lizzie repeated herself in case he hadn't picked up on her impatient understanding of his question's hidden agenda. 'I'm absolutely certain she's a resident of this borough and I've made a note of that on my report.'

In the silence on the other end of the phone she heard the weariness of the social worker's parallel universe: the vortex of lost souls needing housing before God claimed them as his own. Nothing, she thought, could resource the needs of the world. She saw boats drifting on oceans filled with lost populations. The sense of doing something effective receded, as she had known it must. She leaned over the desk and again pressed the heels of her hands into her eyes until she saw patterns.

The drive home saw the mass of Londoners making their way to work through windy streets, pulling their coats tight against the cold morning. Some queued at bus stops. A woman followed behind two small boys in school uniform, both on micro scooters. Drivers cut each other up where the road narrowed from two lanes to one. The cop's narrative played in her head – the minor offences, the stupid risks. These people were living their lives and she realized that she was looking at them as if she were an observer from outer space, as if she was not one of them. This early-morning banality was what she was protecting – their freedom to live their lives and cut each other up pointlessly.

Her mobile rang, shaking her again out of a drift into sleep. She glanced at the screen. *Number withheld.* She put it down on the passenger seat. It continued to ring and then cut. Two minutes later the voicemail pinged. It could probably wait till she got home, but just in case, she pulled over and tapped to hear the message.

It was Kieran. She needed to return to the station. Cosmina had died.

Murder squad had taken over one of the inspector's rooms. A woman was perched on the desk, clutching a decision log and a hardback notebook. She was thin, late twenties or early thirties maybe. She wore a dark trouser suit and had streaked blonde hair. Crow's feet already marked the corners of her eyes. Lizzie briefly estimated all the night duties and long shifts this woman had done to get this far so quickly. A light-skinned black man stood by the window. He wore the department's classic pinstripe, a white shirt, blue silk tie loose at his collar. It was clear that he found time for the gym. No kids, probably, or if he had them, they didn't come first.

Hadley had squashed himself into one of the tiny chairs by the MDF shelving unit. He caught Lizzie's eye. His message was clear enough: *Watch yourself.* Kieran was sitting at the desk, facing his computer screen. He glanced at her and smiled encouragingly.

Lizzie said, 'Guv'nor.'

The woman leaned forward and offered her hand, 'Lizzie?'

'Yes.'

'DS Bradwell. Murder squad. This is my colleague, DC O'Neill.'

O'Neill glanced over from the window and gave her his killer grin. 'Jack.'

Kieran caught her eye from his computer screen with mild amusement. The DS continued. 'Thanks for coming back.'

Lizzie glanced between the people in the room. She attempted a smile and, with as much enthusiasm as she could muster, said, 'No worries.'

'The hospital think Cosmina died from a cerebral haemorrhage,' the DS was continuing. 'We'll have the exact cause of death confirmed by post-mortem. In the meantime, you'll appreciate we're running on a clock. We've got one in the bin and before we interview we need to know more about all this. You two were first on scene. Hadley, I'll have a chat with you. Lizzie, I understand you were the first to find her? I need you to view the body, for continuity. Jack will drive you to the morgue. We need you to do that this morning, before the PM. You OK with that?'

Lizzie pushed the thought of Cosmina alive out of her mind and tried to pre-empt the matter of the autopsy by making her not a person

218

but an object, the mere subject of an identifying statement.

'Yes,' she said. 'No problem. Am I OK to get a coffee first?'

Jack already had the car keys in his hand. 'We'll pick one up on the way. I know a good place.'

Some memories we don't like to contemplate even before they have happened. As the metal gates of the mortuary opened and the car slipped through into the small car park, Lizzie already knew with a heavy sensation that this experience was going to be something she would want to be able to wipe from her consciousness. If you want to be a cop, she told herself, you have to do these things. And every time you do, it will be easier.

A white man was outside, leaning against the wall, smoking. He wore a loose suit with broad stripes. He was tatty and tired, his hair had thinned – fifty years old or more perhaps. By his side on the ground was a metal box of the kind used to hold cameras. They parked up and got out of the car. The man nodded hello to Jack: clearly they knew each other. He was murder squad too. Then she felt his eyes flick to her, appraising her.

'All right?' he said, not unkindly. 'You continuity?'

'That's right.'

He threw his cigarette on the floor, crushed it under his foot and held out his hand. 'Neal,' he said. 'Exhibits. Want a fag before you go in?'

219

She shook her head. 'No – thanks. I'm fine.'

'Very sensible. Come on, then. Let's be at it.'

They left Jack outside and went into an exterior room.

'You'll need to suit up. Shoes, face mask, double glove, the lot.'

'OK.'

She split open the cellophane wrapper he handed her and struggled into the white suit. The zip stuck, caught in the shiny paper fabric. Neal said, 'Here, let me.' His hands were old and, facing him as he struggled with the zip, she felt like a child being dressed to go out into the cold. He met her eyes and smiled. 'Don't worry, love. You need to take a good look and make sure it's the same woman you found in the squat. Then we'll start the post-mortem. She's recently dead so she shouldn't smell too bad. You don't need to do anything. Stand at the back, look away if you want. Afterwards it's just a quick statement. That's all.'

She stood back from the table. There was a shape in a bag, zipped up. Neal and Jack were waiting beside it. Neal had his metal box open and ready. She could see that everything was neatly ordered. Labels already written on evidence bags. Two men in white coats stood by. One was tall, with grey hair. The other stooped and small with a nose piercing. This man, the technician, said, 'Ready, everyone?'

He unzipped the bag.

Lizzie had expected to see Cosmina, but the open bag revealed a shape wrapped in a white sheet. There was a piece of paper attached to the front of the shroud, and someone had written in marker pen Cosmina's name, date of birth and hospital number.

Neal said, 'Lizzie.'

She stepped towards the table. The man with the nose piercing cut through the sheet.

Cosmina, further violated by the rushed assistance of the medics, was briefly unrecognisable. Her head had been roughly shaved and a bolt drilled into the skull just back from the hairline. It reminded Lizzie of a vice, a piece of metalwork from a workshop. A tube snaked around from the back of the head. Her face was bruised, livid, black and grey and yellow like the skin of a vile banana. A sticky yellow fluid ran down from her nose. There was a tube in her neck and a bruise flowered there too. Another tube ran out from between her legs. And for some reason there was a neat stitched incision in her abdomen. Lizzie stared. She had forgotten what her job was.

Neal repeated, 'Lizzie?'

She looked again at the corpse as if it were some discourtesy to answer too quickly. Then she said, 'Yes, I recognize her as the woman I found earlier at . . .'

She couldn't remember the name of the street.

Neal said. 'At Windermere Road?'

'Yes, at Windermere Road. Cosmina.'

She stepped back. She was aware of system and order. Of photographs and measurements. They were busy. She was passive. She was there to witness. She saw Cosmina's body, naked except for the bandage on her right arm. For a short time only it remained, as if in mockery of recovery. Blotched skin. Bruises to her chest and the visible skin of her arms. The skin, Lizzie thought coldly, as she stared at the body, was completely different in death, an unsolvable puzzle. The pathologist narrated the damage as he moved around the cadaver. *Adult white female. Whitened fingernails. Bruises to the inside of the upper arms.* A dictionary of trauma. He examined the head carefully, pressing the bruising, trying to differentiate.

'I don't know,' he said. 'Could be the imprint of the Oscar.'

Neal considered the marks like an art expert examining brushstrokes. He photographed carefully, absorbed in his work.

They moved in front of Lizzie like busy shadows, slipping in and out of activity, giving way to each other, stepping back. The technician slid a block under Cosmina's back. Lizzie remembered diving to the bottom of her school swimming pool. The dark blue tiles and the pressure in her ears as she gripped the corners of the heavy rubber brick. Surfacing to the smell of chlorine.

Cosmina's chest protruded, the artificial light falling across her virescent skin. Her arms and neck fell back, her breasts to each side. The technician began to cut open the ribcage using shears as big as hedge-trimmers. The bones crunched and broke. Lizzie saw the line of the ribs, the cartilage and the marbling of white fat, just like a cow or a sheep hanging in a butcher's freezer. On the outside it was still Cosmina. The breasts now impossibly separated but still human, still Cosmina's. The boys at work called them fun bags. She thought of her own fun bags and how inconsequential they were, just flesh and fat that would hang lifeless off her own body one day. The technician was reaching into the cavity, his arm up high, a tideline of blood against the pale latex of his gloves. He pulled out the organs and Lizzie saw them. Hefty giblets, the claret shine and fat and slip of them. Each weighed and bagged and labelled.

Then there was the head. They spent a lot of time on that, fussing and talking, considering and commenting. The whine of the Stryker saw and the smell of burning. The flaps of skin pulled down either side. The face peeled away. It was a three-man job. Neal taking the weight of the metal vice so that no more damage would be caused and the technician levering the plate of bone away with a chisel. Lizzie remembered her mother slipping the blade of a knife under the metal plate of a pickling jar. The vice lifted. The pathologist leaned in with tweezers, examining, probing. The camera too, pointing in and peering. Eventually the brain: lifted from the skull by the pathologist, bubbles of something like blackcurrant jam emerging from the grey cerebellum. The body was empty. A hollow shell. No purpose to it. But this eviscerated cadaver, this corpse, this meat and bone and gristle, this skin and hair and hands, this seeming, this absence: this *thing* was still, strangely, Cosmina. Lizzie was there to bear witness to that.

Jack was interviewing Lizzie on tape. He took notes. Lizzie sat with her elbows on the table and her chin resting in her hands. Another takeaway coffee was getting cold on the desk beside her. She must have been falling asleep because Jack said, 'You all right to continue?'

She covered her face and yawned. 'Yes.'

'So you put the door in?'

'Well, that is, we got the witness to do it.'

'You got the witness to do it?'

She remembered Hadley's eyes. *Watch yourself.*

'Yes, there were no other units available and neither of us could manage it.'

'Tell me about that.' He was scribbling in his notebook.

She told him about going up the stairs. The first sight of Cosmina, bathed in tungsten light. The relief of the tattoo of her pulse. Joe's laughter and hers.

The memory of Cosmina, feisty, arguing her corner, made her think again, abruptly, relentlessly, of that new image recently garnered from the mortuary's fluorescence. She'd felt something

224

like embarrassment: the ridiculous formality, the time it took to confirm that this was indeed Cosmina. Almost out of good manners she had looked for longer than the identification required, as if demonstrating the act of looking. Now she realized that it was really a kind of hypnosis. The body had seared itself into her and it would always somehow be with her. It was one of those behind-the-curtain moments offered to police. *Here, Officer, look, see.* The corpse held a staring fascination, like a sum that could never be worked out. *Continuity.* Yes, that was the essence of it: Cosmina alive, arguing, laughing. The Gap sweatshirt and the too-tight stone-washed blue jeans. And – the swish of the magician's curtain – the progression. Cosmina naked, dead, silent, hollowed. Cosmina with no more say on any matter and indifferent not only to Stefan's fate but also to the pathologist's tools that sheared her open. The whine of the bow saw, the change of tone as it bit. The smell of burning.

'Hang on a minute,' said Jack. 'I need to clarify this. The witness was inside the crime scene?'

Lizzie felt her face tighten. This was the essence of her job – preserve the scene, avoid contamination. She had not only not saved Cosmina, she had also let down the investigation.

She said, 'I'm really very tired.'

'We're nearly done now.'

'The witness – Joe – he had let himself in of his own accord.'

'It's not a problem,' Jack said, confirming for her that it was. 'And then what happened?'

She saw it through the detective's eyes. Christ, the whole borough had been up there. No excuse. *No one unnecessary in the scene.* Where had her training gone? How many officers had been up there? How many paramedics? The detective was patiently listing them all. Doing his job. She could imagine him talking behind closed doors about how useless the response team's actions had been. Fucking amateurs.

'Tell me about Cosmina.'

'She didn't want to go.'

'Tell me about that.'

'She said she loved Stefan . . .'

From this distance it all felt very different. Then she had been busy saving a life. Now she was seeing all the mistakes she had made.

'And how did you persuade her to leave?'

She sighed with exhaustion and despair. She could think of nothing to say but the truth. 'It was Hadley got her out. He threatened to section her.'

'To section her?'

'Yes.'

'OK.'

The detective made another of his notes.

She remembered Hadley's own words: *Hardly a lawful use of the Mental Health Act, was it? You going to make me face a disciplinary for saving that girl's life?*

★　★　★

She went to the canteen to pick up one last cup of coffee. The DC had finished the interview and left to brief his boss. The murder squad had downloaded the images from the digital camera that she and Hadley had used at the hospital. She had been told to exhibit the prints before going off.

Other officers acknowledged her as they made their way to the tables with plates of sausages and fried eggs. 'All right, Lizzie?' She was experiencing the brief celebrity that went with being a significant witness to a murder. She said hello and thanked them for their interest and support and generally did what was expected of her. Inside was a hidden disintegration. One minute she had thought she was one thing and the next moment she realized she was another thing altogether. Climbing the stairs, finding Cosmina: in her story of herself she had been a heroine. Now it turned out that she had been doing everything wrong. She had not been a heroine at all. She had been a fucking amateur. Not only had she not saved a life. She had also not protected the crime scene of a murder investigation. What was she for, then? What was the point?

She took a deep breath against the tears that threatened. They were brimming up inside her and she felt a tight constriction in her throat. The woman behind the counter handed her a bowl of porridge and Lizzie turned to find a seat. Hadley was sitting at a table at the back of the canteen. He had a full English breakfast and a copy of a tabloid on the table in front of him. He caught her eye and offered her a questioning thumbs-up. She hesitated and then walked over to him.

He said, 'All right?'

She wanted to cry and for a moment she couldn't speak. He tilted his chair back and stretched.

'OK. Bloody sit down, then.'

Lizzie sat. She had a pain in her throat that felt as though it was choking her. Hadley put out a huge paw and held her arm. He said nothing and this, somehow, was the kindest thing in all the world. Then, suddenly, he laughed out loud. It was a huge, generous guffaw, and marvellously genuine. He couldn't speak for laughter and Lizzie found herself smiling even though she didn't know what was funny. Finally Hadley spoke through helpless snorts.

'I can't believe we got that poor fella to put the door in.'

He was again engulfed in laughter, and suddenly she found it funny too. She managed to get out, 'The look on his face when you asked him.' She paused to laugh and then was able to continue. 'You look like a strong fella!'

Hadley said, 'Bet the Met wishes it had sent more bloody units now.'

They laughed till they cried. Lizzie coughed away the throat constriction. They both wiped their tired eyes. There was a brief silence. She took a mouthful of porridge and laughed again.

Hadley said, 'At least we did our best.'

'Mmm.'

Stuffed away in some corner of her mind was that image of Cosmina. The woman was a stranger. She should not have had the right to see her dead on a trolley.

She said, 'Hadley, I told the DC you threatened to section her.'

Hadley shook his head at her. 'Honestly. You are a—'

'I know. I'm a chocolate teapot.'

He gave a grudging smile. 'Doesn't matter.'

'Sorry.'

'No, don't be. Honestly. It won't matter.' Then, after a pause, 'They make you feel bad?'

She began to cry. All at once it had engulfed her and she was able to give into it and admit to being exhausted and out of her depth. All the mistakes she had made, and after it all, Cosmina just dead, dead, dead. The smell of the mortuary. The bag of liver. The glass jar of her brain. What was the point? What was the fucking point? Christ, without Hadley they wouldn't even have got into the house. They wouldn't even have *gone* to the house. And she hadn't managed to keep Hadley out of trouble. Snot was coming down her nose. Hadley handed her one of the canteen's scratchy paper napkins.

'At least blow. You're letting down the uniform.'

She checked to see if he was being serious and saw his sceptical face. He put his paw on her again. 'Do you know what you are?'

She shook her head. 'Like I said, a chocolate teapot?'

'No, a shit magnet.' He laughed again. She felt relief but also an indefinable sensation, as though she were finally giving up on something to which she had always clung with determination.

'Sorry,' she said again.

'You 'fessed up to everything?'

'Yes.'

'The witness in the crime scene?'

'Yep.'

He shook his head. His reaction was ambivalent: she read it as part compassion, part frustration, but was uncertain of the ratio of the ingredients. 'Listen,' he said. 'If you had ever wondered, then there's your reason why we call them cunts. They always know best but they're never there when you need someone to put the door in. Didn't your mum and dad teach you anything?'

She wiped her nose on the back of her hand. Here was no place to try and express the confounding complexity of what her mother and father had taught her. Somehow Hadley's comment was another refutation of everything she had thought she stood for. The world was not a complex place: it was straightforward.

'Don't worry,' he said. 'Fuck 'em. It'll all come out in the wash. You'll see. They'll have their fun – the solicitors, the press, all the know-nothings – casting doubt and criticizing, but it won't make any difference. Stefan killed her. We were the last people she spoke to and you've got it all in your pocket book. I bet you did a good job too, Lizzie. I'm sure you've written a good statement. You can do that, at least. After all the quibbling and griping, the bastard's going down for sure. Life. That's what matters. Don't worry about it. You wouldn't believe the shit I've survived in nearly thirty years in the job. To your own self be true, Officer. We did our best. End of.'

They finished their coffee. Hadley got up. He opened his bear arms and she allowed herself to be hugged. He lifted her from the ground and squeezed her and then put her back on the floor. He stepped back and contemplated her with an ironic smile.

'If I were you,' he said, 'I'd finish off what you've got to do and go home before you confess to any outstanding murders or anything.'

She should have listened to him.

She had sat in the parade room waiting for the terminal to load. It took ages, the blue obstinate screen. While she waited, she flicked through the A4 images of Cosmina that she and Hadley had taken in the hospital. The bruised face, the yellowing skin provoked an uncanny sensation in her. It was some stepsister to horror and grief, an emotion peculiarly alienated by the fact that she hadn't really known Cosmina. It was both to feel and not to feel. Like watching a gripping film without the sound on. All she had known of Cosmina was these bruises, this argument about

231

leaving the flat, her surprising confidence with a digital camera, and then her emphatically dead body. And then she had seen that other thing . . . She shook her head to dispel the memory. The chest cracked open . . . Of course these things were true, but she did not want to see them starkly. Tired as she was, the image of Cosmina on the gurney in the brightly lit tiled room presented itself to her again, unavoidable and emphatic. A woman transformed into evidence, an object for investigation.

Lizzie passed her hand over her face. She turned to the photograph of Hadley and herself that Cosmina had taken in the hospital. They were both laughing, pale under the hospital's fluorescent strip lighting.

'Christ help me,' Cosmina had said.

'Best police force in the world, I think you'll find,' Hadley had answered.

Gazing at the image, Lizzie discovered a sudden new respect for Hadley's claim. She had always thought of him in a certain way, as a type of PC, and she, with her intelligence and her education, she could sum him up – as she realized she undoubtedly had – as an aphorism. He was a dinosaur, an old sweat. Now she had stepped through a looking glass and Hadley appeared altogether different, the hero unmasked. Faced with a firearms incident, an unhelpful Control, an obstructive victim, he had battled single-mindedly to save Cosmina. He had persuaded that young man to put the door in. He had gone into an abandoned house with no backup. He had forced Control to send him more officers, and when Cosmina had refused to go to hospital he had threatened her with an unlawful use of his powers. And in all this, what help had Lizzie really been? She had tagged along, followed his lead. Hadley's readiness to ignore the rules seemed now not something dubious, but rather an act of unpublished courage repeated endlessly, day after day, for twenty-seven years. All that law, all those standard operating procedures: without Hadley they would still be standing outside the door. It seemed to her all of a sudden that courage lay somewhere other than the place she had imagined, and that integrity too was quite a different thing.

Downstairs, Stefan was in custody, waiting. Was he lying on the plastic mattress, catching forty winks? Perhaps he was one of those bastards who made a show of reading the fucking Codes of Practice. Or was he having a custody meal from a polystyrene tray? Coffee or tea? *I asked for sugar!* Was he sitting in an interview room with his lawyer advising him and the Police and Criminal Evidence Act protecting him? Would he say *No comment*, or would he say, *She's always stealing my beer?*

Lizzie exhibited the photos and then wrote another statement on an unrelated matter.

This is a statement concerning arrest inquiries I made in company with PC Hadley Matthews at number 7 Kenley Villas on 23 March.

★　★　★

Later that day, when she finally went off duty, Kieran had opened the door to her in his underpants.

'Lizzie,' he said, in that one word conveying all the inconvenience and exhaustion of a middle-aged man facing another night shift with insufficient time to sleep. He was dead tired. He didn't want this complication right now, with the day full in the sky and the fresh demands of the next shift already in clear view. Lizzie, impatient, pushed the door open. She had had enough of half-measures. She was young and full of desire and her body would be – she knew this with a great and sudden clarity – irresistible. Her flat stomach, her youthful breasts, these were an unfair advantage over the unseen wife who had carried a child in her more exhausted body. But Lizzie herself was exhausted – exhausted by the constant effort of feeling responsible. She wanted at last to throw aside her quibbles. She pushed Kieran impatiently back-wards towards the bedroom. He grinned, suddenly refreshed and delighted to take her behaviour at face value. He laughed at her as though acknow-ledging that she was indeed the thing she presently believed herself to be.

'Hang on, hang on,' he said. 'You're filthy. You stink.'

'OK' she said, conceding that the shift she had just finished – the squat, the hospital, the mortuary – was perhaps not something to take into clean sheets. She pulled him by the hand towards the bathroom. Never letting go of him, she wrestled free of her clothes. The blue police trousers in a pile on the floor, she pulled him into the shower with her. She felt like a faun, undressed and revealed for what she was. She kissed him in the running water and he pressed himself against her, lifting her. Her hand slipped on the wet wall and her mouth filled with water and his lips and tongue. Her hands around his back. His hand clenched on her small breast. *Ah, life* . . . Her neck crooked awkwardly between the shower panel and the corner of the room.

He carried her to the bed and they did it again, astonishing themselves with the energy of their bodies in the face of such a long tour of duty. He kissed her and rolled off on to his back, almost immediately asleep, a Channel swimmer falling exhausted on the shoreline. She curled her left hand around his neck – so strong and reassuring the heft of muscle, so adorable the curl of dark hair at the nape. The fingers of her right hand traced the pattern of the winding rose on his arm.

In spite of the long shift, she could not sleep. She went to the kitchen and stood looking out of the window. Through the flickering tree canopy she could see the lit gabled window of the Victorian house opposite. A woman was standing washing up. The banality of the lonely figure in yellow rubber gloves made Lizzie uneasy. Reality, perhaps, could not be so simply done away with. But she had made up her mind hours ago. She wasn't going to rehearse it all again.

It's not going to be a problem, she told herself. It's all fine.

She made her way back to bed and lay down beside Kieran. He turned in his half-sleep and threw his arm around her. Finally they both slept, their bodies thrown diagonally across the bed, arms outstretched as if reaching together for land.

CHAPTER 27

Collins' chin rested heavily on the heel of her right hand and she appeared to be staring at the door of her office. On her desk was a packet of cigarettes, a set of keys, a takeaway coffee and a half-eaten blueberry muffin. She picked up the keys and unlocked her desk drawer. She removed the working file and searched through it.

Brendan Cormican LLB, of Cormican, Murphy and Khan, had drafted the initial complaint on behalf of Younes Mehenni.

PC Matthews, the solicitor wrote, had entered number 7 Kenley Villas on 23 March without permission. Mrs Mehenni, Younes Mehenni's mother, did not speak English and did not understand the police officers who had barged their way in with no power of entry. The entry to the house was therefore unlawful. Farah Mehenni had arrived to find PC Matthews and PC Griffiths already in the property. Matthews had suggested that the whole family might want to return home – here the solicitor started to go heavy on the quotation marks – rather than remain in London 'pissing people off' and 'creating work' for the 'British' police. 'Do you think the police would put up with any of this shit in your country?' PC Matthews had asked. In the course of questioning Farah Mehenni – a fourteen-year-old girl, Mr Cormican had noted – PC Matthews had called her father both 'Mohammed' and 'Bin Laden'. Farah Mehenni had been very upset. PC Matthews' actions made her fear the police, and when her father arrived home, she was so traumatized that she tried to intervene physically to protect him. This created a situation where PC Matthews used force to remove her from the bonnet of his police car. This distressing and potentially harmful situation would have been avoided if PC Matthews had acted correctly. The family requested a police investigation into the incident, with appropriate disciplinary consequences for the officer.

It was all drearily possible. Collins knew PC Matthews' response almost off by heart, but she turned to it nonetheless and read once again his round state-school handwriting. It was a short statement, and to the point.

On 23 March, I was on duty in uniform. I attended number 7 Kenley Villas on arrest inquiries in company with PC Griffiths. We were looking for Mr Younes Mehenni, who was the named suspect in an investigation into an allegation of criminal damage. A woman who I believe to be Mr Mehenni's mother gave us permission to enter the property. I attempted to speak with her but her English was limited. This being the case, I was unable to get her to sign an entry in my pocket book that she had allowed us to enter. However, she waved us into the property and it was clear that she was giving permission.

Mr Mehenni's daughter, Farah Mehenni, returned home. We were just about to leave the house. She spoke good English and I decided to explain to her our reason for being at the address. I requested her to ask her father to get in touch. She was unhelpful and said she did not know her father's whereabouts. When her father did return home, Farah Mehenni obstructed his arrest by climbing on to the bonnet of my police vehicle. This was a liveried police vehicle and Farah's intentions to obstruct police were clear. I therefore removed her from the bonnet of the car using no more than the necessary force and acting within my powers under Section 117 of the Police and Criminal Evidence Act. Farah Mehenni resisted being removed from the car, but as she is not particularly strong, it was a fairly easy matter for me to lift her from the bonnet and place her on the pavement, which was what I did. This was the full extent of the force used by me. My handcuffs, ASP and CS gas remained in my utility belt throughout.

As I was still hoping to detain Mr Younes Mehenni, I left Farah in the care and control of PC Griffiths while I conducted an area search. I was unable to locate Mr Mehenni. When I returned to PC Griffiths, she told me she had decided to exercise her discretion and not to arrest Miss Mehenni for obstructing police. The usual reports were completed by PC Griffiths on return to Farlow police station.

I understand that a complaint has been made regarding these inquiries. I deny that I said anything unacceptable or was ever rude. At no point did I use racist or derogatory language. PC Griffiths was with me throughout the period that I was with Farah Mehenni.

There were two statements in the file from PC Lizzie Griffiths. The first covered the entry to the property and the use of force against Farah Mehenni. This statement was more detailed than Hadley's. There was more of a sense of the moment when the father returned home, the girl running, the panic attack at the side of the street, the understandable decision not to arrest her. The substance of the statement did not contradict Hadley's – there was a lawful entry and a lawful use of force – but there was an intriguing absence. Lizzie had not covered Hadley's conversation with Farah Mehenni.

Then, eighteen days later, there was a second statement.

This is a statement concerning arrest inquiries I made in company with PC Hadley Matthews at number 7 Kenley Villas on 23 March. I have covered this matter in an earlier statement but have been requested by my inspector to submit a further statement to clarify one aspect of these inquiries. I did not cover this in my first statement as I was unaware that there could be any kind of problem with it.

During the course of our arrest inquiries at Younes Mehenni's home, his daughter, Farah Mehenni, returned home. I was in the kitchen throughout this period and could hear PC Matthews talking to Farah Mehenni in the hallway. He asked her general questions about the whereabouts of her father.

I heard the whole conversation between Farah Mehenni and PC Matthews. PC Matthews was polite throughout. He never said anything out of place and certainly nothing of a racist nature.

Collins put the file down. She rested both elbows on the desk and rubbed her face with her hands. She slipped on her jacket, lit a cigarette and, taking half the discarded muffin with her, stepped out of the window on to the low roof. Sid flapped down towards her and jumped about slowly at a judicious distance. Collins threw a decent-sized lump of the muffin away from her towards the edge of the roof. The crow tilted his head to one side and then hopped away towards the food. Collins pulled her jacket around her and smoked, closing her eyes and leaning back against the wall.

She thought of a child pressing its hand on a window's condensation. If, even weeks later, you blew on it, you could still see the pattern of that hand.

She opened her eyes and gazed at the sky. It was streaked with dispersing jet trails, and in the intensity of colours there was a hint of the day beginning to fade. She thought back to the statements. Events must leave marks on the real world, just as light marked a photographic plate. A man raises his arm and hits his wife with a hammer. The blood splashes on the wall in a particular way. He drives his car from the scene. The CCTV camera catches the vehicle as it crosses the junction. Evidence was impersonal. It rolled out endlessly – as indifferent to meaning as the paper marked by the seismogram's needle. To be a good investigator one had to have a persistent and concentrated interest in finding out what had happened. Eventually the facts would yield to such determination.

Collins threw her head back, stretching and yawning and digging her fingers into the back of her neck. It was wishful thinking. Vanity, even. What did she have? Some discrepancies. A persistent nagging feeling that she didn't know the whole truth. She hadn't come close, she felt, to answering the question Caroline Wilson had asked in her Victorian classroom. What was it that could possibly have provoked Farah Mehenni to take the child?

Sid hopped towards her and cocked his head to one side.

'You're right,' she said. 'Not a good idea for Inspector Shaw to arrive and find me out smoking on this roof.' The crow took another jump towards her. 'Cupboard love,' Collins remarked as she bent down and offered the remaining muffin. 'You don't fool me.' The bird reached out and took the food delicately from her hand.

Steve had escorted them both up from the lobby. The thin black man standing beside Inspector Kieran Shaw was dressed in a dark suit and Oxford shoes. He held out a card and DS Collins scanned it quickly. *Mark Jacobs, LLM, Krauss & Horne.* She handed it back. 'I don't keep them, thanks. I've made a note.' She turned to Inspector Shaw. 'Do you mind if I ask why you've brought a brief here? You're not a suspect.'

Mr Jacobs intervened with a quick smile. 'My client will answer any questions you've got for him on tape. Let's just say he has concerns about the conduct of this investigation and has asked for legal representation. Are you comfortable with that?'

'Perfectly. Although it would have been helpful to have been informed in advance.'

Jacobs smiled again. He was a man who obviously relished his job. 'Helpful? In what way? What difference would it have made?'

It was a game, of course, and she would have to

243

think before she spoke. 'None really, I suppose, but it would perhaps have been courteous.'

Jacobs was pulling out a chair. 'In which case, my apologies, Detective Sergeant. I certainly didn't intend to be rude. May I?'

'Yes, please.'

Collins' phone was ringing. She glanced at the screen. DCI Baillie. She hadn't told him she was interviewing Shaw and she didn't want that conversation right now. She rejected the call and looked up to see Shaw watching her. He smiled slowly and Collins wondered whether Baillie knew about the interview already.

Steve offered to make hot drinks for everyone. Collins accepted: anything to give herself a little bit of time to think. She glanced back at Inspector Shaw. He was wearing a dark grey suit with a light blue shirt and no tie. A good-looking man, for sure, and confident in his looks. He returned her look evenly.

'Do you have any news about PC Griffiths yet?' he said.

'Not yet.'

'You're up on her phone, of course?'

'I can't discuss that.'

They waited while the kettle boiled.

Normally this was the time for small talk. Football. For the more educated suspect, global warming, or even the law. But Collins anticipated Shaw's rejection of any such overtures and decided that under the circumstances silence would be better. Everyone else in the room seemed to be in agreement and so they sat without speaking while Steve fussed over instant coffee, tea bags and milk.

'Are you all sweet enough?'

Shaw said, 'Just one for me.'

Steve dispensed the drinks. Collins said, 'Thank you for coming in so late.'

Mr Jacobs nodded and said, 'Not at all, Sergeant.'

'You're OK to begin?'

'Please.'

'OK.' Collins slotted the tapes into the recorder and pressed record. 'This is an interview about the circumstances surrounding the deaths of PC Hadley Matthews and Farah Mehenni. Inspector, you are not a suspect in these people's deaths. You are not under caution—'

Shaw interrupted. 'How would I be a suspect? What would the offence be?'

The solicitor cut in deftly. 'Kieran, the detective sergeant is just explaining for clarity.'

Steve said, 'Specifically, sir, I think Sarah is encouraging you to feel free to speak to us.'

'And why wouldn't I?'

Collins felt a snap of exasperation.

Shaw was continuing. 'I must admit, I'm a little confused as to what exactly you are investigating and what you need to ask me about. It all looks pretty clear to me.'

Collins said, 'OK. So tell me what's happened.'

'I don't need to, surely. You're the investigating officer.'

'I'd like to hear how you see it.'

'Farah Mehenni was clearly mentally unstable – as the investigating officer, you'll be in a better position to establish that than me – and she just couldn't stand to see her father called to account for his actions. She obstructed police, throwing herself on the bonnet of a police car. She made an unsubstantiated complaint of racism. Then, when none of that worked, she took the boy from the neighbours' garden. God only knows what she thought she would achieve. PC Matthews and PC Griffiths went to the roof to try to save Ben and, of course, Farah herself. PC Matthews died in the attempt but Griffiths recovered the boy safely – for which she should be commended. Instead, she's the object of a witch hunt. No surprises there, then.'

Shaw finished speaking. He sipped his tea and then sat with the air of someone entirely comfortable with silence.

Collins skimmed through her notes. 'So. Let's start with the complaint. Tell me about that.'

'Don't know much about it. The family made a complaint via their solicitor, said that Matthews had used racist language to Farah. As I was part of Matthews' chain of command, the matter was passed to another inspector. That's about all I can tell you.'

'Is it?'

'Yes, as I've just said.'

Jacobs interjected. 'I believe my client has answered the question. Have you any reason to think he hasn't?'

The solicitor was just doing his job, of course. Which was what, exactly? Collins checked herself. She would have to be careful not to be thrown off course by his presence.

'PC Matthews – tell me about him.'

'Good officer. Nothing fancy. Born to be a constable. The amount of shit he'd sorted out in twenty-seven years of coppering. Now he's dead with only three more years to go, and his wife's going to have to finish raising the children on her own.'

'A racist?'

'No. He didn't discriminate. He hated all people equally.'

Collins made a note.

Shaw waited for her to finish. Then he said, 'That was a *joke*, incidentally, and an old one too, but you can make what you like of it. Put a letter on my file if you like.'

Collins looked up, refusing to be riled. 'Was he sloppy, then? A bit careless with language?'

'No. I would have pulled him if he had been.'

Collins paused. 'OK. At post-mortem, Farah Mehenni was found to have PC Griffiths' former telephone number in her back pocket.'

There was a silence. Then, 'No, sorry. Can't help you with that.'

'No idea of a possible explanation? No supposition to offer? It certainly makes the story a bit more complicated than your outline.'

'Does it? Farah had Lizzie's telephone number. So what?'

Collins didn't answer. She waited.

Shaw said, 'She was mad enough to take a child. Why shouldn't she be mad enough to get hold of an officer's private number?'

'Farah made one call that was received by PC Griffiths, on 26 March. Then, on 13 April, Griffiths changed her number. Any ideas about that?'

'No. You'll have to ask her.'

'OK. Tell me about PC Griffiths.'

'What do you want to know? She's a good cop but of a different type to Hadley. She'll go far if you leave her alone.'

'Any special feelings for her?'

Shaw's chin went down and he raised his eyebrows. He leaned back in his chair and looked at Collins with some contempt. After a pause he said quietly, 'Ever thought of doing some real policing?'

'Are you willing to answer the question?'

Another pause. Shaw sighed.

'OK. So, well done.' He pushed his chair back from the desk with the heels of his hands. 'Congratulations. You've dug around somehow and got someone to talk. Who was it?' He leaned forward and flicked his hand dismissively. 'On second thoughts, don't tell me.' He made a sharp, impatient inhale and cleared his throat. 'Yes, I was in a relationship with Lizzie. Yes, I've got – what did you call it – *special feelings* for her.'

'Not your first affair with an officer under your command.'

'No, not my first *relationship*. Yes, there was another one several years ago.'

Jacobs raised a hand in lawyerly protest. 'Sergeant, being in a relationship with a colleague is not a crime. It's not even a disciplinary matter. Inspector Shaw's private life is his own concern.'

'Inspector, you are married and you have slept with female PCs who are under your command?'

'Yes, I have. What are you suggesting?'

'Tell me about your feelings for PC Lizzie Griffiths.'

'What do you want me to say? I *liked* her—'

Jacobs cut in. 'I advise you to answer no further questions about this. It's not relevant—'

'You've been trying to call her.'

'Yes. It goes to voicemail.'

'You don't leave a message?'

'No.'

'Why not?'

'I don't know what to say and I don't want to say the wrong thing. I know she'll get the missed call. Call me back if she wants to talk. I've told you I'm concerned for her safety but you don't seem at all bothered about that. You seem more interested in stitching her up than in preventing her from coming to harm. You're no closer to finding her, I take it?'

Collins ignored the question. 'You didn't want to offer her advice as to how to deal with the investigation, perhaps? Advice that you didn't want recorded?'

Shaw cleared his throat. 'I won't be demeaning myself or you with an answer to that question.'

'Is that a no comment?'

Shaw spoke with heavy emphasis. 'I didn't want to advise her how to deal with the investigation, no.'

'Is that why you organized for her to be driven home after the incident? You wanted to talk to her before we did?'

'Certainly not. Anything else, Sergeant?'

Collins pushed her undrunk cup of coffee away from her. 'Inspector, I'll be frank. The simple account you have offered doesn't quite stack up. I am trying to find out what happened and I don't think you are being particularly helpful on the detail.'

'I've made myself available to your investigation. Ask me what you want to know.'

'I want to know why Farah took such a drastic step.'

'How can I possibly answer that question?'

'If you know about the circumstances—'

'I have no idea why she did what she did. As I've said, she must have been unstable. And, like so many people, she could not accept that consequences follow . . .'

'Yes, OK. Mr Shaw, I haven't finished asking the question.'

The solicitor made a brief movement to intervene – 'DS Collins . . .' – but Shaw batted him away with a hand. 'No, don't worry, Mark.' He turned back to Collins. 'Ask what you want to know.'

'PC Griffiths and PC Matthews got to the roof extremely quickly, too quickly in my opinion. Any idea how they would have known—'

'I don't know what the timings are. I don't know whether they got there *too quickly*, as you say, but even if they did, I wasn't with them. As you are aware, Detective Sergeant, I can only answer questions about things I know about.'

'So you don't know about that?'

'No.'

'Matthews switched his radio off instead of communicating with Control.'

'Again, how can I possibly know why he did that? Maybe he thought a police radio would disturb Farah. Didn't want to scare the horses. Maybe he didn't want Control to start interfering. Thought he could do better talking her down than a superintendent would. Probably right about that too. But that's just surmise, of course. I don't know why he switched his radio off because I wasn't there.'

'Inspector, it's my job to find out what happened. You're a police officer. If you've got any information that can help me, I hope you'll choose to give it now.'

'I've told you everything I know.'

'You didn't tell me about your relationship with Lizzie Griffiths.'

'Because it's not relevant.'

'Anything else you haven't told me?'

Shaw smiled, but a muscle twitched in his jaw.

'You tell me,' he said. 'Looks to me like you think you've got hold of something.'

Collins considered for a moment before speaking without any obvious emotion.

'Inspector, I'm warning you that I have reasonable grounds to believe that you have committed an act to obstruct a police investigation. You went to PC Matthews' locker immediately after his death—'

Jacobs cut in deftly. 'I can't see how this will stack up. If you suspect an offence, you should have cautioned earlier. You specifically told Mr Shaw he wasn't a suspect.'

Collins refused to be drawn. She continued, 'I need to ask you questions about this possible offence. You have a solicitor here but you don't have to answer any of my questions and you are not under arrest. You are free to leave. This interview is being recorded. You do not have to say anything but it may harm your defence if you do not mention when questioned something which you later rely on in court. Anything you do say may be given in evidence.'

Jacobs made a note. Shaw said something inaudible.

Collins said, 'I'm sorry?'

Shaw met her eyes and spoke very distinctly and certainly loudly enough for the tape. 'I don't know how you live with yourself.'

Jacobs cut in. 'I'm advising—'

Shaw interrupted abruptly. 'Mark, there's no point in advising me not to answer questions. It just creates an appearance of guilt. I've been in the job twenty years. I know how it goes.'

Jacobs looked down at his pad.

Shaw coughed. 'OK, Detective Sergeant, I went

to Matthews' locker, yes. Well done for your *detective work*. They would be proud of you at *detective school*. Taken a statement from the asthmatic Mrs Bell in Resources, have you? Poor thing, I bet she can't sleep for worrying now.'

'Thank you for that answer.'

Shaw didn't wait for Collins to ask the next question.

'I wanted to clear his locker.'

'OK.'

'Excited about that?'

Collins shrugged. 'Interested.'

'I shouldn't have done it. OK.' He paused and looked at Collins, and in an instant, his brief appearance of regret had been replaced by contempt. 'You're not *interested*, you're *thrilled*. I can see how thrilled you are. Well, I know how it looks to you, but the truth is I just wanted to protect Hadley's family. I was worried there might be stuff there that would damage his memory, stuff that might perhaps upset his wife. Betting slips from on duty, a bit of porn perhaps. You've seen the headlines, how many thousands of times? Tabloid hype. The usual misdemeanours of ordinary men made to look perverse. "Dead officer kept naked ladies in locker." That sort of thing.'

'OK. And what did you find?'

He smiled at her mirthlessly. 'Absolutely nothing. There was nothing in there, just a load of old pens and a photo of his family.'

CHAPTER 28

On a side street Lizzie had found a charity shop. The door opened on to the musty smell of unwanted items. Crockery with cracked glazing, knives with stained bone handles, a porcelain cat with a chipped ear. Vaguely repelled by the unfamiliar scent of cheap washing powder, Lizzie wrestled behind a curtain in and out of second-hand clothes. The shoes were the hardest thing. There was a pair of heeled brogues that fitted well, but she worried about walking in them and so she plumped finally for a pair of black patent pumps. She matched them with a black knitted dress, a belted coat and a brown leather shoulder bag.

A stranger now returned her gaze in the changing-room mirror: a more conservative young woman with a shiny metallic bob, a woman who spent more time and care on her appearance. It was disorientating, shape-shifting. This woman would have a different temperament and make different decisions.

'Good as new,' the woman with the blue rinse behind the counter said as she piled the purchases into a reused plastic bag. 'And all for a good cause.'

By the time Lizzie stepped outside, the street lights had come on. She had to hurry to catch the shops before they closed. Down the street she found a small chemist's, where she bought a couple of pairs of tights. Further along, and heading west away from the town centre, she looked around her before quickly climbing a low wall into a garden. Crouching down in the shelter of a shed, she pulled on the tights and dress.

The streets were crepuscular, patterned by pools of orange light and the white glare from shop windows. She dumped her old clothes in a wheelie bin on her way back down to the sea. In a separate bin she threw her little backpack. She cut along the side streets, walking evenly and in no particular hurry. She barely glanced at a silver car parked down towards the sea on the opposite side of the street. A man with a shaved head was sitting in the driver's seat; in the passenger seat beside him, another white man with short hair. As she slipped into the shadow of the building, she noticed their outlines – round-headed, broad across the chest, with sloping shoulders.

She did not know what to do, how to survive the night. She had only loose change remaining in her wallet. She began walking along the seafront, east towards Hastings. Out on the darkened beach she could see three men in bleached stone-washed jeans drinking beer. One had his feet resting on a wheeled suitcase. She walked on, past the derelict pier and a crazy golf course where pirate flags hung unmoving in the darkness. The shoes were cutting into the back of her heels and the dress clung to her tights. On her right was an amusement arcade and she walked inside for shelter. It was a charivari – bright lights, loud recorded music. Elvis, a Dracula laugh, the whirr of a helicopter. Lizzie stood in a daze and watched the shove-halfpenny machine shuffling endlessly back and forth, the two-pence pieces shifting incrementally towards the edge.

Things had been going well, that was what she remembered.

It had been the last night duty of the set, and the team were anticipating the four rest days that were finally coming their way. Everyone shared the growing night-duty appetite for carbohydrates and sugar. Arif had made toast. Lizzie spread melting butter on hers and poured honey over the top. Hadley handed her a mug of milky coffee and squeezed his bulk into one of the small chairs. He pushed one of the other chairs away with his feet and, leaning back, affected a Yardie style.

'Hey. Wagwan?'

She laughed. 'Yeah, all right.'

Kieran joined them, late as usual. A slice of toast remained for him and he reached over her and took it. 'Just the one?' he asked.

Arif was already rising from his chair. 'I can stick another one in the toaster, guv. It'll only take a couple of minutes.'

Kieran said, 'Arif, sit down.'

Hadley caught Lizzie's eye and gave her his habitual wink.

Kieran addressed the table, 'Well, ladies and gents, I've just been talking to Mr Reyes on the second floor. Very happy. Homicide have just informed him that Stefan's intending to plead to murder. A very good result indeed. Hadley and Lizzie have both been put forward for commissioner commendations. Didn't they do well?'

There were nods of appreciation, laughter, a bit of back-slapping.

Hadley said, 'Cuddly toy. Cuddly toy.'

Arif caught Lizzie's eye and shrugged, the reference lost on them both.

When the duties were allocated that night, Lizzie was teamed up with Arif. She knew it was a vote of confidence: for the first time she was not paired with someone more experienced. It was a significant event – her initiation into being the senior officer in the car, the one expected to make the call on any difficult decision. She enjoyed the night: the dispatches were straightforward and Arif was good company. They laughed at the ridiculous calls and at three in the morning parked up by the Thames to eat chocolate. Lizzie was happy: something difficult was safely behind her.

It had only been an eight-hour shift and the time had passed quickly. She threw her bag into her locker, already anticipating her bed. As she went outside, two police horses were moving into the yard from the stable. She stepped back to let them pass, breathing in their smell, feeling the heat rising from their flanks.

She had decided to run before going to bed. She would chase away the dirt, the misery, the anxiety, and then collapse into clean sheets to begin her rest days. She pulled on jogging trousers, laced her running shoes, slipped her iPhone into her top pocket and left her flat. The light had been expanding with astonishing speed into an overcast but bright morning. She turned along the gravel path and quickened her pace, running easily, elated, flying through her tiredness. The smell of earth. Ear buds stuffed in, music turned up loud. The air sliced by shafts of light, running as if through the shutter of a camera, fluorescent green and sharp shadow. The ground turned upwards and she felt, like the action of a piston, the strong pulse in her chest deepening as the measures of blood pumped through the chambers of her heart.

That was when the ringtone had sounded in her ears, interrupting her Millie Jackson. She fished the phone out and glanced at the screen: *Number withheld*. She was leaning over her legs, sucking in breath. It was probably a call from the early turn that had relieved her team, a query from one of the dispatches that she had handled during the night. She would take it and then she could run on and sleep undisturbed. She swiped the screen.

'Don't worry. They won't be able to trace this call to me. I'm in a phone box.'

The accent, the youth of the voice – the identity of the caller was unmistakable. Lizzie's immediate impulse had been to switch the phone off without speaking. She hadn't replied, just waited.

'Please don't think I mean you harm,' Farah had said. 'I don't. I like you.'

'You shouldn't be ringing me.'

'You gave me your number.'

'OK, but that was—'

'Yes, that was to help *you*. That was so you could nick my dad.'

'You're angry.'

'Don't start that.' Farah's voice was shaking with rage.

'What? Start what?'

'Never mind.'

There was silence at the end of the line. Then, spoken as though it were merely an observation, Farah said, 'You made a statement. My dad says his lawyer told him. You made a statement.'

'That's right.'

'You said you were there all the time. You heard everything between me an' the other officer. That's what I been told.'

'Yes. That's right.'

'But that ain't what happened, is it? You weren't there, not all the time. You were in the garden and with my nan.'

'Well . . . that's how I remember it. I've got to go . . .'

But of course Lizzie hadn't ended the call. She had been as snared as a fish on a line. There was a pause, and with a chill, it occurred to her that Farah was in no rush to speak: she had known that Lizzie would not ring off.

'I don't know why my dad's bail's not been cancelled.'

'I don't understand.'

'We had an agreement. I was going to bring my dad in and he was going to get a caution.'

'I never promised—'

'You said . . .'

Briefly Lizzie enjoyed the comfort of anger. 'No. For your father to be eligible for a caution, he had to tell the truth. He had to admit the offence and say he was sorry. I made that perfectly clear to him through his solicitor. But he couldn't bring himself to do that.'

There was a pause at the end of the line. Then Farah spoke more quietly, as if she were regretful.

'I don't want to be nasty to you.'

Lizzie felt her role shifting. She too felt sorry, sorry for this girl on the other end of the line who seemed so afraid.

'Look, it'll be OK, Farah, really. It's just a minor offence.'

But Farah snapped in, immediately angry again.

'You don't understand. That bitch is going to take our house away.'

'Farah, please. *Relax*. They're not going to—'

'If you carry on, I'm going to put the phone down.'

Lizzie stopped speaking. She waited.

Farah spoke bitterly, 'What do you know? What do you know?'

Lizzie should have ended the call and lived with the consequences; she knew even then that she should, but still she held on. After a short silence the voice continued, no longer threatening, just factual and a bit nervous.

'My dad says you say you heard PC Matthews speaking to me an' he never said nothing racist.'

Lizzie hadn't replied, just waited for the rest.

'Well, I think you made a mistake. Everyone does that from time to time. My dad did. Your mate did. I think you did an' all.'

'I made a mistake?'

'Yes, you did, PC Griffiths. Think about it. What have you done wrong?'

After the call, she ran again, forcing herself to sprint. The incline peaked and levelled off, opening into wide flat grass. She ran on, turning away from the grass back into woods. The ground was uneven and she had to avoid losing her footing on tree roots and rabbit holes. She slowed her steps, lifting her head towards the winding path. Brambles were sprawling out. Her legs seemed to stop by themselves. The music in her iPod had become nothing but roaring noise. She switched it off and surrendered to the sound of her breath coming in hungry gulps. There was an old wooden bench stranded in the neglected urban woods and she sat down heavily. She closed her eyes, allowing the truth of the phone call to confront her fully. She had a sense of rightness that it had caught up with her. She leant forward, elbows resting crooked on knees, forehead pressing into her hands.

The good officer, she told herself, does not panic.

She went home and showered and went to bed.

But after just a couple of hours it had woken her: the voice of the girl on the other end of the phone. Her recollection of the call was uncanny, eidetic. Farah had not sounded malevolent – that was one of the things that had struck Lizzie. She had been angry, desperate even on occasion, but most of the time her tone had been that of someone putting their hand up in class and venturing an opinion, someone not used to doing that, someone who felt all eyes upon her but who was going to give it a go anyway.

Lizzie could not lie still. She got out of bed and moved to the kitchen. She began to fill the kettle. She was haunted by an eerie sense of déjà vu, as though she had always known that this was going to happen. Hard on its heels came a sweaty sense of fear and shame – a shame so deep that she imagined she would never be able to tell anyone what had happened. She thought, in a flash of recognition, of those moments in interview when she calmly revealed some evidence of which the suspect had been unaware. It could be anything – CCTV, the location of a phone, a quiet voice in the background of a 999 recording. Whatever it was, it was the caught-in-a-lie moment. The pulling-a-rabbit-out-of-a-hat moment. Sim sim salabim, here is the fucking rabbit you had not expected. A feeling of total power, righteousness even – however fleeting – always accompanied that moment. She had perhaps recognized that same tone briefly in Farah's voice. Lizzie's tongue pressed itself to the roof of her mouth. She felt sick.

The kettle was overfilling into the sink. She turned off the tap and emptied half of it out, then set it to boil.

How had she come to this? This . . . error of judgement. That was how she tried to style it at first. Had it been tiredness? Lacking the courage to do nothing? Wanting too much to be liked? Was it really as weak as that? What was Hadley to her that she had done something so . . . so *stupid* for him? That was the word that now repeated over and over to her. Not immoral, not wrong; no, worse than that: stupid. Stupid, stupid, stupid. Weak. Unnecessary. All of this was *unnecessary*.

It was only later that the other words – the moral words that she avoided then – came home to her like baying dogs that would be heard.

Think about it. What have you done wrong?
I have . . . lied.

She hadn't answered the question, of course. In any case, it hadn't been the lie that Farah was referring to. It had been something more practical, an oversight. Suddenly they had been talking business.

'So what do you want?' Lizzie had said.

'What's so difficult to understand? Why don't you get it?'

'Meaning?'

Farah's voice, faint at the end of the mobile's crackling line, had been apologetic, hesitant, childish even.

'What my dad did, it's not a big deal, is it? Not really, you know it ain't. You must have seen a lot worser than that. What that fat copper said to me, that's not a big deal neither. I protect my dad an' you protect your mate. It's just normal, innit? It's just what people *do*. They stick up for each other. You an' me, PC Griffiths, we're the same. Don't you think? We're not bad people. We're *good* people. Well, I'm a good person an' I bet you are too. I really do. Deep down. I bet we could be friends. We neither of us want no one getting in no trouble. Why don't we give everyone a second chance? Everyone gets to start again, what's wrong with that? You can trust me, PC Griffiths.'

Steam had been pouring out of the kettle. Lizzie had flicked the switch and returned to bed without making her drink. She curled up on her side, hoping that the impersonation of sleep would bring its reality. But the problem went round and round in her head, like a buzzing fly trapped in a glass.

No charge, no complaint. That was how Farah wanted to work it. *Lessons learned all round.* It had sounded persuasive for all of about five seconds.

The Crown Prosecution Service had already agreed to charge Mehenni. How to explain to them that suddenly a charge was no longer required? Plus the Chief Superintendent had taken an interest. Carrie Stewart had made bloody sure of that. He had come to see Lizzie in person: he wanted the book thrown at Mehenni.

'Well done, Lizzie. Make sure you serve him with his immigration notice too. Not that it will make any difference, but it does put the fear of God into some of them. And apply to remand, of course. Let me know how you get on.'

No chance of losing the evidence, either. The photos were still on Carrie Stewart's hard drive and Carrie wasn't the type to let it drop.

No, it wasn't going away.

She tried out her defence. She had been mistaken in her recollection. Yes, that was possible. She was in the kitchen with Mrs Mehenni. She might perhaps have missed some part of the conversation between Hadley and Farah. But her statement had been so categorical on this. She had been in the kitchen throughout and had heard the whole conversation.

She tried to clear her mind, counting her breath.

Then she reached to the side of the bed and called Kieran.

'Sure,' he said. 'Yes, I'm just waking up. Come over. I'll make us both pasta.'

In Kieran's flat, she had turned away from the window and walked over to the opposite wall.

Unable to stop herself, she had reached the frame down and taken it over to the sofa, where she could examine the iridescence of the print more closely. The child had a serious face. Kieran, leaning out beyond the nib wall, saw her studying the print, the shine of the glass tilting a line of light across her face.

'Please.'

She turned towards him.

'I'm sorry, Lizzie. Would you mind putting that back?'

Right, OK, OK, put it back. She met his eyes briefly, letting him get a measure of her mood, before she stood up and hung the photo back on the wall. How could she ever have trusted him?

He said, 'Pasta's ready.'

The plates were white china, the glasses etched in green with some funky IKEA pattern. Kieran reached across the table and took her hand, but his touch was uncomfortable now, irritating, so different from how it had been. She drew her hand away and took a mouthful of pasta. It was too heavy on the basil. There was a side salad of cherry tomatoes and rocket. She didn't have enough spit and it was hard to swallow.

He said, 'Do you want to know about my daughter?'

'No, no. It's fine. Tell me when you're ready.'

She took a sip of red wine. There was a brief silence. Then she said, 'OK. Why not? Go ahead then. Tell me about your daughter.'

'She lives with her mother. I see her at the weekends, when I'm not on duty.'

'The mother or the daughter?'

'Sorry?'

She spoke slowly, spelling out what she knew had been obvious to him the first time. 'Do you see the mother or the daughter at weekends, when you're not on duty?'

He looked at her closely. 'I see them both.'

Hey, why the drama? Where was the surprise? She had known this all along. She took a breath of indifference and said, 'OK.'

'We've been struggling. She's moved out of London. It's been difficult. We've been trying to make it work.'

'This isn't a great way to go about it.'

'Agreed.'

She pushed her plate away. 'Not a good evening. Sorry. I'd better be going.'

'What's going on, Lizzie?'

She was silent as she contemplated with some panic the rush of consciousness that would leave her mouth if only she could let it free.

'Shall I drive you home?'

'No. I'll be fine.'

Her hoody was on the sofa and she went to get it. Kieran caught her gently by the arm. He said her name and she thought he would kiss her but she shook her head and pulled away. 'No.' He stepped back and watched her in silence as she put on the jacket and zipped it up. She could not help herself. She said, 'Am I one of many?'

'What?'

'Well. Am I?'

He shook his head and smiled. 'No.' Then, after a pause, more firmly. 'No. Don't be ridiculous.'

She checked her pockets. Purse. Warrant card. 'I'm just one of two.'

'That's right.'

She laughed. 'That's all right, then.'

He laughed too. 'It's problematic. I'll admit that.'

'Problematic.' She left it there.

She was a fool. Of course this whole thing had been much more important to her than to him. A fool. She decided, after a moment's thought, that she could at least let him know about his music collection.

'I hate Pavarotti, by the way,' she said.

'That seems to be a big deal.'

She immediately regretted her remark and could hear its childishness. But his face had cracked into a smile and he said, 'So put something else on.'

She grabbed her phone from the coffee table and slipped it into her pocket. 'No. I've got to go now.'

He walked over and held her gently by her upper arms. 'Lizzie, what is it?'

She shook her head, but this time she did not pull away. He bent over her and kissed her forehead. 'Don't be like this. Stay. Talk about it, whatever it is.'

'No, sorry. I've got to go.'

But she did not move. He stroked her face with his hand.

'Come on, spit it out.'

'That conversation in the hallway, the one I gave a statement about, saying I was there.' She laughed in spite of herself. 'The one where nothing bad was said? That one?'

'Yes, OK. What's the problem?'

'Well, Farah recorded it on her mobile phone.'

He pushed her away slightly. Still holding her arms, he looked into her face.

'OK. Go on. How've you found this out?'

'She called me.'

'How did she get your telephone number?'

'I gave it to her when I went to persuade her to get her dad to hand himself in.'

He nodded. 'OK. What exactly did she say?'

'She said there's a place we can go, the top of Portland Tower. If I get the charges dropped, she'll give me the phone there. She said I could trust her.'

He exhaled and smiled. 'Right.'

'Yes.'

He nodded. 'OK.'

'OK?'

'I'll talk to Hadley about it. Find out if it's a problem. In the meantime, for God's sake change your mobile number. What were you thinking, giving it to her in the first place? You don't want any more calls from Farah Mehenni.'

CHAPTER 29

'Sarah, I expect to be told before you caution a senior officer . . .'

DCI Baillie was ushering Steve and Collins in to his office. The view from the window was an orange city night, a chequerboard of lights that spilled into the river's oily blackness. Baillie gestured swiftly towards the low chairs that faced his desk.

'I left you several voicemails to call me. I wanted an update. What's your explanation for not getting back to me?'

Collins was reluctant to sit, felt the disadvantage of it, but there was no avoiding it. Baillie had remained standing, his hands resting on his desk.

'I'm sorry, boss. I've been trying to move the investigation on. Nobody's had much sleep.'

'Not had much sleep?'

'I'm sorry . . .'

'Really, Sarah?'

Collins resisted an impulse to rub her neck. 'I should have called you. Of course I should. No excuses. I apologize, absolutely.'

'No excuses. That's about bloody right.' He eyed

her for a moment, as if with professional curiosity. 'How do you think it looks when I hear this second-hand?'

'Sir, he arrived with a lawyer. I hadn't intended—'

'You should have briefed me beforehand. We would have agreed a strategy.'

'Of course I should. I apologize.'

'Are you aware of Inspector Shaw's record, Sarah? Do you know what work he's done?'

'Yes, sir.'

'And do you understand that I may well have agreed to you interviewing him under caution; it's the not discussing it with me that I object to.'

'Yes, sir. Of course. I'm very sorry.'

She wondered how many times she would be required to apologize, and whether it would ever be accepted. Baillie was considering her with a furious half-smile, and he now walked away from her towards the window. He looked out, across to the glistening Thames.

'Have you any idea the kind of pressure I'm under?'

She did not reply. Steve was looking down, investigating some mark on his trousers. Baillie reached his arm out to his side and pinched his thumb and index finger together.

'I'm about this close to taking you off the investigation.'

Collins' eyes were momentarily drawn to the panic button on Baillie's desk. For a brief moment – and with the sort of hilarity that happened in childhood – she wanted to reach over and press it.

Baillie said, 'What exactly have you got on Shaw?'

'He cleaned out Matthews' locker within an hour of him being dead.'

'And what did he say about that?'

'He said there might have been stuff there. Stuff that would embarrass. Not bent stuff – betting slips and a bit of porn perhaps.'

'Plausible enough. What's your view on that?'

'It's possible, yes.'

'Possible.' Baillie shook his head as though he couldn't believe what the river was telling him. 'Tell me about PC Griffiths, then. We any further on in finding her?'

Collins did not know whether Baillie was genuinely trying to contain himself by not looking at her or whether he was revving himself up for more fury. It crossed her mind that he really might take her off the investigation. She glanced at the picture of the boy and the fish.

We are normal people: here is my son with a big fish.

'Sir, we've circulated images of Lizzie grabbed from the hotel CCTV, but so far there have been no sightings since she made off from me last night. Two officers are watching the hire car but they've seen no trace of her. I'm considering standing them down. After that footchase I can't think she'd risk going back to the car. There's been no phone use and no financial. We don't know where she spent last night but she must be running out of money.'

'St Leonards? Anything useful there?'

'We've tried the obvious: family and friends. No one seems to live down that way. Mum's helpful but she says her daughter's not been in touch.'

Baillie turned to Steve. Obviously it was still more than his patience could bear to look at his detective sergeant, but to the DC his tone was noticeably friendly: at least somebody in the room was not an idiot.

'Steve, I want you to draw up a briefing on exactly what we are currently doing and any possible further local inquiries that will help us to locate Lizzie. I want a strategy – a proper CCTV trawl, door-to-door, ask questions in local businesses, cafés, hotels. On my desk in an hour, please.'

Steve made a note in his book. Collins waited a moment before saying quietly, 'Understood.' Baillie glanced at her as if slightly surprised to see her still in the room. Collins tried to betray none of the nervousness she was feeling.

'Sir, at autopsy the girl had Lizzie Griffiths' telephone number in her back pocket.'

'Yes, I'm aware of that.'

'Inspector Shaw says he went to the locker to protect PC Matthews' memory, but that's still just his account. He might have been searching for something specific.'

'Yes, OK. So what's he searching for?'

Collins smiled. 'I'm sorry, I just don't know. But I don't believe his account.'

Baillie shook his head in disbelief and then gestured for her to continue.

'I'm not saying I've got the answers, boss, far from it. But I'm sure you'll agree with me that with what we've got so far, this investigation isn't complete yet.'

Baillie tilted his head, waiting.

'And you've always been ahead of me in recognizing that it all pretty much comes down to Lizzie Griffiths.'

Baillie frowned, unimpressed. 'Where's this going?'

'Finding Lizzie Griffiths has to be our priority. Not just for the investigation, but also for her own safety. I've got her at high risk of self-harm. I think you agree with me about that?'

'Go on.'

'The only person close to Lizzie who lives anywhere near St Leonards is Inspector Shaw. He's got a place near Lewes. Shaw and Lizzie were in a relationship. It's quite likely she'd turn to him. I wondered whether you'd consider putting Inspector Shaw under surveillance.'

Baillie's hands closed in front of his sternum. He knitted the fingers together, lengthened his arms away from his body and stretched. He exhaled audibly.

'It has been a long day.'

He turned to Steve, as if expecting the DC to have something interesting to say, and Collins regretted not having warned him of her suggestion.

'Any opinion, Steve?'

Steve – rather comically, given his tired and

worn face – gave the DCI an appearance of attentive neutrality, rather like an obedient and intelligent dog awaiting a command. His expression seemed to suggest that Collins had certainly made an intriguing suggestion, something that had not yet occurred to him but that might warrant consideration.

'Your call, boss.'

Baillie turned back to Collins.

'That's quite a big ask – putting one of our own officers under surveillance.'

'I'm aware of that, sir.'

'OK, let's think about it. I agree that Lizzie might well turn to Shaw, but we have no reason to believe that if she contacts him he won't contact us. And that's the point, Sarah: we don't have any grounds to treat Shaw as a suspect, or even to believe that he is not cooperating with the investigation, and that means we don't have enough to put him under surveillance.'

Collins jumped in, in spite of herself. 'Something's not right, sir. There was a delay before Lizzie made her second statement. We haven't completed the phone work yet, but—'

'OK, it's not complete, I accept that. What have you actually got so far?'

Collins hesitated. 'Just one call from Farah to Lizzie, on the twenty-sixth of March, about an hour before Mehenni hands himself in to be interviewed. There's another call to Lizzie's mobile number on the seventeenth of April, probably just before Farah takes the child. It's from the Mehenni landline. The call isn't connected because Lizzie had changed her number, on the thirteenth.'

Baillie shrugged. 'Lizzie could have had perfectly legitimate reasons to change her number, especially if she was a police officer who had made the mistake of giving out her personal number.'

'We don't know that—'

'Nevertheless, all we have is just one accepted call from Farah to Lizzie, and that call looks perfectly explicable.'

'Yes, sir.'

There was a pause. Collins waited. Baillie cleared his throat. He looked as though he was making every effort to be reasonable.

'So what have we got? Lizzie Griffiths' mobile number in Farah's back pocket? So what. Shaw looking through Hadley's locker – for which he has offered a plausible explanation. And a relationship between Lizzie and Mr Shaw that isn't improper but makes you feel a bit uncomfortable?'

Collins felt she was floundering but she pressed on, pushing for a connection with Baillie, for a language he would understand.

'OK, sir, but consider the context – the public interest is enormous. What happens if we don't watch Shaw, don't follow every possible lead? Then later, much later perhaps, even twenty years on – God knows it wouldn't be the first time – we are found to have missed something or are simply judged not to have tried hard enough. How would that be construed? I'm sure we can agree that neither you nor I wants this coming back to bite us.'

'No, Sarah, no.' Baillie shook his head. 'That's just plain wrong. I'm not in the business of covering anyone's arse. I use my powers within the law. I wouldn't put a civilian under surveillance in these circumstances and I won't do it to a cop.'

Collins began to speak. 'Sir—' but Baillie put up his hand.

'No, hear me out, Sarah. I don't like what you're saying. Not at all. Shaw has a wife and child, remember. You're asking for directed surveillance at his home address, with all the collateral damage that implies. Is that really justifiable, considering how little you have? We have to do things for the right reasons, not because we think – what was it you said? – because we think something is going to come back and bite us.'

Collins winced. Her ill-judged attempt at a connection with Baillie had completely misfired.

The DCI was continuing. 'I'm not talking morality here, not being nice or nasty to officers. I'm talking the law, Sarah. The Regulation of Intelligence Powers Act. But you go ahead – convince me other-wise. Tell me you've got something more than you've already told me.'

Collins took a breath. She had definitely lost this battle, and that being the case, it was best to bow out gracefully.

'OK, sir. I accept what you're saying. My apologies if my language was ill-chosen. You're the boss.'

'Thank you, Sarah. I'm sure you're acting from the best possible motives. Didn't you say you were tired? Why don't you knock it on the head for now? Go home. Tomorrow's another day.'

CHAPTER 30

Lizzie caught sight of herself – a white-faced stranger with a Lulu dark bob – reflected in multiple repeating fragments in the silvered shove-halfpenny machine. The man was closing up the arcade and she hurried to leave before she drew attention to herself. A cold wind was blowing across the seafront and she walked towards the town centre. Two cabs were waiting at the rank outside the station and she jumped into the first one. The driver was a portly white guy, probably in his fifties, with his ID hanging from a lanyard around his neck. She asked him to go to Rye.

'Whereabouts exactly, love?'

'Two seconds please, I've lost the address.'

She switched on her phone, searching quickly on the internet for B&Bs. She read out the address of one chosen randomly and then turned the phone off.

'Would you mind stopping at a cashpoint?'

He glanced in his rear-view mirror. 'All right, my dear.'

The cashpoint gave her £300. Twenty minutes

later, the cab dropped her at the bed and breakfast in Rye.

'No luggage, love?'

It hadn't been much of a question, but Lizzie noticed it.

'No,' she said. 'My boyfriend's bringing it.'

CHAPTER 31

The corridor was in darkness. Triggered by movement, the lights flickered on for the solitary figure of Collins making her way back to her office. The desks were littered with empty boxes, as if the crew of the *Mary Celeste* had been eating pizza when the mysterious event occurred.

Collins sat alone and made herself consider Baillie's viewpoint coolly, as if it had been advocated by someone she respected – by Steve, perhaps – rather than by a bolshie DCI with his eye on some serious career progression. Seen in that light, she had to admit that Baillie had a point. The evidence she had was circumstantial at best, made up of fragments, speculation. And Farah, that shadowy figure, the girl with the cuts on her forearm and the Hello Kitty backpack, had been a troubled child. Perhaps it was just as Kieran Shaw had said – Hadley Matthews had been very unlucky to ever encounter her.

She flipped the switch on the kettle and got out the case file. She thought of her abandoned home: thank goodness she didn't have a pet! She bent

281

over her desk and began to search once more for where the seismogram's needle might have left some helpful tracery on the page.

The mobile she had left on her desk burst into unexpected life.

Collins pulled the window of the office open on to the London night. She lit a cigarette and stepped onto the roof. After just two rings, Steve picked up.

'OK, Sarah?'

'Hi, yes, sorry to disturb . . .'

'Don't worry. Go ahead. What have you got?'

'Sussex Police just called – a taxi driver has gone into Rye police station. He thinks he just had Lizzie in the back of his cab.'

20 APRIL

CHAPTER 32

Collins stirred on the camp bed she had set up in the office. There had been a carefulness about her sleep, an awareness that the bed was uneven and that as she relaxed, her vertebrae displaced. She was careful too about getting up: the last thing she needed now was for her back to go. As she trekked down the corridor to the toilets, she was beset by a burst of intense irritation, a cursed feeling of ineffectiveness and missed opportunities.

The damn trail had been cold, of course. The taxi driver had left it too long before he reported to police. The B&B owner in Rye had told the surveillance team that a young woman matching the taxi driver's description had enquired about rooms but had then decided to look elsewhere. Yes, it had seemed odd, he had told the officers, but you don't call the police just because someone doesn't want to rent a room. Collins and Steve had still given it more than three hours before they gave up. Steve, who had driven to Rye, had got a hotel room in Hastings so he could carry on in the morning. Collins, supervising from the office, had decided there was no point going home and had broken out her camp bed from its unofficial store place in the photocopying room.

She pulled a box of cereal from her bottom drawer and raided milk from the tea club. Her thoughts were elsewhere. It wasn't just missing Lizzie; it was this feeling that she could not knit the investigation into something conclusive. All night, in between supervising the search, she had trawled through the evidence, determined that there must be something, something that would break the impasse. As she ate her cereal, she took the black video tape from the top of her desk and slotted it into the VCR that lived in the corner of the office.

Collins scribbled a note on her pad. *Initial report 23rd March, charged and remanded 17th April.* It wasn't an overly long period for such an investigation, although the remand to court was perhaps a bit unusual for such a minor offence. Still she would look at the timeline again. She put down her pen. Her breakfast abandoned halfway through, she rested her head in the heel of her hand and watched.

The recording was poor quality, the images indistinct and the sound inaudible. In any case, the recording of the custody suite on 17 April from 14:00 hours was unremarkable. The time counter on the top right-hand corner of the screen cycled round as the day unravelled.

It was the usual charging routine. Lizzie Griffiths leaned on the desk with Mehenni standing beside her. The custody sergeant, a black female, worked through the slow procedure. The solicitor leaned in and out of the desk from time to time, making notes on his pad. Officers passed by, busy on other cases. Other suspects came and went. A cleaner mopped the corridor.

Collins glanced at the custody paperwork that she held in her left hand. There had been two charges – criminal damage and malicious communications. She looked back at the screen and saw Mehenni leaning over and signing the computer pad. She looked at the paperwork again. Lizzie Griffiths had applied for a remand on the grounds of preventing further offences and intimidation of witnesses, and it had been granted.Younes Mehenni would be kept in the cells overnight to appear at court the following day to enter his plea. The routine immigration form had also been served. It was no more than paperwork – for such a minor offence, immigration issues would never come to anything. Mehenni would have to do a lot worse than criminal damage to face an immigration tribunal. There was a further note on the custody record and Collins scribbled it down on her pad: the custody sergeant had allowed Mehenni to go outside and explain to his daughter what was happening.

Collins ejected the video and slipped another into the player. It showed the station office, the time stamp displaying the same date at 14:28 hours.

Farah was sitting waiting in her school uniform. People queued at the counter. A man came in with a Staffordshire bull terrier on a lead and three children in tow. Then, in the bottom left of the frame, Younes Mehenni, in the company of a uniformed detention officer, entered the station office from the direction of the custody suite. Farah stood up and Mehenni went over to her. They were small figures at the back of the picture, partly obscured by the man standing at the counter. Mehenni gestured with his right hand and gave some papers to Farah. Then the detention officer came over and touched him on the elbow. Mehenni turned and left his daughter alone in the station office. Farah stood for a moment and then left, her head bowed, studying the papers.

Less than two hours later, she would be dead.

CHAPTER 33

The room had a distant view of the sea. There was a tray on a table by the window with a floral tea set and a cordless kettle. Lizzie had made herself a cup of coffee and piled up the individually wrapped shortbread biscuits on the bed beside her. Eating her way systematically through them, she lay in her underwear and the hotel white towelling dressing gown watching the news.

The same thin man she had seen on the television set in the hairdresser's at St Leonards was being interviewed again.

'. . . The CCTV images we have of her are recent but we have reason to believe that she may have changed her appearance since they were captured. The pictures you are going to see are an artist's impression of how she may look now.'

The screen changed to a chalk drawing of a young woman with a short chestnut bob wearing a dark coat over a dark dress.

It wasn't at all a bad likeness and it confirmed Lizzie's suspicions about the taxi driver last night. He must have got a really good look at her. She remembered standing in the hotel lobby waiting for the cab to leave before she made her excuses and, heart thumping, walked quickly to the taxi rank in Rye. On her way back along the coast towards Eastbourne, an unmarked police car had passed her in the opposite direction, its blue lights flashing.

The television report cut back to the man in the suit and a byline now gave the name of the interviewee: Detective Chief Inspector Robert Baillie.

'. . . I'd like to stress that PC Lizzie Griffiths is not currently a suspect in the ongoing inquiry. She witnessed a horrifying incident and we have concerns for her safety. Any member of the public identifying her is asked to contact police. To Lizzie I'd like to say, call us, or just walk into a police station. Your family and your colleagues want to see you home safe and sound.'

Safe and sound: she tried to imagine how that could feel. It felt extraterrestrial, unreachable by any obvious method.

Someone was moving along the corridor outside her room. Doors were opening. She switched off the television and pulled the towelling hood of the dressing gown up. She opened the door slightly and looked out. A fat blonde woman in jeans and T-shirt was pushing a trolley down the corridor, knocking on doors.

'You want clean?'

Lizzie said, 'Would you come into my room for a minute. I want to ask you something.'

★　　★　　★

290

She stood in front of the bathroom mirror and carefully cut her bleached hair into the plastic sack from the bin. Then she dried it off and gelled it into a scruffy style. She put on the jeans and T-shirt, stuffing the dress she had discarded into the plastic sack and putting that into her handbag.

The chambermaid had said her name was Joanna, but Lizzie didn't know whether that was true. It was as if both women had tacitly agreed that they would believe each other and ask no questions. Joanna said she would have helped for nothing – she too had once had to avoid an angry husband. Nevertheless, returning with the plastic bag from the chemist's and the second-hand clothes, she had taken the money quite readily, stuffing it into her back pocket and making a quick exit.

Lizzie inspected herself in the mirror. She wondered whether she would lose her hair after two colourings in as many days. It had gone a bit yellow, but it didn't really matter; in fact it almost contributed to the look. It was her second transformation and equally disassociating – a young art student perhaps, or someone in a grungy band dreaming unrealistically of fame. She dressed it up with some mascara and red lipstick that Joanna had offered her from her own bag: *No, no, take it. Is my pleasure. Good luck.*

Lizzie had only spotted CCTV cameras in the hotel lobby and bar area, and they were easy to avoid. She slipped quickly along the first-floor corridor and out down the back fire exit.

CHAPTER 34

Alice had called up to the office: Mr Mehenni was waiting for Collins in the entrance hall. 'I'll be down in a minute. I've just got to finish this call.'

She went back to her mobile.

'OK, Steve, sorry about that.'

'So, her phone was switched on briefly in Hastings at 22:34 hours, but it's been dead since. She didn't make any calls, just accessed the internet. The taxi driver who thinks he had her in the car is ex Old Bill. I wish he'd called us immediately instead of waiting to report it at a police station. He says he wasn't sure at the time but, having seen the pictures, he is now. We're enquiring with local taxi firms here to see if anyone took her from Rye, but we've got nothing yet. There's so many cab companies down here, plus the independents. There's a rank outside the station, so if she took a cab, it could have been any of them. There's no CCTV in the B&B in Rye, so we can't get an image. The other bad news is she's got more cash. She withdrew three hundred pounds in Hastings.'

'OK. Baillie's just done a fresh appeal with the new description. She seems to be orientating herself along the coast – can you make sure all the train stations along the line are spoken to personally and provided with posters. I've got to crack on – Mehenni's waiting for me.'

Before she went down to Mehenni, Collins unlocked her desk drawer and withdrew a small evidence bag. She cut it open and slipped its contents into her jacket pocket.

He was standing waiting for her in the entrance hall with Alice. Collins stood back from the glass door and watched.

Alice was a distraction. She streaked her hair blonde and favoured pencil skirts. Today her spike heels were a shiny patent red. She was dead keen – you had to give her that – but she seemed to have no sense of the impression that her fashion choices made on the public. All her weight was on her left foot, the right twisted in front of it. Collins suddenly found herself feeling protective of young, optimistic Alice. In a few years the optimism would give way to something else and the shifts would prematurely age her young, plump skin.

Alice turned and glimpsed the DS through the door glass, and a smile of relief stretched across her face: Mehenni was obviously hard work. Collins had wanted a moment before speaking with him, but now, hiding her disappointment, she stepped out into the station office. Mehenni turned to her. Collins saw a man of small frame and height, clean-shaven, with dark skin and fierce brown eyes. She had, of course, not known him when his daughter was alive. However, it was hard to imagine that the hard set of his mouth, the pinch at the edges, the frown lines between the eyebrows had all arrived overnight. She offered her hand, but he shook his head in refusal. She withdrew her hand without comment.

'Mr Mehenni, thank you for coming in. I am sorry for your loss.'

He had the strict, formal air of a man who was not deceived by her courtesy, and she knew she would not easily get past his rage.

'Can I ask you to come through?' She was pushing back through the glass door. 'Normally family liaison officers are not present during the interview. Will that be all right for you?'

Mehenni did not react to the question.

Collins pressed on. 'Good. Well then, Alice will wait for you and drive you home when we've finished. Alice, I'll call you when we're done.'

Alice, only too keen to be dismissed, walked quickly away. Within seconds she was talking to a flirty officer from another team. It didn't create a good impression. Collins would have to have words. She was pressing her fob against the lift.

'Apologies for bringing you all the way out here. We're separate from general policing, so it's more secure, more independent. We've got recording

294

facilities. It's important I record what you've got to say.'

Younes Mehenni's anger was a river in spate. Collins changed tapes but it did not abate. He denounced the British people, the British police, his neighbour. He was most virulent on the subject of the female police officer, PC Lizzie Griffiths. He had never, never thought, never *imagined* that that woman could have done him so much harm. He lapsed into his own language and then back into English. How could he have ever imagined?

Through all the rage Collins could hear nothing helpful, no valuable information. There was anguish hidden behind all that anger, she realized that, but Mehenni gave no glimpse of it. Like a radio operator with headphones clamped on, she closed her ears to the man's fury and listened instead through the painful crackle for any useful signal. She waited for the tapes to finish and then sealed them, leaving the fresh tapes unopened on the table. There seemed no point continuing with the interview like this. Mehenni was still talking; more rage, more formless blame. Collins leaned forward, gesturing gently but firmly with her palm out for a moment's quiet.

'Mr Mehenni.'

He looked at her.

'Mr Mehenni, your daughter is dead and I am sorry for that, truly I am.'

Mehenni's face hardened. He clenched his jaw.

He was not interested in her sympathy. He didn't want to talk about his dead daughter. Collins waited. She wasn't really offering sympathy.

'Do you smoke?'

He shook his head. She opened the window to the roof. Perhaps out there things would become clearer to him.

'Would you mind stepping out with me while I have a cigarette?'

The wind was blowing strongly and the clouds moved steadily across the sky as if in a hurry to be elsewhere. Mehenni leaned back against the wall and shivered through his jacket. Sid hopped about at the edges of their space, his head cocked on one side. Collins smoked in silence. After a few minutes Mehenni gestured towards the bird. 'You have fed him?'

'Yes.'

'Now you'll never get rid of him.'

'No, I suppose not.' She inhaled, holding the smoke in her lungs. 'I'm not sure I want to.'

He reached out an open hand. 'Could I have a cigarette, please?'

She took the box from her pocket, flicking it open with her thumb and offering it to him. She passed him her lighter. He turned his shoulder to light the cigarette and then leaned back against the wall. He handed the lighter back without looking at her.

'Thank you.'

'You're welcome.'

They smoked in silence for a while, neither looking at the other.

Collins said, 'You do not trust me.'

Mehenni gave a derisory exhale. 'Of course not.'

'Do you understand my role?'

He did not answer.

She pressed on. 'I am the investigating officer. That means I'm the person whose job it is to find out what happened. You don't have to like me or even to respect me, but if you want justice, you will have to help me because I'm all you have.'

Mehenni coughed as though clearing his throat.

Collins said, 'I saw your daughter's body. I saw her on the tarmac at the bottom of Portland Tower and I was present at her autopsy. I know she was just a child. Fourteen. No more than a schoolgirl.'

Mehenni did not speak.

Collins reached into her jacket and took out the little blue horse with the silver nylon mane. She held it flat in her palm. 'This was in her pocket.'

Mehenni stretched out his hand and she passed it to him. She saw it briefly cradled in his brown lean palm. He gave a low, involuntary moan as his fingers closed around it.

'I'm so sorry, Mr Mehenni.'

He laughed. Then he tilted his head so that his back was resting against the wall and he was looking up towards the sky. He swallowed, and glancing to her left, Collins saw that silent tears were running down his cheeks. His mouth was clamped shut. He wiped the tears away with the back of his hand.

She leaned back and lit another cigarette. She waited. Then she said, 'Do you want me to find out how Farah came to die?'

Mehenni turned to her with a sudden clear focus. 'Madam, there is no point in this. I will *never* trust the British police.'

She nodded.

'You could have had a caution,' she said. 'If you'd accepted a caution, that would have been the end of it. All you had to do was admit what you'd done and say you were sorry. But you couldn't do that, could you? You brought Farah with you when you were charged. I saw you on the station office CCTV; handing her the paperwork after you'd been remanded to court. Why did you do that? Bring her with you to the station? The poor lonely girl, you terrified her, didn't you?'

Mehenni didn't say anything.

'So that's it, is it? Really just a simple matter. You put all that pressure on your daughter and, not surprisingly, she broke. You are the reason Farah is dead. You are responsible and your daughter was responsible too: no one else.'

Mehenni cleared his throat with a harsh sound, as if some terrible obstruction pained him there.

Collins threw her cigarette on to the roof and ground it out with her shoe. She surprised herself by being angry too.

'Is it pride that stops you talking to me?'

His voice sounded as though he was struggling with a terrible illness, cancer perhaps. 'Not pride, no.'

'Well what is it? Tell me, please, because I can't understand it.'

Suddenly he was racked. He doubled over, his hands on his knees as though he were on a running track after a long, bitter race. He made a guttural choking sound. Collins felt her own cruelty and it made her sick. She should never have taken him out on to the roof, never pushed him like this.

Then Mehenni was speaking, but she could not understand what he was saying. It was his own language mixed with English. She thought she heard the word *fault*, thrown up briefly and carried on in the current like jetsam disappearing fast downstream. She seized on it, putting a hand on his arm and speaking clearly, loudly, determinedly.

'Whose fault? Your fault perhaps, yes, perhaps partly your fault, but not only yours?'

He was still bent over, gulping as if he had been rescued from those terrible rapids.

'Mr Mehenni, I don't know the whole story yet. I will be honest with you: I'm not sure that I can ever know it. But you can be sure that at least I am in earnest in trying to find it out. What was it made your daughter take the boy, Ben, up on to the roof of Portland Tower?'

Mehenni's right hand was still clutched tightly around the little horse and his knuckles were white.

His jaw was set, his face drawn and smeared with tears.

'Mr Mehenni, the worst has happened. What have you got to lose now? Let's go back inside. You need to talk to me, tell me everything. We need to get it all on tape. Let's go back inside.'

Mehenni spoke for more than an hour. After she had sealed the tapes Collins asked him to sign for the little blue horse that she had given him on the roof. She stood by as he leant over the desk and put his signature next to Steve's entry from the post-mortem.

She said, 'I'll call Alice to take you home.'

He raised his hand. 'Wait . . .' He took a photo out of his wallet. 'I have trusted you Detective Sergeant Collins. I want you to understand that. We are taught that every soul shall taste death—'

He could not speak. Collins waited. Then he handed over the photograph.

'My daughter.'

CHAPTER 35

The shop was empty and there was no one behind the desk. Lizzie stood in front of the shiny display stand of phone cases and headphones. It was a candy bar of pinks and silvers, metallic greens and blues. What fun a phone could be! A tall black man appeared from a door behind the desk and ambled over to her. He was a cool guy – that was the implication of his demeanour. This job was just to pay the bills and no one should take it too seriously. He smiled at her.

'What are you looking for today?'

She wanted to be honest at last. The words could slip out easily: 'Just give me an untraceable phone, please.' She steeled herself instead to show some interest in the different tariffs, how much data, how many free texts.

'A pay-as-you-go, please. I'm a student, so I'm trying to save money on my phone.'

He looked at her for a moment as though sensing something was wrong, but then seemed to shrug it off. None of his business anyway. He lifted a phone from the stand and began to speak. Lizzie could not concentrate on his words; she just wanted to get to the bit where she bought the phone. She said, 'Yes, that sounds great. How long will it take to activate?'

'Oh, no time at all. About ten minutes.'

Lizzie sat on the cold shingle eating chips, waiting for the phone.

She was exhausted, struggling with the effort of concealment and aware that the end was drawing near. This would be the last chapter, the last deception. Then she would see what happened. She thought for a moment that she wanted it to be on her own terms, but then it struck her how such a phrase fitted a different existence. She was in another place now. She had lost herself.

Think about it. What have you done wrong?

I have . . . lied.

That was it: she had lied. She could try to excuse it as a small lie, but it seemed nevertheless irrefutable that with that lie she had surrendered her sovereignty. She had been at the beck and call of others. She had tried constantly to put it out of her mind. And there was the time afterwards, after she had told Kieran about the phone call from Farah. She thought of it as a gap, an interval, a negative space in which the thing had happened unobserved, the thing that she had perhaps assented to but had turned her face away from.

Kieran had insisted that it wasn't a problem – he had spoken to Hadley and Hadley had been adamant that no recording could damage him

302

because he had never said anything wrong to Farah. Hadley had collared her and, in a hushed, angry conversation in the writing room, insisted it was all just a ploy by Farah, just another attempt to get her to drop the charges.

Lizzie had not been able to face him or herself. Her relationship with Kieran had become strained too. She had sensed him tiring of her. Or perhaps that had just been a part of her paranoia, a facet of the uneasy state in which she had lived since the phone call from Farah. She had changed her number and her phone, and had showed up for work. She had avoided Hadley and Kieran. And it must have been in that gap, that absence, that it happened.

Lizzie fished the new phone out of her bag and switched it on. The cell searched for the satellite and then latched on to it. Kieran picked up after two rings.

'Yes?'

'It's me.'

'Where are you?'

'I'm coming to Lewes. Whatever the next train is from Eastbourne.'

'No.'

'No?'

'Get off at Polegate. It's the stop just before. Turn down the high street, carry on down Wannock Road. I'll meet you along there. I'll be parked up just beyond the sign. It's about two miles from the station. My phone will be switched off. You should do the same.'

CHAPTER 36

Baillie was talking on the phone, but he gestured for Collins to come in and quickly closed the call.

'OK, Sarah, what have you got that's so pressing?'

He smiled, and Collins swallowed involuntarily. Her right hand clutched the data she had just taken warm from the printer.

'Sir, I've interviewed Younes Mehenni and I may have an answer as to what Inspector Shaw was searching for in Hadley's locker.'

Baillie raised his eyebrows. 'OK?'

'Mehenni says Farah used her mobile to record Hadley racially abusing her. After Lizzie wrote a statement that supported Hadley's account of the incident, Farah contacted her and tried to use the recording to blackmail her into dropping the charges against her father. Younes alleges that Hadley then took Farah's phone from her. If he's telling the truth, maybe that was what Shaw was looking for.'

Baillie nodded. 'OK, so Farah threatens Lizzie, then Matthews takes the phone from her and hides it in his locker? And that's what Inspector Shaw is looking for?'

'Yes, perhaps.'

'It's a good lead and much better than anything we had yesterday. But isn't it still a bit far-fetched? An officer perverts the course of justice and then hides the evidence in his locker?'

'I agree. It would be a colossally stupid thing to do . . .'

'Indeed it would.'

'. . . but it wouldn't be the first time an officer had been stupid enough to keep evidence in his locker.' Collins stretched out her hand and offered the sheaf of paper. 'Sir, Jez has come through with a bit more from the phone work.'

Baillie took the papers but did not look at them. He was watching Collins.

'I'll put it in context, sir. On the tenth of April, Lizzie writes a statement corroborating PC Matthews' account of his conversation with Farah Mehenni. Two days after this, she gets a call from a number that's not on her contacts. Jez has traced the call and it's from a phone box on Shorefield Street, a short walk from Kenley Villas and on the way to Farah's school. The following day Lizzie upgrades her phone and changes her number. When Farah tries to call her before she takes Ben she can't get through. The phone's been disconnected.'

Baillie's face bore a seriousness Collins hadn't seen before. He said, 'OK. Anything else?'

'Just one thing. There's another call that looks interesting. At 15:52 hours on the seventeenth of April, Shaw receives a call on his private mobile from Hadley Matthews. So, just after Ben went missing and while the incident was in full swing, Matthews took the time to call his boss. Whatever it was he needed to say must have been important.'

Baillie considered Collins for a moment. His eyes were as hard as little blue pebbles. 'Good work, Sarah. Very good.'

On the way back to the office, Collins got a call.

'Steve . . .'

'Inspector Shaw has just received a short call from a pre-paid mobile. He's called it in – says it was Lizzie and he told her to make herself known. Says he has no idea where she was calling from.'

'That's his arse covered, then. Do we know anything else about the call?'

'I'm doing an urgent trace now. The phone was bought in Eastbourne earlier today and that's where the call was made. Shaw picked up in Lewes.'

'OK. Perhaps she's arranged to meet him. The boss has just agreed surveillance and a warrant for Shaw's home address.'

'Damn. I've only just got back to London.'

'Don't worry. I'll blue-light it down to Shaw's house in Lewes and try to keep an eye on him. I reckon I can be there in just over an hour if I put my foot down. Can you get officers on the station at Lewes as quickly as possible, and on any trains going from Eastbourne to Lewes. We need to look at hire cars and taxis too. Hire cars are unlikely – I think, given the time pressure, we should target taxis.'

'Do you want me to come with you?'

'I'd love you to, but I need you here to sort all that out. Is that OK? And tell surveillance to get a bloody move on, please. I want backup as quickly as possible.'

CHAPTER 37

A young white woman in a hijab was wheeling the trolley along the train aisle. She paused by Lizzie and smiled. 'Coffee? Tea?' Lizzie bought a bottle of water and some crisps. The trolley moved on. A group of four women had got their make-up out on the table just a few seats up. They were experimenting with lipstick and different nail varnishes. One of them was complaining.

'Pocahontas,' she said, examining her recently painted left hand. 'It looked good in the pictures, but when it arrived, it was really badly made. Pins and Velcro at the back.'

There was a sound of singing from along the corridor. A woman's voice, a lilting nursery rhyme. *A frog he would a-wooing go* . . . Lizzie glanced down the train. By the door, a woman with dyed red hair was rocking a child. Beside her was a pushchair and a large collection of bags. Her nose was pierced with a single stud.

Lizzie stared out of the train window. The Sussex countryside was rushing past, dipping and rising.

You bastards, you think you can get away with anything.

Mehenni had whispered it to her. She had been taking him through to the custody suite to charge him. Determined to get through the charging process, she remembered, she hadn't even looked at him.

'Sir, you've made your complaint. That will be addressed. In the meantime, I have to charge you.'

After that, he had been ostensibly calm, courteous even. The charge itself had been entirely without incident. Mehenni had asked to go out and see his daughter to explain to her what was happening. Lizzie remembered her unease. She had said she was too busy to accompany him and so a detention officer had agreed to do it.

There was a corner of the station office where it was possible to watch the CCTV relay of the public area without being seen through the counter glass. Lizzie had stood there and watched Younes Mehenni going over to his daughter. As she remembered Younes' angry gestures, Farah taking the papers and shaking her head, Lizzie imagined herself stepping out into the station office, stopping the chain of events that had been set in motion. She would have had to tell the truth. Even now, after everything that had happened, it was still a daunting thought.

The train was pulling in to Polegate station. The mother at the far end of the carriage had strapped the child into the pushchair and was struggling to gather together her bags and push the buggy with one hand. She was an exact match for Lizzie's new look. She got up and walked towards her.

'Let me help you. I'm getting off here too.'

The woman gave a broad smile. 'Thanks. Can you take the pushchair?'

Lizzie asked the name of the baby.

'Megan.'

'What a lovely name.'

Chatting with her new friend, she walked along the platform and out of the station.

CHAPTER 38

Collins drove in a desperate hurry. She came off the A26 and followed country roads before turning right along a narrow lane. There was a ford ahead and she slowed to cross it, dipping into a fast-flowing little brook. The road climbed again. A tractor ahead was ambling along carrying hay in the claw raised above the height of its roof. Collins indicated to overtake but had to pull back: oncoming was a mud-splattered Land Rover Discovery. As it approached, she recognized Shaw as the driver. He saw her too, she was sure of that, and she put her right hand up to wave at him to slow down, but he drove on, barely glancing to his right as he passed her.

After only a moment's hesitation, Collins stuck her siren on. The tractor driver pulled slowly in to the hedge to allow her to pass, the cab rocking as the huge wheels mounted the verge. Briefly she saw a collie in the passenger seat, and as she pulled past, the driver waved.

She turned the car in a lay-by ahead and accelerated back along the narrow lane, siren wailing and blue lights flashing. She hadn't planned for

311

this eventuality, and as she drove, she ran through her mind what she would do if she caught up with Inspector Shaw. She hadn't intended to arrest him; just to park up and wait, to execute the warrant when it had been granted. Still, Shaw was possibly on his way right now to meet up with Lizzie. That would make sense: he had got that phone call. He probably wouldn't agree to accompany Collins back to his house, and he certainly wouldn't allow her to search him. She would have no option but to arrest.

She braked hard for the ford and then accelerated as the lane climbed back towards the main road. Birds scattered out of hedges as if pursued by an army of fanatical beaters. The road curved back round on itself. Ahead and to her left, she caught sight of the Discovery, its roof showing just above the hedgerow. Then it was lost to sight. She accelerated beyond her instincts, hoping to catch it before the T-junction. To take the bend, she changed down a gear so that the engine roared as the car gripped the road and rounded the curve.

Directly ahead was a teenage girl in a fluorescent waistcoat riding a chestnut horse. Collins braked sharply. The car's wet tyres skidded momentarily before the ABS gripped and the car stopped.

The girl was tall and thin. A strand of red hair escaped from beneath her riding hat. She was holding the horse tightly and it was protesting at the tight bit in its mouth, arching its neck and tapping its front right hoof on the tarmac.

Collins put her hands to her face. She had stopped within fifteen feet of horse and rider.

When she took her hands away, the girl had moved the horse into the hedge and was waving her on. Collins drove slowly past and then accelerated towards the junction. There was no sign of the Land Rover.

CHAPTER 39

Polegate was a place on the way to somewhere else. There were broad-leafed trees and hints of the ancient in the names – Wannock and Weald – something Saxon, lost, something never to be tapped. But the past was surfaced by broad, affluent roads, dormer bungalows with Dutch gable roofs and grand 1930s semi-detacheds with new windows.

Lizzie bought a box of plasters for her blisters at a chemist's on the high street. She walked for a couple of miles, the shoes still rubbing like hell, before she saw the Land Rover. There was a dog in the back: she could see its dark, friendly muzzle smearing at the window. Kieran stepped out of the driver's seat and opened the back of the car. The dog, a chocolate Labrador, lolloped on to the pavement.

Kieran and the dog walked ahead, the dog wagging its tail and jumping from side to side. They took a footpath down a lane that turned into a small wood of oaks and beeches. The land climbed steeply, following the undulation of the chalk beneath. Lizzie lost sight of them, but as she rounded a bend, Kieran was waiting for her by a small stone bridge that ran over a stream. The dog was nosing around in undergrowth.

Kieran was wearing a worn waxed jacket and muddy wellingtons. He looked at her in her new outfit, her scruffy bleached hair. He shook his head and said, 'Lizzie, really.' She in turn wondered which was real – the countryman with his dog or the London policeman. She had drawn close to him but neither of them knew what to do. He opened his arms to her, but with something questioning in the gesture. She hesitated, and he reacted swiftly to her uncertainty, tilting his head slightly and saying, 'OK.' He patted his leg and the dog came running over. He began to walk.

'Sorry about the dog.'

'You needed a reason to leave the house.'

'Yes.' Then, after a pause: 'And the dog needed a walk.'

They crossed the bridge side by side, the Labrador running ahead. The path became muddier. There was a feeder for pheasants, and the birds scattered away from them as they approached. Kieran called the dog: 'Pebbles, Pebbles.' It came trotting back, tail wagging broadly. The brook curved round and they came to another bridge. Kieran stopped and took out a package wrapped in kitchen towel. He handed it to Lizzie. She opened it up – a warmed croissant, shiny with oil.

'Thought you might be hungry.'

'Thanks.' She took a bite but found it difficult

to swallow. She put the remains in her jacket pocket.

A field opened out beyond the bridge. The sun was declining and the sheep, shifting around in the field, seemed to almost glow white against the encroaching darkness. Kieran did not walk any further, and in the shelter of the wood, Lizzie thought of the demons that attended her – both the police searching for her and the ballet-dancing girl with the serious face waiting somewhere close for her daddy to come home. Of course Kieran would not risk being seen with her. She imagined him grabbing the lead from a hook in the hall and calling: *Just popping out with the dog.* Then she thought of Farah, flat-chested, waiting for the pathologist's shears.

Kieran said, 'It's been difficult for you.'

She answered in a kind of wonderment. 'Difficult?'

'I'm sorry, Lizzie.' He paused. 'I'd like to hug you but it seems that's the last thing you want.'

The last thing she would want? She wondered whether he had said this as a kind of trick. She felt suddenly very cold again, and incredibly lonely. She wanted to pull her jacket tightly around her but resisted the impulse.

He said. 'Where have you been?'

'St Leonards.'

There was a pause before he spoke again.

'Have you got a plan?'

She shook her head. 'Not exactly.' She looked down at the ground and scuffed it with her shoe.

He shifted his weight. There was something impatient in him. He reached into his pocket and took out a battered black Nokia brick. It looked small, lying there flat in his open palm. The back, Lizzie noticed, was held on with a rubber band. She took it in, the fact of the phone made solid.

'How did you get it?'

'I got a call from Hadley. He said he was on his way to Portland Tower. He asked me to go to the locker and get the phone. I was angry with him, asked him what the hell he thought he was doing. I'd believed him when he'd told me that a recording wouldn't be a problem because he had never said anything to be ashamed of. Now he was telling me he had Farah's phone in his locker. He said he had just been trying to protect you, and that it had been a bloody stupid mistake.'

Lizzie felt her veneer of reasonableness deserting her.

'He'd been trying to protect me?'

'That's what he said, yes.'

Kieran wore the expression of forbearance that Lizzie knew from incidents at work. She had seen him wearing it with unrealistic victims, the mothers of juvenile suspects, officers who weren't up to scratch. Was that what she had become? A difficulty to be managed?

'Did he say what he had done? Exactly how he'd got the phone?'

'He was in a hurry when he spoke to me, Lizzie,

317

and then he was dead, so we never did iron out the exact details.'

She looked at the phone. It was scuffed, the numbers worn away through use.

'Is there anything on it?'

'Oh yes.' Shaw turned it over in his hands and slid off the back, expertly removing the SIM card with his nail. He turned the phone face up and said, 'Look, no passcode.'

It blinked into life and he flicked swiftly through the icons, then passed it to Lizzie so that she could listen. There was hissing and crackling in front of distant voices. Then Lizzie heard Hadley distinctly, a ghost materializing on the Sussex Downs.

'*Yeah, he's . . .*' then nothing clearly, '. . . *erm, better . . .*' Inaudible again, a crackling on the recording, '. . . *needs to . . .*' The sound of Farah's voice, even fainter, '*Not . . . No . . .*' A loud rustle against the microphone. Hadley again, '. . . *should . . . if you, if you . . .*' And then, faintly, but distinct among the crackle, a single word: '*Laden.*'

The recording stopped.

She held the phone close to her ear and pressed play again. She struggled to hear, scrubbing backwards and forward, but got no more than the first time.

Laden. Just one word. Was that it? Was that all that was on the phone?

The triviality of it angered her, overwhelmed her. She couldn't get past it, couldn't make sense of the desperate thoughts raging through her head.

She sat on the low wall that ran down from the bridge. She turned the phone face up in her palm and shuttled through the photographs stored on it. Shaw sat beside her, watching over her shoulder. There was a picture of a tortoishell kitten with pale green eyes. Some girls in school uniform on a bus. A photo taken in a mirror of Farah herself, the phone held up in her right hand, long dark hair falling round her shoulders.

Shaw interrupted her thoughts. 'You feel guilty? Responsible?'

Lizzie nodded without looking up.

'Well there's no reason for it. The girl made her choices. So did Hadley.'

Silence.

Then Lizzie said, 'He says Laden on the tape.'

'Yes. Hardly a racist tirade, is it?'

'It was enough to have got him into trouble.'

'And do you think that's right?'

Lizzie didn't answer.

'Lizzie, do you think it's right that after twenty-seven years of service, Hadley could be dismissed just for calling Farah's dad Bin Laden?'

Lizzie raised herself slightly to slip the phone into her front pocket. She didn't want to answer, but Shaw was clearly waiting.

'He knew the score,' she said. 'He shouldn't have said it. He wasn't protecting me when he took the phone; he was protecting himself.'

'If that makes you feel better.'

Lizzie got up and walked away, stopping at the

edge of the field. 'It doesn't make me feel better, Kieran. Nothing does.'

Shaw had stayed sitting. The dog came over and nuzzled into his hand. He stroked its head.

'Lizzie, you are thinking the worst of Hadley because you're upset, but I believed him when he said he took the phone to protect you. I think if it wasn't for you, he would have just ridden it out . . .'

'And is that supposed to make me feel better?'

'No, I'm not trying to make you feel better right now.' The dog was pushing itself into Shaw's leg and he shoved it away impatiently. 'After all, you hardly helped matters, did you?'

'What do you mean by that?'

'After Farah's little threat, you would barely speak to Hadley. Do you understand what that meant to him? Hadley *liked* you, Lizzie; he thought you had the makings of a good cop. He felt bad, ashamed even, because you'd backed him. He knew how much you would sweat and stress if Farah produced her pathetic recording. I think that's why he took the phone.'

Lizzie picked up a piece of wood and began to strip the bark from it.

After a pause Shaw said, 'Well, I'll always believe that, but the truth is, neither of us will ever know what he was thinking.'

Lizzie considered his words. 'He probably said more than Bin Laden. He probably thought the phone had captured everything he said, and that's why he was so anxious to have it. But it didn't record everything, because Farah had it hidden in her pocket.'

Kieran sighed. 'OK, if you want. It was a torrent of racial abuse. Is that what you remember of Hadley?'

Lizzie shrugged.

'You don't remember Hadley?' Kieran insisted. 'Can you really not trust your memory of him? He wasn't a racist, you know that. He was simply from the street and he talked like the street. You know how he got people to see sense. A bit of pressure here, a joke, sometimes an idle threat. Nothing he said ever really meant much to him. It was all about getting people to do the right thing. It didn't mean anything to Farah either. Whatever Hadley said, it was just coinage as far as she was concerned – a way to protect her father.'

Lizzie snapped angrily, 'Well clearly it went further than that for her in the end. She must have been pretty desperate to do what she did.'

'Or mad.'

'No, not mad,' she insisted. 'Hadley crossed a line, you must see that.'

'Of course I do . . .'

'He took a phone by force from a vulnerable teenager. That's why she's dead. Not because he called her dad Bin Laden.'

'The whole thing's a mess, yes. Of course it is.'

Lizzie's emotions were too much for her. She clenched her teeth together and resumed stripping the branch. The bark was wet and flaked away, leaving the wood beneath white as bone.

The Labrador was rooting around in the under-growth. Kieran walked impatiently over to her. The dog had got hold of something disgusting and was biting at it, rolling her neck. Kieran pulled her out by the collar and dragged her down to the stream. He pushed her muzzle and neck into the water.

As Lizzie watched, it was as if she sensed newly how absurdly she had fallen in love with him. Head over heels: all the clichés. She thought of the warmth and weight of his body, the turn of his hip against her, the winding rose tattoo on his arm.

Kieran let the dog go and stepped back while the Labrador shook herself dry. He looked up towards Lizzie.

'Hadley wasn't a saint, of course he wasn't . . . But he was a decent copper who did a lot of good in his twenty-seven years. He made a terrible mistake, yes, and he's paid a terrible price.'

Kieran squatted down and rinsed his hands in the water upstream, then dried them on a large cotton handkerchief he took from his pocket. Lizzie could think of nothing to say. Kieran walked towards her. He stood opposite her.

'If the world wasn't so bloody crazy, absolutely none of this would have happened. And the girl was mad, utterly mad. You must see that. She took the boy. She killed Hadley, for God's sake.'

Lizzie shook her head. 'No, no. She didn't kill

him . . .' She could feel an intense pain in her throat.

Kieran held his hands out to her. She wanted to resist him but she also wanted his comfort. Then he was hugging her to him. His hands were cold from the stream water. She felt them icy on her neck. Her cheek was against his chest. She inhaled the country smell of the waxed fabric.

'I don't know how to live with it,' she said quietly.

He stroked her hair.

'Darling.' There was a pause. She felt his voice reverberating through his jacket. 'You did OK, Lizzie. You got the child away from the edge. We all fucked up, but you did save the child.'

He pushed her away gently, holding her at arm's length and studying her. He smiled briefly. 'You look bloody ridiculous in those clothes. And that hair, Christ! You look like you should be protesting against the G8.'

She laughed in spite of herself. 'Yes, I know.'

His face fell quickly into a more solemn cast. 'Do you know what, Lizzie, the only really important question now is whether you are going to allow yourself to survive.'

Lizzie looked away.

'What are you going to do?'

There was that question, and Lizzie found herself once again wary.

'I don't know.'

'You'll be interviewed by the DSI.'

'Yes.'

'What are you going to say?'

She opened her hands as if to show there was nothing in them.

He said, 'I hope you won't be landing yourself in it. Hadley would be cross if you did, you know that. If you learn only one thing from him, then let it be this: never give the bastards anything.'

She stepped backwards. Had none of them really done anything wrong? Nothing that mattered, anyway?

'No, I won't be landing myself in it.' And then, after a pause, 'Or you.'

He exhaled. 'I'm sorry?'

She couldn't stop herself.

'Your actions don't look so great, do they? You were my inspector. I looked to you for guidance. You never told me to simply tell the truth. You didn't tell me plain and simple not to write the statement.'

'No, I didn't tell you not to write the statement. You're right. But I did tell you to be *sure*, to be absolutely sure before you backed Hadley, and you didn't do that. You never clarified with him what he said. You still don't know exactly what he said, even now. You just went ahead and wrote the statement. It was your mistake and your bad decision, not mine.'

Lizzie felt angry tears welling up and she choked them down.

'Well that advice might look fine to you, but how do you think it would look to the outside world?'

He stepped towards her, suddenly livid. She was

startled by his anger and she backed away from him, but he had grabbed her upper arms. It hurt. She would have bruises.

'The outside world,' he said. 'What is the outside world?'

Holding her with his left hand, he put his right in her jeans pocket and took the phone. She twisted away from him and he let her go. She saw his hand closed firmly around the phone, and then he placed it in his jacket pocket.

She didn't know what to do with herself. She hadn't planned this and she didn't know what to say. The earth was muddy. Her breath frosted. She couldn't see the phone any more. Kieran's hands were in his pockets, as if he had to keep them there to stop himself striking her.

'For you,' he said. 'I went to search for the phone to protect you. Don't you see that? From the start I only thought of you. The one thing I could do when something terrible had happened was to make sure it didn't get any worse. I put myself on offer and I've been interviewed by the DSI. They interviewed me under caution, for Chrissakes. I didn't need to do that for you. It was always *your* problem, Lizzie, never mine.'

Lizzie felt like she was suffocating. She drew breath in convulsions and then realized she was actually sobbing.

Kieran raised his voice. 'You're not a child, so please stop acting like one. If they'd found the phone, do you think you would have been the woman who was prepared to risk everything to save a little boy's life, or would you have been the bent copper who lied in a statement?'

She shook her head and bit her lip. He grabbed her face and held it so that she had to look at him. 'Listen to me.'

'OK.'

He let her go.

'I know it's shitty: I've got a wife and a child and none of this works out like a fairy tale. But you always knew that, right from the start. I *never* lied to you. I liked you, loved you even, and I wanted to make sure you didn't come to any harm. I was never dishonest with you. Hadley and that girl? I'm not responsible for any of that. Not at all. No.'

Lizzie wiped her hand across her face. Her throat hurt with the effort of trying to stifle her sobs. She spat on the earth. Somehow she seemed to have got earth in her mouth. It must have been that stupid piece of wood.

Kieran was continuing. He sounded more urgent now, more insistent.

'You say you can't live with this. Well what's the alternative? Are you going to die for it? I don't think so. But go ahead, prove me wrong. You going to prison? Really? They'll put shit in your food because you're a cop. Those people on *Question Time*, they'll have a field day with their opinions and their, their fucking applause, and you'll be on the nonce row.'

He paused. She had been listening to him with

something like horror, and now she actually shuddered. He seemed to treat it as a confirmation. He went on.

'Yes, turns out life's complicated and messy, and you've made a mistake. Perhaps *I* made a mistake.' He swallowed and looked at her coldly. 'Perhaps more than one. Maybe I did, yes.'

The dog had picked up a scent and trotted away along the stream. Kieran whistled for her and she stopped and began to move back towards him, tail wagging obediently. He turned to Lizzie.

'So what are you going to do now? Are you going to put up or shut up? Are you going to let this screw you up for the rest of your life or are you going to man up and put it behind you and learn to be a good cop?'

She clenched her jaw and returned his look. 'A good cop, Kieran?' she asked. 'What the fuck is a good cop?'

Briefly he considered her with disbelief, as though she were as alien as a Victorian explorer complete with pith helmet asking questions of the natives.

'Do you really not know? Well for all his faults, Hadley was a good cop. And I'm a good cop too. Those bleeding hearts, they think they want something different but they don't, not really, not when it matters. When the shit hits the fan and their loved ones are in danger, they don't want you, Lizzie. They don't want someone who will worry and doubt and hesitate. And they don't want that frumpy DS Collins from the DSI either. They want someone with balls. They want Hadley or me.'

He withdrew the phone from his jacket pocket and held it out to her. 'I risked keeping this for you so that you would know what bullshit the whole thing was. Bin fucking Laden! I'll be disposing of it on my way home. If and when you are interviewed by the DSI, we never met today. You rang me and I told you to hand yourself in.'

The Labrador was wagging her tail, waiting. He bent down and slipped the lead on to her collar, then stood up. 'I hope you make the right decision. I don't want you to come to any harm. I cared for you . . . no, I *care* for you. *Still* care for you, Lizzie . . .' She felt another sob rising in her chest. She clamped her throat shut harshly against it but it escaped in a ragged bark. He was still talking. '. . . But I want to be absolutely clear that you are responsible for yourself. If you decide to destroy yourself, don't think, not for a single moment, that you can drag me down with you, because you can't.'

He walked away, the dog trotting at his side, over the bridge and out towards the open hillside.

CHAPTER 40

Collins had pulled over a few yards from the house. No one could leave or enter without her seeing.

The evening star was shining in the dark purple of sundown. Warm light spilled out from the cottage windows. A smell of woodsmoke was in the air. A woman came to the window and drew the curtain against the night. Collins caught only a glimpse of her, but the glimpse made sense enough. She was willowy, dark-haired. Her hair, held back in a single thick plait, showed her long, slender neck.

The Land Rover pulled up and Inspector Shaw let a brown dog out from the back.

Collins watched him approaching his front door. The woman she had seen earlier came to greet him. She stood in the doorway in jeans and a T-shirt. A girl, in bare feet, ran out. Shaw lifted her into his arms.

Five minutes later, he left the house carrying a mug, the dog following him. He walked up and tapped on the car window.

Collins got out. Shaw was taller than her and she felt her disadvantage.

She said, 'You failed to stop for me earlier.'

His expression didn't alter. 'I don't know what you're talking about.' He handed her the mug. 'I think I've got this right. You don't take sugar?'

Collins felt the humiliation of it.

Shaw said, 'What are you doing here, by the way?'

'We're getting a warrant to search your house. I'm waiting on the rest of the team.'

Shaw shook his head. 'You've somewhat lost the element of surprise, Detective.' Nevertheless, his condescension did not conceal his annoyance. 'You're bringing this into my home now. What's the point? Even if I had something, it would be gone by now.'

'Yes, I apologize for disturbing your family. It's unavoidable.'

'Unavoidable.' He had virtually snarled the word, but he cleared his throat and controlled his demeanour. He even managed a smile. 'Just leave the mug outside the car when you've finished.'

It got colder.

Collins turned the engine on and slid the seat back.

From her wallet she took out the black-and-white photograph Mehenni had given her. It was a picture of a dark-haired girl aged about eight. She was wearing an Alice band, smiling. She had on a smocked top and jeans. She was sitting on a wall and her legs were swinging. Collins tried to imagine where it had been taken: some city in North Africa, the heat baking off the concrete.

A fog was settling in the valley. Collins was stiff and frozen. Inspector Shaw stood at the window of one of the first-floor rooms. He gazed out at her. Then he drew the curtains shut.

CHAPTER 41

In Caxton Street, some black lads sat in a parked BMW, the car lit up as orange as Lucozade. At first they would not open their window to Lizzie, but when they did, she bought a wrap of cannabis from them for £15. She walked in her stranger's clothes through the fluorescent London night. On Oak Road, a fox trotted beside her down the street.

Someone had left a mattress and a fridge against a wall. A young, lean white man in jeans and grey hoody was crossing towards the building, and Lizzie tailgated him into Portland Tower. He barely even clocked her, walking on ahead, hands in pockets, hood up. The entrance lobby was unevenly lit. Someone had broken two of the orb-like lights so that only one remained. The caretaker's office had long since been abandoned, the victim of ancient cuts that were no longer even part of memory. Lizzie hit the push switch for the stair lights and they flickered on. She climbed to the landing.

The concrete stairs, confined and smelling of urine, bore the usual stains and darkening marks.

She sat on the second stair of the second flight, out of view of the entrance hall. Inexpertly she rolled a joint. She hadn't smoked cannabis since university, and only occasionally then. She hadn't liked it. Now, however she craved the sense of disconnectedness it had given her. She needed some kind of anaesthetic, and alcohol wouldn't do it.

At university, there had been a girl who read the Tarot, laying the cards out in a Celtic cross on the table and turning them over with a satisfied snap. The Lovers, the Fool, the Chariot, the Hanged Man. With incense burning and a joint in her hand, she had liked to invite interpretation from her subject. As the fumes of cannabis surrounded her, she would urge that each arcana be construed in the broadest sense. Death, she had conjured airily, symbolized an ending, and hence a new beginning.

Lizzie reached into her pocket and took out the business card she had been given when she was sitting in the ambulance and carried with her since. She ran her finger over the printed name. *DC Steve Bradshaw.* She remembered the moment among the chaos. The paramedic reading her pulse and the section sergeant outside the door on his radio. The DC with the face like a used paper bag handing her his card. *That mobile's on 24/7*, he had said, *and it's always OK to ring me.*

She was beginning to feel giddy. She rolled another joint and lit it, inhaling deeply. The drug expanded inside her.

Hadley had been an entire Tarot pack in his own right. The Fool, Justice, the Emperor. Or the Magician, perhaps: the manipulator, the sometimes beneficent guide, a stick in one hand and coins scattered on the table. She remembered that he had once said he had a tortoise.

A light came on in the stairway. A woman with her daughter wrapped up in coat and gloves walked up the stairs. She saw Lizzie and looked away.

Lizzie wondered how Kieran had disposed of the phone. Was it crushed beneath his car, burnt in a fire, lying on a river bed or even at the bottom of the sea, turned back and forth restlessly by the tide?

She thought of that recording, the indistinct voices on which so much had turned. Perhaps it could have been worked up into the thing Farah had said it was. Perhaps it could have been enhanced. She imagined some technician pulling syllables out of the silence, and from behind the crackles, words. But she suspected not. That was the stuff of TV dramas. Hadley had kept the phone. In its absences and its presences it had represented perhaps some sort of verification for him.

She thought of his tortoise foraging through the undergrowth. She thought of those Tarot cards with their naïve art deco pictures. The Sun. The Moon. The Tower hit by lightning, with two falling.

She began to climb. It was a long way, and she paused for breath. The stairway light came and went. Along the walkways many front doors were protected by metal grilles. Better to die by fire

334

than to be burgled seemed to be the conclusion of the estate's inhabitants. One walkway was caged off at the end, and an ugly square-headed dog paced up and down by an iron gate.

She sat down again under a pool of stair light. She got out her new mobile and DC Bradshaw's card. She dialled the number. It rang three times before it was picked up. She heard a voice. 'Lizzie? Lizzie?' She closed the call. Within a minute the phone was ringing. She held it tightly, feeling it vibrate in her hand until it went to voicemail. She switched it off. She turned away from the landing and climbed higher. Outside a door, a well-worn dirty doormat bore the words 'Happy Home'.

She passed the last level and continued up towards the heavy metal service door. A remnant of blue and white plastic crime tape fluttered on the handle. The door was locked, but from her coat pocket she took out Hadley's fire door key. She had found it lying on the stairs when she had run up them a lifetime ago and held on to it. She turned the key in her hand. It was like a talisman of Hadley, a symbol of his mastery of the lesser-known skills of policing. The brown lace he'd used to attach it to his utility belt was still looped through it. She slid the key into the slot and the lock clicked.

She imagined Farah ahead of her, and hesitated. Then, with the fear of following a sprite, she stepped out on to the roof.

From the top of the building, a broad view opened. She walked towards the edge, which was bounded by a low wall. Beyond the complex of buildings and small patches of grass, London's lights twinkled out to the horizon. In the distance she could see the very hungry caterpillar of an illuminated tube train shuffling through the landscape. She imagined the people on board, mobiles and tablets out, earphones stuffed in.

The estate was lit in patches of tungsten. The leaves on the trees reflected light as if they were made of beaten metal. Further along was a children's playground. A group of young men in the estate uniform of hoodies and jeans had gathered. It was their manor: a place of rivalry and gangs, of territory, fortification and tribute. The estate was laid out like a maze, and, far better than the police, the drug dealers and robbers knew its many twists and turns, its Elizabethan alleyways and cut-throughs. It came to Lizzie what a fitting place this had been for Farah to bring them. Were we ever, it seemed to say, as bad as this? But in an idle moment Lizzie had googled the estate and found a website of fond memories – black-and-white photos of a street party, working-class men in woollen three-piece suits and flat caps and women in flowery aprons and Sunday-best hats.

A bitter wind was hurtling across the roof. Bracing herself against it, Lizzie gazed out over the city's lights and towards the borough's arteries and landmarks. She had always thought of it as her ground, a part of London that had been entrusted to her.

She saw Ben again in her memory, terrified. His face pale. His piping voice: 'I trust you.'

Farah had wiped his upturned cheeks with her free hand.

There had been seagulls wheeling about in the sky.

She climbed over the wall, holding on tightly. She was shaking. She sat with her back against it, the drop in front of her, the sense of it like a void inside. A plummet into darkness and light. A flash of memory of the boy in the bear suit, the girl with the long dark hair, and the fat policeman trying to catch her eye.

Voices from the playground carried faintly.

Farah had turned away from her and faced out towards the drop. She had been holding Ben's hand tightly, and he too had faced out, as though he could fly.

Lizzie stood up. This was it: the edge. She scanned London's glittering horizon. Then she made herself look down over the drop to the dark concrete beneath.

21 APRIL

CHAPTER 42

Banging reverberated, not only through the custody suite of Northleach police station but even in the offices upstairs and along the station's empty corridors. It was a 1970s nick, just four miles outside the command area where Hadley had served.

Collins leaned into the monitor.

The screen was divided into a monochrome chequer pattern that jumped every few minutes to a restatement of the same, the only variation being the contents of the bleached-out squares. Some were empty, holding only blocks of darkness and grey. In others, a person stood or sat or lay, waiting. In the square inscribed *Male Three* a young man stood, both arms leaning against the wall. A movement at the bottom of the frame showed he was kicking the cell door repeatedly. The pattern refreshed again and Collins peered closely at the cell marked *Female One*. There a young woman lay motionless on the dark grey rectangle of the cell's mattress. Collins studied the image narrowly and then, as the frames changed again, turned away from the screen towards the custody sergeant.

'You've got her on half-hour watches?'

'Yes. But I'm still not happy about keeping her in a cell.'

His breath was stagnant from a long night on duty. It was 5 a.m. and he could probably feel the shift winding down, the imminent arrival of the relief like the turn of the tide. Soon he would hand over his charges and their property. Soon he would make his way across the slowly waking city towards his welcoming bed. But in defiance of the long shift his shirt was still bright: starched white and crisp. He had trimmed sideburns and a large gold watch with spindles and dials that suggested he was the captain of a ship equipped for heavy seas. Ten years in the job absolute minimum, Collins guessed. No wonder he hadn't liked Steve bringing this particular prisoner in.

'I'm sorry,' she said. 'I can't see any way round it.'

Her phone pinged and she glanced at the screen. It was a text from Baillie. He was aiming to be at Victoria Buildings within the hour. Feeling the pressure of the prisoner's custody clock, she turned back to her phone and began texting Steve to meet her at the front gate. They would blue-light it back to the office. But the sergeant detained her. His responsibility for the prisoner in Female One might be about to end, but he wasn't going to let the matter drop so easily.

'I'd like an update as quickly as possible. I want reassurance that her detention continues to be necessary. I've marked that up on the custody record.'

'I'll get back to you as quickly as I can. Let me give you my mobile number.'

A sliver of grey dawn was beginning to split open the dark, overcast sky. Collins stood in the police station yard, smoking. The black tarmac was slowly being obscured by the cars parking up. The early turn's bags waited in piles behind the door, ready to be loaded when the shift changed. The night duty pulled their own bags from their boots and signed back their vehicles. For the most part, the officers looked shabby and tired, making their way single-mindedly towards their lockers and their transformation into anonymity. A few of them clocked Collins standing by the station wall. She imagined them running down the steps to their changing rooms, asking as they struggled out of their uniform and threw their crap into their lockers, *Anyone know who that is?* Word would have gone round about the prisoner in Female One. Gossip could enliven even the most exhausted officer. Collins was used to it. For her part it was a badge of honour not to give a fuck.

She pulled hard on her Marlboro. The heat scorched up the cigarette and the smoke ripped into her lungs. Steve swung the car round in front of her. Collins threw her cigarette on the floor and crushed it underfoot. She slid into the passenger seat. Steve clipped the light on to the roof. The yard's gate rolled to the side and the traffic gave way for them as they turned towards base. Collins pressed her head back against the headrest and closed her eyes. In a moment she had slipped into a deep sleep from which she woke with a sudden jolt. She opened her eyes. The car had braked sharply. Steve was overtaking into oncoming traffic and a car had failed to give way. He hadn't sworn, just waited with no evident emotion for the car to move. The traffic squashed into the side of the road, and as the car pulled over, he accelerated into the gap.

Collins ran her hands through her hair, digging her fingers into her scalp. She stretched back against the seat and yawned. She licked her lips and ran her tongue over her teeth.

'You found her back on the roof?' she said.

'Yes, she was standing on the edge. I thought she might jump.'

'Christ.'

Collins had a brief sweaty flush of relief that the worst had not happened. It was nevertheless uncomfortable to have come so close to disaster. She took a breath and attempted to enjoy the blue-light run. Steve was a good driver, and only rarely did he have to stop. He swerved around traffic islands, slowed for red lights. Momentarily they were stuck behind a geriatric maroon Allegro. The driver had frozen behind the wheel and didn't dare jump the red light to let them through. Steve waited: blaring the horn would only make things worse.

'Come on, Grandad,' he said quietly. 'Live a little.'

They both sighed.

Collins said, 'So how did you get her away from the edge?'

'I asked her if she wanted to ruin my life like Farah and Matthews had ruined hers.'

'And that persuaded her?'

'Well, I said a bit more than that. Anyway, it seemed to do the trick.'

Collins exhaled. After a pause she said, 'Commendation stuff, that.'

Steve gave a disparaging grunt.

'Do you think she was really going to jump?'

'I dunno. I always think the real ones are found dead. But you never know. Pretty crazy thing to do.'

The lights changed. The Allegro moved to the side. Steve pulled the wheel to the right and swerved round. Collins glanced to her left and saw an elderly woman with straggly grey hair clutching the wheel. Grandma, then, not Grandad.

'What did she say?'

'Avoided saying anything significant. She'd been ill. Went to St Leonards to get her head straight. I decided, given her mental state and the circumstances, I'd better leave it all to interview.'

They were back at warp speed, cars pulling to the left to let them through.

'You weren't tempted,' Collins said, 'not even for a second, to give her a damned good push?'

Steve laughed. 'OK, I was, I admit it. But only briefly.'

'Normal reaction. Don't worry about it. The criminal justice system isn't the Catholic Church, thank God. No one's convicted on state of mind alone. If they were, I'd have been banged up years ago.'

'Me too. Came down in the end to too much paperwork.'

'That old chestnut.'

Steve honked his horn in warning at a fat black woman who was contemplating stepping on to a zebra crossing. The woman jumped backwards and put her hand to her chest, and then she was left behind. Collins sighed. She felt relief dropping into her like a soothing weight. She and Steve might both instinctively seek some obscure solace in jokes now that Lizzie had been found – and on the right side of the ledge – but she silently acknowledged to herself how far their words were from the truth of the matter and how terrible the alternative would have been.

Steve accelerated again.

Collins said, 'Can't work out whether the guv'nor would have been angry or pleased if she had jumped.'

'I suppose that depends on how the next twenty-four hours go. What time you meeting the bastard?'

'He said he'd be there for six.'

Collins stood in the deserted canteen, watching the coffee being dispensed from the machine. She checked her watch: 5:27. She had left Steve sleeping in the office. He had sprawled out in her chair, tilting it back, his legs up on the desk, his head thrown back against the headrest. The balance looked precarious but he was out for the count. She glanced over at the flat screen. Younes Mehenni was talking to camera. The man she had last seen drawn and exhausted by grief was now furious. Revived perhaps by the prospect of vengeance, he appeared almost exultant. Underneath, a ticker tape was running. *Portland Tower death fall: police officer arrested.* The cameras were loving it, jostling, pushing into Mehenni's face.

Collins shook her head. Holding her disposable cup, she wandered towards the screen. Mehenni's English, pressured by his emotion, was hard to understand, guttural and staccato. Listening carefully, she could make out '*I came to this country . . . a better life. Never thought . . . my daughter . . . dead.*' The image switched to the closed door of a semi-detached house somewhere outside London. The two police officers guarding it were impeccably turned out. They stood – beat helmets on, of course – with wary expressions of irreproachable neutrality. Hadley's wife evidently knew better than to talk to the press, but the journos were still camped outside, drinking their takeaways. In the foreground a male journalist with a receding hairline and big ears began delivering a piece to camera. The ticker tape running beneath had changed. So-called breaking news about some Premier League footballer who had been cheating on his wife.

347

Collins leaned over to the screen and turned it off. She took her coffee with her to the toilets. She pulled the travel toothbrush out of her bag and brushed her teeth, then splashed her face in the sink.

Baillie was sitting leafing through a copy of the Matthews/Mehenni case file. The photos of the dead PC and the girl were spread out on his desk. He took off his rimless reading glasses and gestured for her to come in.

'Everything tickety-boo?' he said.

'Think so.'

'Good. I've been up all fucking night changing nappies.'

'Sorry to hear that, boss.'

'You had enough sleep yourself?'

'Enough. Just about.'

'Steve found her at the tower?'

'Yes. Standing on the edge.'

'Bloody hell.'

'My thoughts exactly.'

In spite of himself, Baillie smiled. There was a pause.

'Any detail on what she's been up to for the past four days?'

'She said she went to St Leonards to get her head straight. Given that she was found standing on the edge of Portland Tower, it does sound as though she's been in a pretty bad way. But we know she's been in Eastbourne and Rye at least, and we're doing a CCTV trawl now of other stations along the line.'

'What about Shaw?'

'I bumped into him on my way down there. What's to say he wasn't going to meet her? I tried to stop him and I'm sure he avoided me.'

'How sure?'

'I crossed him on a country road. We both had to slow down and the road was narrow. We were within feet of each other. There was a tractor ahead. I put the blue lights on but I had to turn the car round and I couldn't catch him.'

'OK. So pretty sure but not evidentially sure.'

'Yes, sir.'

Baillie wrote something in his book. Collins waited before speaking again.

'The search team are at his address now, but he's had plenty of time to get rid of anything.'

There was the briefest tremor in Baillie's cheek, but he spoke patiently. 'If there was anything.'

'Yes, sir, if there was anything.'

Baillie looked at Collins shrewdly for a moment, and she sensed him getting the measure of her. But she too had made her calculations and estimated that if she did get any hard proof against Shaw, she could count on Baillie to be utterly ruthless in dropping him like a hot brick.

Baillie said, 'So how did Steve find her?'

'She called him on his mobile from Portland Tower.'

'He cell-sited her?'

'No. Didn't wait for that. Pure intuition. Blue-lighted it over there. Talked her away from the edge. Something about enough cops going off the roof of that particular tower.'

'Well thank fuck for that.' Baillie stretched back in his chair. 'Steve's a bloody good officer.'

'Yes, he is.'

At least they agreed on something.

'Where is he now?'

'Catching an hour's sleep. He's not been to bed at all.'

'And you?'

'I slept for an hour or so in the car outside Shaw's house.'

'OK.'

He gestured towards a chair. Collins sat down.

'You're opening up the suite in Victoria House?'

'With your permission, sir. When we're ready to interview Alice and Steve will drive her over: no point before then. DS Halford from team 4 has agreed to act as custody sergeant.'

Baillie nodded. 'Sounds like a plan.' He paused briefly. 'Listen, Sarah, I appreciate the excellent investigative job you've been doing, but I don't want any misunderstandings between us.'

'No, sir.'

'I want this dealt with within the first twenty-four hours. Is that clear? I don't expect you to come to me for extensions. You should have everything you need by now.'

Collins didn't want to make any promises she

couldn't keep. 'I've got some odds and ends to tidy up. And we need the results of the search, obviously. But we should be able to do it all within the twenty-four hours. The interview is key.'

'Of course. And you're taking Steve in with you?'

'Yes, sir.'

'Well, good luck. If you get some hard proof of misconduct you can be sure I will back you all the way.'

'I appreciate that, sir. Thank you.'

CHAPTER 43

Lizzie turned her head and took in the four walls of the cell. The heavy door that opened only from the outside. The marbleized concrete shelf on which lay a thin plastic-covered foam mattress. The low toilet with its constant trickle of blue disinfectant.

She stared up at the concrete ceiling. The usual notice pasted there came into focus like a film dissolve: *Don't want anything coming back to bite you? Take the opportunity for a fresh start. Let an officer know of any other offences so that they can be taken into consideration at an early stage.*

A fresh start: who, lying on this mattress, could ever believe such a thing possible?

Even so, there was something soothing about the enclosed nature of the place. No choices, just waiting. She was pleased to be horizontal and to be alone. She had a sense that everything had led her inexorably to this place.

She'd heard plenty of stories of other coppers who'd been nicked: stories that seemed to evoke a grudging admiration for the hopelessness and sheer stupidity of it all. A delight, even, in contemplating the possible fall, the precipice to be avoided at all costs. She'd heard of one old-timer who had spent his time in custody with his warrant card desperately hidden between his buttocks. He had probably been guilty of the usual transgressions arising from too much alcohol: public order, criminal damage. Then there were the domestic allegations. And of course the offences that put a copper way beyond the pale and made him fair game: sexual offences, child pornography. Officers couldn't distance themselves quickly enough from such filth. She would be something different again. Part of the final category: officers arrested for offences incurred in the course of their duty – violence, corruption, malfeasance, perversion. She would be a figure of ambivalence, a shape-shifter. Her association with Hadley's death would taint her irretrievably. She would be a broken mirror, someone who brought bad luck to the relief.

Hadley had been the sort of copper who seemed to have been born in uniform. The life had been second nature to him. They'd been teamed up and she had been supposed to learn the mysterious craft from him. He'd taken her under his wing. Everyone had known it was a mark of favour. The unspoken expectation had always been that eventually his old-fashioned coppering would rub off on her. Instead he was dead and she was under investigation.

The black toughened plastic of the cell's wicket slid down. It must be the half-hour check. A female

PC appeared at the Plexiglas opening. The girl was Asian and pretty. She had dark hair tied in a bun. Early twenties probably. She smiled apologetically, as if she had locked one of her friends away by accident.

'You OK?'

'Yes. I'm fine, thanks.'

'The skipper wants to know if you smoke. If you do, then he says that me and another officer can take you into the yard for a fag.'

'No, I'm all right. Thanks for the offer.'

'Cup of tea? I'll make you a proper one.'

'No. Thanks. I'm fine. Really.'

'OK. Well if you need anything, ring your bell.'

'I will. Thanks.'

The wicket slid shut again.

CHAPTER 44

Collins parked up a few houses down the road from number 5 Kenley Villas. She turned off the engine but did not move from the seat. 'Now what's the briefing, Jez?'

'Don't be a cock.'

Collins laughed. 'That's right. Don't speak unless you're spoken to. And above all—'

He sounded genuinely irritated. 'I know, don't be a cock.'

'Right again.' She turned to him and flashed him a rare smile. 'Thanks, Jez.'

He smiled back in spite of himself. 'Yeah, right. No worries.'

Jez got the kit out of the back of the car and he and Collins walked together along the street. Most of the press had dispersed, but a lone photographer, realizing they were cops, ran around the front of them and snapped some photos, the automatic shutter whirring. After they had passed, Jez muttered something quietly under his breath.

Uniformed police stood outside the doors to both number 5 and number 7. There was a For Sale sign in the front garden of Carrie Stewart's house. Collins showed her warrant card to the officer on the gate. As she walked down the path towards the front door, the curtain in the window of number 7 twitched. A woman in a hijab was staring at her, and Collins recognized her immediately as the woman who had stood motionless and alone at the cordon to the crime scene. She must be Farah Mehenni's grandmother. Collins wished she had not seen her: she could not stop herself imagining briefly the restlessness inside the house, the desperate emptiness that no justice could ever sate.

There was shrill barking and the Stewarts' spaniel appeared intermittently at the top of the leaded glass of the door as it jumped up. Peering down, Collins could also just make out the top of Ben's head, then the taller shape of Carrie Stewart approached the door. Collins steadied herself. She heard Mrs Stewart remonstrating with the boy – 'I've told you, Ben . . .' – and then the door opened.

Collins showed her warrant card. Jez was standing slightly behind, a tripod and bag slung over his shoulder, but he also had his warrant card in his right hand. Carrie Stewart, pulling the dog by his collar, stepped back into the hallway. 'Yes, come in.' Collins noticed at once the unspoken quality of the woman's supposedly casual clothes – the green cardigan was probably a cashmere mix – and the good set of her pearly little teeth. The teeth were the giveaway. She could dress as casually as she liked, but attention had been paid to the important things from the start. Carrie Stewart was either genetically highly favoured or she had had good dental treatment when it wasn't standard.

Collins followed Carrie down the hallway to the kitchen at the back of the property. The dog was jumping up, wagging his tail. Carrie said, 'Down, Charlie. Down. In your bed.' The dog curled up obediently by the window. Collins noticed the nice stripped pine table. What did they call it on eBay? Shabby chic, was it? An older, tweedy woman was sitting there and Carrie said, 'My mother, Jane. Mummy, this is Detective Sergeant Collins.'

Jane immediately got up in spite of Collins' protestations and offered her hand. 'Pleased to meet you, Detective Sergeant.'

'Sarah, please.'

'Sarah, yes, thank you. I've been staying with my daughter since it happened. She's been so upset.'

'Yes, of course,' Collins said, taking a seat at the table. 'That must be comforting for her.'

Jez sat beside her. He only spoke to accept coffee. He was taking the briefing seriously, and Collins noticed with a smile that the two women seemed to have decided that he was not important enough to warrant a proper introduction. Either that, or their good manners were failing them.

Ben came over and put his head on his grandmother's lap and said, 'Grannykins.' She ruffled his hair and he stole the opportunity to study Collins furtively.

Carrie was moving around the kitchen. She had one of those coffee-makers that needed to be heated on the stove. She turned on the tap and ran the used coffee grounds into the sink. Her back was turned and she spoke brusquely.

'I don't really see how Ben can help you. He's only five. If I'm honest, I'd rather we put it all behind us. I haven't been able to sleep for thinking about it. I keep going over and over what might have happened and of course what *did* happen. The moment I looked in the back garden and he had gone . . .'

Collins looked into the shady garden. There was a bench, a tree, a raised sandpit with a lid. A red plastic tricycle was lying on its side. The area was completely enclosed, separated from the neighbours by rickety wooden fencing panels.

Carrie put a plate of biscuits on the table. Collins glanced at her pale face, the browning freckles, the blonde hair with the slight kink in it. Carrie walked away and busied herself with the coffee-maker. The smell of ground beans filled the kitchen. She opened the fridge door and briefly revealed illuminated a bottle of wine, vegetables, juice and children's healthy yoghurts.

'I'd left him playing. I was upstairs on the phone to a friend. Suddenly I had a sense that something was wrong. I hadn't heard from him for so long. Usually that means he's being naughty. I looked out of the bedroom window and I couldn't see him. Of course I wasn't too worried at that point.

What could possibly have happened? He was in the house, for God's sake. I didn't run down the stairs or anything. I went out into the garden but he wasn't there. Just the dog looking around and wagging his tail. I couldn't believe it. Just couldn't bloody believe it. I thought he must be hiding. I thought it must be a game. I called out his name. God, all of a sudden it was awful. I looked everywhere. I searched the house and—'

The milk was boiling over and there was a smell of burning as it hit the stove top. Carrie swore under her breath with vehemence. 'Oh fuck.' Collins glanced at the grandmother and saw her eyebrows rise slightly. She caught Collins' eye and then lifted Ben up.

'Come on, Ben. I think the *Teletubbies* might be on.'

They waited for Ben to leave the room with his grandmother.

Jez started to get up to help Carrie but she shook her head. 'No, no, *please*. Don't worry.' He sat down obediently and glanced at Collins. Carrie was running a cloth under the water for longer than was strictly necessary. She squeezed it out and wiped the stove top. Steam rose from the cloth and she put it down on the work surface. She put her hands to her temples.

'So then I called the police . . .'

Collins said, 'Yes.' She had listened to the recording of the 999 call. She had heard Carrie's desperate voice, the operator struggling to get useful details from her. She watched Carrie pouring the coffee with what looked like an effort of concentration. Carrie put the nice little earthenware mugs in front of them and sat down. She had poured herself a glass of water and it glinted on the table untouched.

'So I'm still not sure about you talking to Ben.'

Collins took a breath to speak, but Carrie shook her head.

'No, before you interrupt . . .' She left the briefest pause to make sure she had been understood. 'Look at it from my point of view. Ben was abducted from our own home and taken to the top of a tower block, to the very edge. Who knows what that girl intended to do with him. Imagine that, would you? He also saw two people fall to their deaths. I can't bear to think about it, and you're asking us to encourage him to remember it all again. I think it's best that we put this behind us now. I can't see what information you can get from him, and if you don't mind me saying, what's to find out anyway?'

What's to find out anyway? That seemed to be the theme tune of the investigation. Collins waited. Carrie caught her eye. She pushed the biscuits across the table.

'Please, help yourselves. They don't look much but they're very good.'

Jez took a biscuit. 'Thank you.'

Carrie got up again. She stood at the sink and started to scrub the coffee-maker.

'That girl – I'm sorry, I still can't bring myself

to say her name – *that girl* took Ben from the garden and risked his life. That's not in question, is it? I still don't understand why that family wished me harm, why that man hated us so much. She took Ben from the garden, and the policeman, Matthews, went to the roof to find Ben and the poor man fell to his death . . .'

She trailed off, looking at Collins as if asking for confirmation. Collins knew that other officers would offer some word of anger towards the Mehenni family, and that this would be a consolation, but she could think of nothing she felt comfortable saying.

Carrie seemed to wake from a dream. 'I'm sorry. I didn't ask if you wanted sugar. Do you take sugar?'

'No, that's all right, thank you.'

There was a brief silence.

Jez said, 'Great coffee, thank you.'

Carrie smiled briefly at him. 'You're welcome.'

Collins allowed a moment's silence. Then she said, 'If I could talk to Ben, it would be really helpful. I don't doubt that Farah abducted him from your garden, but we need to find out more about what happened on the roof. I appreciate it's painful for you. Nevertheless, two people have died. I can't just leave it at that. There'll be an inquest. I'm sure you understand that I need to discover *why* they died. Farah Mehenni's family deserve that, so does the family of PC Matthews, and so do you.'

* * *

361

Carrie took them through to the sitting room. Ben and his grandmother were sitting with the dog, watching TV. Jane immediately got up to switch the television off but Collins put her hand up to stop her and said, 'No, please. Don't worry.'

Jane smiled and smoothed down her skirt. 'I'll leave you to it then.'

Collins remembered Ben well from the roof: the bear suit and his tear-stained face. Now the boy wore jeans and a checked shirt. She squatted down beside him but he did not take his eyes off the screen.

'You like *Teletubbies*?'

'I love *Teletubbies*.'

'Which is your favourite?'

'Po.'

'Which is Po?'

He pointed at the screen. 'The red one.'

Collins perched on the sofa next to Ben and watched the television. Rabbits came out of their burrows. The Teletubbies had a dance. Ben glanced towards her. 'Who are you?'

'My name's Sarah. I'm a police officer, just like PC Matthews and PC Griffiths. You remember them?'

'Yes. PC Matthews was a fat police officer.'

Ben seemed pleased with the idea that he was being naughty. Collins shunted away the memory of fat, naked, dead PC Matthews that came unbidden.

'Yes, he was.'

362

'If you're a police officer, where's your outfit?'

'My uniform?'

'Yes, your uni-form.'

'I don't wear one because I'm a special kind of police officer. I'm a detective. That means it's my job to find out what happened. The grown-ups still don't know what really happened. And Ben, you are very special because you are the only person who was there on the roof. So you know what happened and you can help me find that out.'

'PC Griffiths knows what happened. She was there too.'

Out of the corner of her eye Collins briefly caught Jez smirking. She pushed him out of her thoughts and pressed on.

'Well that's right. PC Griffiths knows what happened and you know what happened. But perhaps you know bits that PC Griffiths doesn't know. I need you to tell me what happened with Farah and the two police officers.'

She handed him her warrant card. Ben turned it over and ran his fingers over the metal indentations. Collins said, 'That stuff is Braille. It's for blind people. If we show our warrant card to them, they can read it with their fingers and know we're police.'

Ben looked at the warrant and back at Collins. 'PC Matthews is dead.' He handed back the card. Collins returned it to her pocket.

'That's right. PC Matthews is dead.'

'Dead is when you never wake up ever again.'

'Yes.'

'Mummy won't let me wear my bear costume any more.'

'No?'

'I like my bear costume.'

'I remember you wearing it on the roof. Do you remember me on the roof?'

He considered her for a moment and then said, 'No.'

'I arrived after PC Matthews and Farah had fallen.'

He frowned, his soft features barely creasing. 'Dunno, maybe.'

Collins got the video recorder out of her bag. 'Do you know what this is?'

'Camera.'

'That's right. Jez here is going to record what you have to say, because it is so important. Jez is a police officer too.'

'Is Jez a, a *detective* too?'

Collins smiled at Jez. She was tempted to say 'Sort of', and Jez tilted his head back as if daring her, but instead she said reluctantly, 'Yes, Jez is a detective too.'

Jez reached out his hand to take the camera. He had already set up the tripod and now he screwed the camera into the attachment.

Ben's voice was flat. 'Farah's dead too.'

'Yes.'

'She pinched me.'

'You can tell me about that.'

'She pinched me on the leg. I was on the bus with her and I wanted to go home and I tried to tell a lady and Farah pinched me.'

Suddenly Collins heard Carrie's voice. 'She *pinched* you?'

Collins glanced over her shoulder. She hadn't realized that Carrie was still there, but she saw her now, leaning against the door frame. A frown, curiously reminiscent of her son's, had knitted itself into her pleasant face.

Collins turned back to the child. 'Ben, you can tell me all about that in a moment. Do you mind if we turn the telly off? Is that OK?'

'Yes.'

Jez said quietly, 'All set, Sarah.'

Collins leant forward and switched off the television. She turned to Carrie. 'I'm sorry, you'll have to leave us while I do the interview. It's standard – Ben's a child, and so if you're in the room, he'll be influenced by you. He'll pick up on your concerns, try to please you, change his evidence. Do you see?'

Carrie's face was frozen into a stiff, anxious mask.

Collins said, 'Will that be OK?'

Carrie attempted a smile. She looked past Collins to her son.

'Ben, we'll watch *Teletubbies* together when you've finished, OK? I'll make hot chocolate and we can sit together with Granny on the sofa.'

He smiled. 'OK, Mummy.' He seemed to be the one offering comfort.

Collins said, 'Thank you. We won't be long.'

Carrie shut the door softly behind her. The room breathed in her absence. Collins waited to see the light on the camera come on.

'Ben, do you know what the truth is?'

Ben paused. He pulled his lips to one side. 'The truth is . . .'

'Yes?'

He threw his head back and to the side as though the answer was hidden somewhere in the corner of the ceiling behind him. Finally he said, 'I don't know.'

'That's OK. Do you know what a lie is?'

He smiled: this one was easy. 'That's when you don't tell the truth.'

'That's right. Can you give me an example?'

'Like if I said that Charlie had eaten a biscuit when really I had eaten it.'

Collins smiled at the example. Perhaps Ben had had cause to use it already. 'That's good. And why shouldn't you lie?'

'Because then you tell lie after lie and when you do tell the truth no one will believe you.'

The answer had come out pat and Collins suspected that this matter had been explained to Ben on more than one occasion.

'That's right. Any other reason?'

'You might get found out and then Mummy would be cross.'

Collins smiled. 'And that's right too, Ben. OK. Very good. But it's also important to tell the truth simply because it is the truth. Because telling the truth is the right thing to do.'

Ben frowned and Collins regretted her last comment. She didn't want to frighten him. She smiled. 'Will that be OK, Ben?'

He smiled back. 'Yes.'

'OK. And you won't miss anything out? It's important you tell me everything you remember. No one will be cross if you have to say bad words because those bad words might be part of what happened. Do you understand that? I won't be cross and your mummy won't be cross and not even your granny.'

'OK.'

'Just the truth, and no one will mind anything you say.'

'OK.'

'So, tell me what happened from when you went with Farah.'

The dog jumped off the sofa and stretched himself out on the floor. Ben picked him up again and Charlie's back legs dangled. Ben sat down, imprisoning the long-suffering animal on his lap.

'I was playing in the garden with Charlie. Farah came into the garden and she said if I went with her I could have sweets.'

He stroked the dog.

'White chocolate drops, my favourite. I didn't

think Mummy would be cross because she doesn't like the daddy at all but she is always nice to Farah, so I said yes and I did this . . .' he stretched up his arms and stood on his tiptoes, 'and she lifted me over the fence and took me into her garden and she said we had to go to the shop to buy the sweets. We went down her hall. It's dark, not like ours. And there isn't a dog. We went out of her front door and along the street in front of our house. Then she took me on the bus. At first I liked it because I like the bus but then I was frightened. I said Mummy would be cross. I said, I want to go home now. She said, No, Ben. You can't go home now. You've got to come with me. I said to a lady on the bus, I want to go home. But Farah said I was naughty and she pinched me on my leg.

'I was crying. She said, Don't cry. But it wasn't nice when she said it. It was like telling me off. And I was worrying about Charlie because I had left him in the garden. Then we got off the bus and we walked a long way. I said I didn't like it but she pulled me by my hand. She said we would get the sweets soon but we didn't go to a shop. We went into this building. It was smelly and dirty. She made me go up lots of steps, then she put me over the wall and I was crying because I was frightened.'

'OK.'

'I said, I want to go home now. Please. I want to go home. And she said no. She kept saying no and she said I was a naughty boy. Then the fat policeman came and he said hello.'

'Hello?'

Ben nodded.

'Did he say anything else?'

Ben looked at her earnestly. He spoke as though this was the most important bit, as though she had entirely missed the point. 'The policeman fell.'

Collins took a breath. 'That's right. PC Matthews fell.'

'And Farah fell.'

'Yes, Farah fell too.' Collins waited for a moment, then she reached out her hand and touched Ben gently on his arm. 'I want you to think about this bit, the bit when you are on the roof and PC Matthews is on the roof too. The bit before he fell. Are you concentrating, Ben?'

The dog was looking up into his face and Ben pulled his ears at the root.

Collins said, 'Before PC Matthews fell, what happened then? Tell me about that, from the moment that PC Matthews arrived and said hello.'

There was a pause. Then Ben said, 'I was holding her hand very tight. I didn't want to fall.'

'Yes, it was very high and you were frightened. You were holding Farah's hand very tight. Then the fat policeman came, PC Matthews, and he said hello. Tell me as much as you can about what happened next.'

Ben scrunched up his face, irritated. 'I don't know. They were talking.'

'Talking?'

'I don't know. I wasn't listening. I wanted to go home.'

'Anything?'

'The policeman was talking and Farah was angry.'

'OK. Farah was angry. What did she say?'

'I was frightened.'

'Of course.'

He shook his head. He was biting his lip now. She waited.

'The policeman told me to hold her hand. I could see police cars with blue lights and lots of people. I couldn't hear what they were saying. I thought Mummy would be very cross with me and I was frightened. Then the nice police lady came. She said, Climb over to me and hold on very tight like a bear. And then I climbed to the nice police lady like she told me to. I held on very tight.'

'Yes, you did. Well done.'

'Then I was safe but Farah and the policeman fell.'

He started to cry. The dog struggled out of his arms and jumped on to the floor. Ben squatted beside him and played with the scruff of his neck. The dog rolled on to his back. Collins waited.

'We're nearly finished, Ben. OK?'

He carried on stroking the dog's belly. 'OK.'

She put a hand on his shoulder. 'Ben, sit on the sofa again for me, would you? I need you to think very hard.'

He did as he was told. He wiped his hand across his face but he looked still on the edge of tears.

'You can have Charlie on your lap if you want. Yes?'

He nodded, and she passed him the dog.

'OK, nearly done. Just go back a bit. Tell me what they said. That's very important. What did PC Matthews and Farah say?'

'He told me to hold her hand.'

'Did he say anything else?'

Ben shook his head. 'I don't know. I was frightened.' His features puckered again into a soft frown. 'Are you cross?'

'I'm not cross, no. Why would I be cross?'

'Anyway, you can ask the nice police lady what they said because she was there.'

'Ben, I know you're trying really hard and it's really, really difficult. It would be difficult for a grown-up too. I would like you to try for just a moment longer. Then we're done. Tell me everything you remember, because you might remember something important. Will you do that for me?'

His face was constricted, as though someone had pulled it tight with a drawstring. Collins was worried he was going to start crying again.

Jez said quietly, 'Sarah . . .'

She looked at him sharply, but her voice did not betray her. 'We're nearly finished.'

Ben said, 'I can't remember.'

'All right.'

'The nice police lady came. She was kind. Kind to me. Kind to Farah.'

'Kind?'

He pressed his lips together.

'Can you remember what she said, the police lady? What did she say?'

'She told me to trust Farah. Farah said she could fly. She said, I can fly. Do you believe me? The police lady said I should trust her so I said yes, but I didn't really. Anyway she couldn't fly, could she? Then the police lady said, Hold tight like a bear. She said climb over and I climbed over. I held on very, very tight.'

'Farah said she could fly?'

'Yes.'

'And then PC Griffiths told you to climb over?'

'Yes.'

'So, I'm sorry. I'm not clear, Ben. Farah *let* you climb over?'

'Yes. At first she wouldn't let me and then she did and I climbed over.'

'So what changed? Why did she let you climb over?'

'I dunno.'

A pause.

'OK.'

Another pause.

'Ben, do you think Farah really thought she could fly?'

Ben smiled. 'Of course not. She was kind of showing off.'

'Showing off?'

'Yes.'

'And she said, I am innocent too.'

'I am innocent too?'

'Yes.'

'What did she mean?'

'I dunno. I just remember it because she said it so loud.' He raised his voice. 'I AM INNOCENT TOO.'

'OK. That's really good. Can you think of anything else, Ben? Anything.'

He shook his head. 'No.'

'And then, after you climbed over, then what happened?'

'I was holding on to the police lady.'

'And PC Matthews and Farah? What were they doing?'

'I don't know. The police lady was cuddling me. Then she made a funny noise and I turned and the policeman and Farah weren't there any more.'

Jez had a lollipop in his trouser pocket. He pulled it out and showed it discreetly to Collins. 'Do you think it would be all right?'

'Probably better not. Not without Mum's permission.'

Collins left Ben in front of the telly. Jez packed up the equipment.

Carrie and her mother, both in aprons and yellow rubber gloves, were at the kitchen table cleaning silver. There wasn't much – a rose vase, a battered silver plate, candlesticks. Jane looked up from a tall, twisted candlestick and said, 'I'm sorry, Detective Sergeant. We didn't know how long you'd be and we've always enjoyed cleaning the silver together. Silly really.'

'That's all right. I turned the telly back on for Ben. I hope that's all right.'

Jane said, 'Could I ask you something, Sarah?'

'Certainly.'

'I'm sorry to ask. But you can imagine, it's difficult.'

'What is it?'

'The family next door, is there any chance they'll move now?'

Collins remembered the For Sale sign in the front garden and felt a sudden stab of sympathy. She knew that the local authority had offered Mehenni a move but so far he had turned it down. She said, 'I don't think so. Not in the foreseeable future anyway. You know property is really difficult in London.'

Carrie pushed a stray hair away from her face distractedly and smudged her forehead with her dirty glove. 'All done, then?'

'Yes. Thank you for letting us speak to Ben.'

There was a pause.

Collins said, 'Jez has got a lollipop. Would it be all right for him to give it to Ben?'

Carrie smiled but she looked exhausted, pale and worn. 'Yes. Why not? This thing has put lollies into perspective.' She was pulling off her gloves. 'I'll show you to the door.'

With Jez and the camera equipment it was a squeeze in the hallway. The dog had followed them out and was threading between their legs. Ben was hanging back, sucking at his lolly.

Jez gave a little wave. 'Bye, fella.'

He went ahead, down the pathway towards the car.

Carrie offered Collins her hand. 'I'm sorry if I was rude earlier. I'm pleased you came.'

'You weren't rude.'

'Did you get everything you need?'

'Well, Ben did his best—'

Carrie interrupted. Her face had tightened up and her voice had the sudden urgent whisper of a confidence being given. 'I just can't believe she *pinched* him. It's a detail, I know, nothing in the scheme of things, but somehow . . . I don't believe in capital punishment and I know it's terrible, but I can't help myself. I'm pleased that girl is dead. I am. I am.'

Jez and Collins sat in the car in silence. Collins turned the engine over.

Jez said, 'You did a good interview, Sarah. He was just too young.'

'Thanks. And thanks for helping me.'

'Not a problem. You're doing a good job. It isn't easy.'

Collins indicated left but still she did not pull away from the house. She found it hard to let go of her hope that the facts of that conversation on the roof could be retrieved from the imperfect palimpsest of the boy's memory.

CHAPTER 45

The interview room was conspicuous by its neatness. There were three cups of water, pre-written tape seals, a pile of fresh tapes, a box of tissues; no scraps of paper, no discarded tape wrappers. A closed lever-arch file waited on the table.

Steve was showing Lizzie in, and as they took their seats, Collins unsealed the tapes and slotted them into the machine. She pressed record and the machine buzzed.

'We are in Interview Room One, Victoria House. My name is DS Sarah Collins. Also present is . . . If you would introduce yourselves, please.'

'DC Steve Bradshaw.'

Lizzie looked across at the detective constable. His notebook was open in front of him and he waited for her to speak, pen in hand.

'PC Lizzie Griffiths.'

Collins resumed. 'PC Griffiths, you've been arrested on suspicion of perverting the course of justice and misconduct in public office. Do you understand the offences?'

'Yes.'

'You don't have to say anything but it may harm your defence if you do not mention when questioned something which you later rely on in court. Anything you do say may be given in evidence. Do you understand the caution?'

'Yes.'

'So you'll understand me then when I tell you that saying nothing can be just as harmful as giving an account.'

'Yes.'

'Do you want to tell me why you've declined legal representation?'

'Because I don't need it.'

'You can change your mind at any time.'

'Yes, I understand that.'

Collins leaned back in her seat and took a moment to consider PC Lizzie Griffiths. Her appearance had changed significantly since Collins had seen her first on the roof of Portland Tower. She wore faded jeans and a dark T-shirt. Her hair was peroxide bleached, a little yellow, cut short and scruffy. She looked thinner, pale and tired, and yet somehow, in spite of everything, she had remained pretty in the way that was only available to the young. It was an unconscious splendour, a healthy excellence that had survived all assaults and was, perhaps, even sweetened by her fragility.

Steve said, 'Lizzie, we just want to know what happened.'

Collins said, 'Sometimes people do things that are wrong for the best possible reasons.'

Lizzie made no reply.

Collins took out a bunch of photographs and laid them on the table. Lizzie picked up one of them and stared at it for a while. Farah was lying on the pavement with her arm outstretched. Lizzie put it back on the table. Collins handed her another: Farah naked before the post-mortem. Her body was astonishingly unmarked by the fall. Her unblemished skin was sallow, her breasts just budding.

Collins said, 'I've attended many autopsies but I've never got used to them.' She sought out Lizzie's eyes and paused, but Lizzie avoided her gaze, looking down at the table. Collins went on, her tone matter-of-fact: they were both professionals. 'The point is to establish the cause of death, as you'll know. In Farah's case there were no surprises. Sudden deceleration. That's always, in some shape or form, the cause of death in a fall. The human body hitting the hard ground too fast. On the outside she appears almost untouched. Inside she's mush. It's like hitting the internal organs with a hammer.'

Suddenly Lizzie shuddered, and in an instant Collins saw her as she had been up on the roof. Shocked, horrified. She had to suppress an unexpected impulse to forgive.

She said, 'We just want to know how this came to happen.'

Lizzie looked up. Her face was set like stone, hard and tense. She said, 'Could you put the pictures away, please?'

Steve gathered them up carefully and slowly, slipping them into their plastic folder. Collins waited.

'OK,' she said, taking a breath. 'Let's go back to the beginning. You attended Farah's home address to make arrest inquiries. A complaint resulted from that against PC Matthews. Farah said he was a racist.'

Lizzie's right hand fluttered briefly like a butterfly against a closed window.

'No.'

'No?'

She trapped her wayward hand beneath the firmer left one and rested them both on the table. 'I don't think Farah said PC Matthews was a racist.'

'No?'

'I believe the allegation was not that Hadley was racist but that he had said racist things, or things of a racist nature, something like that, but I'm not sure.'

It was an interesting objection, and perhaps fruitful. Collins glanced at Steve's notes.

'Racist things, or things of a racist nature. What do you mean by that?'

Lizzie hesitated, perhaps aware that she was being drawn into a conversation that could do her no benefit. 'I was never shown the complaint.'

'But if you could explain your phrase, please. What did you mean?'

The gap between Lizzie's eyebrows puckered into a little frown.

'Nothing really. It's just that Hadley – that is, PC Matthews – he had a way of saying things that could be misinterpreted.'

'Misinterpreted?'

'Yes.'

The impulse to forgive had vanished. 'What do you mean?'

'He put pressure on people. Some people might put two and two together and make five, but Hadley was no racist.'

'But he may have said racist things?'

'No. He may have been misunderstood.'

'But how could he have been misunderstood? In your statement you say . . .' Steve opened the lever-arch file. Inside it was neatly ordered and colour-coded. He handed Collins a typewritten sheet and Collins put on her glasses and scanned it. 'Yes . . . Here we are. *I heard the whole conversation between Farah Mehenni and PC Matthews . . . He never said anything out of place and certainly nothing of a racist nature.*' She paused. 'If he never said anything out of place, let alone of a racist nature, then how could he possibly have been misunderstood?'

'I don't know.'

Collins could see that Lizzie was getting anxious. 'Perhaps we could clear this up by you telling me exactly what he did say.'

'I can't remember much detail, but if he had said something racist I would have remembered it. What I'm saying is, it would have stuck in my

381

memory, definitely. I would have been shocked. He said he needed to speak with her dad. We'd have to keep coming round until we'd spoken with him. That's all I remember now. It's in my statement.'

'OK.'

There was something here that was bothering Lizzie, some grit that irritated, and Collins waited for her to speak.

Lizzie said, 'But . . .'

Collins couldn't help smiling for just a brief second. 'Yes?' she prompted gently.

'Well, his manner . . .'

'His manner? Collins scanned the statement again. '*PC Matthews was polite throughout.*'

Lizzie shrugged. 'Polite, yes, but . . .'

'Yes?'

'But firm.'

It was time to move on. This might be helpful stuff, but at the end of the day it was just quibbles, circumstantial material that would only assist if it was supported by something more definite, some damning fact or omission. She needed to keep the interview flowing.

Collins said, 'Well, we'll come back to PC Matthews' manner later in the interview. But there's nothing in your statement that suggests Farah Mehenni could have in any way misunderstood him. The other explanation, of course, is that Farah was lying in *her* statement.'

Lizzie frowned. 'I don't want to say she was lying.'

'Oh, why not?'

Lizzie coughed and wiped her hand across her mouth. 'Because she's dead, Sergeant Collins. Because she was just a child.'

There was a pause. Lizzie put her head in her hands and gripped her hair tightly.

Steve said, 'Are you OK to continue?'

Lizzie didn't look up. Her voice was strained. 'Yes. For Christ's sake. Let's get this over with.'

Collins said, 'You're sure?'

Lizzie let go of her hair and looked up. She took a breath. 'Yes.'

Collins looked at Steve, worried for a moment that she could lose the whole interview if she were judged to have overstepped the mark or to have continued when the subject was in no state to answer.

Steve said gently, 'Lizzie, you're sure you want to go on?'

Lizzie spoke impatiently. 'I'm OK. I've been assessed. I'm fit for interview.'

Collins said, 'OK. We'll continue. Your statement . . . Hadley said you would corroborate his account. But you didn't provide a statement until nearly three weeks afterwards.'

'I provided an account of the arrest inquiries . . .'

'Yes, in which you didn't mention anything about this overheard conversation.'

'I was asked to give a clarifying statement, because of the complaint.'

'Who asked for that?'

'Inspector Shaw.'

Lizzie glanced across the table. Steve was making a note in his book.

'I hadn't realized that the conversation in the hallway was of any significance,' Lizzie said. 'I had been more anxious to cover the pursuit of Younes Mehenni and Farah's attempt to obstruct us – her climbing on to the car. That was the stuff that seemed worrying at the time of writing the statement.'

'Eighteen days. Eighteen days between the arrest inquiries and the date on your second statement.'

'Once I'd been asked for it, it took me a while to get round to it.'

'To get round to it?'

'Yes.'

'Why was that?'

Lizzie opened her hands slightly. 'I was busy. We were always busy on team.'

'I don't believe that.'

Lizzie threaded her fingers and brought her palms together. She did not answer.

'Top of your class at training school. By the time you were only six months in, you already had one commendation under your belt. Doesn't sound like you're the type of person who takes time to get round to stuff.'

Lizzie glanced at Steve as if looking for help, but his face was dispassionate.

Collins said, 'A mentor, someone who took you under his wing – that's how everyone describes

PC Matthews' relationship to you, but it takes you eighteen days to write a statement supporting him.'

Lizzie nodded. DS Collins leaned forward.

'You'll have to speak. The tape doesn't record anything it can't hear.'

'Yes. It took me eighteen days to write the statement.'

'What's the explanation for that? What are you? Lazy? Selfish?'

'Neither.'

'No, I don't think you are. Quite the opposite.'

Lizzie's eyes flicked to Steve again. He was looking down, writing.

Collins said, 'I think it took you so long to write the statement because you couldn't bring yourself to lie but you also couldn't bring yourself to tell the truth. Either you heard Hadley say the things that Farah accused him of or you simply didn't hear the conversation at all. So for eighteen days you did nothing.'

'No.'

'Remember to speak up for the tape.'

'I've answered your question.'

'I don't think you have. A usually diligent officer—'

'I just didn't get round to it. And OK, no excuses for not writing the statement sooner.'

'Lizzie, it's not a question of excuses. I'm looking for an explanation. A normally conscientious officer fails to write a statement. And not just any old statement – your colleague PC Matthews *needed* you to make that statement. But for eighteen days you were silent.'

Collins stopped and waited. Lizzie spoke so quietly that she could not be heard.

Steve looked up from his pad. 'I'm sorry?'

She shook her head. 'Nothing.'

Collins tapped the desk impatiently. 'Come on, Lizzie, tell the truth. We all know it's never going to be all right to call people Bin Laden. Those days are over. Hadley already had a warning on his file for a similar incident. If the complaint had been upheld, he would have been dismissed from the service. Gross misconduct. All the disgrace of that and, with only three years to go, the loss of his pension. Not a good prospect after thirty years. That's the crux of it, isn't it? He asked you for your support?'

'No.'

'He asked for your support and you quite rightly refused.'

Lizzie caught herself chewing the inside of her lip. She shook her head and then remembered that she needed to speak. 'No.'

'And then, after eighteen days, something changed, didn't it? What changed?'

'Nothing.'

Lizzie sipped her water. There was silence.

Collins was reading again, her finger tracing the line of typeface. 'He asked her *general questions.*'

She looked up. 'General questions? What *exactly* did he say?'

'I can't remember, not exactly. It's a long time ago. He asked where her father was. Hadley had a way about him. I'm sure the other officers will have told you. A way of . . . of getting what he wanted. That's why I think the girl might have thought he said something racist. But he didn't. He was the same with her as he was with everyone else . . .'

'Yes, and he had a warning on his file for this way of getting what he wanted – as I've mentioned.'

'I didn't hear him say anything reprehensible.'

'Perhaps you didn't hear him say anything. You were with the grandmother.'

Lizzie remembered being outside in the cold yard. The scrubby pruned buddleia sprouting out of the concrete. The persistent angry voice down the phone. Then, when she had moved back into the kitchen, the shadowy figure of Farah in the hallway.

'No. I was in the kitchen. I could hear what was said.'

'Lizzie, I've read your other statements and they run to several pages. You don't usually generalize. There's no explanation for this one being so short.'

'I was tired. It had been a long shift.'

Collins removed her glasses, holding them in her right hand. 'I know about that long shift. Cosmina was your first murder? You did well, you and Hadley. You were both up for commendations at

387

the end of it all. But one minute you're talking to Cosmina and the next minute she's being cut open. Your first post-mortem. As I said earlier, I've still not got used to them. Pretty harrowing, was it? And after a long night like that, you found the time to write a statement on an unrelated matter. Impressive.'

'Is there a question there for me?'

'It was a long, hard night and at the end of it you decided to back Hadley. It's an understandable mistake, Lizzie. You were inexperienced and under a lot of pressure.'

'No.'

'Tell me about writing the statement. You wrote it sixteeen hours after you'd gone on duty. It had waited nearly three weeks. Why couldn't it wait one more day?'

'I remembered I hadn't done it. I'd gone past tired by that point – why not sit for another thirty minutes? And yes, it did feel more important to write the damn thing. Hadley had tried to save Cosmina. We'd been on our own for a time. Hadley got a civilian to put the door in and we went into the house. After that I realized how important it was to back him, that he was a good copper and that we needed to stick together. But that doesn't mean I lied, only that I finally sat down and wrote it. Perhaps that's why the statement's so short. I was exhausted and I wanted to bash it out and get to bed after a very long shift. Or perhaps it was short because there simply wasn't much to say.'

'A very long and difficult shift. You were upset. You made a mistake.'

'No.' Lizzie folded her arms across her chest like a child: she had said all she was going to say on the subject. But when Collins did not ask another question, she blurted out angrily, 'That conversation in the hallway: it was the biggest non-event ever.'

Collins raised her head. 'Two people dead at the end of it all. That's not a non-event.'

She reached in her handbag and took out a tube of Polo mints. She offered it across the table. She said, 'For the tape: I am offering PC Griffiths a Polo.'

'No thanks.'

She pushed a mint up with her thumb and popped it into her mouth. The interview was going well. Lizzie was riled. She needed to keep the pressure up, keep manipulating the pace and the disclosure of evidence. Steve took a mint too. He tilted his notebook towards Collins and she slipped her glasses back on to read.

'*We needed to stick together*? Could you clarify?'

Lizzie looked at Steve. He said, 'Well, Lizzie?'

'Yes, we need to stick together. To stand up for each other. But not beyond a certain point.'

Collins interrupted. 'A certain point? Where's the line, then?'

Lizzie allowed herself to be exasperated. 'The law, obviously. That's the line. Bloody hell, why else am I here? Support each other, yes, but not beyond the point where we are breaking the law.'

'The law, then, that's the line?'

'What do you want me to say? OK, integrity, that's a line too.'

'But might there be a conflict perhaps between integrity and obeying the law? Or perhaps . . .' Collins searched for her exact meaning. 'Perhaps integrity sometimes feels like sticking up for people rather than telling the truth . . . and then the law feels . . . well, how can I put it, not quite the point? That's understandable. Perhaps saying you'd heard a conversation you hadn't didn't seem like such a big deal after you'd recently seen someone's chest cavity secateured open. In the grand scheme of things that might have felt, well, like how you described the conversation in the hallway – a non-event.'

Lizzie remembered the heft and purpose of the body's deconstruction under the mortuary's stark fluorescence. The whine and smell of the saw. The body like cuts of meat, of bone and cartilage and brain. The plastic bags and jars. The gloves slimed in blood beyond the elbow.

Collins prompted gently, 'Did it, Lizzie?'

'No.'

'No?'

Lizzie looked up. She was emphatic, her voice loud for the first time in the interview. 'I didn't lie.'

It had been the emphasis perhaps of someone determined to see the interview through, but nevertheless it was no confession. Collins had felt as if she could almost reach out and take it, but it was like the twist of a fish in water that offered only the sensation of movement, an intimation of the thing itself.

'Did Mr Shaw have a view on any of this? He's an experienced officer. Did he talk to you, perhaps, about *sticking together*?'

'No, he asked me to write a clarifying statement. That's it.'

'You were in a relationship with Inspector Shaw.'

There was a pause. 'Yes.'

'You were in love?'

Lizzie shrugged.

Collins leaned back in her chair. She allowed Lizzie's reluctance to use the word *love* to sink into her, and the youthfulness of Lizzie's caution expanded within her like a flavour. She was so young, so young for so much to turn on her.

'Well, did you love him?'

Lizzie sighed. 'I don't know. I think so. I thought so.'

There was something there, and Collins gave herself a moment to consider it. Then she said, 'Something has changed between you?'

Lizzie looked at her and her eyes narrowed. 'A lot has changed, Sergeant.'

Perhaps that question had been a mistake. Lizzie's defiant tone suggested that it had steadied her. Collins turned to Steve.

'Would you get out the CCTV images, please?'

Steve unclipped a plastic folder from the file and took out some full-colour images. He passed them across the desk. They were screen grabs of Lizzie on Polegate station, walking beside the woman with the dyed red hair and pushing a pram.

Steve read out the exhibit numbers. 'SJB/5, SJB/6, SJB/7 . . .'

Collins said, 'Did you meet Mr Shaw yesterday?'

Lizzie passed the images back. 'No.'

'Did you call him?'

'Yes.'

'You used a pre-paid mobile. Why?'

'I didn't want to be found.'

'What did you talk about?'

'Not much. He told me to make myself known to police.'

'So what were you doing in Polegate yesterday?'

'Wandering.'

'Wandering?'

'Yes, I've been all over. St Leonards, Hastings, Rye, Eastbourne . . .'

'Let's talk about this not wanting to be found. After Hadley and Farah died, you went absent without leave.'

'Yes.'

'You ended up standing in the darkness on the edge of Portland Tower.'

Silence.

'You thought, perhaps, of jumping?'

There was no reply.

'Tell me about that.'

Silence again. Then Lizzie said, 'I can't.'

'You can't? Why not?'

Lizzie closed her eyes. Here was something at

last: the darkness. Collins sought the question that would reach into it. She waited. Lizzie opened her eyes, as if recollecting herself, but she said nothing.

'Why would you despair?' Collins said.

Lizzie bent over the table and pressed her forehead into the heel of her hands.

Collins said, 'I only want the truth. I just want to know what happened.'

Lizzie did not move.

Collins waited. The time stretched and was alive and then, incontrovertibly, became lifeless. Lizzie would not speak.

Collins said, 'Seventeen twenty-five hours. I'm suspending the interview.'

Steve offered to put Lizzie in her new cell and sign her back while Collins updated the boss.

They met in the canteen and sat opposite each other with coffees. Collins had got herself a muffin but did not eat it.

She said, 'This interview is the only thing we've got.'

'You're getting very close.'

'Let's give her five more minutes on her own. That might be all she needs.'

'Eighteen twenty hours. I'm resuming the interview. DS Collins present. Also present . . .'

'DC Steve Bradshaw.'

'PC Lizzie Griffiths.'

'You're still under caution, Lizzie. You understand that?'

'Yes.'

'You're still entitled to legal advice.'

'I know.'

'Tell me about the roof.'

'I was drawn back to it.'

'No, the first time, when Farah was there with Ben. You got there very quickly?'

'Yes. I broke the law. I drove on blue lights.'

'Why did you do that?'

Lizzie looked suddenly directly at Collins, and Collins saw something new in her expression, a determination, as if Lizzie had newly resolved on some frightening enterprise, like scaling a rock face or jumping from a significant height, and in spite of her trepidation was set upon seeing it through.

'About five days previously I had received a phone call from Farah Mehenni. She was upset with me. She thought I'd promised her father a caution and I'd let her down. She said she was desperate about him being charged and she wanted to talk. There was a place she liked, a place she had found that no one knew about.'

It was rubbish, nonsense. The call had been about the phone. Collins had to compose her expression to hide her angry contempt. But Lizzie's story was in deadly earnest and there was just enough truth there for it to hold. The only way to show the lie was to treat it as if it were the truth, to probe its fault lines until it fractured.

Collins said, 'And that place was the roof of Portland Tower?'

Lizzie looked at her with a tiny frown before answering. 'Yes. I charged Younes Mehenni at about two o'clock in the afternoon. I was in the police station putting the final touches to the case papers. When I heard the description of a five-year-old missing boy, I knew straight away it was Ben.'

'Because of the bear suit?'

'Yes. When we reported the initial allegation at his house, he was wearing a bear suit. And then I heard there were some figures on the top of Portland Tower . . .'

'So you realized at once that the incidents were linked, and you were so worried that you used blue lights when you weren't authorized.'

'Yes, I did. Everything I knew about Farah was worrying—'

Collins interrupted. 'And PC Matthews, had you told him about the phone call from Farah?'

'No, I didn't tell anyone.'

'I ask because PC Matthews . . . Well, you were *quick*, but PC Matthews was . . .' Matthews was a fucking time lord, she thought. 'PC Matthews was even quicker. How did he know Farah and Ben were there?'

'I don't know.' Lizzie sighed as if suddenly exhausted by it all. 'You'd have to ask him.'

Collins brushed aside her own irritation at Lizzie's sarcasm. She needed to stay on track, to keep the pace of the questions up.

'And how had Farah got hold of your telephone number?'

'I'd given it to her. I gave it to her when I went to persuade her to get her father to hand himself in.'

Collins cursed herself: the story was firm, organized. Bits of it were true, other bits false, and it was proving impossible to sift out the lies. That time in the cell was supposed to have led Lizzie closer to a giving-up of the truth. Instead the opposite had happened. The story had emerged fully formed, flawless. It was as if in the short interval, while Collins had sat in the canteen with Steve, Lizzie had remade herself.

'The phone call from Farah. The one where she asked to meet you. You reported it, of course.'

'No.'

'Why not?'

'I was embarrassed. I had been warned not to give witnesses or suspects my personal mobile but I'd gone ahead and done it. I'd had a bet with Hadley that I could get Younes to hand himself in and I'd been too keen to win it. After the call I told Farah not to call me again and changed my number. Of course I regret not reporting it now.'

'And did you tell Inspector Shaw?'

'No.'

The interview, it seemed to Collins, was a skein of denial, and yet everywhere she applied pressure, it held.

She said, 'There was a recording.'

Lizzie didn't answer.

Collins insisted. 'Farah's father says there was a recording.'

Lizzie looked her directly in the face but did not speak.

'Farah's father told me that she recorded that conversation with Hadley in the hallway—'

Lizzie interrupted, allowing herself to be impatient. 'That's different, of course, from there actually being a recording.'

'If you'd let me finish—'

'But that's just nonsense.'

'No, what you are saying is nonsense. That phone call from the payphone – that was to tell you about the recording. You panicked because you had given a false statement and so you told Hadley about Farah's call. Younes Mehenni says Hadley took the phone from Farah by force.'

Lizzie's hands were clasped together and she dug her thumbnail into her palm.

Steve said, 'Is that what happened, PC Griffiths?'

She blinked slowly.

'No, that isn't what happened.' She paused. 'I've told you what happened.'

Collins resisted the nagging presentiment that the investigation was in fragments: at the centre of it, a void that could not be knitted together.

Years ago, on holiday with her parents, she had swum over the drop of a loch and seen, beneath her childish white legs, the land shelve away to unknowable depths.

She said, 'Tell me what happened on the roof.'

Lizzie tilted her head towards the ceiling. When she looked back at Collins, her face was tight with tension.

'I find it hard to think about it . . .'

'Well, do your best.'

'I can't remember it.'

'Nothing?'

Lizzie bent forward. She cleared her throat and then began to cough, as if something was stuck in her throat. It was quite clearly genuine and the coughing was getting worse: she retched, and Collins was afraid she might even be sick. Steve got up and patted her on the back. He offered her water. She took it and gained control of herself, wiping her mouth on a tissue from the box.

Steve said quietly, 'Shall we stop for a bit?'

Looking down at the desk, Lizzie shook her head. 'No, no. Let's finish. I want to finish.' Then, after a pause, she said quietly, 'I don't want to remember.'

Collins nodded. 'Farah said, "I am innocent too." Do you remember that?'

Lizzie looked up but she did not reply. Her face was pale and smeared.

Collins said, 'Why would she say that?'

There was a pause. Lizzie wiped her face with the back of her sleeve. She looked drained, utterly exhausted.

'Well, I think I said to her that Ben was innocent and she didn't want to harm a child, and maybe she said it then. She let him go. He climbed over to me.'

Collins felt herself releasing her hope of revealing the truth. It was like opening her hand and watching a stone fall away into deep water.

'Let me guess,' she said. 'You didn't see them fall?'

Lizzie looked her in the face, and in spite of herself, Collins felt an unexpected compassion.

'That's right. I didn't see them fall.'

Collins remembered those two bodies on the concrete, and Lizzie pale and shaking on the roof.

She said, 'About twenty minutes before she took Ben, Farah tried to call you. But you had changed your number.'

Lizzie looked down at the desk and shook her head. She mumbled something and drew her hand across her face.

Collins said, 'I didn't catch that.'

Lizzie continued to look down. 'I don't know. I don't know.'

Collins waited but Lizzie remained silent. Collins said, 'Your training sergeant at Hendon described you as an idealist.'

Lizzie looked up and a shadow of a smile passed briefly across her troubled face, as if she had glimpsed a memory long gone. 'Did he?'

Collins did not return the smile.

'He did. But perhaps you've changed.'

There was a silence.

Collins took a small black-and-white photograph out of her handbag and pushed it across the table. It was the picture of the dark-haired girl sitting on a wall, wearing a headscarf.

'Mr Mehenni gave me this picture of Farah.'

Lizzie's face tightened up and her voice had a note of protest that Collins feared for a moment might be justified. There was, after all, no question attached to the image of Farah.

'Why are you showing me this?' she said.

'Farah's father gave it to me because he wanted me to understand. I suppose I want you to understand too. I'm asking you to tell the truth.'

There was a pause. Lizzie did not speak.

'Are you telling the truth?'

Lizzie cleared her throat and put her hand on her voicebox, as though it hurt her. She nodded slowly.

'The tape can't hear that. Are you telling the truth?'

Lizzie's eyes flickered briefly over to Steve. Then she said, 'Yes. I'm telling the truth.'

Collins wondered how Hadley had taken the phone. She remembered his big hands at the post-mortem, and how small Farah had been.

She said, 'Hadley was the type of cop who gives the rest of us a bad name. Wouldn't you say that was true?'

'I can't answer that.' Lizzie shook her head. 'No, I won't be drawn into that. It's not relevant. It's not a proper question.'

CHAPTER 46

Lizzie was the only prisoner at Victoria House. The cell was immaculate – no smell of detergent, no banging or fighting from outside – but Lizzie was in any case blind to her surroundings. She saw only the turmoil of her mind. Steve had told her they would be as quick as possible in making the charging decision. They could take as long as they liked as far as she was concerned. She could not imagine being free, could not think of the nuts and bolts of beginning to live again.

She thought of that photo of Farah Mehenni, sitting on the wall in that faraway place. She had looked so small but so lively. *Full of beans.* That image was another thing that would never leave her now.

Before she took Ben, Farah had tried to call her . . . No, she wouldn't think about that. No. Not now.

As for Hadley – what had the detective sergeant called him? *The type of cop who gives the rest of us a bad name.*

Lizzie could conjure him only in snapshots,

fragments of the man. His large hands on the steering wheel of the panda car. His upright thatch of salt-and-pepper hair. Sometimes she hated him.

She had a sudden memory of a routine call. The threadbare upholstery of the police car, the plastic door wells stuffed to bursting with used blue plastic gloves and discarded breathalyser tubes, the whiff of stale clothing and body odour. Perhaps someone had put a vagrant in the back. It had been bitterly cold but the windows were wide open. Hadley had turned on the heating full blast. Still the car stank, still the cold air rushed in. She had scanned the screen of the data terminal.

'Left here. Number thirty-one.'

It hadn't really been necessary to tell him the number: of all the houses in the street it had been bound to be this one. The net curtains at the window were grey. The steps leading to the front door were chipped and dirty. There were several entry bells but they hadn't needed to ring. The shadow of someone moved around behind the narrow frosted-glass panes that gave on to the communal hallway. As soon as they approached, the door opened. A woman – in her forties, perhaps – stood wrapped in a light-blue towelling dressing gown. She was thin and wore no make-up. Her face was lined and her mousy hair was streaked with grey.

'He's in there with the other kids,' she said. 'He won't let me in.'

The woman was standing on the dirty tiled floor of the entrance of what had once been a grand Victorian house. Uncollected post lay scuffed and gritty underfoot.

'Has he ever hurt the other kids?' Lizzie said.

'Lord, no.'

'Has he got a weapon?'

'No, he just won't let me in.'

'How many other children in there?'

'Three.'

Lizzie name-checked the boy. He was known to police but not for anything particularly violent. A bit of public order, some drugs possession, but no dealing and no serious violence, at least not yet. She knocked on the door to the flat.

'Jack, it's the police. Let us in.'

'I'm not going to let you in. You're going to arrest me.'

His voice had the uncertain timbre of a larynx only recently broken.

'Jack, let us in. If you don't, we'll have to break the door down.'

'Are you going to arrest me?'

'I don't know. We're going to get in one way or another, so you may as well open the door.'

'I'm not going to open the door unless you tell me you're not going to arrest me.'

Hadley spoke up. 'We're not going to arrest you. Let us in.'

'I don't believe you.'

With a dismissive paw, Hadley waved Lizzie away from the door and took her place.

'Jack, we're not going to arrest you. I want to get off on time and an arrest would hold me up. But you need to let us in or we'll have to break the door and then I *will* arrest you, mainly for annoying me but also to stop me being the one who has to wait for boarding up.'

Lizzie raised her eyebrows. Hadley stepped away from the door, which opened slowly.

A shelving unit had been overturned. The phone was smashed. Jack, a thin teenage boy, was wearing jeans, a T-shirt with the words *Game Over* and a baseball cap turned backwards. They followed him through to the kitchen. Three children were sitting round the table. One was cuddling a tortoise. Scrambled eggs and a broken plate were on the floor. There were images of saints on the wall and a framed print of some tapestried scripture. *Dearly beloved, let us love one another, for charity is of God.* On the side was a porcelain Virgin Mary.

'You've got a pet tortoise?' said Lizzie.

'Oh yes,' said the mother. 'They make grand pets, don't they, kids?'

The children, staring at her and Hadley, made no reply.

Lizzie said, 'Do you want to show me where you keep him? Is it a him?'

The mother said, 'We're not sure. It's difficult

to tell. Off you go, Catherine, take the officer through and show her where Archie lives.'

The solemn girl shook her head, not fooled and wanting to stay where the action was. The mother said, 'Catherine, I'm *telling* you, not asking. Go on, kids, go with the officer. She wants to see the tortoise.'

The children's bedroom was dark, the curtains still drawn. It smelled of sour straw and damp. Lizzie asked to hold the tortoise. When she got back into the sitting room, Hadley had already heard most of it.

Jack, alternately furious and distraught, was saying, 'Please, Mum, please let me stay.'

Lizzie didn't need to know the details. Dad, of course, was long gone. Years ago he had left this woman to raise his four children on her own. The mother had had enough but she needed reinforcements to implement a decision born out of sheer exhaustion. Any army, no matter how important the struggle, will give up after too long marching.

'No, Jack,' she said. 'I can take no more of this.'

'I've nowhere to go, Mum.'

'Perhaps you could call a friend?' Lizzie suggested. 'They'll understand, help you out.'

Jack, suddenly incandescent, turned to her with a howl of outrage and contempt. 'That is the most stupid thing you have said so far.'

The most stupid thing . . . Hadley, plainly delighted, smiled broadly from ear to ear. Lizzie, who had said next to nothing, had somehow managed to say many, many stupid things, and of the many stupid things she had said, this had been identified as the most stupid.

'Stupid?' said Lizzie, somewhat riled by Hadley's amusement and also puzzled by Jack's reaction, which seemed to contain something she could not easily pin down. 'Your friends will understand. Why's that so stupid?'

'You know *nothing*,' Jack howled. 'NOTHING.' Hadley again caught her eye with a look of enormous gratification. Jack turned to his mother, simultaneously furious and plaintive. 'If I OD, Mum, it will be YOUR FAULT.'

Hadley rubbed his eyes and covered what appeared to be a genuine yawn with both his enormous hands cupped over his mouth and nose. As usual, his disclosed emotion when dealing with the public appeared to be no more than an all-conquering weariness. Why did everyone disturb his rest? Why did everyone get in the way of him sitting down and eating? The conspicuous emphasis was that he would do whatever looked like being the least trouble.

'All right, Jack,' he said. 'It's been fun and all that, but if you can't sort out somewhere to go, we will have to arrest you.'

Jack turned to him, dismissive. 'But you promised you wouldn't arrest me.'

'Well . . .' There was a pause. 'Well, April Fool then, I suppose.'

'It's not April the first.'

Hadley laughed out loud.

The boy, furious, spoke to him as if he was an idiot. 'Go on, arrest me then,' he taunted with a desperate adolescent swagger. 'What you going to arrest me *for*?'

Hadley suggested with an almost apologetic shrug that this was, in the end, a practical matter: somewhat irritating, like all the other things that stopped him from watching Manchester United, but ultimately as easily solved as a broken alternator or a blocked sink. It just required a bit of effort. 'Well,' he said, sighing out loud and apparently stirring himself into considering the possible solution to this moment's particular problem. After a moment of contemplation he resumed in the manner of a thoughtful discourse. 'We could start with criminal damage, I suppose, or breach of the peace, perhaps. I'm sure I'll be able to think of *something*.'

Outraged now at his powerlessness, at the trick, at the mockery, at the possibility of a broken promise and above all at Hadley's apparent indifference to it all, Jack squealed, 'You *said* you wanted to get off on time. You *said* you wouldn't arrest me.'

Hadley was unmoved. 'As I said, I'd much rather not. But you can always force me to change my mind. And if I do have to arrest you, I should warn you that I'll be most pissed off.'

From the moment Jack began to squeal, it had

been a done deal. It was just a question of waiting it out. When he finally agreed to call his friends, his tone was unrecognizable from the anguished scream to which he had subjected Hadley, Lizzie and his mother for the past ten minutes. On the phone he was low-key, streetwise: nothing much was going on in his life. He was certainly not someone who ever howled or pleaded. He grabbed a grey hoody from the back of a chair.

'How's it going, man?' he said, arranging to meet up in town, and doubtless to find some trouble before the day was out. 'Safe.'

As he opened the door, his mother said, 'You need a coat.'

Jack was a man now. 'Mum, this is *me*. You'll have to decide. You can't kick me out *and* tell me to wear a coat. Up to you.'

Lizzie caught a glimpse of his mother's face, suddenly stricken.

She stood at the communal doorway and watched Jack stomping off angrily down the street, just a skinny kid with no coat on. She went back inside the flat. Hadley was sitting holding the tortoise in the flat of his palm. He stroked the animal's shell and made small talk, allowing ten minutes to make sure Jack did not return.

Jack's mother said how surprisingly friendly tortoises were: they would even eat from your hand. Hadley said he had had one as a boy.

'Really?' Lizzie said.

She had imagined him briefly and convincingly

as a boy in grey shorts, straight from a Hovis ad. He smiled at her ruefully. She had missed the point again. Who knew whether he had ever had a tortoise?

He had turned back to the mother and added, not without sympathy, 'They can be a devil to find.'

CHAPTER 47

Baillie stretched back in his chair.
'So what does the Crown Prosecution Service have to say?'

Collins handed him the paperwork. 'Not in the public interest to prosecute.'

Baillie glanced through the prosecutor's report.

PC Griffiths has put forward a consistent account with no discrepancies and this account has been tested thoroughly at interview . . . There is considerable and convincing evidence that Farah was unpredictable and given to disproportionate reactions to events . . . Significantly there is no clinching piece of hard evidence to support a prosecution . . . In spite of the execution of warrants and thorough searches, Farah's phone – if it ever was unlawfully in the possession of police – has not been recovered.

The prosecutor notes that Mr Mehenni has made allegations. These can be aired at inquest. The prosecutor does not believe, however, that the public interest would be served by the expense and burden of prosecution when there is no realistic prospect of conviction.

Some of PC Griffiths' actions – her absence from duty, her lack of timeliness in writing her second statement, her failure to report Farah Mehenni's phone call to her – might be the appropriate subject of disciplinary procedures, but this is not a matter for this charging advice.

Baillie put the report down. 'That's pretty conclusive.'

Collins aimed for a neutral tone. 'Yes, sir. It is.'

'You did a good interview, of course. And she answered all your questions?'

'She said she couldn't really remember the roof. Didn't want to remember it.'

'Well, that's understandable.'

Collins nodded. 'Yes, sir.'

'And there was nothing left unresolved?'

She didn't answer.

'Well?'

'Yes, that's right, sir.'

A shadow flitted across Baillie's face, but it was only momentary and he quickly smiled. 'But you're still not happy, are you, Sarah Collins?'

Collins looked down. 'Well, I wasn't convinced, sir. Particularly not by her account of Farah's phone call to her from the payphone . . .'

'But in any case we haven't recovered a recording?'

'No. The search team reported back a couple of hours ago. They haven't found anything at Shaw's house.'

The detective chief inspector went over to the window. Behind him the Thames snaked, brown and estuarial. Presently he said, 'You will have to let it go.'

Collins wasn't sure she had heard him correctly. 'Boss?'

Silence for a moment.

Baillie's back remained turned. Collins waited. Finally Baillie said, 'Is it not at all possible that what she's saying is true?'

'It is possible, of course.'

'Well.' He turned back with a half-smile on his face. He sounded patient, kindly even. 'Sarah, as the prosecutor says, she's given a consistent account. She hasn't requested a solicitor to be present when she's been under caution and she's answered every question.'

'Yes. She has.'

'Are there any outstanding lines of inquiry?'

'No, sir.'

'I understand Mehenni entered a guilty plea to the charges and the court has agreed to offer a token community service on condition he accepts the move away from Kenley Villas?'

'Yes, sir.'

'Well, that's good.'

Collins had an uncomfortable sense that Baillie knew already how this conversation would

413

end. She didn't want to volunteer the conclusion for him, but she could think of no effective objection.

Baillie said, 'You've done a very thorough job investigating this, so please don't be offended. Nevertheless, I think it's fair to say that at the end of all your efforts we are back where we started. We don't know exactly what PC Matthews said and it's clear we'll never know. And do you know what? Perhaps it doesn't matter that much.'

'Sir, it's only part of a bigger allegation—'

Baillie put his hand up as if he was stopping traffic. 'Hang on, Sarah. Please give me credit for understanding that. Hear me out. Perhaps we should take stock, review the bigger picture? These are some facts we do know for sure. We know Farah's father started it all with his hatred for his neighbour. We know that Farah abducted a five-year-old child and risked the child's life. And PC Matthews lost his life, we know that too. These are some of the things we know.'

There was silence again.

Collins cleared her throat. 'And we know that Farah is dead too. Let's not forget that.'

Baillie exhaled. 'You think I have no sympathy for that?'

He waited, but Collins did not reply. He continued.

'OK, so Farah is dead too. I agree with you, Sarah, let's not forget that. It's a tragedy, it is indeed, but there's nothing we can do to undo it. PC Griffiths has given an account and she's also

414

shown that she sticks to that account under pressure. Griffiths went to the roof and her actions probably saved the child's life. Surely she deserves credit for that. If we have no evidence we can put before a court against her, then she is innocent. Isn't that the law?'

Collins held his gaze. He was right. Even on her terms, he was right. She thought of Shaw. If she could have stopped him on that country road, then perhaps . . .

Baillie said, 'It's time to put this to bed, Sarah. There's nothing to be gained for anyone in dragging it out. It's in everyone's interests to begin to move on.'

He turned back towards the river, perhaps giving Collins time to consider his words. She looked at the boy with the fish on the wall, considered the operculum frozen out in an extended gasp for breath, opening desperately for the flow of water over that strange internal fleshy corrugation, and suddenly she worked out the detail of the photograph that had been bothering her. Of course the fish wouldn't die. Anglers did not kill their fish; they photographed them and then they threw them back into the water.

The DCI had walked over to the coat stand in the corner of the room. He was pulling his jacket off a hanger. There was barely the inflection of a question in his voice. 'So, is it white gloves at the funeral, Sarah?'

There was a pause.

Collins spoke quietly. 'Yes, sir. It looks like it is.'

He was slipping his arm into the sleeve of his jacket. 'Good. I'll go and tell the DAC in person. Bit of a treat for me. Not often I get the opportunity to deliver good news. He'll be pleased with you too, DS Collins, you can count on that.'

He straightened his lapels and took a step towards her. He held out his hand. It was warm and strong. Genuinely warm. He could afford to be magnanimous, she thought. He smiled broadly.

'Well done on your hard work. Thank you for being so thorough. You've shown yourself to be a very talented investigator and I've taken note of that. A relief, as you said earlier, that we've covered all the bases.'

CHAPTER 48

Steve escorted Lizzie through the building's corridors. She was small and compact beside him and she brought to mind a Lowry painting, as if she were a matchstick figure. He couldn't but think of her as a girl although she was of course an adult and had power of arrest. There was something ridiculous about her yellow bleached hair and her too-large jeans, although he had to give her credit – she had done a good job of evading police.

She did not make small talk and neither did he. He considered offering her a cigarette or a coffee, but the slide into a casual conversation might prompt her to disclose finally what had happened and he didn't want to hear the full story. Still there were things that needed to be said. They were at the heavy glass door to the building.

'I'll walk with you as far as the river. There's a little kiosk down there. Got to buy some fags.'

He leaned in to the doorway and lit a cigarette. They walked out into the shadow of the building. The wind was blowing bitterly. A street cleaner in a dirty fluorescent jacket was pushing his metropolitan barrow. A Chinese DVD seller was sitting at an empty pub table sucking on a cigarette. In the wind, crisp packets and cigarette wrappers blew across the paving parallel to the river's stretch. Steve buttoned his jacket.

Lizzie said, 'How did you find me?'

'Guesswork. You called me. I made a lucky guess.'

'You're good at guessing?'

'I s'pose so, years of practice. But I think it helped that you wanted me to find you. That's why you rang me.'

She did not reply. There was shame in standing on the edge and not jumping.

'So, Lizzie, that's the end of it now.'

It was both advice and a warning.

They had arrived at the steps to the bridge. Steve stopped and held her wrist briefly. The grip was soft but it was clear he was detaining her.

'Do I need to say anything?' he asked.

'No.'

He seemed unsatisfied with this. His grip tightened slightly. 'Do you understand me?'

She licked her bottom lip. 'Yes. And you don't need to say anything else.'

They walked together up the steps to the bridge. A man was sitting with a dog on a rope. Next to the dog, an upturned hat. The street sleeper clocked Steve and did not even attempt a request for money. They turned on to the bridge and walked out a few paces. It was colder here over the river. They stood side by side. The water's grey swathe was corrugated in sharp waves, opaque.

Steve said, 'I've got a question, Lizzie.'

'OK?'

'Why did you go back to Portland Tower. Why did you stand on the edge?'

Lizzie didn't answer immediately. She was leaning against the railings, looking downstream. Then she put her hand across her eyes. Steve waited for her and after a minute she took her hand away and spoke slowly.

'I don't know. I don't *think* I wanted to jump. Maybe I wanted to prove to myself I could do it.'

'Do what?'

'I told Farah that if she would let Ben go I would stand next to her. But I never got the chance. I wanted to know that I could have done it.'

Steve leaned back against the railings. He reached inside his jacket pocket for his cigarettes but then thought better of it. 'What will you do now?' he said.

'I don't know. Resign probably.'

'Don't do that. Move on. Everyone makes mistakes when they are young in service. Hadley and Farah found each other. Neither of them would back down. You thought other people knew better than you. Now you know not to make that mistake again.'

DS Collins took her cigarettes out of her coat pocket. She pushed open the window and stepped out on to the roof. The crow was nowhere to be seen and she missed him. She walked over to the edge. There was no boundary, just the unsheltered drop. She had always been scared of heights. She thought, not for the first time, that the problem was not falling, but rather the desire to jump. That was something she shared perhaps with Lizzie. Birds were flocking and swooping, dark keystrokes let loose against the fading sky. With her feet on the edge, Collins looked out towards the river. She could see two figures standing on the bridge.

Steve and Lizzie leaned on the railing, the river was flowing fast beneath their feet. Steve reached out and put his hand briefly on Lizzie's. She glanced at him. He was a man whose face invited truth-telling, but she knew that this impression was deceptive. He was a cop, not a priest, and there would be no value to either of them in a confession. They had both worked out the consequences and they were too great.

Steve said, 'Don't resign, Lizzie. Stay in the job and be a good cop.'

They were quiet.

Then Lizzie said, 'Thanks. For everything.'

'Just doing my job.'

He offered her his hand and she shook it.

He turned and walked away, a thin, anonymous man in an anorak and sensible Clarks shoes. As he made the turn on the bridge's sheltered steps, he threw a coin into the beggar's hat.

The day was dimming and the city's lights were glinting, triggered by a million cadmium cells. They glimmered pinkish against the nacre sky.

Still Lizzie could not think of the roof.

She remembered the uncertain voice on the end of the phone: *You an' me . . . We're not bad people. We're good people.* After all, everybody thought they were good. Lizzie had thought she was good when she wrote the statement backing Hadley.

The Thames swept out beneath her, grey and cold. She leaned against the balustrade as if she would allow the wind to snatch her away into the water. She imagined the pull of the current, the impersonal muscle of the river rolling her up with indifference into the to and fro of its tides.

CHAPTER 49

'**D**o you want to tell me what you said to her when you found her on Portland Tower last night?'

Steve was hanging up his coat. He paused momentarily and then finished what he was doing before he turned back to the detective sergeant. She was sitting with her desk covered in papers.

He put his head a little to the side. 'What?'

Collins did not move. 'Lizzie's performance in interview was very assured all in all. What did you say to her on the roof?'

'It's in my statement, Sarah. Read my statement.'

Collins picked up a piece of paper from the desk. 'I have read it. You received the phone call from her at 01:53 hours but you didn't book her into custody until 03:12. Even allowing time for you getting there, that's a long interval.'

Steve shrugged.

Collins felt she should not put these suspicions into words, perhaps, but she could not stop herself.

'Stopped off at a twenty-four-hour Maccy D, did you, for a bit of unofficial disclosure, or did you just drive the long way round? Told her what we had, talked her through the interview, how to handle it? Something like that? It wouldn't be a big deal, would it? Not interfering with evidence, nothing like that. Just a bit of advice. When we stopped the interview and you put her in her cell, did you have another little word with her? A bit of encouragement, some advice perhaps, something to get her through the difficult part?'

'Don't be ridiculous.'

'Ridiculous? You walked with her on to the bridge just now. I saw you from the roof.'

'Yes, I did. So what?'

'*So what*? Because the interview was everything we had: our only chance. You knew that, and if you helped her get through it, if you told her there was nothing to worry about, if you advised her to simply deny everything, not to hesitate to show Farah in a bad light . . . well then, that offers a very good explanation of how well she did.'

Steve placed his index finger on his lips in the universal gesture for silence. 'I would stop now if I were you.'

Collins went on. 'And all along, Baillie has known everything I've done. I thought it was Inspector Shaw's friends, but it wasn't, was it? It was you.'

Steve's face flushed. 'Reporting the progress of an investigation to a senior officer—'

Collins interrupted impatiently. 'Is that how you see it?'

He inclined his head slightly. 'Yes. How do *you* see it?'

423

There was silence.

Then Steve said, 'I feel sorry for you.'

Collins could feel her jaw tightening. 'That makes sense.'

'Even if I had done what you've said, so what?'

'Steve, really. *So what?*'

He replied with an impatient flick of his hand. 'Yes, so what, Sarah? The girl's in her twenties.'

'And she's a police officer.'

'Have you ever seen those cases reported on the news? Have you read what the judge says in his sentencing remarks when he sends them down to live with the nonces for three years?'

'You'd put away a shoplifter—'

'Sarah . . .'

'But you don't have the balls to put away a police officer who has perverted the course of justice?'

She had raised her voice and immediately regretted it.

Steve looked at her for a moment as if considering whether to go on. Then he said, 'So that's what you would charge her with, is it? Perverting? Because she was inexperienced and backed a colleague? That's all she did.'

'It isn't all she did, although lying is serious enough. They took the phone—'

'Lizzie didn't take the phone.'

'As good as.'

'No.'

Collins raised her voice. 'Farah Mehenni, a desperate, vulnerable teenager, is dead.'

There was silence. Then Steve said gently, 'And I'm sorry for that.'

Collins tried to order her thoughts, to speak calmly.

'Lizzie's inexperience is just mitigation. Mitigation is none of our business.'

They had stopped speaking. Collins sat at her desk as if she had some work to get on with. Steve went back to the peg to get his coat. He was still for a moment and then, with his back turned, he said quietly, 'No wonder you're so fucking lonely.'

'It's our job to put the evidence in front of a court.' She had thought she was insisting but was shocked to hear that her voice sounded pleading.

Steve turned back to her. He blew out his cheeks. 'Is that what you joined to do? To send such an inexperienced and young woman to prison for making a stupid mistake. To destroy her? Who else would pay such a price for such a mistake?'

Collins was furious. 'It's not for us to start deciding what our damn job is, and it's for the court not us to consider mitigation . . .'

'Oh really. I repeat my question. Is that what you joined to do?'

'To do my job? Yes, it is. Why? What did you join to do?'

'Well not *this*, that's for fucking certain. It wouldn't give me any pleasure at all to put that girl in front of a court. No pleasure at all. I joined to put away the bad guys—'

'Lying, bullying cops – they *are* the bad guys. A teenage girl is dead—'

'And I'm sorry for that, but her own fault it is too. Her own fault.'

Collins' head swam. What was this bloody thing she insisted on? It was over. No further action. Did she just not like being bettered?

After a silence Steve said, 'Sarah, I've put in for a move.'

Collins nodded downwards, as though it was the desk that had spoken to her and she agreed with its hard, implacable surface.

'Bet you've got it too, have you?'

She knew it was petty. She wished she could think of something else to say.

Steve was pulling on his anorak. 'I've not had much sleep. I was going to suggest a drink, but instead I'm going home to the beer in my fridge.' He threaded his second arm into the sleeve. His tone was discursive now, as though they were both sharing experiences.

'I remember when I worked on murder squad. Tavena Smith – I'll never forget her. A little black girl shot by accident by some rude boys showing off in a chicken takeaway in Hackney. We knew who they were but we couldn't get the bastards: every line of inquiry followed up and still getting nowhere. Made me long for the time when we could have a word with them in the back of a van. Then the boss spent about half a million on a forensic review and some conscientious boffin found a droplet of blood on one of the suspect's jackets. God, the satisfaction a few corpuscles can give a man, I tell you. That droplet – it gave me a fucking hard-on. Go to prison, you bastards.'

Steve zipped his anorak up. He felt in his pocket for his warrant card, flipping it open as though checking it was still his face inside.

'Can't think I'd ever get that satisfaction from a mobile phone recording of some fat copper saying *Bin Laden*. Particularly when the fat copper in question is dead. What about you?'

He slipped the warrant back into his pocket.

An unvoiced argument rose inside her. She remembered something unrelated: how in the playground she had ushered the boys away from a daddy-long-legs but then had not known what to do with its writhing, tortured body. Steve had walked towards the door. His hand was on the handle but he turned back.

'You're a very good detective, Sarah, really you are. But your talents are wasted. Any complaints you have about me, put them down on paper. I'm going home. I've got the kids this weekend and I'm taking them go-karting. Probably drink too much Coca-Cola and eat too many chips. What are you doing, Sarah? Anyone to see? I am sorry for you, that much is true.' He paused as if considering his next comment. 'Get yourself a dog. Yes. That's my advice to you.' He looked her clean in the face. 'Get yourself a fucking dog.'

30 APRIL

CHAPTER 50

The streets were bordered with a black ribbon of police uniforms. On the route approaching the church the officers chatted and killed time. Some occasionally stamped their feet to keep warm. All were in dress uniform with white gloves. Their black shoes had been worked to a military shine. Motorcycle outriders in fluorescent jackets and white helmets appeared first, moving slowly round the turn in the road. Behind them, the round headlights of the Daimler came into view. As the motorcade approached, the officers fell silent, and as the cortège drove slowly past, they all came to attention. The hearse's polished window reflected back to them their black uniforms and silver buttons. Then, as the hearse turned at a bend further along in the road, the light switched and they caught sight of a wreath of white and red carnations spelling out Hadley's shoulder number.

The graveyard was carpeted with daffodils. Among the grass and the lichen-stained headstones the flowers shone like fragments of yellow glass. Six officers acted as pallbearers. Hefted to their shoulders, the coffin – draped in a Union Jack with a police helmet on the top – made its way slowly up the path. Ten officers from Hadley's response team formed a guard of honour at the entrance to the church.

Deputy Assistant Commissioner McFarland stood in the suburban graveyard and read a prepared statement to the press. Collins stood next to Baillie in the background. She wore a Marks & Spencer trouser suit and a dark silk shirt. McFarland's uniform was perfectly pressed. His white shirt gleamed. The wind blew across his face, lending him an air of determination. He spoke into a microphone, which blustered with the buffeting of a wind that threatened to snatch his words away. 'PC Matthews spent his professional life serving and protecting the people of this great city. The thoughts of all of us are with his wife and four children.'

Hadley's wife, Mandy, was seated at the front of the church. On either side of her were the four children. Two already young adults. The other two, Collins knew, were aged eight and ten. Richard and Ian. Two blond boys usually dressed in football strips but today smartly turned out in miniature jackets. One of them had inherited Hadley's thatch, and it was already springing up and mocking the hairbrush. Officers approached the family. They shook hands with Mandy and the children. Mandy thanked them and smiled, although her face, when it relaxed, was drawn. It was easy to conjure the disturbed sleep, the crying and worrying since Hadley had died.

Collins glanced over to the pews on her left. Carrie Stewart was there, seated beside Ben. She had dressed him smartly in a suit. In Ben's lap Collins could just see the ears of a brown teddy. PC Lizzie Griffiths was nowhere to be seen.

As the coffin entered the church, a sound system blasted out 'Glory Glory Man United'. Everyone made their way back to their seats. The officers placed the coffin on the catafalque in front of the congregation and the music faded out on the words *Wem-ber-ley! Wemberley!*

The vicar said 'Neither death nor life, neither angels nor demons, neither the present nor the future, nor any powers, neither height nor depth, nor anything else in all creation, will be able to separate us from the love of God that is in Christ Jesus our Lord.'

Collins recalled Younes Mehenni's words: 'Every soul shall taste death.' In her wallet was the black-and-white photograph he had given her of his daughter. Perhaps he had not intended for her to return it, but she would.

The family approached the coffin and placed flowers. The children left a Manchester United scarf. Carrie Stewart went forward with Ben. He placed a police teddy on the gleaming surface. Carrie reached out a hand and touched the wood with a flat palm.

Inspector Shaw got up to give the tribute.

'Hadley would have wanted me to say something funny . . .' He glanced at the coffin, and Collins saw, with surprise, that his eyes had filled. He struggled for a moment, swallowing hard. 'I'm sorry, Hadley. I can't for the life of me think of anything funny.' When he looked back towards the congregation, he had composed himself. 'All I will say – and I know, Hadley, you would have wanted this – is that I haven't run what follows past senior management. So I hope that's acceptable.'

There was a rustle of approving laughter from the congregation, and Shaw acknowledged it with a slight nod before continuing.

'After Hadley Matthews died, I went to empty his locker. Mandy had found it too painful to consider doing it herself. When she rang me on my mobile, she asked me if I'd mind. She said, "You know Hadley. It'll be a complete mess and there'll probably be something in there that shouldn't be."

'There's something about an officer's locker. This is where you keep your stuff, and what is inside is between you and your maker. That is, unless the DSI decide to spin it.'

This was greeted with another murmur of laughter from the pews. Collins pressed her lips together and blurred the image before her eyes. She imagined the reality of him at that locker. The hurried search. The phone, perhaps, in his hand.

'I went down the steps to those lockers. There's probably a fancy phrase for this that I can't find.

Something that captures how it felt going to that basement room with Hadley's key. The rows of grey metal lockers, the relief out on patrol, and me with one to empty . . .'

He caught Mandy's eye. It seemed to give him strength, for he continued in a more matter-of-fact tone.

'Firstly, of course, Hadley had *two* lockers.' He shook his head in mock disapproval. 'And this at a time when management are telling us to hand them back.' His voice had an edge of aggression now. 'And for any members of the press who've managed to smuggle themselves in here uninvited, don't get excited. There's nothing sinister in him holding on to those two lockers: no hidden secrets, just that after nearly thirty years in the job, a man *needs* two lockers.

'What was inside them then, these two unofficial lockers?

'In one, a very extensive collection of Met-issue black biros. I gave up counting when I got past a hundred. They're probably of historical interest. A copper's always got a pen, and you've got to hand it to Hadley, he seems to have grasped that point at least. What else? Oversize Met shirts – too many of them. It seems he ordered new but never got rid of the old. Well, it is hard to part with an old shirt, we can all agree on that. Stuck to the inside of the first locker door was a photo of his wife and children. I won't tell you what photos some officers have taped to the inside of their locker

435

doors, but Hadley, that least sentimental of men, had a picture of his wife. Mandy saved him, he always said that. They've raised four children together.'

All heads turned towards the family, an obeisance to their loss.

'Now Mandy's going to have to finish that job without him. Boys, I know it's tough, but Hadley knows he can rely on your mother and I know that in your hearts you know this too.

'For those of you here who don't know Mandy, she's another of our so-called little people. The press and the politicians call people like Mandy and Hadley "unsung heroes" – that is when they're not stitching them up and voting themselves pay rises. Mandy is a state registered nurse. She's spent her professional life mopping up after people she doesn't know, holding their hands and doing her best. Hadley knew good sense when he saw it. So Mandy, it might not feel like it right now, but I know that somehow you're going to get through this.

'Hadley didn't have rank and he didn't work in a glamorous squad. No murder inquiries, no hiding out, none of that Jedi knight stuff. No scrambled egg on his shoulders either. No one ever called him sir, nor would he ever have wanted them to. He was a day-to-day copper. Early turn, late turn, night duties: all his working life answering 999 calls. He never worked out of uniform. He had a contempt for CID and was fond of pointing out that uniform dealt with and solved more crime. He could wax lyrical about that. He could in fact *go on*.

'He was a great believer in simplicity – right from wrong, punishment fits the crime, that sort of thing – and his way has been out of fashion in recent times. He had principles and they were principles that people who aren't in the job probably won't understand. He'd never call anyone with rank sir. They were always "guv" – and that went right the way up to the commissioner. "Guv" indicates respect, but not too much. Constable was the most important rank in the Met: that was his opinion and he was right.

'When he arrived at work, he was invariably wearing tracksuit bottoms and some awful football shirt. Anyone seeing him enter via the station office would think he was returning for bail. He was at his funniest when he smartened up for court. I relished those moments – Hadley emerging from the locker room with his shoes shiny, his hair Brylcreemed down.'

Shaw broke off and found Collins in the congregation. He looked her full in the face as if defying her. A few heads turned to see who it was that had caught his attention. Shaw coughed and there was some confused laughter. He resumed.

'In the police room at court, Hadley's tunic was buttoned up against all the odds. "Waste of taxpayers' money to order a new one," he told me once as he struggled with the buttons. "I'd only have to get a new one in six months. Don't know what it's down to either, because I bloody love lettuce." By the time he got to give evidence, a button would have gone and his hair would have sprung up again. I think it must have been made of wire. I remember him swearing in the gents', trying to enforce some order on his appearance. If I happened to catch his eye, he would say, "Not a word, guv. Not a word." But in spite of his losing battle against the phenomenon of his own body, when he went up the steps Hadley always impressed. He impressed because he himself was impressed by absolutely no one. He had no particular axe to grind, just a weariness with the pervasive bullshit of most human beings and a simple and unfeigned sympathy for those beset.

'I'm going to miss him. Of course all the coppers who worked with him will miss him too. But I'd say that there are also lots of people who will never know that they are missing him. They won't know that an old-fashioned copper doesn't patrol the streets of London any more. They won't know what they have lost. He won't be there to talk sense to youngsters. He won't be there to turn a blind eye when that's the right thing to do. He won't be there to find an unorthodox way round a problem. He won't be there with simple kindness. And he won't be there to remind the rest of us of how to do it: the old-fashioned coppering that has always been London's secret enemy against both tyranny and idiocy.

'Don't worry, I'm nearly at the end. In a minute

we can all go and have beer and sandwiches. Just one last thing. I haven't told you yet what Hadley had inside the other locker. Some of you will know already, but for the rest of you . . .'

Shaw met the eyes of his audience.

'Now calm down, everyone, there's nothing to worry about. No nasty surprises. Any guesses, then?'

His eyes found Collins and a flicker of a smile passed over his face. He was still looking at her as he resumed speaking.

'Taped to the door of the second locker Hadley had a photo of the 1968 Manchester United team.' He turned away from Collins towards Hadley's wife. 'It's a great photo, and if you don't mind, Mandy, I've kept it. It's already sitting framed on my desk. What a glorious moment it captures. Matt Busby, Bobby Charlton, Denis Law, George Best, just twenty-two years old and stuffed to bursting with brilliance. Hadley told me once that in the footage of Man U at the European final at Wembley 1968, there's a very small boy behind the Manchester goal, and that was him. George Best on the field: he was Hadley's inspiration. A player who cut effortlessly through the bullshit and who could spot a good and a pure thing when he saw it.' Shaw swallowed hard. He could barely speak the last words, and the congregation leaned forward to catch them. 'And that is how I will remember Hadley Matthews: a man who would fight for a good and a pure thing.'

★   ★   ★

The officers milled around in the graveyard, dark uniforms among the headstones. Mandy was having a brief conversation with Carrie Stewart. Collins, standing alone, watched them hug. Ben was running among the daffodils and Carrie called out to him not to climb on the graves.

Collins was longing for a cigarette. Jez came over and stood beside her.

'You did a good job, Sarah. You gave it your all.'

'Thank you, Jez. I really appreciate that.'

'Come on, no point hanging around here. Let me take you for a drink. I promise not to be an idiot.' Jez glanced over towards Inspector Shaw. The contempt in his voice was ringing. 'And George Best, by the way, was a terrible drunk who threw away everything good he was ever given.'

CHAPTER 51

A cold evening was setting in. Lizzie got her coat and her wellingtons and unlocked the door to the fixed caravan where she had been staying.

Her father had taken them to Pagham when her mother left. It was a place where she had been *allowed* – all the usual rules had been suspended. No one had to wash and you could have as many ice creams as you wanted. It had been a brief time of blistering heat and the noisy screams of children as they plunged their sunburned skin into the sea.

In April, however, it was a colder, quieter country. The beach stretched away, grey-blue pebbles and mist. Strange salt-brave plants with spiky leaves and globular fruits held firm in spite of the shifting terrain. The horizon was a blue mist. The seafront, a deserted border of bungalows and auto repair shops, was divided only by shingle from the vastness of the sea. The water swelled out into cold blue, deepening into darkness.

The thoughts pressed on Lizzie continually and at unexpected moments. Brushing her teeth, starting her car: there it was. Falling, falling through space, through blackness. It was neither willed, nor considered. Rather it was something unavoidable, inescapable, a possibility that she had already rejected but that nevertheless rose within her against her will. A dark image that presented itself like an offering, the image of herself, joining them. Her own body silenced, on sand or pebbles or concrete.

It was clear she could not work. Disciplinary procedures had been suspended for the time being. She had been signed off sick.

It was true what she had said to Detective Sergeant Collins. To begin with, her memory of the roof had been darkness, with only sensations and fragments inside that space. The face of the boy. The bitter sensation of the cold wind. But her recollection had slowly filled and deepened, each detail brimming with meaning. Here, alone at Pagham, she had let it slowly uncoil, like drawing out a thread from deep within her.

She remembered the police radio standing upright on her desk, chattering away as she completed Mehenni's case papers after she had charged him. She had worked out that that must have been the gap of time in which it happened. She had watched him going to his daughter in the station office, angrily showing her the charge sheet and the immigration papers, telling her he had been remanded and then leaving her as he turned back with the detention officer towards the police cell.

She imagined Farah Mehenni returning alone to that alien kitchen with its flowery linoleum and pine panelling. She wondered if the grandmother had been at home or if the house had been empty. Who knows what darkness, what fears had turned inside Farah? Certainly it must have felt, if nothing else, bitterly unfair, bitterly lonely – her father in a cell and no consequences for Lizzie or Hadley.

And Farah had tried to call her.

Lizzie still shied away from that piece of information: Farah dialling her mobile number and discovering it had been disconnected. Her last betrayal.

She imagined Farah walking into her neglected garden. She could see the stained paving slabs, the wild buddleia, the sandpit abandoned by some other long-gone family. Over the fence the wrought-iron bench and the trough of bluebells. Ben in his bear suit playing with the spaniel, Charlie. She imagined Farah inching towards her momentous action, talking to him, persuading him, lifting him quietly over the fence.

Lizzie hadn't even noticed the first time the dispatch was transmitted over the radio. It was only the second time that she had paid it any attention.

'White male, aged five years, wearing bear suit. Believed taken from his back garden. Missing approximately twenty minutes. Any units available?'

And then she had heard the other call, the supposed suicide risk on Portland Tower. Understanding immediately, she had not transmitted.

She had run instead down the station steps to her car. The car had kicked into action and the station's gates cranked open before it. The traffic gave way to let her out, but the road she had turned into was stationary with traffic nose to tail. She hit the middle of the steering wheel and the siren wailed. She was doing fifty up the bus lane, and a camera flashed her. The radio traffic crackled and scorched. She had prayed then intensely that there would be no consequences, no consequences and no damage, please God, no harm to the five-year-old boy in the bear suit.

The bus lane ended at the junction. She had been forced to push and bully the cars out of her way, honking her horn and pulling into oncoming traffic. She turned off the main road into the estate, weaving through its width restrictions and mini roundabouts and pulling up outside the communal entrance door to Portland Tower.

The block had towered over her, framed by a bright blue sky.

The frosted-glass panels of the entrance lobby were reinforced with hexagonal wire mesh. She pulled on the heavy door. It barely moved against the sturdy automated lock. She keyed in the number of the first flat and pressed call. It rang out with a loud, insistent buzz. There was no reply. She hit the wall with frustration, then keyed in another number. The buzzer rang out again, harsh, indifferent. *Christ.* Never had she been so frustrated by how bad she was at getting into buildings.

Hadley had a fire key: she needed him now when she most hated him.

But then, there it had been: the customary hostile voice of estates. The question that gave nothing away and made no promises.

'Yes?'

She had held her warrant card up to the camera. 'Police.'

No response.

She keyed the number again. The buzzer rang.

'What do you want?'

'Let me in. It's not for you. I've got a power of entry, and if you don't let me in, the courts will want to know why.'

The lock slipped with an anonymous click. She pushed the door quickly and the darkness of the lobby revealed itself. With a foot in the door, she reached back on to the pavement and propped it open with a Coke can. She started climbing the stairs, flashing in and out of the late sunlight as she hit the open walkways and then dipped back into the darker stairways. At the top landing was the dark maw of the service stairway leading to the roof. She leaned over, resting her hands on her thighs, drawing in breath. After a brief pause, she climbed the service stairs quietly. The metal fire door was locked, but she saw, in the corner of the uppermost step, the fire key with the brown lace looped through it – Hadley's.

The door opened inwards. As she stepped from the darkness of the stairs, the sunlight threw everything into an indecipherable brightness. She shielded her eyes against the rapidly pinkening wash of sky. Then the scene condensed and made itself clear to her scorched eyesight.

On the edge of the roof was Hadley. Beyond him was the girl, Farah, and beside her the small figure of Ben. The child's back was towards Lizzie. She could make out the shape of the bear suit, the little furry ears.

As she reached the lip of the wall, Lizzie saw that there was about a metre of hard surface between the edge of the wall and the drop. It was on this that all three stood.

The wind was cold and bracing, whipping remorselessly across the high surface, as if they were on a mountaintop. The consequences of the drop, falling away, were a physical sensation inside her. Hadley turned to look at her over his shoulder. His drawn and fearful expression unnerved her. Then Ben turned too. His face was stretched with fear, and close up she could see that he had been crying.

'Hello, police lady.' His eyes were unspeakably wide, and in his fear he gave the impression of a child relying on his very best behaviour. It had filled Lizzie with an almost uncontainable terror to see him so.

'Ben, you're doing really well. I want you to stay calm. Can you do that for me?'

The only sign of agreement had been the smallest dip of his nose.

'And hold on tight to Farah's hand.'

Again the nose dipped: he was going to be good and everything would be all right.

Briefly she caught Hadley's eyes. He seemed to be trying to communicate with her as if by telepathy, seeking some sort of shared strategy perhaps. At first her terror stopped her thinking: they were all so close to the edge. But then, suddenly, the awful simplicity of it struck her. She imagined the phone somehow taken from Farah, snatched from her hand or forced from her pocket.

How could she stop this terrible, stupid game?

She said, 'Farah, I'm sorry.'

The girl looked at her evenly. 'Sorry now.'

'I didn't know . . .'

'You didn't know, but you told him, didn't you? What did you think would happen?'

Lizzie looked at Hadley and she saw that his eyes had shed their customary complacency. It was unnerving to see him so unmanned. In a barely perceptible gesture he turned his hands slowly outwards, but Lizzie could not read the movement.

Farah said, 'I've told him not to speak. He's said enough.'

Lizzie struggled to think of the right thing to say or do, but all that came into her mind was a silencing terror, a premonition of enduring catastrophe. Then another thought dawned. Perhaps Farah had been waiting for her. Perhaps her arrival had made the audience complete. How did this end? She could not see Ben's face, just the child's back – his bear suit and the two ears.

Farah in any case was glancing down at Ben. She said, 'Do you trust me, Ben?'

Again there was the slightest movement of his head, the slightest assent.

'Would you trust me if I told you we were going to jump out together? You'll be perfectly safe. I can fly.'

Ben turned slowly to look over his shoulder towards Lizzie. His eyes were wide open with a question. Lizzie did not dare to interrupt, was afraid of any word or gesture that could be construed as disrespect. With as much confidence as she could muster, she gave him the gentlest nod. *Yes, Ben, you trust her.* And he turned back to Farah and said in his piping boy's voice, 'Yes. I trust you.'

Farah looked out again towards the drop. Lizzie saw her hand tighten around Ben's. She spoke quickly. 'Farah, let me stand on the ledge with you. That would be fair. Ben's not played any part in this, but I have. You're right: I am sorry now. Very sorry. You let Ben go and I will stand next to you.'

Farah was still looking out. Ben was clutching her hand tightly, as though they were about to cross a busy road. Lizzie had told him to hold on to her, and he was doing what he'd been told by the lady in uniform. Lizzie glanced at Hadley, but Farah had rendered him powerless. He dared neither speak nor move. Still there was something watchful in him.

Lizzie said, 'It was unfair; I can see that. We bullied you and we didn't think there would be any consequences.'

She could hear how inadequate her words were, but she could think of nothing else to say. Farah muttered something under her breath. Lizzie couldn't hear her. She said, 'Please—'

Farah spoke over her, louder. She sounded desperate, frightened. 'I trusted *you*. I didn't think you were like *him*.'

There was a silence. The wind whipped around them.

'He *mocked* me.'

Hadley made a slight move, as if to speak. Farah raised her free hand: *Don't.* The boy bear gave out a tiny nervous squeak as though he knew instinctively the exact measure and beat of the music that was playing out on the roof.

Birds were wheeling overhead, buffeted by the wind. The sky was streaked with jet streams.

Farah said, 'I used to come up here, after school. It was a place I could be alone. But a couple of days after I called you, he was waiting for me on the stairwell, in the dark. I don't know whether he'd followed me or not, but he was there. He took the phone out of my school bag . . . He said – Farah glanced across at Hadley, her eyes full of loathing – '*Isn't that just like a wop – brings a knife to a gun fight.*' She turned back to Lizzie. 'I didn't know what it meant so I googled it, and it's from a stupid film. *The Untouchables*. Can you believe it? Can you believe he said that? Did he think he was being *funny?*'

Lizzie could not bring herself to look at Hadley. She was so angry. Why had he said that? Bravado? Intimidation? *Had* he actually thought it was funny?

She said, 'I'm so sorry, Farah. Really, I'm so ashamed. If you step back over the parapet, you can talk about it to someone independent. I'll tell the truth this time. I promise.'

Farah shook her head. 'No you won't. You don't understand. I *hate* you. Why ever would I trust you after all this?'

Echoing up from the concrete plaza below, Lizzie could hear sirens wailing.

'Look, you think there's no way back, but that's because you're young. I know it feels terrible, but none of this is worth dying for. There *is* a way back. Let me stand next to you, then you can have time to make your mind up. I know it's not fair. If someone has to pay, please, let it be me, not Ben. He's innocent.'

And then Farah had shouted out wildly and suddenly: 'But I am innocent! I am innocent too!'

Ben wailed with terror. Farah had placed her right hand on the wall to steady herself and then looked down over the edge, pulling him forward with her. Even this slight action was perilous; the tiniest adjustment of balance could be fatal. Her

450

left hand was still clasped tightly around the boy's. Struggling to master her terror, Lizzie took another step forward and knelt down by the wall. From here she could see the crowd gathering on the concrete below.

'Farah, please, you are innocent, yes, yes. But he's a child. I remember you saying – what was it you said – that you were *good*. I believe that, Farah. I believe you are good. I don't believe you want to harm a child. Hold on to him and I'll put my hands round his waist and guide him over. Or I can stand next to you first and we can pass him over together. I'll come and join you on the ledge. You can decide then what to do.'

The closeness of the calamity was making Lizzie's arms shake, her hands sweat.

Suddenly Ben spoke, his voice a frightened squeak. 'Please Farah.'

Farah looked down at him. She placed his hand on the wall with her own hand on top. Slowly she squatted down opposite him. 'Ben, I'm going to let you go. But I want you to remember that I let you go. Will you remember that?'

Ben's eyes flicked to Lizzie. She nodded quickly.

Ben spoke slowly. 'Yes. I will remember that you let me go.'

Farah loosened her grip on his hand. Quickly, before the girl could change her mind, Lizzie leaned forward and wound her arms round his waist. The boy turned in to her. His breath was warm and shallow on her face. He burrowed

451

against her, warm and furry in his bear suit. Still Lizzie feared that Farah would change her mind or that some terrible mistake would happen.

She said quietly, 'Ben, climb very carefully over the wall. Use your hands. Hold on to me. Hold on tight. You can grip me as tight as you like. Don't let go. Not for a second.'

She locked the fingers of her left hand around her right wrist so that the boy could not fall. Whatever happened, she would hold on to him. She would never let him go. He was climbing and she held him tightly. His small hands were on the top of her head and on her shoulder. He put a hand over her left eye and squeezed her cheek. It was like a game. One leg was over the parapet wall. She ducked her head so that it was not in the way. She could feel his weight shifting, the warmth of his body. He was moving towards safety. Everything would be all right. She would stand on the ledge and Farah would agree to turn back from disaster.

The boy had both feet on the roof beside her. His weight was still leaning in on her. Lizzie turned to her right. Hadley caught her eye, and she realized at once that of course he would never let her step out on to the ledge.

He said, 'I'm sorry, Lizzie. I'm really sorry.'

Farah too seemed to know how it ended, for she glanced at Lizzie and then leaned out. There was something sorrowful about the movement, and Lizzie's voice was ripped out of her in a terrible noise that was unknown to her. She tried to grab at the girl, but she was too far away. Hadley's arm was flung out too, his hand open as he sought to catch hold of Farah and was lost.

And then there was just absence. Lizzie heard the terrible sigh of the crowd beneath.

The boy was standing next to her. She could not breathe. He had his arms around her.

'Don't cry, nice police lady.'

Kieran had been there when she could make no sense of anything.

He did not hug her. Clear in this moment of disaster, he chose instead to say, 'A call came from a member of the public that she was up here on the roof.' She did not understand why of all things he had said that, but she understood his reasons now. He had wanted her to be able to explain her presence on the roof if she hadn't heard the dispatch to Portland Tower.

The boy was in her lap. She was shaking, but she held on to him tightly. She was getting colder and colder. She had needed to hold on to him. He was her consolation. But his mother was at the scene, waiting for his return. The female detective had explained, kneeling down beside her: she had to let Ben go to his mother. The boy was peeled away from her. Separating from him made her sob.

In the ambulance, the paramedic had wrapped a silver blanket round her and told her to lie down.

He asked for her name and date of birth. She knew the routine of the questions, but they were strangely inapplicable to her. She was not injured. She was not a victim.

She said, 'I'm fine.'

The paramedic had a clipboard and a yellow form that he was resolved to complete. She felt the numbness spreading. She closed her eyes. His voice was like the distracting whine of a mosquito. She felt the possible consequences driving deep into her life and spreading out like the shock waves from a bullet.

That was what she remembered: the shock coming in waves, like the roar of the sea held to her ear. The tide ripping out the rounded pebbles from beneath her feet.

She began to walk along the beach. The pebbles, in shades of grey and blue, crunched and shifted beneath her.

If Farah had taken her offer, had stepped to safety over the parapet, would Lizzie have been true to her word? Would she have told the truth about the statement and the phone, the whole shameful episode?

Well, that was the past. Farah had not taken the offer. She had leaned out into the drop, and now she was gone. Lizzie had decided to do what anyone else would have done. She had decided to get away with it. Now she had somehow to remake her idea of herself.

Hadley would be in the ground by now. Lizzie

imagined the mourners gathered around the grave, the sound of the fall of earth on the coffin and then the cold loneliness of the graveyard. She remembered him sitting with the tortoise in the flat of his hand, the perfect hexagonal geometry of the animal's shell.

The phone in her coat pocket buzzed. She pulled it out and read the text. It was from Kieran. He was worried about her. He wanted to meet her.

Lizzie looked along the shoreline towards the lights of the beachfront café. She imagined Kieran sitting before a cup of tea, waiting for her. She turned slowly and began to walk along the beach towards him.

The sea rushed and lapped restlessly. Lizzie could not fathom her feelings. They moved within her, deep and shifting beneath an unknowable weight of water.